Merely
Academic

R. A. Miller

PENSIVE PLATYPUS

Merely Academic

First published in the United States by
Pensive Platypus Publications
Copyright @ 2017 by Rod Miller
TXu 2-043-582

Excerpt from *The Intellectual Life*, A. G. Sertillanges. TAN
Books, Charlotte, NC (www.tanbooks.com) used with
permission.

Quote from THE SCREWTAPE LETTERS, by C. S.
Lewis © copyright C. S. Lewis Pte Ltd 1942 used with
permission.

Quote from "A Little Learning" by Evelyn Waugh.
Copyright © 1964 by Evelyn Waugh, used by permission
of The Wylie Agency L

Published in the United States of America

A note on smoking:
Tobacco pipes are discussed in the book. The author wants to make it clear that pipe smoking is one of the great joys of life. His favorite pipe is a gently bent *Mastro de Paja* but his best smoker is an *Il Vellero* wide stem, filled with Kingsbridge, and enjoyed during meetings with good friends of the Diogenes Society.

Cover design by Emily Depre

Cover photo, Magdalen College, by author

Pensive Platypus Logo by Verity E. Miller

For Will

Brother in tweed

CONTENTS

Part One

Part Two

PART ONE

COLLEGE À LA MODE

Is it not natural, given these conditions, that the man of vocation should put away and deliberately forget his everyday man; that he should throw off everything of him: his frivolity, his irresponsibility, his shrinking from work, his material ambitions, his proud or sensual desires, the instability of his will or the disordered impatience of his longings, his over-readiness to please and his antipathies, his acrimonious moods and his acceptance of current standards, the whole complicated entanglement of impediments which block the road to the True and hinder its victorious conquest?

A. G. Sertillanges, *The Intellectual Life*

Dr. Brian S. Mossworth, Ph.D., Professor of Art History, referred to as Mossy by his students when they were generous and BS when they were not, grew slowly conscious of the itchy press of carpet into the side of his face. Forcing open his eyes he focused variously on the shadowly legs of his desk, to flooring, to nearby bookshelves. "Ah." His office floor. Not yet dawn. Mossworth sniffed. A fetor of gin hung about. "Uh."

The Morning of the Shoe.

Yesterday.

It began with Mossworth trimming various erruptions of bodily hair utilizing his German gentlemen's tools.

"Snip, snip."

And he was set. But the shoe. Sitting on the edge of his bed, left handmade Alden oxford on, right being tied. Only it wasn't working out. The right laces were soon a mess and as his forty-something eyes could not focus at that depth anymore, the only thing for it was to attempt the risky buisness of removing a shoe tightly knotted. On the third try, with full force, he pushed the heel down, down, pulling, pulling; it broke over the bottom of his foot and released with enough pressure to smack him in the face.

He went to the bathroom to discover a bright red welt across his cheek and a darkening eye.

"Bloody shoe."

With a cool cloth he dabbed at his face. Felt soothed but took on more color. "How am I supposed to teach?" Mossworth reached for his cell; the department secretary would be there.

"No. No. I am a professor! I shall endeavor to do my duty."

So he moved to the kitchen and put the kettle on. Or, rather, he attempted to. Upon switching the appliance a nasty flash ended most of the electrics and provided Mossworth a burning sensation in his right hand.

"Bloody hell!"

Back to the cold water in the sink.

After drying his hands he attempted putting on his second best Harris tweed sportcoat only to hear the inner lining give way.

"Bloody jacket!"

During the drive to work he dodged a pickup only to hit the curb and give his Morris a terrible shimmy.

"Bloody drivers!"

He could not get his favorite parking spot.

"Bloody car park!"

He had no good mail in his mailbox.

"Bloody post service!"

The copier jammed.

"Bloody paper copying machine!"

Housekeeping had jumbled his pipe rack when they dusted his office.

"Dammit!"

As the last curse escaped his lips he glimpsed a figure in his doorway: Professor Van Engelen-Van der Bauwede, distant relative of the Baroque choirmaster, Stephane Van der Bauwede, Ethyl and Claude Ott Distinguished

Professor, Chair of Gender Studies, founder of the Hardley College Center for Sexual (X)ploration Studies, feted supporter of the Arkansas Marxist Society, College representative to the Arkansas Lesbians-at-Risk Task Force, ordained priest at St Guthlac's Episcopal (and co-founder of their pet celebration Sundays), a south-east regional Aikido medalist, erstwhile seventies porn star, art department Chair, and the current bane of Mossworth's existence.

"Hello. Brian."

"Oh, ah, morning."

"It is school policy not to swear in front of the students."

"Well, yes, that is, it was not swearing about students…"

"And I have no doubt that had a female student overheard that comment, she would have taken it as insult to her as a woman, denigrating to her feminine identity, as she might chose to define it."

Mossworth blinked a few times.

"But of course, Brian, I'm not here to review your continuing struggles with patriarchal sexism…"

"Oh, well, that is…"

"I'm here about class."

"Class?"

"Generally we ask faculty not to dismiss classes before their allotted time."

Mossworth took a long inhale, "I say, Evangeline…" but she was gone.

The class?

The Class.

Western Art History Survey I. Could teach it while sleeping. Yesterday probably had. Mossworth stood below a projected image of a resplendent marble goddess. Mossworth enthused with his muddled trans-atlantic accent: "The glorious Venus. Yes, the glorious Venus. Here she stands, revealed, nude, splendid, delighting our

3

eyes which now witness the marble handiwork of, ah, craftspersonship, thinkers of a magnitude that have enchanted and beguiled countless..."

"Excuse me, Dr. Mossworth?"

"Oh, ah, Yes?" asked Mossworth.

"I have a question about Venus."

Mossworth's head nodded. "Ah, yes, uh, but this isn't the time for questions. I, ah, that is to say, I am not ready. We shall have time for questions at the end of the lecture."

"Oh, oh, okay..."

Mossworth shuffled his papers. "Sorry, sorry, I don't want to be one of those professors who doesn't take questions when they are asked right in the middle of his organized lecture. No, that's not me. It's all about the learning." He scratched at his chin. "Happy to answer your question."

"It is a question about love."

Mossworth pursed his lips. "Love? Love. Ah, yes?"

"Sorry," the voice said, "I just...you know, this is Venus."

"Yes?"

"Well, it was a hard thing to make."

"Uh, um?" answered Mossworth.

"She is, I mean, you know, the goddess of love."

"Yes, yes, and..?" asked Mossworth.

With a tremor the voice quietly asked: "Is love...real?"

Mossworth squinted into the darkened room. "Well, you see, while that is a good question, it is at its base an inappropriate art historical question. When questions are brought to the classroom, and they are encouraged, to be sure, I, ah, am not one of those sorts of teachers, no, but, well, it is important that the question reflect something of the material at hand. But, that is, I do hope you will keep thinking about, the, ah, subject."

Mossworth continued: "... that have enchanted and beguiled countless visitors and viewers and raised questions about technique, marble, history, and the lives of ancient people. And so we begin today's journey into the world of living marble, evocative and delightful forms which continue to please discerning viewers of taste even today, as they have done for millenia."

No further questions emerged from the darkness. Habit kept his mouth working yet he found himself gripped by a gnawing doubt regarding the entire purpose of art, his career teaching art history, and his very human existence. He also had gas. A mild panic gripped the good doctor when he realized there would be no subtle ventilation. And then it was upon him: Mossworth's inner workings echoed through the lecture hall and into college lore.

With nothing else for it, Mossworth peered in the darkness of the now silent room and shouted, at no one, "You are rude, sir, plain rude!" He then departed the room, neglecting to turn on the lights, and left behind both darkness and an atmosphere of putrefaction.

The Morning of the Shoe.

But that was yesterday. From his current position sprawled on the floor of his office, he coughed, cleared his throat.

"Stupid students. Love, love! As if that, as if that…"

Rolling to his knees, he clutched at his desk and hoisted himself up.

"Evangeline…if she only…she's just…"

Moving to his feet he found the whole world making his head spin.

"Bloody…Tolkien didn't have problems like this."

He shuffled over to the tiny gothic-framed mirror hanging behind his door. Mossworth starred, pulling and rubbing at the pale skin around his red eyes. He pushed his brown hair and removed his untied bow tie. "Yes, ahem, yes, well…" Nearby lay an empty bottle. "Hm." Mossworth lifted his chin and tilted his nose upwards, sniffing. "Um, yes…" Quickly his hands reached for the window latch and with an unintended flourish he threw open both windows. A fresh breeze ruffled the dingy curtains.

Along a perimeter, defined by the arc of the impending sunrise, splatters of the warmer colors waved and shimmered through high altitude clouds. Twinkles of starlight flickered between the delicate play of blues. Upon his wall opposite the window, shadows thrown by the leaves of a nearby tree grew in relief as the dawn approached. A breath of morning air moved the tree slightly, the shadows of the leaves wiggled a bit. Slowly Mossworth turned away from the wall, removed his eyeglasses, and began cleaning them with his pocket handkerchief. "Oh, my goodness, my goodness," he mumbled, "what a stimulous of shadow and color." Then, as his eyes landed upon student papers awaiting grades he added, "As if those students know anything about love."

He flopped into his desk chair and looked to his bookshelves, filled with dusty volumes, arranged alphabetically and by color. He flipped a small remote activating a series of tiny lamps inside a particular, glass-covered section of shelving. Mossworth could make out two of his grandfather's pipes, a vintage beer stein from Mossworth's ancestral German home (to which he'd never been), and two books: a first edition C.S. Lewis (unread) and an autographed Evelyn Waugh (read but long forgotten). Behind all of these, mounted in a vintage gilt frame, was a poorly rendered nineteenth century print of the Oxford skyline from South Park.

Sighing, head thumping, Mossworth slumped. Questions of office drunkenness were swamped by nagging suspicions about art and the world of art history. Mossworth felt a need to wrap himself in comfort. Standing, he fetched from a tremulous coat rack his wooly Jesus College, Oxford scarf; crimson and black it esconced him in wooly stripes of something like history. The stripes reversed on the back, a fact that no one would notice except for Mossworth and perhaps anyone who had graduated from Jesus College. Mossworth had graduated from the University of Louisville. Louisville's colors were also red and black but the only scarves they offered featured a cartoon bird mascot. Sitting, touching this bit of the Old Worlde, reminded him of those glorious old school days of yore...that others had experienced at good schools with uniforms, rugby teams, and summer holidays.

"Taste, the true measure."

A rumble from his innards alerted him to other pressing issues. Through his mind dashed a myriad of causes for continuing discomfort: age, food, that Vietnamese curry from yesterday lunch, too much drinking, too much Van-Whatsit, never having attended Oxford, too little exercise, "and dumb questions from students about love." Yet that wasn't quite it, either. Mossworth eyes alighted upon his desk. To one side sat a pipe rack. "But which pipe, which pipe?"

He settled upon a cheap bent apple he had picked up in Rome, the fit of which pleased his hand and the shank of which spoke volumes regarding breeding and habit. After a bit of fussing with a tobacco jar, a match flamed. He sucked the burn down into the tobacco, a heady mix of leaf. The superheated rush blasted up, cooled a bit by the stem, and wafted onto his anxious palate, satisfying that odd urge that only burnt leaf can. Smoke wreathed his head; the dazzling dawn light now pouring into his office caught the smoke and illuminated the particles creating a halo effect. "Mm, a bit like late Massacio." He took another long draw. "Like a late Massacio who happens to teach in central Arkansas."

Gripping the shank profoundly, he turned to gaze in a deeply thoughtful manner out the window. From behind a hedge the slobbery gob of a she goat appeared. She set to on the weedy grass. "A goat. Splendid."

Mossworth blew smoke towards the goat then turned back to his desk. Goats. Dumb students. Intestinal distress. Drunk in the office. Stalled career. Mossworth blew smoke across his desk.

Really? Stalled career? Time to head out?

"Yes, these have been joyful years but, perhaps, my talents are needed elsewhere."

Briefly he contemplated his prospects. Then a deep puff on his pipe lifted Mossworth high up in the clouds. Another puff sent his head spinning, flying even higher and, then, he pictured himself standing, clad in a variety of historic tweeds, just outside the Eagle & Child pub in Oxford. The sun shone brilliant exactly as it never quite does in Oxford. Mossworth watched the afternoon traffic, consisting mostly of double-decker red buses and Morris Minor autos. He turned as he heard a shout. Emerging from his own cloud of smoke was J. R. R. Tolkien, smiling, waving.

"Tollers, Old Boy!"

"Mossy, friend!"

Before too much breeze could be shot, there were more shouts and greetings as a myriad of tweed-clad gentlemen approached. Lewis was guffawing, Chesterton laughing, John Ruskin pontificating, lots of back-slapping and joking and pipe smoking and intellectual this-and-that. Surrounded by these men, Mossworth joined in the laughter and smiles.

He was sent down from Oxford by his pipe's deposit of a hot coal onto his crotch area. A few moments of leaping, and the necessary vigorous patting, settled the excitement. Fully awake again, and yet fully hungover, Mossworth nodded. He sat again and flipped open the notes from yesterday's class. "Yes, yes," he mumbled through his pipe-clenched teeth. "I shall bring these students up! Perhaps they are not yet developed to the level of Taste." Reflection brought him to consider changes to his teaching method. "I shall endeavor to move beyond Taste. Jolly good." And he right then determined to rework his notes and courses writing atop the notes for the next lecture, in red ink: PASSION. "That's how I was taught art history and look where it got me. They don't want Taste, not ready for Refinement, well then, emotional stimulation they shall have come Monday." Hardley would remember him long after he departed for greener fields.

"Greener fields?"

Was that what he needed, a new start? A new college at which to actually reach students who were capable of being reached.

"Daft students."

From a distance, church bells rang. Mossworth checked his watch, then his calendar. "Wait, Saturday. Sunday? Sunday. Oh, bloody..." Quickly Mossworth closed the office windows and gathered up the two empty bottles from his wastebasket. After locking his office door, he stepped outside, threw the bottles in the dumpster back by the sculpture studio (where the students threw their bottles) and went to his car, mumbling invectives about the singing birds, the brilliant morning sun, and his thumping head. Above all else, Mossworth realized during the drive home, he must buy a new pair of shoes.

Shortly thereafter, a relatively odor-free Mossworth entrenched himself in the St. Swithson's Seniors Sunday School, linoleum-tiled, classroom. Elderly congregants with pulled woolens shuffled in. Surrounding him gathered wrinkled well-wishers and smiling faces. Mossworth engaged.

"Morning Mrs. Wheeler, you are looking well today."

"Hello, Mr. Blair, have you had your hair cut?"

"Ah, my dear Mrs. Satko, the lentil soup recipe you offered was an absolute delight."

"Well, hello professor!" A wee woman with a round face, ruddy cheeks and twinkling eyes greeted him. She held out a thin, pale hand that Mossworth shook happily.

"Alma Lee, you are looking lovely this morning."

"Thank you, professor. I like your coat."

Mossworth beamed. "Harris. My favorite color combination. Did you know that the tweed was handmade in the Outer Hebrides, those are islands off the west coast of Scotland."

Alma Lee managed to smile towards Mossworth. Then someone in the front of the room began to speak and heads were bowed. Mossworth did likewise. With his head down he noticed his shoe. Very smoothly he removed a hanky from his pocket and polished up the dull toe of his brogue.

After a few sharp gasps and a sob from the room, Mossworth paid attention to the prayer.

"...how what we ask for isn't always what we get but let us, Lord, let us just remember you are Sovereign. Keep Becky and that baby in your hands, Father, just...please, Lord God, please. We don't understand, we don't. But know that You love her more than even we do. Please, God, please."

A very long time followed wherein most sniffed, sobbed, or quietly pleaded. Mossworth shook his head at agreement with the sentiments of the prayer. Mrs. Patterson put out a hand and patted Mossworth's back. Mossworth jerked with the unexpected touch and found himself tearing up. "Yes, yes, yes," Mossworth prayed, "the feelings and emotions are very strong this morning."

Upon the end of the class, Mossworth quickly made his way past lots of people to stand at his usual site: the coffee bar. He helped himself to a large cup and then considered the folks entering the lobby. "Not sure who that was, but what a sportcoat!" Eventually, the numbers moved towards the sanctuary and Mossworth followed.

Inside, he took up position, one worked out over several years: seventh pew on the extreme left side. Mossworth sat, starring, up at the massive beams composing the decorative ceiling trusses. The truss beams were not actually oaken timbers hewn by devout Medieval pilgrims but were pine slabs covered with thin oak-stained veneers and installed in 1951. The effect worked from a distance. His strategic seat provided Mossworth the best view of the beams as well as the rose window and surrounded him with most of the people from his Sunday School class. As the service began Mossworth relaxed down into the pew with a soft smile, casting his benificent gaze down upon the balding grey heads nearby. With the swelling of the organ, Mossworth fell quite asleep.

The shuffling movements of others standing woke Mossworth at the end of the service. He stood slowly and moved into the aisle, nodding and shaking hands, and wiping sleep from his eyes. Off to one side, several other congregants had formed into intimate groups, a few bowed heads and prayed together. Mossworth took this in as moved towards the exit.

"What do they think this is? This is church."

At the door, Mossworth inhaled deeply of the aging oak pews (recently oiled) and the slightly mouldy carpets. Smelled like church. He shook his head as he started down the aisle. "Yes, yes, good Sunday. Good Sunday. Strong emotional appeal. I shall miss St. Swithson's."

The serious wooden door heaved open providing Mossworth a face full of sunshine. He lifted his hand to shield his eyes. "Ugh." Moving quickly, Mossworth began his twenty minute walk home. Even with his summer weight herringbone Harris tweed he grew slightly warm by the time he arrived at his neighborhood. He rounded the corner to his street passing by the Widow Wimberly's house. Mossworth slowed his step, hoping.

"Hello there, Mr. Doctor Mossworth. You reckon you got a minute or two?" cheered a creaky voice. Mossworth looked up and towards a tidy front yard where Mrs. Wimberly knelt in the flower-bed, trowel in hand.

"My dear Wimberly, looking forward to those azaleas this year," said Mossworth with a smile and a wave.

"Mr. Mossworth, I was about to make some tea. Perhaps…"

"Oh, I couldn't, thank you."

"Well, I don't want to keep the good doctor."

"Quite alright, not a, uh…maybe..?" said Mossworth not slowing.

"Scones are in the oven."

Mossworth stopped. "Scones?"

"Ginger scones…"

Mossworth trembled slightly. "Ginger?"

"Just about done. And I got some preserves, strawberry, from my nephew's farm in Menifee."

"Ginger?"

Monday morning Mossworth sat in his office reading online newspapers and enjoying the second pipe of the day, when the phone rang.

"Mossworth."

"Brian," said the voice on the line, "Free for coffee?"

It was Couch. "Ah, Couch," thought Mossworth, "Good chap, Couch."

"Yes, certainly, please do pop 'round."

"Uh, okay, see you."

Mossworth immediately stood and donned his dark green and grey Donegal tweed coat. He liked the way it hung and, after years of smoking, smelled. The tweed made a dashing ensemble with his drab flannel wool trousers. Catching a glimpse of himself in his mirror he mugged once. His face had always been on the lean side but now age lent it crags around his mouth and, he thought, deeply meaningful crow's feet. Moving in closer he removed his narrow rectangular glasses and squinted a few times provoking a deeply theoretical appearance. His was, he determined, a marketable face. Replacing his glasses he flashed a smile in the mirror, nodded, and then scanned around his shelves for...ah, yes, Milton. The book cracked nicely upon opening; Mossworth imbibed the yellowed-paper scent.

"Um, Milton, tremendous literary skill." Then, with his pipe firmly entrenched, Mossworth leaned into the musty Milton. "Of mans first disobedience..."

"Knock, knock." Couch stood at his door. "Ready? Oh, sorry, you look busy just now. Should I come back later?"

"Not at all, not at all, I was just catching up on some Milton," replied Mossworth. "Let's be off. Is it cold out?" Couch nodded. Mossworth wrapped his scarf about.

"Righto, mate, after you."

Weather beaten, faded, and shaped by two clapboard houses pushed together, The Coffee Cup stood just a block from the main campus and a hundred yards from the door to Mossworth's building. Manifesting all that one desired in coffee house ambiance, it managed to make up for that by serving what one might inadequately refer to as coffee.

As they strolled, Mossworth noticed that Couch wore a vividly handsome and unique black and charcoal tweed sportcoat, one with an unusual angled weave.

"I say, Couch, is that a new jacket?"

"Oh, yes, thanks. Lucy picked it up when she was in Scotland last month. Haven't worn it much since. " Couch paused and smiled. "What do you think? I know you are something of a tweed authority." Mossworth stopped walking and reached out to brush Couch's lapel.

"Mm, yes, quite. Er, Marks and Spencer's?" asked Mossworth.

"No, actually, it's from up there. Made up there, I mean."

"What? Where? Made where?"

"Oh, you know, that island below Harris and Lewis, ah, Uist."

Mossworth, walking again, tried not to look at Couch's jacket, at the way the light captured the weave with a shimmering, hebridean textural depth. "Can't be from there. Harris just labels the tweed fabrics and sends them to manufacturers around the globe."

"Well, Lucy said the man in Uist had a rack of them, a special kind of jacket actually made there, by the weavers, or their wives, of a special, heavier, kind of historic sort of weave. Only made them that one summer, apparently. Some sort of anniversary or something. See, here? Here is the special badge inside."

"Um, yes, very nice."

"Oh, here, coffee." Couch opened the door for Mossworth. A coffee-like smell assailed their nostrils.

"Good morning, Dr. Mossworth and Dr. Couch," said the girl behind the counter.

"I'd like a cappuccino with a double shot."

The girl behind the counter stared at Mossworth blankly.

"Wow," said Couch, sotto voce, "I thought you were done with their coffee. Going to give it another shot?"

"Well Old Man, I thought that one shot just wouldn't do," replied Mossworth with a droll grin.

"Ha!" laughed Couch. "Well, this is a special day."

"Um, yes, quite."

Leaping into action, the young woman ground, dumped, pressed, steamed, poured, and frothed with exceptional care. While she worked several of the other employees glanced towards Mossworth. One mumbled, "Nearly six months..."

With a last whoosh, the espresso machine finished up, the woman carefully sprayed cream into a flowery shape, and flicked chocolate powder on top of the elegant pile. Steam rose agreeably from the cup and an aroma of moist cocoa swirled near Mossworth's nose. Mossworth said nothing but accepted the cup, carefully examining the contents. His eyes began to sparkle.

"Hey," said Couch, "that's looks pretty nice."

Discreetly, the counter girl and the other workers kept their eyes on Mossworth and Couch as they moved across the shop and sat at a chipped table near the front window. The curtains were drawn and the sun peeked out from behind the clouds and fell neatly on Mossworth's mug, illuminating the steamy vapors dancing above it. He paused for a moment, noticing the steam, the cocoa smell, the warmth. The room grew quiet and tense, as when squirrels intuit a major change in the weather. Timidly, Mossworth lifted the mug upwards, his mind racing, "this time, this time…" Imbibing the steam, tongue touching the chocolate sprinkled cream to make room for his lips. A mild slurp. Those behind the counter eagerly gazed. Mossworth put the cup down gently and cleared his throat.

"Yes," he spoke in a voice loud enough for all to hear, "That's…lovely, quite nice, thank you, thank you very much…"

A collective sigh went through the employees and patrons of the coffee shop. Morning papers were shuffled and began to be read again. Conversations were started. Work resumed.

Then Mossworth suddenly, yet quietly, stood. "Oh, look at the time. I've got to run." Couch nodded and stood knowingly.

Ten yards from the coffee shop, Couch spoke: "That bad?"

Mossworth removed the plastic lid from his cup and poured the contents into the gutter. "It was hot and runny and colored something like burnt umber," replied Mossworth. "It also tastes a bit like burnt umber."

Couch laughed.

It flashed through Mossworth's mind that better coffee might be found in other coffee shops near other campuses, ones far, far away.

Standing in the front of the darkened classroom, head down, hands clasped, Mossworth began, slowly, with a deep resonance: "Just after the turn of the seventeenth century, slightly past the aberrations of Mannerism, lurked the pleasures and luxuries of...Bernini!" Upon the screen behind Mossworth suddenly appeared the twisting, muscular form of Pluto, giddy with delight, in the act of seizing the voluptuous Persephone. Mossworth paused again, then changed images to reveal a close up image of Pluto's fingers pressing into the tender, forever-young flesh of Persephone's thigh.

"Ah..." began Mossworth. He licked his lips. "Yes..." He gestured to Pluto's marble fingers. "Notice how...the...fingers..." Mossworth coughed. "Notice, if you will, and this is important..." He looked out towards the darkended space wherein he knew students lurked. "Persephone's thigh, you see, it is...that is to say..." Persephone's thigh, soft, tender, silky, yielding...

"Dr. Mossworth," said a voice from out of the darkness.

"Oh, what? Yes, a question? Yes, yes?"

"What does this sculpture mean?"

Mossworth squinted into the darkness. "Mean? How do you mean, what does it mean? Mossworth could just make out the form of...someone-or-another, an overly enthusiastic freshman. He knew her by her voice. He did not know her name. Or maybe it was a male student.

"What is it about? I mean, I know the myth, but why a sculpture of the myth, why now, in the Counter-Reformation?"

Mossworth stood tall. "That is, indeed, a very pertinent question. The use of classical mythology was quite popular in the seventeenth century, as it had been, of course, earlier, and would continue to be, later. Here we see the passion displayed in the evocative flesh..."

"Yes, but..." came the voice, again.

"But what?" said Mossworth.

"What is this work about? I guess I mean, why does it matter?" came the voice.

Mossworth did not answer. "Ah, yes, well, it matters because it is important, a masterpiece." There grew a subtle shuffling on the part of the students. A glimpse at his watch explained. "Yes, well, good question, very good. Let's rejoin this when next we meet, shall we?" Mossworth quickly exited the lecture hall. Various papers and an umbrella under his arm, Mossworth headed to his office, mildly desperate for tobacco.

"Flick, flick...fffumf...fffumf." Mossworth pushed the lighter button again and sucked the flame down into the briar. But the flame went nowhere.

"Is it important? What sort of a question is that? Did they not see the thighs?"

Working the lighter rapidly Mossworth could not light a fire.

"Dammit!"

The lighter flew across the room. "This is art history, not some fluffy cat poster!" Rummaging through his middle desk drawer, he grasped a box of matches and shortly a cloud of white smoke hung dully in the room. "Yes, um, yes. Evocations of the flesh didn't seem to enlighten them. Hm, yes, what next, what next," he grunted. "Humph, humph" he puffed. Mossworth flipped open one of his windows. "I will write and clear my mind!" He spun back to face his computer.

"Click, click, thud, clickity, click, click." Fingers running lightly, Mossworth began typing rapidly on another version of an article squeezed from his dissertation subject. Over the past eight years he'd managed to get two articles published, one in the Society of Architectural Historians' academic journal entitled: The Journal of the Society of Architectural Historians. That was a coup for him although he was unsure how it was received, as of the few people who read the Journal of the Society of

Architectural Historians none were actually architectural historians. Mossworth had published a book three years ago. It was a minor guidebook to the architecture of a moderately prestigious New England college campus. Winning the commission had been a great soother to his ego; realizing the cost of research trips would fall to his own pockets and that his royalties were only about twenty-five cents a book and after three years sales topped out at four-hundred and twelve copies steadied him a bit. Worst of all, his book was currently number 1,877,784 on Amazon. His only other publishing success was with the radical leftist online journal, Noxious. While it paid him a hundred Dollars the article appeared nowhere on his C.V. "Noxious," he sneered.

He drew a long pull on his pipe. "But my class, my art history class...taste...passion..." Smoke entered his body at the same rate as the class exited his mind.

Golden, warm, late winter sunlight filtered past the trees, down between the slats of the blinds and into Mossworth's office. His eyes closed and a vision appeared of English schoolboys playing football out in the field, then rugby, then cricket. After a gentle, yet warming, afternoon rain, the boys as all sat for tea and crumpets...in a room with huge arched windows and sunlight pouring in...

"No, wait."

Mossworth forced himself back to reality. "I've got to..." Sitting upright in his chair, pipe firmly clamped, he considered his morning class. "Taste was a failure, they aren't ready, and the grasping of aesthetic stimulation, even that as erotic as Bernini's just left them flat. Right, right." Mossworth stood, paced his office. "What they need is a good dose of facts. Facts will be just right. Can't argue with the facts. It was how I was taught art history." But then a heaviness of factuality descended, one tinged with angst, mid-life recognition of mortality, and a frustration with paucity of good pubs. Perceptions of facts arrayed in front of Mossworth's mind but found no order there.

Jarring him from melancholy was a familiar click-clack from down the hall: the well-heeled footsteps of Professor Van Engelen-Van der Bauwede. Quickly his snuffed his pipe; his office windows were already open. Mossworth remained still, twitching slightly, as a worried hamster, and attempted to listen for...

"Hello. Brian."

"Oh! Oh. Hello Evangeline, what can I..."

"Brian we really would prefer if you did not smoke in your office."

Mossworth smiled. "But Evangeline, I do not smoke in my office. I smoke outside and then come into my office. The rules are clear."

"Yes. Quite clear."

Professor Van Engelen-Van der Bauwede kept her grey eyes locked on Mossworth and her mouth a thin line. "Brian, it has come to my attention that images in your class this afternoon were of a nature offensive to some, particularly in your masculine way of exigesis and phallo-centric class-structure."

"But..."

"Please do try and fulfill your college duties with the utmost respect for collegiate justice and equality, remembering the diversity of the students in your class, particularly those who are more diverse than others."

"Evangeline, I think it only fair..."

But she had gone.

Mossworth stood and closed his door, extra firmly. He ground his teeth, shuffled his feet, and shook his head. Then starring down the hall, he relit his pipe with extra-deep inhales, and created a huge cloud of smoke.

"If I ever..."

"Someday, I'll..."

"As if she knows what she is talking about!"

Soon the fit of rage passed and Mossworth returned to his keyboard. With brilliant thought hovering on the edge of his consciousness, however, he happened to look out the window to catch a glimpse of the typically inebreated student worker and that could mean but one thing: campus mail delivery. Mossworth stood, dusted grey ash off his trousers, and skipped to the Department Office. A catchall, the art department office overflowed with the detritus of forgetful academics: invitations and international postcards, dirty coffee mugs pilfered from the dining hall, and experimental creative objects from faculty and students. Hanging opposite the door resided a painting the college purchased from a visiting artist, at Mossworth's urging. Following in the tradition of the abstract schools of the fifties, the work portrayed nothing recognizable but did so in seven ineffable shades of yellow with sections of red and white stripes and irregular black shapes. Indeed it lent to the room a certain ineffable quality, one that cost Hardly College a very effable six-thousand Dollars. Today, as he did most days since encouraging its purchase, Mossworth passed it mumbling, "hm, yes, vibrant composition and dynamic liberation of the canvas."

In his mail box Mossworth found the typical assortment of book announcements from tragically awful university presses, office furniture catalogs, a small ordered box of tinned tobacco ("ah, Kingsbridge!"), the daily postcard from the postcard factory announcing that it was a good idea for the department to buy postcards, and surprisingly, two regular, hand-addressed, letters.

After tossing all but the tobacco and letters into the recycling bin, Mossworth noted that the first letter came from an old graduate school friend. The second letter featured an envelope with a crest above the return address, a crest that Mossworth knew by shape, the blue and gold colors, and all of its deeply symbolic references: Oxford. His hands shook.

Flashes of towers, finials and warm golden stone, echoes of quiet quads and cozy pubs, witty banter around fireplaces with sherry and tea... Quickly he skipped down the hall to his office. Shutting the door behind him, Mossworth sat at his desk, set his computer to play Handel's Watermusic, and relit his pipe. He first opened the letter from his friend, deftly wielding his Turkish meerschaum letter opener. After the initial well wishes and greetings, the letter read,

Did you hear about the opening at Bleary? I heard from one of the French profs who knows someone in the Dean's office. Turns out the former Chair embezzled most of the funds for the search, as well as their department's operating budget, and they missed the posting dates. Bet you could get an interview, as there won't be many applicants! Give it a shot. You'll be closer to the action and Carthage is a lovely town. I look forward to seeing you on campus.

Mossworth sat back slowly. "Providential. Providential! And Bleary...not a bad school. But Georgia? Well, I'm bloody well in Arkansas now so what's the difference?" He quickly googled Bleary, got to their Human Resources site, and scanned for the job: there it was, a perfectly bland and detail-less three sentences announcing the opening. Closing date was three days hence.

"Oh, bloody hell, bloody hell!"

Mossworth clicked open his Personal file and set to updating both his C.V. and his cover letter, last revised in 1995.

One and one-half hours later, application complete, Mossworth stood with a great back stretch, yawned loudly and passed a modicum of gas. He inserted his arms into his Australian drovers coat, grabbed his reproduction 1929 army air corps briefcase and headed down the hall. "Interesting, interesting," he murmured, "Bleary could be just the place, just the ticket, Old Boy." As he left the building a wind whipped around his head and his nostrils took in the heady ozone. Dark clouds loomed. Mossworth's eyes darted upwards and he quickened his step towards his 1954 Morris Minor drop-head coupe, pale yellow, mostly. "Yes, new pastures and students eager to learn."

By the time he turned up his street, the trees waved dangerously. An extraordinary flash of lightning crashed nearby, illuminating the house fronts. The boom rattled the Minor's windows. Mossworth jumped. Then the heavens opened up such a deluge that the remaining few blocks became a challenge, particularly with the Minor's aged headlamps. The electric garage opener ungratefully opened; the Minor wheezed and puffed inside. "Bleary. Dr. B. S. Mossworth, Bleary College Art Department..."

Mossworth skipped into the house, threw his briefcase and coat onto the floor of the spare room, and made for the kitchen. With a well practiced move he flipped on the lights, oven, and kettle. Hoisting a half-eaten package of stale, imported Hob Nobs, he moved to the living room. The previous week he had received a package containing the six-volume, 13 hour, made-for-BBC version of Evelyn Waugh's war trilogy. Filmed in the mid-eighties in some remote area of Soviet Czechoslovakia, the mini-series was panned by critics and public alike for being cheaply produced, badly acted, and painfully scored. Mossworth pushed play and let the magic begin, shoving a couple of Hob Nobs into his mouth. Thus far he had made it through the first four hours.

"Roger, I want you to know...if anything happens...I want you to send this letter to my...to my...wife...in Cirencester..."

Mossworth's modest domicile resided in a modest subdivision, Pineapple Cliffs Shores, on the west side of town. It had been highly touted in 1973 for the unique use of narrow brick. The developer thrilled to the concept of narrow brick; the thinner bricks were half the weight of their full-sized counterparts and saved in shipping. He neglected to realize that houses would merely need to use twice as many of the narrow bricks. When bankruptcy threatened he named the neighborhood for his three favorite elements of Hawaii and moved to Hot Springs to avoid prosecution.

"Charles, please send this division to the front. We need the men there."

"But sir, we clearly know that scouts have found enemy emplacements there. We dare not send troops to their death!"

It stood distinctive from his neighbors' homes for two reasons: a yard that demonstrated an utter disdain for anything even approaching yard work and an American's idea of an English decorator's touch inside. Outside Mossworth tried to plant trees that would kill off most of the grass. It worked with limited success. Inside, the ranch-style house one might notice that the walls appeared slightly irregular; Mossworth had spent an entire summer slathering wet plaster to the sheet rock to lend it a hand-troweled texture.

"George, you've been my batman for what now, eighteen months? Can you still not grasp that I prefer my tea without milk?"

The master bathroom, resplendent in dulled brass fixtures, purple shower curtain and green and yellow flowered wallpaper, housed a toilet of historic origins. The square tank, mounted about six feet off the floor, Mossworth rescued from an old farmhouse sale. Technically speaking, the Victorian unit was not actually for auction the day of the sale. In fact, Mossworth, so enchanted with the thought of such a device contributing to his personal hygiene, unscrewed the unit, carried it, dripping, out to his car, and simply drove away without offering to pay anybody. Eventually, Mossworth ordered restoration hardware (at a cost of several hundred dollars) and rigged it to work. The result pleased Mossworth to no end: its wheezing, dripping, condensing, squealing, squeaking and clanging operated, in fact, much like a genuine Victorian toilet.

"And so, our division was called up to southern Italy, this time for the big push. We knew that our lives were on the line, that..."

The roar of the electric kettle moved Mossworth back to the kitchen. He selected a brown betty from several other teapots, grabbed two bags of Yorkshire tea and his Magdalen College mug. A splash of the boiling water into the pot warmed it nicely. He dumped it out just as he had learned to do by real English people. "And now dinner!" He removed a twenty-nine cent chicken potpie from a freezer full. He had learned that if he cooked the pie for about an hour, then froze it again, and then blasted it for two minutes in the microwave, it passed as a suitable substitute for Lancaster hot-pot purchased at Tesco.

Steeping time allowed Mossworth to enter his closet, remove his work clothes, and hang them upon different cedar hangers made for trousers, shirtings, and sport coats. Hangers were pushed about to create an even amount of space between each garment. Pulled from a shelf came his Marks & Spencer's gentlemans pajamas. As he draped on his English housecoat, tan with brown and beige piping, he heard the timer beep. Soon he situated himself comfortably by the remotes, a cozy woolen throw around his feet, tea in hand. Mossworth lifted his steaming mug upwards, lips aquiver, but another crack of thunder cast him into utter darkness. "Oh, damn," sighed Mossworth. He carefully sipped his hot tea and held the cup between his hands.

Half a cup of tea later, however, the world still lay unlit for Mossworth. "Oh, oh for...this is just a bloody outrage." Booming thunder and a blinding flash silenced him. He could smell the slightly warmed pot-pie. Then came the pounding rain. Then came the tornado sirens. Mossworth stood, then sat, then stood again. "Closet, right, closet," he reached for his tea, took a quick slurp, spilling only a tad upon his housecoat. Stumbling down the hall, Mossworth could make out the sound of massive hail hitting the windows. His teacup rattled. It rattled considerably more after he tripped over his feet and spilt hot tea, seriously scalding part of his leg. Writhing on the floor, the sound of wind whipping the trees, Mossworth managed to just drag himself to the innermost closet.

Inside was darker. Mossworth rubbed and dabbed at his burned leg. Lightning splashed odd silver light across his face. "Something...something..." mumbled Mossworth. Another burst of lightning flickered, booms echoed down the street. "What the devil did I for...?"

A burst of lightning cracked right outside his house, shaking the foundation.

"Oxford!"

Without a moment's hesitation, Mossworth reached up for his creased and ironed jeans and thrust one leg in before he realized his PJ pants were still on. It didn't matter. Mossworth donned his rarely worn Alden boots and his less worn rain slicker, and made for the garage. The Morris turned over, and over, and then seemingly aided by the shouts and curses of Mossworth, cranked as much to life as a Minor might.

The Morris began down the drive as flashes of lightning flickered and pounded. Wind howled and screamed along with the sirens. "Oxford, Oxford! What do they want? It wasn't personal, was it? Is it?" Rotted rubber wipers and fifty year old vacuum actuators did their best for the Morris' windscreen. A branch crashed onto the roof startling him and causing him to stomp the accelerator. Only moderately did this increase the Morris' speed. "Why are they writing to me, why me? Did they read something of mine?" The Morris began to slow. "What if they want me, they want me to..." Lightening banged again.

More rain fell. Void of other drivers, Mossworth found the empty roads strangely relaxing. The road's shimmering surface dissolved into smaller and smaller circles of light where the street lamps beamed. "I'll bet it wasn't for me at all. Bloody accounts office, they'll have buggered it all up and here I am..." Another crack of lightening struck a mammoth pin oak. The shock of it temporarily blinded him which worked out well as one whole side of the tree blew apart and landed upon electrical lines leading to the nearby street lamp, snapping the line, and casting the street into utter darkness.

"Damn it!" Mossworth shouted. Still driving, albeit at about ten miles-per-hour, the Morris rocking violently with the winds, he pressed on. "Oxford! And the Queen!" he shouted in a sort of delirium. "God save our mighty Queen, master of everything, God save our Queen...la, la, la, la, la-la, la, la, la, laaa-la-la, la, da, ah, ah, ah, daaaa-di-da, God save their Queen." Across the hood of the Morris sped something large, grayish, and furry that may have been a goat.

Another blast of lightening showed Mossworth the driveway to the art building. Through the windows he could make out the battery operated emergency lights. Leaving the marginal safety of the Morris, he leapt out into a deluge. Instantly Mossworth received a drenching, his boots filled with water, yet he carried on. Snapping branches whipped this way and that. He ran, stumbled, and went down into mud and goat droppings, slid down the slight incline, got back to his feet, and made it to the door. With shaking hands he maneuvered the keys from his pocket and got the door unlocked.

Inside, a relative calm. Emergency lamps threw new shadows high up on the walls; down below splashed novel lit angles. "Oh, a recommendation? No, wait a minute, who do I know who is at Oxford?" The next moment he stood in front of his desk, dripping, hair draped indecorously across his forehead, hands shaking.

"What if it is a...a..." He ripped into the letter, not even bothering to use his meerschaum letter opener. Leaning into the light spilling from one of the emergency lamps, Mossworth drank in the Oxford stationary:

Dear Art History Teacher,

As you may know Oxford University is home to many summer learning programs in the arts. This year we are particularly pleased to offer a new, intensive, three-week program in art history of the British Isles. The program is situated at one of the Oxford Colleges and participants will enjoy the experience of residing in actual undergraduate housing. Experts, among the best in the world, will provide lectures and tours. By the end of the program all students will have not only a better grasp of the history of art in Great Britain but also memories of time spent among the gleaming spires of Oxford.

Mossworth flopped, soggy, into his chair. He crumpled the letter and tossed it into his wastebasket. "Oxford." Slumping down into the recesses of the chair, Mossworth yawned. His mouth continued to move, as if to speak. He kicked off his soaking boots. He found his Jesus College scarf and covered himself. Outside, the sirens ceased and the wind began to calm. Hail ceased to rattle his windows. Then the electricity returned, shutting down the emergency lights and easing Mossworth into near total darkness. Before he much responded to the lack of illumination, the building's cooling system regained power. A breath of air tickeled his brow, the whisper from the vents slowly lured Mossworth even further into his leathery chair and towards sweet oblivion.

The next morning, before sunrise, Housekeeping showed up to clean. Mossworth was first alerted to the presence of Emma Mae by the shattering screams that leapt from her mouth upon finding a damp man sprawled in Dr. Mossworth's office, stocking feet on his desk.

Emma Mae only screamed a few more times before she recognized Mossworth and maybe a few more times after that.

"Sorry, I didn't know it was you," said Emma Mae.

"Oh, oh, don't mention it." Mossworth yawned, fully awake now. "I, er...I...well, that is, good morning."

Emma Mae nodded, lifted his trashcan and dumped its contents into a plastic bag.

"Oh, yes, ah, just a minute, if you don't mind." Mossworth leapt up still quite damp, and rummaged in the bag until he'd located the Oxford letter. "Thank you, thank you my good lady. I do bid you, good day."

Emma Mae waved him off, shaking her head.

After cleaning himself up at home, and two gin and tonics, he managed to miss both his morning classes. Working tirelessly from home, however, Mossworth completed the Oxford summer program application, drove it to the downtown post office, kissed the envelope and dropped it gently into the slot. He wandered the two blocks of historic downtown, passing by the bridal shops, strange boutiques run by bored middle-aged fat women, and a Mexican food store. Sighing, he remembered the only place to eat: Bob's Grill. "Not quite the Eagle and Child, but it will have to do, No doubt there are better places near Bleary."

His two-hour lunch left him in a tender mood upon returning to his office. Cradling a glossy black French pipe, kicking back into his worn chair, Mossworth enjoyed a usual respite from the life of a college professor: giving deep thought to actually doing some writing work. His desk phone rang.

"Mossworth."

"Mr. Brian Mossworth?"

"Yes, this is Dr. Mossworth."

"Ah, well sir, my name is Shane, James Shane."

"Yes, how can I help you Mr. Shane?"

"Well, actually, it's Special Agent Shane, Dr. Mossworth. I'm calling in regards to some help we were hoping to get from you."

Mossworth licked his lips. "I'm sorry, what?"

"This is kind of a big deal for us, Dr. Mossworth, and I know it is a lot to ask, but it will really only work if you are here in person," said Shane. "Maybe you could come down to our offices in Little Rock?"

"Ah, uh, what? What are you a special agent of, exactly?" asked Mossworth.

"I'm sorry," said Shane, "I work for the FBI. Mostly I'm involved in transnational money laundering and some field work in bank fraud." Shane hastily added: "but I have worked a few cases with art fraud."

"Well, yes, of course, I'll help any way I can," replied Mossworth.

"Great. Thanks. Maybe...let's see, next Tuesday? Does that work for you?"

"Fine. Yes."

"Okay, so why don't you come just a few minutes before twelve and that way we'll be sure everything is ready for Pete. Wow, I really appreciate this, Dr. Mossworth. See you Tuesday. Bye."

Mossworth sat for just a minute with the receiver in his hand, his mind ticking over and again. "Pete? Who the hell was Pete?" Slapping his hand on his desk he shouted, "Wait a minute! I do know a Pete!" So the law has finally caught up with that, that..."

Looking out his window, Mossworth remembered back to the tenure of one Dr. P. D. Roome. Roome was department of English; early in his career faculty noticed he was in trouble. Rumors of his classes abounded. Students hated him. Students loved him. Whenever one met him on campus, the poor Dr. Roome looked fierce. One hardly knew what to say. At the Coffee Cup once,

Mossworth had just finished ordering when he looked up to see Roome staring blankly at him.

"Good morning," said Mossworth.

"Really?" replied Roome, "what do you mean by 'good'?"

Mossworth retorted: "By 'good' I mean it gives me pleasure. It feels good. That's what I mean."

"Ah," sighed Roome, and walked away.

Mossworth recalled his feeling both angry with Roome but also frustrated that he may have missed something. "Roome," he hissed.

Standing at his window, Mossworth remember the last time he, or anyone at Hardley, had seen Roome: the final faculty meeting of 1998. While professors were still finding their seats, Roome walked to the front and picked up the microphone.

"Hello friends," he began, "I'm sorry to burst in like this but I want to ask you all a question that has really been at me lately." The entire room stopped talking. "Do any of you," continued Roome, "have the slightest idea why we are here? I mean, what are we doing here? We're supposed to be teachers, but what are we supposed to be teaching? I'm supposed to teach American lit, well, which? Which lit? Which is best? What I say is best? What the journals say is best? No one agrees anymore so what should it be? So what am I doing?"

Most of the faculty looked at Roome and some nodded and mumbled not unsupportive things In a corner the science faculty continued to chat together.

"Think about this, think about this!" said Roome. "We spend our time here, telling our students things they think are true, they think we think are true! We give them examples of great literature but never explain what we mean by great. They believe we are enlightening them! Can you imagine? Some students think that Sphanktor's thoughts on Marxism are really true! What are we doing, what the hell are we doing?"

The intellectual audience shuffled in their seats. Professor Sphanktor, basking in his normal glower, mumbled something to the person next to him about Roome's obvious inability to "think outside the capitalistic box." That person next to Sphanktor was Mossworth, who blinked at Sphanktor's comment. (Sphanktor, Mossworth recalled, died tragically the following year during an accident involving a domestic electric can opener.)

"Look, " Roome continued, "we all..." and then he stopped. Slowly his eyes drifted across the shifting faculty, taking them all in, taking it all in.

"Hey, Roome," shouted the stately Dr. Mooney (Spanish and Philosophy) from the back half of the room, "what exactly are you on about? You've been ranting and raving but you have yet to make a point. Do you, in fact, have a point? Do you?"

Roome dropped his eyes, then his shoulders, and then put his hands in his pockets. "No," he whispered, "I don't suppose I do." Then he walked up and out of the auditorium and no one at Hardley saw him again.

Mossworth sat back in his chair and stroked his beard. "That must be it, that must be it. Hm, the Feds will jolly well have a thing or two to say to him."

For a brief moment Mossworth considered what he might have to say to Roome, if he were to see him again. Interrupting he let his eyes land on his teaching notes. "Oh, bloody..." With tremendous effort he roused from his desk to fetch the notes and consider the class. "What did they want? What was their problem again?" Lifting his pipe in a rakish manner: "Right then, the prats did not grasp for any sort of appeal to taste, passion left them hanging. Facts, right, it was facts. Nothing else will ever be of any service to them.

He began humming while flipping through his notes.

"Jolly good, early Modern. Stick to the facts, sir! I'll bet Bleary students would appreciate the facts!"

Mossworth sat back in his chair and let his eyes roam the bookshelves filled with fact-laden textbooks. And then it was lunch.

Hulen Hall stood as a ravishing example of mid-seventies design. Aluminum framed the huge windows, aluminum panels with cutout flower designs separated the serving and dining areas, the latter festooned with aluminum tables and chairs. Avocado carpet lend a languid glow to the dull metal furnishings. Mossworth sighed. It helped that the college paid for his lunch. A dean had suggested that Hardley give a number of free lunches to the faculty in order to encourage faculty/student interaction during the meal hour. Rare was the faculty member who wanted to sit with a student during lunch; rarer still was the student who wanted to be anywhere near the faculty a second longer than was necessary. But no one really wanted to take the lunches away from the faculty and, in fact, later administrations had found adding lunch credits a way to avoid salary increases.

From the faculty tables buzzed a congenial mix of public chatter and private gossip. Mossworth floated over with his tray of food, accompanied now by a tepid mug of tea. He aimed for a seat between Green (Chemistry) and Stern (Theater). Before he could sit there, however, two of the Profs suddenly moved in to hear some very serious private gossip and that left the only open seat between Hoffmeyer (Accounting) and Charolais (Biology).

This unanticipated seating change did not, in fact, suit Mossworth well. Gossip had abounded for some time now that Charolais had designs upon him. And Charolais did have her charms. Mossworth thought her to have a most remarkable appearance. It wasn't that she was fat, although she was full-bodied; it was that she looked like a cow. Somehow her hairstyle, which had not changed the entire tenure of Mossworth's time at Hardley, managed to convey cowness. Her nose was somehow squashed a bit, nostrils readily apparent, and her eyes were huge and brown. She also had gigantic breasts that didn't seem to know how to stay in the middle of her chest. No one thought her ugly, in fact, most of the male faculty thought she was attractive, rather in much the same way a dairy heifer might catch one's fancy.

"Hellooo, Brian," Charolais intoned, and continued, slowly, to munch on her green salad.

"Charolais," said Mossworth with a nod, "Term going well?"

"Mmmm," replied Charolais, with a mouthful of salad, "Yooou?"

"Quite, although I've been buggered by some more than regularly annoying students."

Charolais stopped chewing, took a sip from her glass (of milk) and looked intently at Mossworth. "Really, I've had a share of whiners, too, this term. I swear, they are going to drive me ooooover the edge." Mossworth looked up at her from his lasagna.

"Mine are less whining as they are...annoying," he said.

"Well, I can't stand it when they come up to me after class, asking about things I'd said twice already, wanting to know when the pop-quizzes are, what is on the test. Oooo, say, why don't we talk about this over dinner? Saturday? I'm a great cooook. Six o'clock. I'm right on the corner of Green Meadows and Grassy Glen. See yoooou," and then she stood with her tray and left.

Mossworth sat motionless, lasagna lingering on his fork. He looked at the suddenly quiet table; they were all looking at him.

"Damn, Brian," said Marlboro (Dean) "I never saw a woman act so fast." The other faculty nodded. Then, when Marlboro saw there were no women faculty present he added with a grin: "I guess you'll be having beef tonight." A roar of male laughter went up from the table.

"Yes," Mossworth started again, "I am in a bit of a fix."

"C'mon, Brian, you can do better than that," said Marlboro with a grin.

"Well," began Mossworth, himself begrinned, "I supposed I could have milked it for a bit more." More male laughter followed. Mossworth laughed at the joke, but not at the situation.

THE TÊTE À TÊTE

Definition of a College professor: someone who talks in other people's sleep.

W. H. Auden

Late Saturday afternoon, Mossworth lay in his exceptionally hot bath. Salts from his gentlemens toiletries shop in London perfumed the waters.

"She is a charming woman but...what do I feel for her? Certainly she possesses a wit and some measure of charm."

"Mere sexual pleasure? No, out of the question, my deep Anglican conviction."

"But those breasts..."

Mossworth heaved himself out of the tub and, dripping, had a long look at himself in the mirror. He placed his hands on the sides of his neck and pulled the skin a bit tighter down across his chin.

"Hm."

Mossworth reached for the bottle of Geo. Trumper cologne. Mossworth splashed his hand and rubbed his neck releasing the citrus aroma much in the same way, he imagined, Churchill had upon his own jowels.

Sartorially, Mossworth selected his best pair of dark-green moleskins. Above these he buttoned up a pure white Oxford shirt and tied a purple/red/orange silk regimental tie. Mossworth noted the color coordination between tie and the flecks of color in his Harris tweed jacket he slipped over his shoulders.

With one last check of his hair and breath, Mossworth skipped to his garage, hopped into his Morris, backed out of the drive and headed down the street unawares that he had forgotten to put on any socks.

Standing at Charolais' house, daisies in hand, Mossworth's trembling finger reached for the bell and then stopped.

"A relationship?"

Suddenly the door was flung open and there gleamed Professor Charolais, resplendent in her black and white silk blouse. "Brian, you made it. Well, please dooo come inside. I'm starving, are you hungry? I hope so." From behind her, Mossworth glimpsed a warmly glowing dining area, candlelight dancing. He detected aromas of actual cooking that aroused at least one part of him.

"Er, thank you indeed. In fact, I am famished. Oh, and these are for you"

"Brian, they're lovely. Thank yooou." soothed Charolais, "Say, is that a tweed sportcoat?"

Mossworth tugged at the sleeves of his jacket and, slightly, smiled. Looking up at Charolais he replied, "Yes, and do you know, I picked this up at a rummage sale down in Little Rock. I knew it was a good one, you see, because of the way the collar and pockets hang a bit limply; it was handmade!"

"Really?" asked Charolais, big brown eyes twinkling, "how interesting!"

Sunday morning found Mossworth deeply meditating on the interior elements of St. Swithsun's architecture. A splendid array of Sunday morning colors danced from the one stained glass window, an image of the Good Shepherd. "Mm," mused his subconscious, "just like a London church, or Oxford or something…"

He sat with a blissfully dull smile as the minister, a visitor from Northern Ireland, preached in a sonorous Belfast accent: "When we act, we are to act in a particular manner. This seems a simple enough concept but, in fact, it is quite complex. How do we act? Perhaps we have some vague notion of acting in a manner that is pleasing to God, but what exactly is that?" The minister paused, giving the congregants a moment to digest his words. Mossworth noticed the flickering and twinkling of the dust particles caught in the sunbeams. A peppermint tin made its way down the pew.

The minister continued, "We are to act as free men, St. Peter tells us. Free men. We are free. We know that. In fact, we know it only too well nowadays. All we do is act freely. But for what? To know that we are free and that we can act free tells us little about what it is exactly that we ought to be doing." Mossworth yawned without covering his mouth, rustled with the peppermint, and continued to gaze longingly.

"Here is what Peter says: you are not to use your freedom for evil. You are to use your freedom as a bond slave of God. We are free but we are to act as slaves. What a sweet irony there is in that. Of course, it is by our indebtedness to God that we become free. Then our actions take on a meaningful nature: charity and compassion given as free slaves to love."

Candles. Wine. Crackling fire. Food. "Oh, the food," Mossworth moaned, and then pretended to cough. The peppermint tin was handed back down the pew. Mossworth's stomach rumbled as he recalled the arsenal of edibles Charolais had prepared the previous evening. She had set out her best china. The candles and the fire warmed the room very nicely and illuminated the table with a golden flicker. She served an honest meal, with courses, a massive dripping roast with gravy, and Yorkshire pudding.

"Yorkshire puddings!"

Mossworth tingled to remember the English puffed pastry. For afters she had fashioned, from an online recipe, a trifle. Mossworth knew the word from a variety of BBC programming but he had never eaten one. After Charolais offered him a third helping his eyes welled slightly.

They finished with tea, real English tea in neat little square tea bags without strings. Later, sitting very near each other on the sofa, Charolais put on a scratchy old record of Noel Coward. Finally, when she got up to flip the record over, she returned with tiny Waterford crystal glasses brimming with a not utterly cheap port, and sat even closer. He wanted to stay longer and asked for Charolais to put on another Coward album; she did not have another. So they listened to the first again and, when Charolais tilted her face up towards Mossworth's, deep brown eyes needing, it was only natural that he should embrace her with his whole will. Their lips met, their arms wrapped, their bodies tingled. He lifted Charolais' hand to his lips and kissed it. He thanked her for the wonderful evening and then drove the Minor home in a way uncharacteristically slow for even it.

"Brian?"

Mossworth blinked into the eyes of the Swithsun's minister, the Reverend Halp.

"Mm. Mm?"

"How are you?" Reverend Halp repeated.

"Ah, splendid," replied Mossworth.

"Great. Dunlop is a terrific speaker, isn't he?

"Yes, yes. By all means, wonderful vicar, wonderful," said Mossworth dreamily.

"Well, he certainly seems to have gotten your attention. I only hope to get through to folks half as well as he did. Oh, hey, don't forget next week: it's the annual blessing of the pet companions service."

"Yes, yes. Pet companions. I won't forget."

"Er, Brian?"

"Hm?

"You do know that the service ended...quite some time ago?"

Mossworth looked around and saw that only three or four parishioners remained at the back of the church.

"Um, yes."

"Okay. Well, why don't you just let yourself out when you are done?"

"Yes, sorry. Splendid. Yes. Grand."

And then the Reverend Doctor Halp departed leaving the church silent and empty, Mossworth sprawling in his thoughts. Briefly the possibilities of sexual encounter with Charolais tickled his conscience. "Oh, oh, but, no. I am a church-going man, faith is a defining part of my life. And the sexual, that, well, you know. She is beautiful. She is Beauty."

"Just like that of Venus herself."

"Venus with purity."

"Venus revealed in her full naked..."

Mossworth stood and ambled towards the arched wooden doors that formed the exit; he passed through them began the walk home. Sunbeams danced around his strolling person, flickering shadows of young leaves twinkled.

"Okay, okay, don't get yourself too caught up, Old Boy."

"It was a lovely evening, to be sure, but it was just one evening."

Then Mossworth suddenly reflected upon the possibilities of other wonderful evenings and shivered. He also happened to notice the day, the wonderful day, a Sunday afternoon glimmering and glowing with the anticipation of spring, blooming azaleas, and blistering heat. Mossworth sucked up two nostril-fulls of the warming air.

"I must find her a nice wee something, something that is as wonderful as she." Mossworth mulled over a myriad of options to give Charolais, items that could communicate his feelings, and by the time he entered the end of his street, Mossworth concluded his thoughts: "She must have a complete set of Wodehouse."

"Excuse me, Dr. Mossworth."

And there it was.

Mossworth reflected over today's experiment with The Fact; it did not appear to be going as swimmingly as he aspired. As soon as he announced that the next quiz would feature memorization of names, dates, and locations, the class moaned as one. Now that student, that annoying female voice in the darkness:

"Dr. Mossworth, which facts? If art history is about the objectivity of historical facts, how do we determine which works of art are good or bad? And if that doesn't matter, if good and bad are merely our own preferences, what value is the study of art? I mean, what is the value of art for humans?"

Mossworth forced a smile. "Penetrating questions, all, to be sure. Perhaps we might consider that it is worthy to study good works of art because they are good?"

The female voice: "What makes Rembrandt good? What makes his paintings so great?"

Mossworth stood tall and straightened his tie firmly. "Well, let's talk about how you respond to them."

"What do you mean?"

"Ah," said Mossworth, "have a look and just let the image work upon you, let it affect your visual perceptions and dance lightly upon your emotional reactions."

"My perceptions?"

"Quite."

"Well, I see Jesus sitting at the table…"

"But how do you know that is Jesus, and…?"

"Because the title is 'Supper at Emmaeus'."

"Ah, very good, you've been reading ahead. No, you will wish your emotions to just let loose, to seek to be stimulated by the handling of the paint, the composition…"

"The formal qualities of the work."

Mossworth shuffled on his feet and straightened his tie even more firmly. "Yes, that's right. How do the formal qualities of the work, ah, work?"

Silence. "Do you mean, how do they work on me?"

"Yes, yes, that's what I mean, how do the formal qualities work on you?"

The student cleared her throat. "Well, I'm not sure they are working on me."

Mossworth sighed and smiled. "Not to worry, not to worry. It is through art history class that we learn how to let the works, the formal qualities, work upon us. Now, Rembrandt's career was marked by extreme hardship. His children all eventually died, his first wife died, and then he was not permitted to remarry because of a prenuptial agreement that granted him certain stipends. Even then he had tremendous financial difficulties." Mossworth paused for a breath.

"Um, yes, but his painting…?"

Mossworth bit his lip. "Little rich twits," he thought. "I had to sweat it out during my undergraduate years in Reading during the War, Oxford on the weekends, holidays in Brighton, mother working in a munitions factory. Oh, wait, that wasn't my life." Mossworth sighed, loudly, and scratched his chin.

"Yes, well, the paintings." Sotto voce he muttered, "Bleary's not like this." Clearing his throat, he peered into the darkness. "Susan is it?" he asked.

"Cynthia."

"Yes, Cynthia, why don't we talk about this in my office after class? Actually, we're out of time now anyway so the rest of you, please read chapter 13 on the Realists. We'll discuss them next time." Mossworth put his laser pointer in his pocket, flipped on the lights, flipped off the projector, and walked out of the room. He did not notice that Cynthia followed behind. She overtook him fumbling with his office keys.

"So, what I meant..." started Cynthia.

"Ah!" jumped Mossworth. He quickly composed himself. "Ah, Susan, you startled me! You certainly have a lot of questions."

"Well, I really like art and I want to know, you know, how art has meaning for humans."

"Yes, yes. Wonderful," said Mossworth, unlocking his office. Upon opening the door he immediately put down his items and reached for his Burberry and umbrella.

"Oh, Dr. Mossworth," said Cynthia, "I thought you said we could talk about Rembrandt now."

"No, I'm afraid not," replied Mossworth. "Did I give you the impression we should talk after class?

"Yes," said Cynthia, with a chill. "You said just a minute ago that we should talk about my questions after class."

"Oh, yes, sorry. What I meant was not *immediately* after class but rather *sometime* after class. Perhaps later this afternoon?

"I have lab this afternoon."

"Hm, well, perhaps another time then, at your convenience, of course. Now if you will excuse me, I've important college business to attend to." Mossworth stepped quickly down the hall and out the lobby door leaving a red-faced Cynthia by his office.

Having escaped, Mossworth worked his way out the building, past the stand of live oaks, and towards the dining hall. This day was blossoming into something quite good, sunny, twittering birds, and sparkling dewdrops. Mossworth took it into his soul and then missed his step, stumbled precipitously, jerked crazily to one side of the footpath and led his oxblood brogue lace-deep into springtime mud. Hardly missing a beat, Mossworth left the footpath entirely, coming quickly to the grass, and subtly walking and dragging his left foot, managed to scrape off most of the mud without anyone noticing.

"Damn footpaths!" he muttered. Reaching the dining hall vestibule, he took in the odors of industrial school cooking. Down the hallway, through the aluminum entryway that separated the hall from the dining room itself, Mossworth spotted Charolais. She was wearing a soft, almost furry looking light brown sweater; her huge eyes looked up just in time to connect with Mossworth's own. She winked.

Mossworth moved into the lunch line and soon his pale green plastic tray overflowed with overcooked roast beef, undercooked rice, damp yeasty bread, tepid tea, and starchy pudding. "Yes," he mumbled, "yes, jolly fantastic." Deftly he maneuvered between students blinded by hunger, and kitchen workers annoyed by blinded students, towards Charolais. As he placed down his tray he noticed that Charolais had placed both her brown sweater and her cream handbag on the neighboring seat, items she now quickly removed for his convenience. Mossworth sat.

"Hello, Dr. Charolais. How nice to see you."

Charolais looked at him conspiratorially. "And you, Dr. Mossworth. I trust the term is treating you tolerably?"

Mossworth talked while looking at Charolais, hand reaching for fork. "Yes, yes, the patient practices of past...pursuits have paid off...profitably." Mossworth smiled at Charolais and took a mouthful of greasy roast.

Charolais grinned back, subtly, and leaned in a bit. "Well, I hope the hapless hoards in your history hours have heard… honorable and helpful hints, not...hearsay."

Fork halfway to mouth, greasy bit of roast dangling, Mossworth's mouth was agape. He stared.

Breaking the spell, a voice from across the table asked, "Brian, how was the show?" Ignoring the voice, Mossworth continued to stare at Charolais' eyes, those endless huge pools, lakes. Under the table, Charolais reached a hand across and gave Mossworth's own a wee squeeze.

"Brian, the show, what did you think?" Mossworth snapped out of his reverie and turned to Crowder (Theatre) across the table. He noticed that Crowder wore clip-on suspenders.

"Oh, the show...the show. Yes, well," he began, "the story line was cleverly manipulative but the sets and costumes were so awful that it was difficult to get past them."

Crowder shook his head, "I gathered as much from the reviews, but I wonder, was not the theme of the story of sufficient merit to consider?"

"What?" Mossworth coughed. Under the table, Charolais nudged him with her knee.

"Well," said Crowder, "what I mean to say is: the play may have not been the most technically astute production in the world but at least the writer, a local fellow you know, was courageous enough to explore issues of faith and meaning. I think he seriously asked the audience to consider how culture would be shaped without God, and I think he did a fair job."

Mossworth looked up at Crowder. "Do you mean to say that you liked it?"

"Liking has nothing to do with it," replied Crowder, "I said I think he did well in addressing important concepts."

"But those awful costumes!" said Mossworth, "Remember the girl's best friend? What was with that over-dyed hair and the shimmering dress? It was just stupid. I didn't like it at all."

"Ah, well," said Crowder, standing up with his tray, "See you later."

"Bye," said Mossworth.

"Bye," said Charolais.

There was a moment's respite after Crowder left as the other Profs at the table conversed with each other. Mossworth shifted in his seat to face Charolais more directly. They munched in subdued silence for a few minutes. "Hello," he said at last.

"Why, Brian, what is with you today? You are positively effusive."

Tugging the sleeves of his tweed jacket, Mossworth glimpsed about the hall to make sure he would not be over heard. "When, when...?"

"Yes, when what?"

"When can we watch TV together?"

Charolais stared at Mossworth and then quickly picked up her napkin to catch what seemed to be an extended cough. "Brian," she quietly replied, "we can watch TV together anytime you'd like." Then with a wry grin she added, "But let's take one thing at a time, alrighty?"

Mossworth's smile drooped just a bit. "Yes, yes, quite right, quite so, I didn't mean to, well, you know, come crashing through the door."

"No, no," said Charolais, "you're fine, you're okay. Everything is fine."

"Oh, okay," stammered Mossworth, "I just, well, you know."

"Mm, yes, I know. Brian, don't you have a committee meeting this afternoon?"

"What?"

"Like, now?"

Mossworth glanced at his Hamilton watch. "Oh my, I…"

"Quarter past one."

"Ah, well, I must be off. But...is...I mean to say..."

Charolais laughed gently at him and sent him off with a last, quick, subtle hand squeeze. Mossworth pressed through the crowd of students. Charolais continued to watch him as he made his way out. Then she turned back to the table, and her food tray, took a large bit of lettuce and methodically chewed it, head hanging down. Hatterwas-Smith (psychology), a diminutive woman with straight brown fringe, fussed with a bowl of peaches and cottage cheese. She had been sitting next to Charolais, and listening.

"Mm," snorted Hatterwas-Smith.

"Mmmmm," moaned Charolais.

"How many times have you seen each other?"

"Yeah, once."

"Honey," said Hatterwas-Smith, "you've got your hands full there. Nice recovery, by the way."

"Am I crazy," asked Charolais? "I mean, he is sweet, but...is it worth it?"

"Well, let's see: how old are you again?"

Charolais grunted in assent, then snickered a bit. Hatterwas-Smith joined in the grunting and snickering, and then coughed. A small bit of Hatterwas-Smith's cottage cheese lunch suddenly shot itself out of her nose and across the table onto the back of an utterly unaware student. With that, and a few more stifled snorts, Hatterwas-Smith and Charolais picked up their trays and quickly exited.

Mossworth, hastened to the event: the monthly meeting of the Committee of Records and Proportionality, a group that seemed to work very hard and diligently towards unknown ends. These innocuous events were always held in the Chambliss Chambers, a locked room that was built to look exactly like Senator Gustavus Chambliss' Senate office circa 1974. Sadly, the Senator's reputation fell rapidly after photographs were published of him frolicking in a D.C. fountain late one evening with a voluptuous damp woman other than the Mrs. Senator Chambliss. Rumor at Hardley quietly circulated that after the scandal broke supplemental donor funds fell off and, too far along to be halted, Chambliss Hall construction continued. The difference in funding led to a substantial narrowing of the building; faculty ended up with offices only four feet wide. Of course, the proposed fountain out in front never even received formal drawings.

"Har, har!"

Mossworth took a deep breath and forced a smile as he entered the paneled office and greeted the Chair of the committee, Maloney (Chemistry).

"Har, hurrmp, heh, heh, bleat," started Maloney, "We all need to remember just why we are here, what we are trying to accomplish for Hardley, snort. Without oversight like ours, informational systems and institutional guidance, could suffer tremendously, hunk. Ours is a substantial responsibility, blurt, to inform, and direct...although, of course, our committee, has not genuine authority. Yes, we are only to inform the administration of our, findings..."

"Yes," thought Mossworth bitterly, "and after all of our work the administration does whatever the hell it wanted to in the first place. Not a shred of credit!" he burned, and then his thoughts were interrupted by the delicious and captivating visage of Charolais, moistened lips speaking softly.

"But what was with her comments at lunch?" he wondered. "Too fast, too much? TV isn't too much, isn't? And we've already listened to Noel Coward!" Rising before his mind came an image of his last brief relationship, undergraduate days. What did the girl say? "Don't assume you know what a woman wants or what a woman feels. You must talk to her"? "Well, it was something like that."

While considering the merits of past dating wisdom, shooting into Mossworth's head came a long buried memory. He a skinny nineteen-year old with patchy skin, she a bubbling twenty, brown locks, wide eyes, smooth arms, standing alone in the street in front of the Mossworth family bungalow outside Philadelphia.. A warm June evening surrounded them with promises of no classes, sunny afternoons at the Jersey shore, and fresh summer love. The girl looked up at him, pools of moonlight in her young eyes, and mumbled some words. He found his mouth dry but would not have known what to say anyway. Then she moved, or he moved, and they were together, skinny arms wrapping tightly, lips pressing, bodies squeezing, and the earth shook, the stars rang, and their minds burst into fireworks of naive passion. But it ended quickly after his second year, she moving to another university. There were letters, at first. He tried to recall the end, what had been said, or thought. All he could remember was a vague detachment; no anger, no retribution, rather a creeping dullness.

"Charolais?" he considered. Years ago, shortly after his tenure, she was interested. "I'm not stupid," he assured himself. But little about her had attracted him then. Now he couldn't stop thinking about her. "She likes Noel Coward? Wow, that cup of tea! Does she really think I move too fast? Hm, did I? Would she move to Bleary with me?"

Wait. What?

Mossworth merged his conscious thoughts onto the chaotic highway of his subconscious angst, vanity, jealousy, and inadequacy in an attempt to make sense of his life. As close as he got was: "What do her breasts look like?"

"...with surveys conducted by us, and filled out by nearly half the faculty, we've gathered some valuable information. It seems that more than half of the respondents think that surveys are a good method, for communicating their, bleat, concerns to the body at large..."

"I'll bet they are slightly drooping, heavy, white..."mused Mossworth to himself. "What am I thinking? I'm not ready for that yet. I need to sort out the relationship first, the, uh, relationship, yes the relationship...the look in her eyes..."

Eventually, Maloney's bleating slowed to the point at which the committee members who were still awake knew it was time to depart. Amongst those in the room only three conclusive decisions had been made, none of them public: Maloney decided that he was, indeed, qualified and popular enough for the position of assistant provost, Herbert (English) decided that he would again attempt to have some sort of sexual relations with yet another of his male and/or female freshmen students, and Mossworth decided that he would go this very evening to Charolais house and sing outside her window.

Mossworth hurried back to his building hoping to pick up a few things before heading home. As he opened the door to the lobby, a blast of Hermes' 24 Faubourg hit his nostrils like a German gas attack at the Somme: Professor Van Engelen-Van der Bauwede.

"Hello. Brian."

"Ah! Oh, oh. Hello Evangeline."

"Brian, I do hope you recognize that your committee responsibilities require you to attend your committee's meetings in a timely manner, no matter what your masculine sensibilities may have to say about punctuality. Oh, even that word, 'puctual', as if time can be punctured. Obviously phallic."

Mossworth licked his lips. "So, Evangeline..."

"And when you are doing your job, your nice little job, of attempting to teach art history, at least as you see it, please remember that some students may be interested in knowing how art has meaning for humans."

"I don't believe...wait, what?"

"And Brian. I do look forward to reading your evaluations from this semester. Please recall that in your last review several issues with organization, communication, masculine gesturing, and textual harrassment arose."

"I am quite well aware, but what did you mean..."

"...as well as issues of anger, timely return of student work, classcist attire, threatening auras, gender discretion/sexual personna, personal hetero-normativity gesturism...

"Evangeline! When you said 'how art has meaning for humans' what did..."

"Professor. Mossworth. In the future you will refrain from raising your voice to me, and doing so in a manner unprofessional, offensively masculine, and lurid. Good day!"

Professor Van Engelen-Van der Bauwede clicked down the hall in her Manolo Blahnik heels. Mossworth's head vibrated back and forth while his lips tried to make noise.

Mossworth fumbled his keys, hands shaking, but managed to gain entrance into the private sanctuary. Mind awhirl, he slammed shut his office door and locked out all of the world's miseries. He paced the room.

"I knew it! She has been provoking Susan, uh, Cynthia! That...that..."

Suddenly yawning, he stretched and flopped into his chair, reached for a pipe and began to chew on the stem in a most angry manner.

"What is happening? Of course, I'm not the world's greatest, I recognize my pedagological and intellectual limitations, that goes without saying. My courses are moderately well attended and my evaluations are not total rubbish. And I dress a damn sight better than most of the faculty!"

A trembling hand reached for the tobacco jar.

"Why are Cynthia and that horrid Evangeline trying to get me?"

The last time Mossworth had felt this put upon was back when he turned thirty. To kick-start his intellectual life and sooth his younger wounded self, he headed up to Boston for a summer conference; upon his return, he got a haircut, shaved off the beard, bought a pair of very expensive, genuine English-made, olive-green moleskin trousers, and started a three year subscription to *This England*. His depression subsided after that summer. Vaguely he realized that was the summer he began to familiarize himself with the liquor stores in the neighboring wet counties. Landscapes viewed when he made the drive to the county line reminded him of

England, England meant comfort, English comfort to Mossworth meant drink, and all of this make him think file cabinet. He yanked open the squeaky drawer and reached in the back.

As his first scotch smoothed down, he noticed that the lowering sun had painted an orange glow across his office wall. With his second glass he gave his attention. Leafy trees outside his office caught a breeze and suddenly Mossworth noticed the dancing shadows but neglected the lambent glow between the shadows. He reclined back in his chair, yawned again, and drifted into his third glass and sleep.

Mossworth dreamed himself on a plane, dressed impeccably, his hand holding a very expensive glass filled with very expensive drink. He lifted the glass to his lips and glanced over the rim at the unwashed masses not in first class.

Something was amiss. The airhostesses darted about the cabin; up front a few of them checked a passenger list. Now one of the flight attendants stepped up on a teaching platform and dimmed the lights. Mossworth's eyes narrowed as he stroked his grey-streaked beard thoughtfully.

"Ladies and gentlemen," the attendant began, "Western would like to thank you for traveling with us. We are, however, experiencing some small difficulties that may or may not affect our lives. We need some help." She paused dramatically as her eyes searched the cabin. "Are there any art historians on board?"

A low murmur developed amongst the throngs of passengers. Mossworth adjusted his perfectly round Le Corbusier eyeglasses, tugged on his sleeves, straightened his bow tie, and stood: "Ma'am, I'm an art historian."

Quickly the flight attendant came to his side. "Please, sir," said the attendant with gravitas, "Follow me."

As Mossworth stood he felt the impressed stares of the other passengers. Certainly he overheard at least one passenger state: "What a useful man!"

The flight attendant moved towards the cockpit door and gestured at Mossworth to draw closer. She whispered, "Sir, we really need your help. You are the only one who can save us." Then, with trembling hands, she flung open the door. "Please, sir, do something with these!"

Mossworth blinked as he took in the pilots. One had a large, stony head of smooth white marble with curly hair and a wrinkled brow. The other pilot stared strangely with two eyes on the same side of its divided head.

"Ah, of course," began Mossworth, "quite simply, this is Michelangelo's, David, 1501, and this is a Picasso, *Femme Assise Dans Un*, 1941, a more developed cubist work demonstrating his attraction for abstractions of the human form." The aircraft suddenly bucked wildly.

The flight attendant looked at Mossworth blankly. "Well, yes, sir," she said, "we know what they are. The facts aren't actually helpful. We were rather hoping you could explain them to us."

"Oh, right, right," said Mossworth, "the cool marble of the David works upon my senses creating a sublime response..."

"Sir! No one gives a damn about your responses!"

Mossworth's eyes batted back and forth from cubism to classicism. He noticed that a warning klaxon, sounding a bit like one of Bach's fugues, began to wail; At the same time, a lamp hanging from golden chains began to dim. "What's happening?" he blurted just as the plane began a steep decline.

Grabbing a microphone the flight attendant flipped a switch and began shouting into the device, "Western is going down, it's going down! Help! Help!" She turned to Mossworth with pleading eyes, "Please, sir. You're a doctor, do something!"

"Yes, uh, of course," he began as the plane tilted even further. "Well, David was begun in the mid-sixteenth century from a piece of flawed marble thus explaining the unusually narrow midsection..."

"That-isn't-helping!!" shouted the flight attendant.

"Perhaps...perhaps you might share how the work makes you feel?"

"Ahhhhhhh!" screamed the flight attendant.

Mossworth's mind leapt to, but not fro, as the plane tilted ever more precipitously and before he could say anything more, the plane seemed to flip over; he awoke to find himself flipping backwards out of his aged office chair and onto his office floor. He lay for a moment, winded, eyes swimming. "Damn," he grunted.

The phone suddenly, and quite unexpectedly, rang.

"Mossworth. Hello." A few crackles were all that Mossworth could discern from the line. "Hello? Hello?" Then the line was closed. Mossworth sat back again. "Who might that have been calling at... Good Lord, it is almost nine!" Leaping up, Mossworth shut down his computer, donned his Burberry, grabbed his briefcase, umbrella over his arm, plunked a ratty old grey-green trilby upon his head, glanced at himself in his hanging gothic arch-framed mirror, pushed his hair under his hat, and quickly left only to discover that he'd locked his door and his keys had fallen out of his pants pockets.

About forty minutes later, after Campus Security unlocked his office, Mossworth gripped his Morris' wheel, directing it along damp, darkened streets with just a tad of alcohol induced ineptitude. The clutch pedal felt a bit slippery through his shoes, even with the wetness of rain, and automatically he reached down to touch the clutch pedal only to be rewarded with a finger-full of a sticky, brown ooze. Mossworth recognized this from his shortcut across the field to his car and shouted in rage, "goat..., really? Really? Goat crap!?" Grabbing the window crank with his left hand, Mossworth steered with his knees and flicked the offending matter off of his right hand. A miserable, drizzly rain began to sink down in earnest. Mossworth rolled up the window and flipped on the wipers.

A few more blocks found him passing in front of Charolais' house. He did not stop. "What about...what about when I move, when I take the job at Bleary...what would she... I mean, should I think...?"

Continuing around the block he managed to enjoy a few more pulls from a handy flask. Then he was approaching her house again. Staring hard out the rain-slicked windows, he hoped, if it were possible, that by sheer will alone he could attract Charolais' attention enough for her to look out, see him driving by, know it was his car, and come running out towards the street, in slow motion. "Yes," he muttered, "come out, come out." He imagined her chasing him down, wet, damp rainwater pouring in slow motion across her clinging blouse.

However, during the last pass, Mossworth's gaze lingered for a fraction too long. He looked up just in time to see the side of a rusting Chevy pickup intimately meet the front fender of his Minor. Mossworth reacted immediately but the painful grinding and scraping, plus a few sparks, told him all he needed to know. Quickly shutting off his lights, he drove straight towards a few darker roads. Breathing quickly, Mossworth scanned the streets ahead for other drivers and piloted the Minor directly home. Five minutes later his garage door opened and he drove the car in. Five minutes after that his double whiskey found its way to his still-shaking right hand, as he stood in a steamy shower. "Jolly, bloody awful, jolly bloody awful. Nobody saw, nobody saw," he kept repeating. With the help of his steely resolve and two more whiskeys, Mossworth managed to extricate himself from the shower, dry himself, and slip into his Pure New Cotton pajamas. His bed warmed quickly as he worked out the last thoughts of that day along with his prayers. "Our Heavenly

Father, forgive that stupid truck driver, uh, parker. And please help those skinny black kids in Africa get, some, you know, food. Amen."

The next morning, with a vibrantly alive head, Mossworth stood in his unopened garage, staring intently at the right side of the Minor. A variety of deep scrapes ran the length of the car revealing the six layers of paint underneath; the door was notably buckled. The outside mirror was nowhere to be found. "That won't do, not at all," he mumbled. Mossworth picked up a hammer. Mossworth put the hammer down. Then he picked up a piece of sandpaper. He scratched at the side of the Minor to negative effect. With a huge, dull screwdriver he managed to pry out just a small bit of the door getting it to open and close well enough. Feeling lucky, Mossworth deftly flipped the screwdriver over and attempted to push back the pulled out metal from around where the wing mirror had been; the screwdriver slipped up and into the door window hard enough to leave a crack from top to bottom.

"Damn it all to hell!" he screamed and threw the screwdriver across the garage and into the wall where it didn't stick like a neatly thrown knife but hit butt-end and left a dent in the sheetrock. He removed himself from the garage.

"Okay, okay." Mossworth flipped through the phone book. "Automotive...repair...body..."

He dropped the phone book.

He picked up the phone.

"Art department, this is Jean."

"Hello, Jean, Mossworth here."

"Hi Dr. M. What can I do you for?"

"Jean, I'm afraid that I'm not feeling well today and won't be in for classes."

"Well, I'm sorry to hear that Dr. M," said Jean, "I hope you feel better soon. Shall I put up your usual sign?"

"Thank you," said Mossworth.

"Dr. M," said Jean, "you've not forgotten about your meeting with the FBI this afternoon, have you?"

"Ah, well, yes, actually. I'm afraid that I had forgotten."

"Do you want me to call them and tell them you are sick?"

"No, no," grunted Mossworth, "I'll go, I'll go. I have to go. My country calls."

"That's the spirit, Dr. M. Anything else?

"Thank you, no. Goodbye."

Mossworth put the phone down and stared out the window, shuffling his feet. "Damn the... bloody...." Mossworth did the only sensible thing that an anglophilic gentleman could do. He put on the kettle and readied himself for a really hot cup of tea. Soon, with his steaming PG Tips in front of him, Mossworth weighed his options. After more than seven and a half minutes of deeply contemplative meditation, he decided, he would get the Minor repaired professionally and have a second cup of tea. With the second cup now steaming (ever so slightly less hot) in front of his nose, Mossworth relaxed a bit further and knew what he had to do next. He again picked up the phone.

"Morning, Conway Police Department."

"Good morning. My name is Brian Mossworth and, well, I think I'd like to report an accident."

"Okay sir. Just a minute. Right, what was your name again?"

"Brian Mossworth. With an "i.""

"What? You what?"

"No, no, the letter "i." My name is spelled with a letter "i."

There was a slight hesitation on the other end of the line. "Brian," the officer said, with a slightly slower pace. "You mean, B-R-I-A-N?

"Ah, yes, that's it. Brian. Brian Mossworth."

"Is there another way to spell Brian?"

"Oh, well, I..."

"Okay, Mr. Mossworth. Where did..."

"Doctor."

"Pardon me? Are you injured?"

"No, sorry. Doctor. Doctor Mossworth."

"Oh, right. Thanks. Doctor. Where did the accident occur?"

"I, uh, think it was near Stone and Briarwood."

"You don't know where the accident occurred?"

"Well, actually, I'm not sure what to think about it."

There was a longer pause on the other end. Mossworth could hear what sounded like whispers on the line. "Mr. Mossworth," said a new voice, "this is Sergeant Bickwick. When did the accident you are somewhat describing take place?"

"Yes, Sergeant. Ah, it was, last evening. Around ten...past ten."

"Mr. Mossworth, you know exactly what time the accident occurred but you don't know where it occurred?"

"Well, it was raining, and dark, and I didn't think I'd hit another car."

"You hit another car?"

"I'm not sure, I'm not sure what I hit."

"You just said you hit a car."

"Did I? I thought I said that I didn't think I'd hit another car."

"How do you know you hit anything, Mr. Mossworth?"

"This morning my car had dents on it, on the side. I knew I hit something last night but I didn't know what it was. Now, when examining the damage in the light of day, it is clear that I hit something, ah, hard."

Mossworth could hear some low talking on the other end. "Mr. Mossworth," began Sergeant Bickwick, "were you drinking last night, sir?"

"Wh, what?" stammered Mossworth, "I mean, yes, but not while I was driving!"

"Of course not," replied Bickwick. "What about before you were driving?"

"No, no, no," pleaded Mossworth, "I had a few after I returned home."

"Mr. Mossworth?"

"Yes?"

"Was the vehicle you hit dark red?"

"Uh, maybe."

"We've had a report this morning of a dark red Chevy pick up that was damaged during the night. Owner lives at 2445 Stone Road. Sound like that might have been you?"

Mossworth sighed. "Yes. That must be it."

Bickwick cleared his throat. "Mr. Mossworth, we'll have an officer at your home within the hour to file a report."

"An hour? I have a meeting to attend in Little Rock." There was a pause on the other end of the phone. Mossworth continued: "It's with the FBI."

"Mr. Mossworth," said Bickwick, "an officer will be at your home within an hour and I strongly suggest you are there to meet him, sir. Goodbye."

By ten Mossworth, fully dressed in his second best wool blazer, had signed the paper work that would require him to not only pay four hundred dollars in fines but for the damages, estimated at more than two thousand dollars, for the Chevrolet that was itself worth only eight-hundred. The police officer had assured Mossworth that he was free to pursue the matter in traffic court before a judge. Mossworth smiled thinly. Twenty minutes later the interstate greeted he and his newly battered Minor on their way to Little Rock and the FBI. Traffic was heavy this time of day, which, though of some consequence to most of the vehicles, made little difference to the Minor.

Another twenty minutes of crowded driving brought the Minor to the exit for downtown Little Rock and the

Federal Building. Pulling carefully into the parking slot nearest the door, Mossworth backed up, then pulled in a second time making certain to be exactly centered. Checking his watch, Mossworth stepped quickly up to the front door, confirmed his ID to the guard, and skipped into a just closing elevator door. Tapping with impatience, he wondered what exactly was going to happen to Pete. Suddenly Mossworth caught his breath and considered that he might actually be seeing Pete.

"What would I say? What do they want me to say?" he mumbled to himself. Would he have to sit in some sort of tribunal against Pete? Would he be testifying and then sending Pete to...well...prison? "Yes," Mossworth carefully pondered, "they should have contacted me years ago. I would have given them an earful. Now Pete has gone and...done something that...got him in trouble. Well, he'll have to pay for that, no doubt. Stupid git." The elevator stopped and Mossworth stepped out into an imposing reception area.

A suited man stepped immediately up to him. "You must be Dr. Mossworth."

"Yes, yes," replied Mossworth.

"Well, I'm James Shane, Dr. Mossworth. I can't tell you how thrilled we are that you made it. C'mon, I'll introduce you to the team." Shane led Mossworth through a long corridor off of which opened frosted glass windowed doors at regular intervals. They all had painted lettering with titles that sounded dreadfully exciting. Mossworth grew disappointed when he happened upon one of the doors that was opened enough to give him glimpse of a huge office space with dull grey desks covered in lots of paperwork.

"So, Dr. Mossworth, what are you working on now?"

"Uh, well, currently I'm attempting to sort through some documents related to Jensen, an early twentieth-century American architect, his domestic work. It seems that a number of letters between he and one of his clients turned up when a country library outside of Hanover got refurbished recently."

"Ah, Jensen again, eh? Great, great," said Shane, "I was up in New Hampshire last fall on an investigation. Pretty country up there. I was really impressed with the Dartmouth campus. Know much about it?"

Mossworth put his finger inside of his collar and tugged at it a bit. "Sure, a bit."

"Baker Library, fantastic building. Know who designed it?"

"Oh, uh, no, I'm afraid not."

"Well, seems like it should be famous. With that tower in front it looks very much like Independence Hall in Philly. Very Georgian, don't you think?"

"Yes, yes, very Georgian. I would say it's very Georgian. Interesting, ah, massing." Shane looked over at Mossworth and was about to speak but then noticed they had reached their destination: Bank and Accounting Fraud Unit.

"Here we are. Boy, Pete is really going to love this. Okay, he doesn't know you are coming so he won't be expecting you. But the rest of the team is inside," said Shane.

"Well, it is certainly a jolly strange experience for me," replied Mossworth.

"And listen, we know that the frontispiece of your book is glossy so Nickels brought a paint-pen," said Shane, reaching for the doorknob and then turning it. Quite before Mossworth could digest the necessity of his book and paint-pens the door was opened and there stood nearly thirty professional persons with Styrofoam cups of coffee and sagging paper plates of yellow cake. Shane led Mossworth through the chatty crowd towards a fit, white-haired man standing near the cake-table and wearing a pointy party hat.

"Pete, Petey, I want you to meet someone," shouted Shane above the din. The white-haired man looked over to Shane and then to Mossworth and put out his hand.

"Hi, I'm Pete Donovan," he said. Shane looked with a grin as Mossworth blinked a few times and then shakily put out his hand.

"I'm Brian Mossworth." Donovan looked more carefully at Mossworth and suddenly the dawn of recognizing a face, from years of training, broke upon him.

"Mossworth, the Mossworth?" he cried, "I've wanted to meet you for ages! Oh, Jimmy, how...wow, thanks, thanks a ton!" Then turning back to Mossworth, shaking his hand even more vigorously, he continued, "Has Jimmy told you how much your book has meant to me? What memories, what memories. I was at Glower from about 1958 until 1963. Stayed on an extra year for a foreign study program. What a great school!"

Feet shifting and hands wringing, Mossworth smiled slightly and kept nodding. His eyes shifted about the room.

"...and Jenkins Hall, remember that one? Boy, changed a lot since my day. When was the last time you were there? Ninety-four? Good grief, that's a lot of water under the bridge. Do they still have..." Shane brought down Donovan in mid-sentence.

"Petey, there's something else," he began as he removed from a bag at is side a pristine copy of Mossworth's book. "The good Doc has agreed to sign it for you, too." And with that, Shane produced an odd-looking pen filled with permanent paint. "Here you go, Doc." Mossworth fumbled with the lid and managed to get some of the black paint upon his fingers. "That's all right, here, take this napkin. Now, hold the pen like this and then push down to let the paint out. Practice a bit. Hey, Mickey, Ted, come here and meet Doc Mossworth." A few other agents came over and greeted Mossworth. None of the others had attended Glower but all had heard about it from Donovan.

"Very good," mumbled Mossworth, "I think I've the hang of this. To whom should I make it out?"

"Me!" exclaimed Donovan. A few of the agents snickered lightly.

"Okay, "muttered Mossworth, "Happy Birthday..."

"Birthday?" said Donovan, "who told you that! Jimmy, did you tell him it was my birthday?"

"No, no," laughed Shane, "I don't believe I told Doc Mossworth anything about your birthday." Shane turned to Mossworth, "it's Petey's retirement. The old weasel is leaving us here and we all wanted to do something nice for him."

"You couldn't have thought of anything nicer than this," said Donovan.

"For Pete...P-E-T-E-Y?" asked Mossworth.

"How about Peter, just Peter," replied Donovan.

"For Peter on the Occasion of your Retirement. Best Regards, Brian Mossworth." With a flourish, well practiced, Mossworth attempted his signature. The paint pen brought rather mixed results. Before it had dried completely, Mossworth closed the book and handed it back to Donovan.

"Thank you, thank you very much. I...you don't know how much this means to me," said Donovan. Mossworth looked away at some of the other agents, a few of whom had begun to gather around Donovan.

Then, looking back at Donovan Mossworth replied, "My, uh, pleasure."

"Doc," spoke Donovan quietly, "the memories, the feelings from Glower... so strong, so very strong. Know what I mean?"

Mossworth looked away briefly, licked his lips slightly, and looked back. "Yes, oh yes, strong feelings."

"It's those college days. We live a thousand years in only four and when we are on the other side of it we realize that we only lived a blink. But that blink, well, it shapes us, it shapes us in ways we only begin to realize later in life." Here Donovan sniffed and rubbed his nose. Then, speaking more loudly, addressing more of the agents who had gathered around, he said, "Part of the reason I am...was, the agent I was is because of what I was taught at Glower. Professor Jerry, failed me for writing a sarcastic paper on Death of a Salesman. Told me, I'll never forget: "Brilliant perhaps, but not the right time and place." Made me write again." Donovan drifted off for a moment and then looked up, smiling, at Mossworth. "You know what I mean. It is what your students are saying about you. It's how you shape them."

Mossworth nodded and glanced around the room and found that the agents nearest him were listening to Donovan, nodding in agreement. There was a moment's quiet pause, but the agents were not nervously shuffling. Someone cleared his throat. Donovan rubbed his nose again. Shane patted Donovan on the back. Mossworth took a step backwards and managed to extricate himself from the group's intimacy. With excellently timed delivery, someone from behind Donovan said loudly, but kindly, "And the Bureau shaped you, too. Just look at that shape!" The room burst into warm laughter and many backs were patted. Mossworth took another step back, found himself near the food table, and grabbed a slice of the yellow sheet cake, assuming it to be the plastic-flavored delights sold by Kroger. With a slightly wavering fork, Mossworth shoveled rather a large bite into his mouth and discovered that the cake was homemade and spectacularly tasty. Two more violent bites and he made the end of it.

Glancing about the room Mossworth mused, "bunch of sentimentalists, bunch of sentimental cops. Wonder how long I have to wait around?" Then he grabbed a styrofoam cup and nursed a tragically sweet iced tea.

It turned out that he only had to wait about twenty-three minutes before he could make his escape. After a firm handshake with Donovan, lots of backslapping from various agents, and a quick trot down the hall with Shane,

Mosworth was back in the Morris. His cheeks tired from extended attempts at smiling, he relaxed in the non-comfort of the Morris. After shaking for a few minutes, Mossworth rubbed his hands, passed some gas, cranked up the Morris and began the serious brooding for the drive home.

THE INSPECTION

A well-informed mind is the best security against the contagion of folly and of vice. The vacant mind is ever on the watch for relief, and ready to plunge into error, to escape from the languor of idleness.

Ann Radcliffe, *The Mysteries of Udolpho*

"When seeking an onanistic subjectivity for the exercise of my own interior ur-fururism, I exponentiate validity by perceptive apprehension. This developed conceit thrusts a cognitatative dissonance via application towards painteristic totalities."

Three things Mossworth had so far gleaned from the visiting artist's lecture: the artist liked painting, he had once read a book on Taoism, and he found the color robin's egg blue erotic. Leaning forward, ears attuned, Mossworth desperately attempted to actually gain insight, meaning, direction, or even just comprehensible verbage. But these events ended always the same, filling him with frustration as he could not admit to his own lack of understanding about what the artist was saying not yet could he condemn the visiting artist as an imbecile. So he meditated on pipes.

"If I were to attend that conference in Munich I could visit Pfeiffer Huber and pick up another one of those handmade briars. Application for funding ends next Thursday…"

Disturbing his meditation, eventually, came the sound of applause notifying that the visiting artist had competed his requisite presentation. Mossworth, with perhaps even less understanding of what the artist's work was about than at the start of the lecture, joined the dozen or so others in shaking the artist's hand, wishing him well, and extricating themselves as quickly as possible from the artist's presence so as to avoid any more impenetrable droning.

Quickly ensconing himself in his office (door slightly ajar to inform students that he wasn't really in the mood but open enough that he could have said, if asked, that his door was always open), just about ready to light up, Mossworth began to feel, at last, a bit more relaxed. He even managed to bury himself, for twenty minutes, in a volume on Manet, one he had last opened three years back.

"Hi, Champ, howyoudoing?"

Mossworth looked up. Dean Marlboro stood in his office doorway.

"Mind if I steal some of your time, Champ?"

"Oh, ah, no, not at all," said Mossworth with no attempt at courtesy but carefully removing his pipe to a desk drawer.

"Great, good, okay. Listen, Sport, I'm just gonna close your office door, okay?" At this, Mossworth sat up.

"Right, well, look Buddy, we got a small problem. Not a problem really, just an issue. Okay, well, maybe just a small issue, just something, something has come up."

Mossworth sighed deeply. "Great," he thought, "they aren't going to approve my grant to study commercial banking architecture in Maui. Figures."

"Know Cynthia Gravely? She's in your Survey of Western Art course. Know her, know which one she is? She's kind of a medium sized girl with brown hair," said Marlboro.

"Cynthia. Cynthia? Oh, yes, yes, of course I know her. Has she been killed, or something?"

"Ah, well, no, no, not really, no, she's fine, she's just fine," said Marlboro.

"Well, that's a relief," said Mossworth, "er..."

Marlboro shook his head. "Yeah, yeah. Yeah, look, she's, she's been complaining, well, not complaining really, more like just talking, yeah, she's been talking, complaining..."

Mossworth asked, "What exactly has she been complaining about that concerns me?"

Marlboro's attention was fully directed at Mossworth. He shook his head then scratched his chin. "She's been complaining about your teaching. Not real happy, no."

"Really? What has she said?"

"Hm, yeah, well, she said, 'Mossworth sucks. '"

"What?"

"Oh, sorry, sorry, well, she didn't exactly say that, she said..."Mossworth really sucks" but, well, she said, she said that you were not answering her questions in class, that you refused to meet with her after class, and you were 'rude, obnoxious, and a total...' oh, well, I won't repeat that. Then she said 'Mossworth really sucks.' And she said something about you being 'quixotic' but I'm not sure she really knows what that means."

"Well," said Mossworth, shifting in his seat, "I must say I find this something of a surprise. Cynthia has been a very good student and her marks in my course reflect that."

"Yeah, that's right, that's the spirit, Champ, that's what we're looking for, we want to know she's doing well. But..."

"Yes?"

"Well, she's not so much thinking it's a grading issue as it is a learning one," said Marlboro flatly.

Mossworth did not move. His mouth was feeling the need to wrap itself around some sort of liquid. "What, exactly, does she mean by, 'a learning issue'?" asked Mossworth.

Marlboro pursed his lips. "Well, sir, near as we could understand, it seems she did not understand the criteria for artistic greatness. Uh, and more to the point, Sport, she didn't much think you could, either."

"Rubbish," spluttered Mossworth, "I've been describing artistic quality all through the term. It is clear which influences were most profound and which were mere derivatives. Has she even read her text? You know, her writing assignment, come to think of it, didn't inspire confidence in her essay skills. And someone, was it Hoarsley, thought that she was doing drugs..."

"Uh, yeah, look Champ," interrupted Marlboro, "I didn't want to get you all worked up about it. Just do what you can and see that we can help her out of here with as little pain as possible. She is supposed to graduate this May. See what you can do. Catch you later." Marlboro had already begun his movement towards the door. Around Hardley rumor said that Marlboro had never actually stayed in an office, any office, including his own, for more than three minutes, twenty seconds. Someone in Physics once timed him.

Mossworth stared about his books, then his pipes, then his computer, then his Oxford trophies. "Just perfect," he thought. "Stupid little...why could she not have just come and talked to me? Any time, any time she could have come into my office and sat down and I would have let her talk! Bloody...! To go over my head like that...!" Whirling quickly about in his chair, Mossworth turned towards his computer. "Hm, Hardley students. Not at Bleary, no sir, not at Bleary. Then, it was time to console himself with some really rather intensive Ebay searching. Narrowly avoiding the temptation to purchase an 1878 oak and mahogany armoire from Sheffield, Mossworth immersed himself in the search for antique fountain pens when the phone beeped.

"Mossworth."

"Brian. Couch here. Up for coffee?"

Mossworth sighed and rubbed his head. "Oh, my. Bloody hell, yes. I'm buying," he said, "see you in five."

Mossworth, instead of waiting for Couch to come to his office, walked out to the front of the art building. The sun was just beginning to warm up the day and, in typical Arkansas Spring fashion, the chilliness of the morning was giving way to a heat and humidity that would conquer even the most stalwart. Strutting purposefully along the sidewalk, kicking acorns and rocks this way and that, Mossworth paused. For a moment, it seemed, the chirping birds had quieted and the sun, radiating a delicious afternoon light, played behind Mossworth's downturned face. He noticed the dancing shadows along the sidewalk. Then something grew near Mossworth's consciousness, a sort of gentle peacefulness neared itself. Mossworth took a breath.

"Ah, the shadows. The reflective darkness must be lending me a particular aesthetic experience."

And yet.

He intuitively knew this particular sensation expected grasping; he also knew that to grasp it, to take it, to embrace it, would require some action on his part, some change, some belief. In an instant Mossworth clearly perceived that he would not take that action, not now, maybe not ever. To take the step would require admitting something about himself; instantly he knew he could not. Or would not. Still, the sweetness lingered. Its proximity felt good even if tinged with the knowledge that closeness was not possessing.

Then it passed. The birds flew away, the wind ruffled his hair, and Couch strolled up.

"Hey, Brian. How you doing?"

Mossworth, startled, lifted his eyes, grunted a greeting and began walking down the street.

"You jolly well won't believe the kind of a day I've had," began Mossworth, "first, last night I... this morning I... Do you remember Pete...? I was down in Little Rock at the... That is to say... Oh, damn it, forget it, just forget it!"

For a while, they walked in silence. Couch looked ahead steadily. Mossworth walked, head down. Couch asked: "Thoughts for your next sabbatical?"
Mossworth looked at Couch and then laughed aloud.

"Thanks, Couch," said Mossworth, "You're a good mate. I'm buying today." The sun was still beaming down brightly; Mossworth walked looking ahead now. "You know, Couch, I may even spring for a cookie."

"Feeling flush, are we?" asked Couch.

"No. In fact," replied Mossworth somberly, "I had something of an accident last evening."

"What?" said Couch, "A wreck? A car wreck? You didn't bust up the Minor, did you?" Mossworth nodded grimly. "Oh, I don't believe it. Didn't you just get it put together last summer?" asked Couch.

"Two summers ago," said Mossworth as they rounded the corner, "but I never had it done properly." The two of them walked up to the Coffee Cup. Couch opened the door.

"Well," said Couch, "I hope it wasn't too badly damaged. What happened? Did someone pull out in front of you?" As Mossworth made to reply, he looked up to notice that Today's Special was a Brazilian decaf, that the last of the homemade toffee-chip cookies had just been purchased by a Hardley student with three nose studs, and the student Mossworth recognized as Susan but who was really Cynthia Gravely, hot coffee in hand, was turning from the counter towards him. Cynthia looked up, recognized Mossworth and started to open her mouth to speak, but paused. Instead, she just stopped and looked directly at Mossworth. Too late to ignore her, Mossworth moved around her, twisting his body (crotch side away) to reach the counter.

"Two..." started Mossworth.

"Excuse me, Dr. Mossworth," said Cynthia, "I'd like to come and see you today. If that is possible."

"Certainly," said Mossworth, turning to face her. "I'm always available for students. I'm here to help. That's my job."

"Wonderful," said Cynthia. "What time?"

"How about three, Susan?"

"Cynthia."

"Cynthia."

"Three is fine."

"See you then."

"See you then."

As Cynthia departed, Couch let out a held breath. "Man, that was...chilly."

"Yes, yes, young Cynthia is a bit miffed, I must say," noted Mossworth. "I can't imagine what has gotten up her craw, poor young thing."

"Gosh, well, I don't know. Evans had her last term for Gen Chem. and told me she was an incredible student, really gifted. I can't believe she'd speak so rudely to you."

"Yes," mused Mossworth, "it is strange." He and Couch turned to the menu board. The happy-faced young barista behind the counter waited for the professors to make up their minds. He was new. "Ah, yes," said Mossworth to the young man, "we'd like two frappamochachinos, please. Decaf. And those last two chocolate muffins as well."

"You got it, docs," replied the barista cheerfully.

Mossworth turned back to Couch but before he could speak, both he and Couch noticed a change in the air. The clips and snips and clops and hisses from the barista's actions chimed in a way, somehow more melodic.

"What's this?" whispered Couch, eyes wide, voice atremble.

"I don't know, I don't know," gasped Mossworth.

The barista banged the strainer, clanked out the espresso powder, jammed it into the machine and flipped the switch in one smooth and fluid movement. Milk frothed, steam danced, the angels sang and in an impossibly few seconds there were two glowing mugs of warming goodness. Reflexively, Mossworth and Couch reached for them.

"Ach," chirped the barista, shooing their hands away. With a last flourish, he produced a chocolate syrup bottle from behind his back and squeezed into each mug a floating treble clef. Then he stood back and looked at Couch and Mossworth: "music major."

Couch and Mossworth, hands shaking, gently lifted their mugs and started towards a table. Mossworth couldn't wait; he lifted the mug up and inhaled deeply. Then, remembering the muffins, Mossworth accomplished four nearly simultaneous movements. Stopping suddenly caused a Boba tea toating Professor Van Engelen -Van der Bauwede, who was trying to avoid Mossworth, to walk directly into him. This jostled Mossworth's elbow sending his mug up and the cappuccino mostly into his face thus signaling an uncontrollable spasmodic reaction in his right leg that produced a violent kicking straight into a nearby steel column breaking three of his toes, sending him howling to the floor, whereupon he caught his descending mug squarely on his nose, thrusting him into oblivion.

"Brian. Brian," a female voice gently intoned. "Brian. You can wake up now. That's a good fella. There you go."

Slowly Mossworth's eyes opened. He glimpsed into a very young and pretty face. His eyes drank in her youthful beauty. "Are you...an angel?"

"Yes," said the young nurse, Julie.

"Am I in heaven?" asked Mossworth dreamily.

"Yes, yes you are," replied Julie, "and now this angel is going to remove your diaper and give you a sponge bath."

"Okay...bath..." and with that he drifted off again. This time, however, calming repose sent his thoughts into another direction entirely. Mossworth saw himself in an operating room, dressed in scrubs, masked. The patient laying on the table looked entirely familiar.

"Gentlemen," he began, scalpel in hand, "the patient is fully sedated and we are ready to begin the procedure." Above and around Mossworth-the-Surgeon, seated in theatre, dwelt a vast host of Very Serious Young Students. Some were dressed in green scrubs; some were in black wooly nineteenth century jackets and ties; a few looked to be Italian Renaissance men, *l'Uomo Universale*, resplendent in dark gowns and hoods. Buzzing in and out among the students flew a number of Rafaelesque *putti*. They wore nothing.

"Now, as we gaze down along the ribs we see that the first incision must be made at a slight angle, like this." As the surgeon began the cut, Mossworth felt it keenly along his chest. Mossworth-the-Patient realized, with a start, that the patient in his dream about to have his chest opened was himself.

"Here, gentlemen, we see the ribs blocking the main cavity, so we insert the spreader, clip the sternum, and begin to crank the ribs apart." Mossworth-the-Patient felt each turn of the spreader.

One of the Renaissance men, a hairy chap resplendent in green and gold gown, leapt up and exclaimed, "Look, look, the cavity is empty! No heart, no heart!" The others in the gallery began to chatter nervously amongst themselves. "How can he not hae a heart?" shouted a gentleman from nineteenth-century Edinburgh: "He couldna function without it!" "A French professor, perhaps from the eighteenth-century, flipped back his lovely powdered wig and flatly stated: "He cannot function. He is but dead."

Mossworth-the-Surgeon raised his hand to the animated audience. "Gentlemen, gentlemen, please, I'm the teacher here! I will say who is who and what is what. This man merely doesn't have a heart. Since when has that been necessary for living?"

The students weren't having it at all. One of them, who looked an awful lot like Cynthia Gravely, shouted out, "don't you see, the doctor doesn't have a heart!" At this, Mossworth-the-Surgeon put down his scalpel and lifted a large bone saw from a nearby table.

"Listen, listen to me! The heart is nothing! What is important is the head! The mind, the brain. That is what matters! That defines it all, that is what motivates and guides and explains! So, watch!" With that, he yanked a cord on the side of the saw and it began buzzing loudly. The spectators settled as Mossworth-the-Surgeon neatly sawed open the skull of Mossworth-the-Patient. With a deft flip of the wrist, the top of Mossworth-the-Patient's skull popped off and revealed the innards.

A dark hush fell upon the students in the gallery. A diminutive man with balding head and thick glasses stood and pointed: "that patient," he said, "is without heart and without brain. In short, it is not a man." With that the gallery broke into utter chaos. Mossworth raised his hands but to no avail.

"Gentlemen, please, gentlemen!"

They continued to shout.

"Brain! Brain! Where is the brain?"

"Brian?"

With a snap, Mossworth starred into the wide and warm face of Charolais.

"There you are. Having a nice dream?"

"Uh. Mmmmm."

"Well, sorry to yank you back into the real world. But it isn't that bad. The doctor says you will have to walk with a crutch for a month or so and that he'll want you back in a week to remove the stitches, but that's about it."

"Mm."

"You are a piece of work, Brian Mossworth, I'll have to give you that," Charolais began, "If you don't like the coffee, why do you keep buying it and getting mad about it?"

"Mm, ka, ka, fe. Mm," whispered Mossworth breathfully.

"Okay, well, we can talk about it later. Doctor says you've got to stay here tonight but I can take you home tomorrow." Then, catching an odd glance from

Mossworth, she added: "Yes, that's right, me, taking you, home. I am taking you to your house. I am going to look after you. There is no one else." Leaning in to Mossworth, her huge bosom dangerously close, Charolais whispered, "I hope that doesn't...upset Dr. Mossworth."

Mossworth did his best to make his only partially controlled face muscles smile.

"Good, then sleep well and I'll pick you up tomorrow." Charolais kissed Mossworth warmly on the cheek and left.

Things seemed to be looking up. His foot ached like bloody hell but a week of healing under the gentle ministrations of Charolais lent Mossworth a vaguely warm domestic feeling. Charolais arrived with breakfast in bed each morning, cleaned his house, laundered his garments, and changed the dvds whilst he reclined on the sofa. Mossworth managed, with little difficulty, spending the week not teaching his classes. He read a bit. Memories of the dream he had none.

When the stitches from his foot were removed, Charolais took her leave citing the need to sort her classes and do some chores of her own, but mostly to rest. Mossworth felt himself well enough to check in at his office. Victorian ebony walking stick in hand he entered his building and received several well-wishes from students and colleagues. From a distance he glimpsed Van Engelen-Van der Bauwede down the hall, entering her office. After checking his mail, he puttered in his office, collecting a couple of different pipes and some fresh tobacco. Then he called Couch and set off down the block to the Coffee Cup.

A smiling Couch waved him to the table by the window.

"Alright, alright," asked Mossworth, pulling up a chair, "tell me it was worth sacrificing my toes, Old Boy."

"The coffee? Heavens no," said Couch. "I could not enjoy coffee thinking about what happened to your foot! I've not been back since."

Mossworth nodded. "Cheers! You're a true mate, Couch."

"You know," said Couch, glancing over his shoulder towards the counter, "I called ahead to tell them what we wanted." A moment of silence passed between them. The edges of Couch's mouth twitched up slightly. "We have a name for the new drink."

Mossworth snorted.

Timothy, the skilled young music major/barista, walked carefully over, balancing a tray with two steaming mugs. Each of the coffees had a long broken cookie stuck in the side. Timothy observed their glances. "We broke 'em on purpose. Broken cookie and double shots. Part of the new drink: 'Mokkha Kickker'."

"Splendid, splendid," said Mossworth, "I could not have asked for more profound recognition of my greatness."

"Yes," intoned Couch, "you always put your best foot forward." They laughed gently and then grew serious.

"Well, this is it."

"Indeed."

Mossworth lifted his mug carefully to his trembling lips. Slowly, reverently, he pursed, grasped, slurped, and tasted. A warm, enriching glow slid down his gullet, tickling his taste buds along the way. Like a golden wave of Sahara heat was the chocolate; like Swiss Matterhorn cocoa processed by virginal elderly spinsters nuns in a remote berg; like Juan Valdez himself, deified, apotheified, descending from Olympus with Aphrodite as a goddess of The Bean, roasted by Vulcan, ground in a machine of Athena's creating to music from the harps of Apollo. For a moment, Mossworth's eyes rolled back in his head. Couch made a sort of gargling, moaning noise. Sparkling beams of sunlight danced about the room through windows from which rushed Spring-fresh breezes.

Timothy smiled at the two professors. "So, you like it then?"

Couch continued to moan softly, his eyes blinking rapidly. Mossworth moved his lips: "Mm...mah...mah."

Timothy nodded his head, pointed a finger gun and clicked it at them, and returned to his post behind the counter.

Both Mossworth and Couch continued drinking, nary a word spoken between them. Their respective mugs were soon drained and, as best possible, licked dry.

"My, my, goodness, that, that coffee was of a magnitude..."

"I hear you, yes, I hear you," said Couch, "it was like, like..." Then the two fell silent again and longingly starred into their mugs. Couch cleared his throat, "not that I would want to suggest any sort of behavior that, uh, you know..."

"Yes? Yes? Yes." said Mossworth, "Keep talking, keep talking. I think I know where you are heading, Old Boy."

"But how do we, ahem, not appear to be too...," said Couch.

Mossworth looked serious. "Yes, a bit of a tough nut. Perhaps..." But just then Charolais entered the Coffee Cup.

"Hello Doctors," said Charolais, leaning in to kiss Mossworth on the cheek.

"Hello, Dr. Charolais," said Mossworth, "You are just in time for coffee. Dr. Couch and I were about to order. Timothy!" Vaulting over the counter, Timothy reappeared.

"Ready for coffee, doctors?" he asked.

"Yes," started Mossworth, "this time we'd like..."

"This time?" asked Charolais.

"Yes, yes. Two Mokkha Kickkers and Dr. Charolais will have an iced cappuccino." Timothy nodded and leapt back into action.

Charolais raised her eyebrow. "So, you boys been drinkin' a lot this afternoon?"

Couch grinned sheepishly. Mossworth smiled. "It's not a bad thing, is it, to want to have more perfection?"

"Not at all," answered Charolais, "that's why you want to spend more time with me."

"Oh, dear lady," mooned Mossworth, "you have no idea."

An hour later, dizzy with caffeine, Mossworth and his walking stick made their way slowly back up the street towards the art building. The late afternoon sun filtered its way through a few thick clouds, bursting this way and that, making the heavens closer than usual. With the taste of otherworldly coffee still on his lips and the glow of Charolais' lips still on his cheek, Mossworth felt. He grew aware that he was feeling, that the feeling stimulated him; he warmed with pleasure and also with something he could not name. Briefly thoughts of Bleary entered his consciousness but he manged to push them aside.

He entered the art building with a smile, turned down the hall towards his office, and spotted Cynthia Gravely standing by his door. Pausing for just a moment, he leaned heavily on his cane. He smiled stiffly, nodded his head, and moved to open his office door.

"Ah, good of you to come, Cynthia."

"Well," Cynthia began, "I, uh, thank you. Is this a good time? I hope you are feeling better now."

"Thank you. You are too kind. My toes are healing nicely. Goodness, hard to believe it was only a week and a half ago." Mossworth opened his office door headed inside. "And I believe that I owe you an apology. I was quite inexcusably rude to you before and I cannot offer any reason other than mere stress of the job. I do hope you will forgive." He waved generously towards the plaid guest chair opposite his desk.

"Sure, Dr. Mossworth, thanks. And I'm sorry that I came across as pushy. Sorry," said Cynthia.

"Not at all," said Mossworth, relaxing into his chair, "you were just pursuing a line of thinking and that is a good thing. Please, sit down. There, yes, now, let's see if we can get a handle on what it is that I can teach you."

Cynthia sat, not altogether stiffly, on her chair's edge. She removed a small pink pad of paper from her backpack and readied her pen. Her eyes focused sharply onto Mossworth. "It's not really a big deal, you know," she said, "I just want to know why some artists are better than others." She paused. "No, that's not exactly it. Really, I guess what I want to know is why some stuff is called art and other stuff is not called art. Yes, that's it. How is it that some things are art and put in museums and written about in books and other stuff is not?"

Mossworth leaned forward, nodding. He inhaled deeply, reached across his desk to his neat pipe rack, and selected his magnanimous French bent apple, all the while avoiding Cynthia's gaze. Tapping the stem against his lip he muttered, "I see, I see." then he leaned back and chewed thoughtfully on the stem of his pipe. Across his mind flashed an image: sitting in his rooms at Cambridge, looking out across the "backs" of his very own college, stone mouldings around the windows, fire in the fireplace, port at hand, eager young students in tweedy clothes thinking him brilliant. "What you want to know is: how are values for things that are material determined? That's a good question and one that has frustrated..."

"Actually, no," interrupted Cynthia, "what I want to know is not about monetary value. I want to know why, or who, or how..."

"Well, the who is easy," replied Mossworth, tapping his lip with his pipe. "You see, when one attends graduate school, there are several options offered in the course of study. One can pursue the purely theoretical, so to speak, art history. Or one many seek to receive training in the practical field of curatorial sciences. It is those people who make value determinations." Mossworth leaned into his chair, facing Cynthia. "Does that help?"

Cynthia leaned into her chair, facing Mossworth, her lips pursed. She nodded a few times and then shook her head. "No," she said flatly. Then she leaned back, rubbed her chin, and glanced about the room. For twenty-eight seconds no words were spoken. Cynthia, leaning in again, her face eager, but not angry, began: "Dr. Mossworth, all semester you have been teaching us about works of art from other cultures. We've looked at the ancient Greeks, the Egyptians, we have seen work from ancient India, Japan, China. Next week we're supposed to look at sculptures from Africa. We have learned many... Hm, well, we have learned about those works, we've learned facts about them, but isn't there, I mean, isn't there...something else? There is some reason why these things are all thought to be valuable, in some cases, priceless, but I can't find that information anywhere. Isn't there more to it all than just...I don't know...the objects, the facts?"

"Um, hm. Um, hm," nodded Mossworth, "I see where you are going now." He chewed on his pipe and glanced wistfully out the window. "Yes, I see, I see. I think you want to learn about their cultures, right?"

"Maybe. I'm not sure what you call it," said Cynthia.

"Right, right. Okay, well, works of art are examples of the highest skills of mankind." At this, Cynthia's face seemed to droop a bit. "Ah, yes, sorry," said Mossworth, "personkind. Art represents the highest works personkind can achieve. Think of the glorious spires of Chartres, rising up towards the sky. Think of the stunning stained glass windows, how the light they let in colors the whole space, flooding it with...color! And the stories told in the windows also lend an air of mystery, but also of history. Illuminations of various craftsmen... people... persons... uh, craftspersons performing their jobs admirably! All fitting together into a unique and utterly original design and shape. And, don't forget that it was once burned down.

Twice, actually, and rebuilt by God knows who." And here Mossworth's voice hushed dramatically: "People came from all over France, it is said, so that Chartres might be reconstructed, might become a great work of art. It takes one's breath away, doesn't it?"

Mossworth sat back a bit, the wooden part of his chair creaking and the leather part under his bum making a disagreeable noise. He allowed Cynthia to take in his brilliance slowly, enjoy it, chew it up and digest it. Cynthia did not look at him. She gazed up along the wall, past his etching of Wells Cathedral, along his fake-wood bookshelves, and down to her shoes. Finally, a hiss of breath escaped her lips and she spoke. "Dr. Mossworth...why? Why did the people of Chartres, of France, rebuild the Cathedral? Why did they rebuild it just like that? Because they liked it? Is that it? They liked those colors and those materials and big tall towers and...just put it together that way? Where is the...meaning? Yes, yes, that's it, the meaning, where is the meaning?"

Mossworth sat up again, rubbing his pipe, its spherical bowl gleaming with the effort. "Cynthia, I think I underestimated you. What you are seeking is not normal undergraduate fare. I'm sorry for doubting you. You see, what you ask is quite complicated...but let me see if I can make it plain for you. When I say the word dog, what do you think of?"

"Uh, a dog."

"Yes, of course," said Mossworth, "but what kind of dog?"

"I don't know," started Cynthia, "I just think of dog generically, kind of keeping the options open in case I need to make a decision one way or another."

"Oh. Very well. What about if I say the word green?"

"Right, I think of green."

"Good," intoned Mossworth, "and what shade of green might that be?"

"Okay, okay," started Cynthia, "I think I see where you are going with this."

"Good, again. Now what I mean by the word green isn't what you mean by the word green, is it?"

Cynthia looked pointedly at Mossworth. "Well, surely we both must mean something similar or we could not use that word at all."

Mossworth shuffled in his seat. "Well, what I mean to say is: my use of the word green corresponds to something in my mind, some concept of greenness. That concept isn't the same as yours. What that leads us to is that the word green is merely a...sign, yes, that's it, a sign. It does not really correspond to anything in reality." Mossworth sat back again.

Cynthia began to lick her lips and then gnaw at them. "I'm not sure I follow. If neither the word nor the concept in our mind correspond to anything in reality then how can we have a conversation?"

"Ah, yes, well, that is a good question. More to the point, of course, is the connection with art and it's lack of ultimate meaning. You see, what the artist intended to portray, or paint, or sculpt, or include in his painting, for example, is not really what is there. Furthermore, when you or I come to that work, we are so full of our own experiences and biases that we cannot really talk about the work having any sort of meaning of its own. Any meaning one derives from a work is merely that, derived. So we could talk about meaning, but in truth, it just isn't there."

With this, Cynthia grew quite still, her eyes narrowed, and she remained silent for a good seventeen seconds. Mossworth inhaled and then blew a large cloud of smoke except it was imaginary as, caught up in the moment, he had forgotten he wasn't smoking.

Cynthia opened up her backpack, inserted her notebook and pen, and suddenly stood. "Dr. Mossworth, if there is no meaning in art, if all there is what we bring to it, if there is nothing there to discover in it, why study it at all? What's the point?"

"Well, yes, I see..."

"In fact," Cynthia interrupted, "I am done trying. Thank you, Dr. Mossworth. Goodbye." With that, she turned and walked out the door, not closing it.

Mossworth leaned down and pulled his socks up tight. "Um, hm, yes." Then, with his good foot, he gave his rubbish bin a solid kick. "What does she want? I gave her the answers. Ingrate."

He pondered, "I brought her through aesthetics, the historic facts, modern formalism, and even post-structural theory." He reached for an older pipe, his poker, but did not fill it. "Everything, I gave her everything! The whole history of it!"

Rolling the pipe in his fingers his eyes lingered upon the orderly grain, the gentle curve of the shank, the modest reflection of the polished briar. "Um," he grunted, "the simplicity of the pipe. Even it has aesthetic appeal." At this Mossworth stood again, holding his pipe aloft, gesturing with his free hand.

"If for but a moment one could permit their mind to grasp the simplicity of the aesthetic, the pleasure and the delight would follow quickly. Here we see a simple form, yet that form has been worked, has been altered, consciously or not, via the artist's desires. Produced at the end, after years working with materials, careful consideration of the forms, we the viewers are the beneficiaries of training and effort which has produced this work of art!"

Mossworth held the pipe higher and modestly looked about his classroom which, in this case, was his office. With the perception that only years of graduate training can bring, the professor realized his office void of an audience and the object of his contemplation, mono-teaching, and passion was but a tobacco pipe. Standing there, pipe held aloft, color rose in Mossworth's cheeks and he quickly sat down.

"Yes, yes," he muttered, placing his pipe gently into the pipe rack. "Hm, hm. The little bitch understands nothing."

THE TOILETTE

Everybody who is incapable of learning has taken to teaching.

Oscar Wilde

"Damn you, Hardley College."

Very late the following afternoon, Mossworth stood by his window, smoking. As he puffed, he huffed about the unsatisfying meeting with Cynthia, at the unfairness of the faculty meeting later, and at the goats defecating on the turf out his window.

With the aid of prodigious tobacco, Mossworth constructed an ivy and Gothic vision of Bleary College before his imagination.

"Hm, Bleary. Good old Bleary."

Then a deep rumbling from his innards interrupted.

"Oh, bloody hell!" Mossworth rubbed his belly gingerly.

Typically, only one solution presented itself as suitable for this sort of event, at this time of day. Mossworth picked up the latest copy of the Journal of the Society of Architectural Historians on his way out the door. Outside, Mossworth noticed that the twilight weather did not suit him. Heavy, roiling clouds sparkled with the orange flecks of a sun low on the horizon; it smelled of rain. A twisty breeze, warm and full of vigor, played about Mossworth's face. He drew his coat tighter about; thankful for the way the cotton fibers had been deeply saturated in a highly technical (and yet Olde World) way with pure carnauba wax. Amid this dance of nature, Mossworth strolled towards Old Main. Lights along the walk paths suddenly lit, here and there, winking on with the coming evening, illuminating the darkest corners. Mossworth kept his head down and pressed on quickly.

Old Main was still open, thankfully. Mossworth's need had grown slightly more pressing during the stroll. Deftly, leaping the aged marble stairs, first storey, second storey (always with an e) and then, third, top storey. The stairwell door squeaked closed behind a panting Mossworth. Darkness enveloped most of this level; light entered only from the dormered window alcoves. Just as he pressed quickly on down the hall, the sun's last gasp poured through these windows casting a burning warm glow across sections of the marble floors, shadow, light, shadow, light. Out of the corner of his eye, Mossworth found himself startled by the dark shadow of himself following him along the wall. He did not notice the light. Then, thankfully: The Toilet.

The story on campus suggested that Old Main had originally been constructed as an office building for one of the first banks in the region, an institution that ended up earning a fortune during the Depression by repossession of debtors' farm properties. No one on campus, not even Mossworth, had surety as to the accuracy of this claim; what had been confirmed, however, was that the only part of the building left unscathed from the rampaging fires of 1923 and the rampaging design aesthetic of the 1960s was the third floor, more specifically, the third floor gentlemen's restroom. One need only give a gentle push upon the original oaken door, feel its profoundly smooth action upon thick brass fittings, to know a different world. Inside, the floors, and the lower portion of the walls, glistened in resplendent grey marble panels. Covered in the original tin tiles, the ceiling dully reflected the dim light emanating from the copper light fixtures. The delicate ceramic castings of the sinks made one think more, "basin." Mossworth moved, quicker now, towards the last stall, the only one on campus with its own window and windowsill (for papers, journals, and coffee). The marble-paneled door moved ponderously permitting Mossworth ingress into the chamber; it shut, all the way to the floor, enclosing Mossworth in utter privacy.

Situated, seated, Mossworth opened his journal and relaxed. Flipping through the table of contents, he scanned for names he knew. He mused for a moment over the decision not to get a hot cup of coffee before coming over. "A nice hot cup and all is well," he thought. Now, seat more comfortably warmed than before, the quietness of the room settled upon him. Dimly he grew aware of the gentle creaking of the aged pipes, the subtle whispers of evening breezes upon the windows, and a faraway drip-drip that added a rhythmic quality to the presence of the room.

The warmth, the general ambiance of the men's room, and the post-caffeine crash lulled Mossworth to a certain psychic state and slowly, restfully, a dim sort of image grew in his consciousness. There he was, young athletic schoolboy during his younger days at Eton. Although his father had been killed in The War (some war) his mother had bravely worked nights and days at the sweat factory, tirelessly sewing together sweatshirts for the troops. Young Mossworth had little, had fought and grown out on the streets, wise, yet brave and compassionate among the street urchins. He'd been discovered in the first form, while performing differential equations upon his wee student chalkboard. Quickly, the authorities that regulate brilliant minds whisked him away to Eton and then up, up, up to Oxford...

Mossworth snapped back to find that he had momentarily dozed, slipped off the seat, and rammed his right hand and most of his arm into the commode water.

"Oh, oh, damn it! Damn it! What the...? This! I!"

Mossworth stood awkwardly, pants down, checked the room was empty, and then waddled over to the sinks. Slowly he began washing what he could and then dabbing it with clumps of paper towel. At one point he caught a sideways glimpse of himself in the mirror, hair disheveled, pants around his ankles, his right sleeve soaked, and a look on his face that he could not place. For a very brief moment Mossworth felt the bright and keen desire to roar with laughter, but quickly this jumped, or was pushed, into an aggravated frown and boiling anger. Kicking the stall door loudly, with his good foot, Mossworth stomped and threw soggy paper towels against the wall.

"Damn you...to...hell!" he roared to the aged tiles.

Then he noticed that he had been stamping upon the leg of his trouser, helping it to absorb more of the dampness off the floor, and that steadied him a bit.

"Bollocks. Bollocks, bollocks, bollocks," he intoned as he lifted his pants and then zipped, and buckled.

More carefully, now, he cleaned his sleeve as best he could, arranged his hair, gathered his things, and sighed. With a last glimpse in the mirror, and a last sigh, he strode confidently out of the restroom and directly into the President of the college.

"Oh, good Lord," cried Mossworth, "I'm terribly sorry."

"Not at all, not at all," replied President Larson, "Here a bit late, aren't you?"

"Yes, well...rather," answered Mossworth with a shrug.

"Ah, of course… the third floor mens..." suggested the President Larson.

"Um, yes, you know, it is, ah..." bumbled Mossworth.

"The stuff of legends, to be sure." President Larson took a look at Mossworth. "How are things Dr. Mossworth, Brian?"

Mossworth blinked a few times.

"I recently stumbled upon an essay of yours from a few years back in, ah, Aedifictoria Esoterica? Something about an American architect and his work at, was it, Hanover College?"

Mossworth, finding himself simultaneously flattered, embarrassed, and damp, managed to say, "why, yes! 'Wholly Architecture: How a Swiss cheese Magnate

Funded the Hanover East Campus.' Let me tell you, I was quite surprised that they decided to publish it. Uh...did you, um, like it?"

"Hm, what's that?" asked the President, "like it?"

"Well, yes, of course, liking and...the like..."

President Larson let the silence hang for a moment. "Yes, liking and the like...what?"

"Oh, oh, well, I mean to say that liking, liking and how we like, are, you know, merely reflections..."

"Reflections? Reflections of what?"

Mossworth licked his lips. "Goodness me, look at the time. Sorry, perhaps we can continue this another time?"

Without waiting for a reply, Mossworth turned on his damp heels, flapped an arm wave, and trotted off.

"Good evening to you, Dr. Mossworth," said President Larson as Mossworth exited. Larson stared down the hall towards the door which Mossworth had exited, shook his head slowly, and then moved himself towards the lavatory.

Mossworth, for his part, headed out of Old Main and across the lawn, missing entirely the heady night air. "Damn pretentious git," he muttered, "Like, like....like! That's all I meant! It was about liking. Does he not understand that some things are likable and others are not likable and that's what liking is about? Liking is about liking! I guess it's just too difficult for some people to see."

Liking came easy for Mossworth particularly with the thought of breakfast for dinner, a Hardley tradition before monthly faculty meetings. While most faculty found these celebrations of tedium, some took solace with the expansive, hot breakfast foods. Mossworth often found it cheering to be addressed as Dr. Mossworth by the dining hall staff. He exchanged trivial gossip with them in the sort of way an eighteenth-century manorial baron might have quipped with his hounds' keepers.

"Good evening, Dr. Mossworth," greeted an elderly man as Mossworth entered the dining hall. Mossworth had known him for many years, but not by name.

"Care for some bacon, eggs and grits? I made the grits myself."

He neatly dished out some eggs, tossed on some bacon, and then dumped a ladle-full of cheesy grits onto a styrofoam plate.

"Ah, yes, Sir, thank you. You look in good form," said Mossworth, receiving the plate. "How is the missus?"

Before the man, whose wife had died six year's earlier, could reply Mossworth turned away, shuffling across the hall towards the auditorium. On his way there he casually tossed his entire plate into a nearby receptacle. Then thought better of it and reached into the trashcan for a piece of bacon. "Grits," he muttered.

At that very moment O'Fenlon (European History) happened upon Mossworth. "Brian, looking for research material?" Then O'Fenlon laughed his drunkard's laugh and settled himself down near where Mossworth had intended to sit. Mossworth kept moving further to the back, all the way, in the corner, where the badly designed lecture hall illumination shown dimmest. He munched his cheese-grit-covered bacon in silence and alone. The meeting began.

Mossworth knew beforehand that he would not be paying the slightest bit of attention to the meeting. He surmised that no one, other than the Politics faculty and that one woman in Gender Studies, ever paid attention. "What is the point?" he mused. Eyes wandering over the crowd, Mossworth began to consider them, each, as institutional types. He ruminated over the differences in attitude based upon their respective ages and time of service. Without at all considering into which group he might fall, Mossworth worked up several categories: those young and green enough to still think they are smart and have something important to offer the world, those who still experience a rush of pleasure whenever they are publicly addressed as, "Doctor," those who are beginning to suspect that they are nothing special and have never had an original thought, those who had been around enough to know that no one in nor out of the academy gives a fig for what they think, and finally, the embittered old timers, those tragic few who have seen their pay stagnate almost at the same pace as their societal respect and are wracked with the guilt at how they wasted the golden opportunities afforded them in the academic life by shirking their precious time and shortchanging their many students.

"Yes, yes," Mossworth thought to himself, "shortchanging their students. If only they understood, if only they got it." Mossworth was able to spare his subconscious the last part of that thought, "...as I have" by some wonderfully clever contortions of his ego. He didn't exactly entertain the thought that he might or might not have had whatever it was that he assumed he had but didn't want to admit to not having, when a flustered Charolais plopped down into the seat next to him. She stared straight ahead, pretending to really listen, but meanwhile giving Mossworth a reassuring and secretive and tickling pinch to the knee causing him to suddenly thump his wounded foot.

"Oh, sorry, sorry," whispered Charolais, "I wasn't thinking. Sorry."

"Um. It's okay, fine," whispered Mossworth through gritted teeth, "I was just trying to get what they were talking about, I was thinking about the meeting, about what they were discussing."

"Dental plans?"

"Uh, yes, and besides, you weren't supposed to be here. What happened to the SPCTABNA meeting?

Charolais glanced around to make sure they were not drawing attention. They she gave out a bit of a snort and a suppressed laugh. "Ooooo, Brian, Denise and Margaret were there, discussing the rights of urban domestic fowl..."

Mossworth wrinkled his brow.

"Chickens?"

"Chickens. And pea hens and some game hens, anyway, right in the middle of their presentation a group of...well, I'm not sure who they were, some construction worker types, walked in thinking they had reserved that room for their party, and they had at least six buckets of the Colonel's finest. It was more than poor Margaret could handle."

"Fried chicken?" Slowly realization came to Mossworth's face.

"The last thing I heard was one of the men says something about her being pretty cute for an animal rights lesbian."

Mossworth attempted to picture Margaret, a scrappy, full-bodied woman by any measure, being spoken to in such a manner. "Do you think," he asked with a coy grin, "that the local constabulary has yet been contacted?"

Charolais let out a squeal and had to cover it up with a fit of coughing. A few heads turned. Eventually she calmed down enough to lean in a bit closer. "Sorry for not asking: how was yesterday? Heard that student was waiting to see you."

Mossworth opened his mouth to begin several times but could not quite find the words. He stared off at the droning speaker. "It was...not...good."

"Sorry, sweet thing," said Charolais, "what about I meet you later in the parking lot for a quick... snog?"

"Snog." thought Mossworth, a smile coming to his lips, "she knows what snogging is?" He could not have been more pleased, on several levels. "That would be," he replied, "my extreme pleasure." And after that, so as to avoid any subtly disturbing gossip, and potential nepotism issues, Charolais turned in her seat, her brown wool pantsuit rustling softly.

Later, long after the meeting, and after the breathless and risky encounter in the dark parking lot, Mossworth found himself at home, in a quiet mood, accompanied by an impulsively opened, very cheap, and now mostly gone bottle of Wiederkehr sherry. Softly glowing in the gas-burning fireplace flickered the flames of gas burning. A battered old brass floor lamp glowed in the corner. Clad in his green plaid PJs and matching dressing gown, he sighed contentedly. His eyes smiled, then drooped.

"What a good day. Hm, this calls for something to remember." Mossworth stood, swaying just a bit nearly knocking over the bottle, and moving towards one of the not-quite-square built-in bookcases he had built in. He reached up and removed a dusty Moleskine notebook from the top shelf. He fell back into his chair, flicked on the green-shaded desk lamp, and then picked up a sparkling Pelikan fountain pen, a green and black striped affair he had given himself. Opening the Moleskine, and flipping through several dozen pages, he considered how, after his reputation was established as a world-class mind, graduate students from around the world would wish to know how his original and clever wit had functioned before he became famous. Keeping the journal had not been for reflection but for progeny. Taking up the pen, he began to write: "Life has been..." Then the pen, little used, ran out of ink. Fifteen minutes later, after lots of swearing and several tissues used to soak up drips, Mossworth continued. "...good as of late. My career has been simply taking off, launching as the case may be. I find that really valuable thoughts are coming more easily now and I'm more able to deal with the difficult issues of the field, of art history, than ever before. It feels good. But what feels even more good is the new love of my life, Charolais. How I feel about her? If I could but count the ways. She is lovely and special and really wonderful. She is pretty and attractive and I am ever so fond of her."

"Yes," he said aloud, waving his sherry glass about, then drinking it, then filling it again, "yes, life is good, life is good. I'm sure glad that my life is good. I've got everything." With such complex and heady thoughts, Mossworth took himself and his plaid PJs off to bed. But as he lay in bed, dreamy thoughts about to overtake his relaxing mind, he suddenly envisioned Charolais, then a possible move to Bleary, then thoughts of school reminded him about Cynthia Gravely, and with a wave of nausea, he recalled that his monthly reading group would hold its final meeting. "Only one more meeting, only one more meeting..."

"It's not that the author is attempting to persuade the readers that lesbianism is normal," began Visiting Professor Chutes (Unknown Interdisciplinary Field), "it's more that he, or I guess we should now say, she, has grasped that lesbianism understood as a non-sexual phenomena of sociological anti-conditioning is really transcended by our combined, that is to say, the sociologically combined, efforts of the communal id." Mossworth was privy to the rumor that Chutes, Professor and Feminist in Residence at the Center for Art and Knowledge Transfer, University of Applied Arts, Vienna, was pulling down at least ten grand for this one-month gig at Hardley. Faculty attending the workshop could count on a hundred Dollars, a poor-quality ballpoint pen, and a mint. Funding for her visit had been arranged by Professor Van Engelen-Van der Bauwede.

Chutes was permitted to reside, for the duration of her residency, at the mysteriously lavish Barphy House. No one on the Hardley faculty knew for certain the exact function of the Barphy House. It held neither classroom space nor offices for professors nor administrators but all knew of The Apartment. Chutes must have been enjoying herself immensely, thought Mossworth, what with the huge bedroom suite that opened onto its own private and enclosed verandah. Legend heard tale of the flowering vines, the fruit trees and the well-stocked bar.

"Right," droned Chutes, "who also found that the work touched their own lesbian side? And remember, by lesbian, I don't necessarily mean a female-to-female sexual relationship. Non-coital, non-vaginal, lesbianism is just as legitimate even if it is between two men, or perhaps especially so." Several of the faculty shifted in their seats. As it was, through what must have been an effect of subconscious institutionalized sexism, only male faculty had signed up for the reading group. Coincidentally, the entire male faculty present wished they were not. Chutes eyes roamed the room. What made her gaze even more disturbing was her uncanny ability to never, ever, wear proper supportive undergarments; no matter where one looked at her one saw little nipples. Men tended to look askance at her, eyes moving in opposite directions, so not even a hint of interest in her mammary accouterments would register.

"Well," began Hitchens (Music), clearly starring over Chutes' head, "I found the author's use of the imagery to be a bit, you know, uh, erotic."

Chutes locked her eyes, a bit like some kind of missile technology, onto Hitchens, somewhere near his heart. "But isn't that the whole point?" she said. "When we speak of the erotic we are speaking merely of our own, conditioned, socially determined, or programmed, responses. There is no more than that. Ergo, the sexual, or the erotic, or the pornographic, and of course, notions of gender, cross-gender, or trans-gender, or perhaps even hyper-ur-genderenomoly, merely reinforce the reigning patriarchal structures that originally served as a conduit towards the whole black/white, male/female, good/bad nexus."

"Hm," mused Mossworth to himself, "this might be a chance for me. I'll knock one over their heads. Yet I wonder if they will have the wit to grasp my insight?" Then before he could quite stop it, Mossworth's ego stepped up to bat. "Yes, yes, quite," grunted Mossworth. Several pairs of bleary eyes turned towards him; many seemed to be pleading for him to say something, anything, that one could actually deem comprehensible. "Uh, I...the phrasing of the text..." Here he removed his glasses and began to clean them with his pristine white handkerchief. "It has a certain...structure..." Frantically his mind raced for technical words all the while repeating the mantra: "not nipples, not nipples, not nipples."

"Mm," voiced Chutes, "Mm."

"And… that structure...finds a sort of resonance...in the deconstructuralist...ah..." Mossworth's eyes swayed back and forth, looking, hoping, for somewhere to land, "...that is to say, the semiotic...you know, manipulation...between, ah, the genders, that is, the constructed genders, that eliminates...er..." Mossworth's eyes twinkled slight and he mused, "this is going very well. Dazzling."

"Yes, yes," said Chutes, "I like where this is going." Conner (Anglo-Irish Lit), Parish (Pure Maths), and Zandi (Mideast History) all perked up a bit, scooted to the edge of their seats, removed glaze from their eyes and looked harder than before at not her breasts.

"Yes, well, that eliminates what was once...you know, thought to be non-coital, but now finds a more pure, more felt, expression..."

"Emotion!" shouted out Duncan (Physics).

"Yes, emotion, a more pure emotion," continued Mossworth, "that symbolizes..." not nipples, not nipples, not nipples, "...the obfuscatory nature of merely... a conjugal union between a husband and wife." Mossworth gasped for air, his chest heaving, smiling grimly.

A heaviness hung in the room. Eyes turned, quickly, to Chutes. Well, near Chutes.

"Mm, yes. Mm," she mumbled, "conjugal union, eh?"

Eyes to Mossworth. "Yes, ah, yes. That's exactly it."

Eyes to Chutes. "Very interesting."

Eyes to Mossworth. "Really?" asked Mossworth.

Eyes to Chutes. "Well, no. I didn't get a word of it. I think it utter bunk. Really, Dr. Marcus, you must do better. We've been at this for four weeks now and you surely grasp at least the rudiments of the English language, don't you?"

Mossworth's mouth moved but only a bit of a stale odor emerged. A ripple of disappointment rolled across the room, discouraging everyone, excepting Chutes, even further. "Right then," said Chutes, "that's our time. Hard to imagine that we have reached our final meeting. (The room perked up quite a bit at that.) It has been a great experience for me and I'm sure it has been for you, too. And I must run to catch a flight to Paris. Ta, ta, my lovelies!" With that she grabbed her red NOW canvas tote, gave one last thrust of her pointy chest as she twisted herself into a ratty old brown trench coat, and whirled out of the room.

No one else moved for a while. Then Duncan stood up and walked to the door, peeked out the tiny window, and returned to the table. "She is, apparently, gone. Checks will be in your mailboxes soon. Admin wanted us to fill out evals for this book club, too. Here." Duncan passed out forms and the table set to. The room grew even quieter and soon all that could be heard was the scratching sound of pencils on paper.

Breaking the quiet someone, Mossworth thought it Parish, asked, "how do you spell 'Satanic'"?

And then it was Sunday morning. Mossworth broke his antique razor, over-steeped his tea, burnt the toast and eggs, badly, and finished up his best Trumper's cologne. He then decided to avoid the Sunday school class entirely; He sought something like quietness. Entering a back door, avoiding personal contacts, he took his regular seat in the mostly empty sanctuary. Upon sitting, his right leg began repetitive bouncing. Recognition of some kind fell upon his mind; flashes of Gravely, annoyed students, Charolais, Chutes, bad coffee, and general mid-life angst whirled. The grinding machinations of his intellect came to bear upon his conscience that cast reflections over his will and attempted to stir deeply the shallow waters of his heart. With his mind thus preoccupied, he prayed, as sincerely as he could force himself to be, his head hanging moderately down.

"Lord, Father...God...here I am. Find me at repose within the confines of your House, oh Lord...I...I see I am not...that is to say...Gravely...Quench my... ah, work and students...please...those idiots...I am...filled with anxious... if they would just...and direct my feet, uh, foot steps so that I may... upon Your Ways trod. I now embrace the forgiveness and permit myself the joy, uh, the bounteous joy of finding You again. Amen."

Mossworth sat back in the pew and breathed deeply. Within a few minutes several familiar congregants began to take seats near Mossworth.

"Well, hello Brian, how are you today?"

"Dr. Mossworth, lovely to see you again."

"Brian, did you hear, we're finally getting that east window replaced. I put your name in to be on the committee."

To each of these Mossworth extended a hand and beamed a broad smile. In his mind he repeated with each greeting: "today is a good day." With the start of the service, Mossworth sat up firmly furrowed his brow in concentration. "Today is a good day, and I shall be good today. I shall do better." His passions settled. He offered a peppermint to an elderly gent even though the man did not have a sport coat. When the plate passed he inserted a crisp twenty Dollar bill. During the music he felt the cords resonate some deep feeling, although he could not have named the feeling. The sermon admonished the congregation over the subtleties of sin. Mossworth embraced the conviction with authentic emotion, deeply concerned about the state of his soul. He took a deep breath and prayed, "Thank you, God, that I am feeling better, that you have touched my heart. Lord, helps those who are not as moved emotionally as you caused me to be."

At the closing hymn, Mossworth stood even taller, lifted his head even higher, and bellowed his baritone. His smile beamed about, to the group upon his right, to those seated upon his left. As the last stanza intoned, Mossworth caught a glimpse of President Larson, three rows back. Twisting about, leaning and bending just so, Mossworth enabled himself to catch Larson's eye and give a devout nod of his head. "Today is a good day. Larson will like me better." With comforting pride Mossworth saw Larson nod back; then Mossworth noticed that Larson's gaze lingered and he was attempting to extricate himself from his pew.

"Oh, god, he's coming here," muttered Mossworth.

In a blink Larson stood in front of Mossworth, hand extended.

"Good morning, Dr. Mossworth. Lovely to see you so soon again."

"Oh, yes, good morning, President Larson."

"Please, call me Paul."

"Very, ah, kind, yes, thank you, Paul."

"I believe I owe you an apology for our…encounter…the other evening. Not fair of me to put a professor on the spot about their research. I ought to have known better."

"Not at all, not at all. Please don't think twice about it. Rather a rough day."

Larson nodded gently. "I am sorry to say that I did not realize you attended St. Swithsun's, too. How long have you been visiting?"

"Oh, I, ah, that is, just a…couple of…years…"

"Well my dear Dr. Mossworth, please forgive me doubly for not greeting you at church before this. I had no idea."

"Yes, well, that is, it isn't at all, ah… I usually rather sit, behind, over…"

"As it is that I have missed you for the passed few years, and no doubt that is due to my own selfish nature, as our good pastor discussed this morning, perhaps Mrs. Larson and I might tempt you for luncheon at our house? A few other folks may join us. We'd be most delighted."

Mossworth licked his lips and rubbed his hands, his eyes darting. "Well, so kind of you and, I am so very, ah, tempted, thank you, thank you much. Alas, I have a vast amount of work to catch up with today, not the least of which is some work on my recently, ah, damaged auto."

Larson nodded, "Of course, I am very pleased to know you are working hard. Perhaps some other time?"

"Thank you, yes, some other time."

"Very well, goodbye, Dr. Mossworth."

"Goodbye, uh, Paul."

Mossworth made for the back of the sanctuary, moved quickly through the narthex, removed his handkerchief to dab at his forehead, and then he was out, in the sunshine, heading towards his neighborhood.

Dancing across his mind whirled various outrages and annoyances. "Why didn't that man have on a jacket, at church? Who told Mrs. Dunwoody that it was acceptable to sing quite so loudly? What parent of that child could not control them and get them out of the sanctuary? Lunch? Why would he, I mean, really, to invite someone like that. I can't imagine what we would converse about." And suddenly he did not feel good.

The glittering sun flickered in the young leaves as he stepped onto their sidewalk strewn shadows, even faster along his route, past the homes of Mrs. Wemberly, Mr. Shutt, and Miss Wendy. "Not today, not today, not today."

"Why hello, Doctor," came the sweet trilling of Miss Wendy from her porch.

"Oh, Miss Wendy. Lovely to see you again. Lovely." He kept moving.

"Doctor, you are so kind. What about an ice tea? Got some biscuits from breakfast, sausage gravy."

Mossworth stopped. He forced a smile. "I, oh, well, thank you, Miss Wendy."

"No trouble, no trouble. C'mon up."

Mossworth stepped up on to a decrepit porch.

"Now you take my hand, Doctor."

He reached over to shake the steady hand of an astonishingly wrinkled woman.

"Now you just sit yourself down there, Doctor, while I fetch some of them biscuits."

A faint smile grew at the corners of Mossworth's mouth.

"You know which chair, Doctor."

"Indeed I do, Miss Wendy."

With grace, Miss Wendy stepped through the doorway of her house. The sound of plates being taken down echoed down the hall.

"And do you want gravy on the side or on the tops?"

Mossworth's smile increased just a bit. "On the side, Miss Wendy."

"And will you have some butter, too?"

"Yes, Miss Wendy."

"And you take two sugars in your tea?"

"Yes, ma'am."

For a brief minute, no more questions emerged from the kitchen. Mossworth leaned back in his chair, smiling broadly.

"Oh. Doctor?" said Miss Wendy.

"Yes, Miss Wendy?"

"I wonder if y'all wouldn't mind having a look here."

"What would you like me to look at, Miss Wendy?"

"If it's not too much trouble, that is."

Mossworth was already on his feet and moving towards the kitchen.

"Miss Wendy, it is no trouble at all."

"Well, I've got this light bulb here in the kitchen. Burned out on me last week and I hadn't had no one to replace it. My boy, Johnson, said I can't go up the step ladder no more."

"No, Johnson is right. You indeed cannot go up the step-ladder. Bulb, please." In a snap illumination filled the room. Miss Wendy smiled. Mossworth smiled.

Miss Wendy clapped her hands and exclaimed, "Thank you, Jesus!"

Mossworth's face twitched.

Miss Wendy smiled at Mossworth. "Now, Doctor. You know that while you changed my bulb, it was the Good Lord that gave you them arms."

"Yes, ma'am."

"And He gave you them arms so you could help me."

"Yes, Miss Wendy."

Stepping into the sunlight from the kitchen window, Miss Wendy stretched her arms to catch the warming rays. "So we thank Jesus, Doctor, and that is a beautiful thing."

Mossworth nodded his head. For a moment, his eyes softened, and he took a deep breath.

"Now, my friend Doctor, I can do a beautiful thing for you. Why don't you sit back down while I get you some biscuits? The sun has popped out again on the porch. It'll feel good."

An hour later, Mossworth cheerfully stepped down Miss Wendy's walk and towards his home. His face relaxed and his step was easy. Rounding the corner, his house came into view. Comfort, peace, and something akin to joy floated around him. Very close upon the edges of his mind he toyed with fitting church, Miss Wendy, and the simple grace of a sunny afternoon, into some kind of system. Before anything so profound might occur, he entered his home, discovered he had no one to greet him, smelled the mung of the burnt breakfast, remembered Cynthia Gravely, and headed straight for his liquor cabinet.

Mossworth sat at the very edge of his office chair. Before him lay an unopened tome of nineteen-fifties scholarship on Michelangelo. The day was just shifting from afternoon to evening. The sunlight just started to cast orange during that quiet hour or so after all the students and most of the faculty have left. A struck match lit up his nicely yellowed Turkish sultan's head meerschaum. Mossworth attempted to reflect. He looked at the Michelangelo volume. He looked at his computer screen. He reflected. He looked out the window in time to see one of the campus goats eating grass and bits of paper. He looked back to his book. He sucked hard on the pipe and felt the bite of the smoke. He opened his mouth and let the spent smoke drift indolently. He heard a clunk from down the hall. With a sigh he stood and limped down the hall, keeping careful eye out for any trace of Van Engelen-Van der Bauwede, to the main office. There he found, amidst a dozen advertisements for self-published art historical monographs, a hand-addressed letter from Bleary College. Limping back faster, Mossworth closed and locked his office door. Valiantly he wielded his meerschaum letter opener to discover:

Dear Dr. Mosswroth,

Upon very strong recomendation it is my distinguished plesure to offer you an on-campus interview here at Bleary. We are gratful for your application and would deem it an honor if you could fly over and visit with us about your future at Bleary next week. As you probably know, we are behind schedule on this search and would like to move the selection process along as quickly as we can. Please contact our department secretery at the number below.

"Secretery?" he mumbled. He very deeply reflected over the spelling. "Well, no need to be pedantic," he blurted to no one, while standing. "Bleary sounds a delight." And how could they not want him? He was still young, agile, loads of teaching experience, he'd been to England twice and watched hours of BBC television. "Really," he mumbled on, "I am at my peak." But by having verbalized the words he momentarily forgot that he actually then had to hear them. That activated rather another portion of his mind that wasn't at all sure about the claim. So he kept further thoughts of this nature firmly within his subconscious and considered instead the well-known rumor that Bleary had buckets of cash ready to spend.

Mossworth spent the next hour booking his flight and replying to the invite. He glanced over at his collection of art books, even those few that he'd actually read. He looked out the window and sighed. He stood up, locked his office door and went outside. Pausing in the lot, he very loudly took in a deep breath of air. Mossworth waved a cheery hello to several students, none of whom waved back. "Yes, yes, I shall miss this place, this part of it anyway. The campus, under an early April sunset, with thriving...green...leaves of... leafy leaves. And the delights of young minds...the wonderful students. Oh, I shall remember Hardly College fondly. Good memories, good memories."

Mossworth hopped into his Minor and toodled his way home, smiling. He pulled into his garage, closed the door, and went inside whistling "It's a Long, Long way to Tipperary." After checking the clock, noticing it was just past seven, he tossed two pot pies in the microwave and put on the kettle. Then he made his tea, grabbed several bottles of cider, and sat down to watch more of his made-for-BBC miniseries. Around him, through the evening's course, settled the remnants of greasy pies, empty cider bottles and shot glasses, and his licked-clean authentic Magdalen College pudding basin in which had lain a most nummy custard. Mossworth ever so slowly drifted towards sleep, lulled by the gentle ambient noise of mindless television. At the last second before plunging into oblivion, he dreamt of cows.

At a quarter-past eight the following morning Mossworth arrived on campus to empty grounds and halls. Glancing about he rushed to his office and scanned his calendar; it was neither holiday nor Saturday.

"Oh, my god, no. No."

He reached towards a dust-covered tray on his desk. It held correspondence from admin, some dating back more than a decade. He stopped. It would be in there but what was the point? Even without the letter, Mossworth knew the drill: The campus-wide convocations always started at half-eight.

With a sigh, he looked to the hook on the back of his office door. The only good part of convocations came from getting to wear his gown and hood, custom made. Soon he gleamed resplendent in a tropical-weight bright red wool gown adorned by the scarlet and black hood cascading down his back, a virtual homage to silk and fine tailoring. Crowning the ensemble splayed the cap, an elaborate affair ordered from his favorite Cambridge supplier: a long brim twisted upwards and pointed sharply towards the front, gold thread weaving a not-so-subtle line crossing the rear of the cap, the section pointing downwards. Seemingly effortlessly draped across the top and around the exceptional brim glowed the whitish fur of an ermine breed now extinct. Mossworth admired himself in his wee office mirror. "Hm, quite the part, no doubt," he mumbled as he did up the traditional frogs, "this is by far the best fitting article of clothing I own!" For the moment, anyway, Mossworth managed to forget that his red gown was also the most expensive article of clothing he owned.

By now he really needed to hurry. Tardiness was not civil, he mused, and limped quickly Past Old Main and down the green towards Clips Auditorium, a building that saw rare use excepting for visiting donors convocations. Mossworth closed in on Clips and caught the flash of one of the glass doors just closing. "Oh, bother, oh, bother," he grunted and sped up slightly. A handful of students moved slowly towards the doors, watching, Mossworth could just make out, the tail end of the faculty processional. One of the students held the door open.

"Almost missed it, Dr. M.," he grinned.

"Yes, yes, rather, and thanks," replied Mossworth, just sneaking into the lobby and running directly into the back of the Hardley College Marshall, Wilcox (Maths).

"Hey!" Wilcox hissed as the Hardley College Mace slipped from his fingers, which were sweaty as usual. The Mace fell to the floor, chipping one of its decorative wooden moldings. Mossworth reached for it immediately, but not as quickly as Wilcox, and managed to ram his outstretched hand into the back of the Wilcox', giving him a nice bloody scratch with his fingernails. Wilcox shot Mossworth a desperate glance and then looked up to see how things were progressing; fortunately, the crowd had its attention directed towards the front of the auditorium. Then, sniffing at Mossworth, Wilcox managed to suck the back of his hand while hoisting the Mace to its proper position and continue down the aisle. Mossworth, glancing about, nearly lost his step again; he groused as he noticed Wilcox' composure but could do little as he moved back in line behind Wilcox other than quietly pass gas.

Few in the crowd of mostly faculty noticed the incident as their eyes were fixed, already, upon today's speaker. Elias Whittaker, a diminutive man, held a Doctor of Education from the School of Continuing Education, a branch of the Night School of the Community College of South Arlington, one institution of the Dallas County Community Colleges. Soon, the President of Hardley would drape a hood over Whittaker's head. But none of that explained the faculty's rapt attention. Like cats fascinated by the dance of a pointed flashlight, the eyes from a hundred brain-filled-heads found themselves mesmerized by the flickers of reflection twinkling from Whittaker's thick leather belt which sported a pair of silver-plated Whittaker .357 pistols.

Whittaker's money, money that the Hardley administration eyed for many years, came from the firearms industry. Featherguild (Sociology) happened upon an article in the Sociological journal, *White Death*, and then presented to the faculty that the "Pocket Pete" was the handgun of choice amongst early inner-city gangs, was typically sold with a buy-one-get-one-half-price discount, and had originally been marketed during the 1930s under the name, "Nigger-Killer." Naturally, the faculty, upon hearing of this news, could barely contain its outrage. The Provost, in a particularly apoplectic manner, explained that the invitation had already been given and approved by the trustees. What counted, continued the Provost, were the several millions to be donated and those funds, at least thirty percent of them anyway, or at least a percent of that thirty percent, were to be directed into faculty salaries.

After that things sailed more smoothly. Certainly, Mossworth approved.

As Whittaker warmed to his monologue, Mossworth scanned the faculty ahead of him. There was McMurphy (Chemistry), a relatively junior faculty member whom Mossworth had not really gotten to know, in his rich blue gown from Yale. "Sure," thought Mossworth, "it's got a lovely color balance, but who does he think he is?" Slumping back into his chair, Mossworth managed a hand into his shirt pocket for his Altoids tin. For good measure, he rustled the paper extra loudly and helped himself to two peppermints.

Whittaker was still at it. "It's guns that made America what it is. Not the bleeding hearts who think government is here to take care of us and not the girlie men who want to take 'em from us 'cause they think all guns do is kill people." Keats (Gay and Lesbian Studies), Mbnmknukkua (African/African-American Studies), and Kloner (Studies of Studies) shifted in their seats and seethed quietly. Bouvier (Gender Studies) stood halfway up before nearby hands forced her back down.

Mossworth continued to eye the gowns of several faculty who had not attended American colleges or universities. He lolled the two Altoids about in his mouth and adjusted his Cambridge cap to a more rakish position. At that moment, his attention swerved back to Whittaker for the room had grown very still.

Whittaker was handling one of his gleaming silver pistols, waving it about his head. "And just to show you how safe and non-dangerous it is..." Whittaker started firing into the ceiling.

"Blam!"

Utter silence

"Blam!"

Scream from...was it Harrison-Doogle (Ceramics)?

"Blam!"

Campus security, under the leadership of a former Green Beret, attempted to tackle Whittaker. Whittaker, assuming a communist plot, soundly beat one of the guards with the butt end of his silver pistol; in turn he received for his troubles a couple of good whacks with a nightstick and then a tazing. The faculty sat, silent, at the events unfolding before them. Jenkins (Theater) stood up, shouted, "bravo!" and began clapping loudly. He would not stop and the rest of the auditorium guessed that it would either be rude not to join in the applause and that the whole incident had been some bizarre performance art.

As his flight approached Atlanta, Mossworth lifted his second drink and snickered, remembering the Whittaker event. "Yes, I will indeed miss those good old days at Hardley." Atlanta sprawled out below him, cars moved methodically, along the highways. Mossworth noticed houses with pools, large warehouses with expansive roofs, and curvaceous interstate exchanges spread like wild flowers. "Hm," he grunted, "I wonder what Bleary pays?"

Once outside the airport Mossworth noticed a young man in dirty coveralls, holding a "Mosswroth" sign. "Sorry," the young man explained, "Dr. Conover couldn't make it out from campus. He's got some meeting with a consulting firm from Boston...or something. Oh, and my name is Karlfour."

Mossworth strolled next to Karlfour. Behind Mossworth his Genuine Swiss Army suitcase no longer rolled smoothly, as the Swiss would have wished, due to some violence on the part of a baggage handler who didn't care for the Swiss nor for rich prats with fancy luggage.

"Karlfour, a pleasure," said Mossworth, shaking hands. "Now, ah, am I to understand what you said, that Professor Conover is meeting with some folks from Boston today?"

"Oh, no," replied Karlfour, leading him towards a battered Buick, "he is in Boston today meeting with some folks."

A profound and unexpected annoyance worked its way into Mossworth's gut. Carefully had he sculpted his appearance so as to look the part of a successful college professor for Conover.

"Right, okay, right. So, Karl...er...tell me about Bleary," suggested Mossworth, as they climbed into the car.

Once underway, Karlfour waded into his own tedious story, one that Mossworth utterly ignored. Eventually the car stopped by a Bleary administration building. "Here you go," said Karlfour with a grin, "hope I didn't bore you too badly with the story of my family and Bleary. I feel strongly about this place, it's a good place."

"No, no, no, not at all," replied Mossworth while yawning "In fact, I'm very...uh...grateful...for the chance to...ah...get to know such a dedicated and impassioned Bleary student."

"Oh, sorry," replied Karlfour sheepishly, "I meant to say, I'm not actually a student here. I was in the army for two years, and then discharged for medical reasons. Dean's office is in there. See you." The engine gunned and Karlfour evaporated. Mossworth looked up at the grey, grimy, pile of institutional seventies architecture. He dragged his suitcase towards the front door.

Inside Mossworth consulted the huge address board. He found the Dean's office and his name, or what he thought was his name: Ahrupthaboopanian, Phil. Moving abruptly to the elevator Mossworth suddenly hissed: the elevator was inoperative and Ahrupthaboopian's office was on the fourth floor

By the time Mossworth and his luggage arrived to the fourth floor, his left knee burned, his right shoulder burned, and his hips didn't swivel anymore. His hair and shirt were soaked through from the exertion and the fact that the building's cooling system didn't actually produce what one would consider conditioned air. Mossworth set down his bag and coat, took off his sport coat, mopped his brow with a hanky, and composed himself. After a moment, he entered into a delightfully cooled room (with its own a/c unit buzzing happily in the window). A young woman glared at him as he entered. "I'm sorry, but the Dean is no longer interested in any, ANY further life insurance, thankyouverymuch."

Mossworth put on his best snob smile and glared a sweaty glare back. "I'm Dr. Brian Mossworth and I'm here for an on-campus interview." Mossworth saw, for a split second, the young woman wince. "So, if you aren't too busy, I wonder if you might inform Dean...ah...Assa...Ahhnan...the Dean of my arrival."

Immediately the young woman picked up the phone. "Yes, I'm sorry sir. A Dr. Mossworth is here for his interview. Yes. No. Wait, let me check." She looked up at Mossworth. "Dr. Mossworth, are you here for the biology position?" Mossworth shook his head and started to reply. The young woman continued speaking. "No sir, not biology. I'm sorry? Oh, okay, got it." Swiveling about in her chair the young woman viewed a computer and clicked a bit. "No, not for today. Okay." She paused listening for a moment and then roared with laughter. That stopped suddenly when she looked up at Mossworth.

Quickly interrupting, Mossworth spurted, "I was to have met today with Dr. Conover. This is for a position in the art..."

Talking over him, the young woman spoke into her phone. "Okay. Very good." After setting down the phone and leaving a lingering pause in the air, the young woman addressed Mossworth. "I'm sorry Dr. Mossworth, we have no scheduled time for your interview with the Dean today nor was the Dean notified that you were to be on campus. Nor that there was a search in art. He informs me that, however, he should be very happy to squeeze you in sometime tomorrow. I hope that is convenient."

Mossworth looked at his watch and then back at the secretary. "How does one get to the art building?"

She looked at him over her coke can: "Which one?"

First there was the broken sidewalk, then the series of terraces and steps that lead to the higher ground. Arriving at the first of the gates, as the Dean's secretary had described, Mossworth found himself surrounded by an installation project consisting of eight-foot tall phalluses constructed entirely out of pinecones. Pressing on led him to the first of the art buildings. He entered to find no directory but a student prone on a florid green sofa who explained that Mossworth needed to go to "Upper Art East Three" atop the bluff, third building east from "Center" whatever that was. Turned out Center was the pinnacle of the stairs/terraces, featured a tiny sitting area under a ripped and torn canvas roof and was marked by a fifteen-foot tall overtly male sculpture constructed out of discarded and broken cinderblocks. Heading east Mossworth had to leave the concrete footpath. He then passed through a thickly forested and strangely overgrown series of berms. During his stroll along that path Mossworth espied two snakes, a family of weasels, and what he took to be a cougar. Eventually, a building that must have been "Upper Art East Two" came into view, the base of it a massive curvaceous form; the towering vertical center pile thrust itself high into the sky.

Inside the building there was neither directory nor room numbers. Most of the light bulbs were burned out. Carefully negotiating the dim hallways, Mossworth followed a trail of clay dust, assuming it would lead to the office of the art department Chair, Professor Sheep, a teacher of ceramics. Mossworth was rewarded by the sound of a human voice: Sheep was on the phone. Of the second member of the department, Dr. Conifserson, Mossworth had no idea.

"Okay, okay! Now your talking about what I'm talking about!" Sheep, a sixty-something, squat, thick, with long grey locks and a skuzzy grey beard, chittered on his cell. He noticed Mossworth and waved him in. "Right, hey, Michel, I've got some department work I've got to get to. Let's just agree that we are in the neighborhood of one-sixty, okay? Is that okay? I mean, you're getting a deal at one-seventy! Right, right, okay. Well then Monday, for sure. Bye."

"Dr. Mossworth! So sorry to keep you waiting. I feel terrible." Sheep stood and moved from behind his desk, bits of plaster and clay dust falling in a steady cloud off his denim pants and apron. He wiped his right hand upon his pants, making a larger poof of dust, and offered it to Mossworth. "Very sorry, man, very sorry. Sorry about the mix up with Conover. Well, I guess it wasn't a mix up, really, but just an important change of plans on his part, anyhoo, and just now I had a call from out of state. It's a gallery from Florida and they are hot, hot on to a couple of my pieces. Couldn't not take it. Anyway, how are you? Good flight and all?"

Mossworth blinked a few times. "Oh, by all means, lovely flights. There was also been a bit of confusion in regards to my scheduling with the Dean.

"Really," queried Sheep, looking out the window.

"It seems he had no notice of my interview at all."

"Wow," said Sheep, looking out the window.

"And the walk up the bluff..."

"The bluff? Oh, the trails. Did they not tell you about the shuttle bus? Every fifteen minutes from admin. Don't ever walk that trail. Hastings from physics died up there last year. Really. Horrible campus design. What were they thinking? Hm, but I guess they did have some design criteria at work. I'd not wish to question their aesthetic choices, of course. And, well, the buildings, they are astonishingly good, don't you think?" Sheep flicked his dusty hands, reached into a drawer and removed a thick scrunchie, pulled his great grey locks back behind his head and scrunchied them into a droopy grey ponytail, except more like one might see on an ass. "And don't worry about the schedules. No one on campus runs much through Phil's office. Really, he isn't calling the shots anymore around here. Between you and me, the whole power structure has shifted to the Area Deans. Been that way for some time, since the early nineties anyway. So, no sweat, no sweat." Sheep paced towards the door. "Now, Conifserson's tardiness, that's another issue. I swear... Hey, would you like a coke? Let me get you something."

"Ah...tea?"

"Sorry, only what's in the machine. Mountain Dew?" Sheep reached into his pockets for change and just then a heavily breathing thin, pasty and very sweaty man swept into the room and flopped into a dirty grey armchair. The man was clad in ultra-lightweight running gear: fluorescent yellow tank that exposed his hirsute armpits and fluorescent yellow short-cut shorts that provided a bit too much information regarding his hirsute upper thighs. He appeared to be in his early fifties, lightly balding, with eyes that didn't seem to quite focus on anything. After catching his breath, he stood up, oozing moisture, and approached Mossworth with an outstretched damp hand.

"Hi, I'm David Conifserson. You must be Dr. Mossworth."

"Please," said Mossworth, "call me Brian."

"Okay, Brian. Here, why don't you sit here across from me?" Conifserson motioned to a chair opposite the dirty grey one, obviously his own desk chair. Mossworth sat. Conifserson pulled a towel from a stack on a bookshelf and proceeded to dry his face, neck, and underarms. "So, you and Conover are pals, eh?"

"Yes," said Mossworth, "we met in grad school. He's a good, ah, mate."

Conifserson smiled, in an odd way, and nodded. "Hm, hm. Righto, grad school. I remember those impassioned days...and nights. Right, right? Know what I mean, right?"

The corners of Mossworth's mouth twitched up, then down. His eyes darted about. "Oh, ah, well..."

From the other side of the room, Sheep let out a bleat of laughter. Mossworth turned to look at him but could not quite tell if he were looking at Conifserson or out the window.

"Brian, why don't you give Sheep and I your own life story regarding your journey towards the arts?"

"My, uh, my, uh...journey?"

"Yes, yes, by all means. It's very important, and I think I speak for the department, that Sheep and I have some insight into a candidate's inner vision for artistic desire. Don't you think so, Sheep?

Sheep nodded enthusiastically. Then, abruptly sitting down a bit more closely to Mossworth than he would have preferred, Sheep leaned in, dropped his voice and said: "we're all about vision here. That's where it is at, man. Not some hackneyed conceptual surface, no way. We're after the real deal. Know what I mean?

Mossworth bobbed his head up and down. "Yes, of course, it is authenticity that makes the, ah, artist. That's what you're really after here."

Sheep nodded vigorously then sat back suddenly. He flipped his ponytail around and nibbled on the end. Conifserson leaned way back in his chair. Both looked at each other. Mossworth leaned in, awkwardly, and in a semi-conspiratorial tone suggested: "for me, of course, and here I cannot speak for my current employer nor department, but for me, on a...uh...conceptual level...you know, there has always been, conceptually, a base of thinking that...seeks the inner with a more authentic and..."

"...and structured way," finished Conifserson. "Exactly, that's exactly what we are talking about." Conifserson looked knowingly at Sheep. Sheep nodded. Mossworth noted the movement with approval. Then he noted Conifserson lean all the way back into his chair and put his feet upon the coffee table that separated them. Finally, and with a slight twinge of nausea, Mossworth noted that, in that position, with legs slightly askew, he had a clearly structured and authentic view of Conifserson's dangling man bits.

"Please," Conifserson intoned, "continue."

"Ah." Mossworth blinked about, trying to focus somewhere behind Conifserson's sweaty head. "Ah. Well. The inner vision...it seeks a more, you know, ahem, delicate balance...one that, ah, seeks an equilibrium, that is to say, a knowledge of...er...the paradigms of structure, of the spaces, the, ah, often gendered spaces, that is, those gendered and socially constructed spaces of depth...like, ah, the layering of a painting..."

Mossworth took a deep breath and glanced at Sheep and Conifserson. Sheep now starred intently out the window, hand on chin and pinky finger in his mouth meditatively; Conifserson had both eyes fixed, but not quite directly, on Mossworth and he appeared to blink less often than a normal human.

"Hm, huh," moaned Sheep.

"I hear you, I hear you," intoned Conifserson, "but more to the point, I feel you. Know what I mean? I feel you."

Man bits.

"Uh..."

Coniferson leaned way back. Sheep starred out the window. Coniferson leaned way in. "I feel you. Are you with me? Are you with me? Do you feel me?"

Man bits.

Mossworth leaned in, and then out, and then blinked much. Without much subtlety he caught a glimpse between Conifserson and Sheep.

Sheep looked across the room. "Do you feel?"

Mossworth steeled himself. "Yes, yes, by all means. Feeling, I mean, you know, who doesn't?"

Man bits.

"But," began Conifserson, "do you feel me? Don't you want to feel me?"

The next day Mossworth was not feeling his interview with Dean Ahrupthaboopian. This meeting had consisted of the Dean waving him in, ordering him to sit opposite his huge desk, and then asking Mossworth, "what are your questions?" After a few instantly conceived questions about sabbaticals and tenure ("Oh, tenure, very hard to achieve here"), the Dean received a phone call and the interview ended. Mossworth, however, received rather a different reception with his final event: the lecture. The room was cold, the blinds did not keep out all the light, and the seats, based on the shuffling among the committee members, must have been uncomfortable. And yet, as his enthusiasm grew for the paintings of Raphael and the sculptures of Bernini, Mossworth perceived those in the room engaged fully.

On his last flight home, at the end of his second Bloody Mary, Mossworth discerned that the entire interview had gone brilliantly. He thrilled to recall Sheep's words to him as they walked to the shuttle van: "I've had a word around the committee members and, there is no doubt, all of them thought you did a spectacular lecture, truly demonstrated a narrative essence of art's embrace and conceptual insight." Then Sheep moved his face to within an inch of Mossworth's. "It is safe to say, you are our Prime Selectoriate." With a fresh third Bloody Mary in hand, Mossworth took "selectoriate" as a good thing. On his drive home from the airport, he massaged his ego by laughing about the absurd behavior of Conifserson and Sheep. "Hm, well, they are nice chaps, to be sure, but they are not art historians. Change is sure to come when I take over the Chairpersonship. The theoretical branch is rather a different breed." Just at that moment, he noticed some different breed of heifers grazing just off the highway and his heart rate increased. "Ah, love," he said aloud, "sometimes the warmth is filled with, ah, great pain." He then resolved to call Charolais sometime the following day, or week, or soon.

A few mornings after his return, and after an unexpectedly quiet eight o'clock class, Mossworth found himself in his office, hard at work, rummaging for tobacco. The antique jar on his desk sat empty. He located a shriveled plastic bag hidden in the back of his file cabinet containing a bit of over-dry leaf. He packed a pipe anyway, and lit up. A particularly angry striking of a match, an enthusiastic sucking in of breath, and a dramatic expulsion of unusually hot smoke attempted to heat his creative energies. Wheeling his chair to his computer, he opened up a fresh document and began to type titles for his next project. "Work, yes, work. A new day, a new day. Get back on track... Bleary will be amazed." His first title, ARCHITECTURE AND THE AMERICAN MIND was rejected as too broad and quickly became, ARCHITECTURE OF THE AMERICAN MIND DURING THE NINETEENTH CENTURY. Then Mossworth remembered that he really didn't know that much about the Nineteenth century so he changed it slightly to, AMERICAN ARCHITECTURE OF THE LATE NINETEENTH CENTURY. Mostly good, it needed just a bit of geographical tweaking to, RURAL EASTERN ARCHITECTURE OF MID-TO-LATE NINETEENTH CENTURY AMERICA. Still, that didn't quite get what he was hoping for. Eventually, after several more tries, he arrived at: WHITE, HETEROSEXUAL, MALE SECONDARY SCHOOL BUILDING ARCHITECTURE OF SOUTH-WEST BROOKLYN FROM 1893-97. Mossworth's fingers reached for the keys, "In 1893..." Then, good fortune arrived for any potential readers: the phone rang.

"Mossworth here."

"Hi Dr. Mossworth, this is Sharon from Dr. Jennings office. I'm calling about your previous physical exam and your next appointment."

Mossworth shuddered with a memory of himself at his last physical.

"Uh, yes?"

"Dr. Mossworth, Dr. Jennings was pleased with most of the results of your tests, although he mentioned something in his report about alcohol and tobacco consumption. However, of more immediate concern were some irregularities in your stool."

"My...oh," said Mossworth. "What does that mean, exactly?"

"Well, sir, Dr. Jennings would like me to schedule a colonoscopy for you as soon as possible. It is a quick and painless procedure that should only take about an hour of your time and an afternoon to recover. We'd like to get you in on Friday, sir."

"Friday...?"

"Yes, Friday at six a. m. sharp."

"Six...?"

"Very good, see you then, Dr. Mossworth." With that, Sharon hung up. Mossworth took a deep breath, flapped his lips silently, then looked up to see, resplendent in her black and white pantsuit glory, Charolais. She winked at Mossworth.

"Hi there, matey."

"Oh...matey..." said Mossworth, trying to smile.

"What's up, why the frown?" asked Charolais.

"Oh, well, I, that is, I mean, well, I...I...Friday. Friday."

"Hey, me too! Okay, Friday, what about you make me a nice meal to remember? I've heard you're quite the cook. Friday, at seven. I'll bring something for desert. Maybe, after dinner, we could curl up with a nice documentary on the Victorian age?" Charolais grinned at Mossworth. "C'mon, it will be fun."

Mossworth smiled a bit. "Friday, yes, Friday at seven. Jolly good. I'll see what's in my video collection."

"Jolly good," said Charolais, "but now I've got to run. See you, matey." And with a quick kiss she blew out the door.

After a moment's contemplation, Mossworth stood up and grabbed his coat. "Whew," he said to his books and pipes, "nothing like a bit of writing to get up an appetite. Yes, Friday, Friday...hm, perhaps a goose? No, no, a rack of lamb! Oh, bother, I shall have to go to Little Rock to get lamb. Well, nothing else for it." And so, after a day of blistering work at the office, Mossworth escaped, driving towards the thriving semitropolis of Little Rock, all the while "matey," ringing in his ears and thoughts of Bleary conveniently shoved aside.

THE LADY'S DEATH

He knew he'd had a narrow escape and in later years was fond of talking about "that inarticulate sense for actuality which is our ultimate safeguard against the aberrations of mere logic."

C. S. Lewis, *The Screwtape Letters*

Thursday morning, en route to his art history survey class, Mossworth considered the impending dinner. "Yes," he mumbled quietly, "yes, me and thee...and a roast lamb...and a nice bottle..." Mossworth practically vibrated across the parking lot towards his office. A glowing and warming sun sparkled up the dewy grass. Sparrows chirped. Crows cawed. Goats bleated. He smiled.

"Morning Dr. Mossworth," came the greeting from a cheerful freshmen. Mossworth remembered him as Arnold, or Eric, or Aaron, something like that.

"And good morning to you, sir," replied Mossworth with a bigger smile.

Away towards the back of the building, Mossworth caught a glimpse of Professor Van Engelen-Van der Bauwede entering her office.

"And a bad morning to you," he mumbled.

In his office, Mossworth carefully hung his organically natural white linen jacket upon his coat stand. Quickly checking his watch, he noticed that a mere ten minutes remained until the start of class. (The tardiness had something to do with rack of lamb preparation and a second pot of tea.) "Ach," he mooned, where does the time go?" Mossworth glanced at his desk, at the several books he thought about reading over for today's lesson (shift from Realism to Impressionism) and opened the digital presentation on his desktop. After a moment's lip pursing and head scratching, Mossworth reached into his desk for his green laser pointer, grabbed his dog-eared class notes, and wandered down to the department office to make himself another cup of tea.

"It was at this moment, this very moment, that western art began the tremendous shift from an attempt to portray that which was visually accurate to that which was individually visually accurate, so to speak, to one's own perceptions. So, here we see Courbet's, Rock Breakers...a work of anonymous laborers at heroic work. Notice the way in which the workers are reduced, that is to say, the manner in which the artist has painted them with the same attention to detail as the surroundings. They are part of the landscape, nothing more. Very well, the shift moves from this blunt, if you will, realism, to this work by Monet, Impression..." But as Courbet's workers flicked off the screen, nothing replaced them. "Ah, well, yes," began Mossworth. He clicked to move the presentation to the previous image, then to where he was. No image appeared. "Well, my apologies. I'm not sure why this image is not appearing." Mossworth tugged his collar and shuffled his feet.

"It's because you are using a Mac," shouted someone from the darkness. "The PC version doesn't accept all versions of images, some TIFF and some JPEG but not all."

"I can fix it," said another. A young man appeared from the darkness and set to work on Mossworth's laptop. "Yeah, here."

Mossworth swallowed and smiled. "Thank you for clearing that up." He turned to the class while waving his arm behind him. "Monet's Impression Sunrise. The hazy sun rising above the Seine on a working morning, bridges and fishermen barely visible, the flickers of light..."

"Excuse me, Dr. Mossworth," came a disembodied voice from the audience.

"Yes?"

"How do we know that is the river Seine?"

"Well, well, of course, Monet lived in Paris for many years, he would have had ample opportunity to view the Seine."

"Sure," came the voice, "but we don't know it was really the Seine."

"I'm fairly certain," continued Mossworth, "that scholars have identified the, uh, bridges, uh..."

"But are we really sure?" asked the voice.

"Well, I, um, most likely...but it doesn't matter, really, does it?" said Mossworth, eyes attempting to penetrate the darkened classroom.

"Why not?"

"Ah, well, you see, art is not merely about the factual representation, it is about the manner in which something is represented, the mode, the style. That is why, in short, Monet entitled this work, Impression Sunrise. It's not so much about the location as it is about his own optical sensations regarding the sunrise." Mossworth paused, magnanimously, then: "and before you ask, no, he did not originally name the work, Impression Sunrise. That was a derogatory comment placed upon the work by a contemporary critic. Monet through it appropriate and kept it."

Another voice: "It's just about Monet's impressions?"

And yet another voice: "Why did the critics want to put a derogatory label upon it? Did they not like the work?"

Another: "Did they think it was bad? Why did they think it was bad?"

Another: "If they thought it was bad, why do we think it is good?"

Mossworth raised his hand and smiled, slightly, his lips tight. "Right, well, good, good questions all."

"Uh, excuse me, Dr. Mossworth," came a voice he recognized: Annalisa, a student Mossworth could always count on to ask sensible art historical questions about dates and locations.

"Yes, Annalisa, do you have a question?" asked Mossworth approvingly.

"Well, not so much a question. I've been thinking..."

"Yes?"

"Will this, this discussion, be on the quiz?"

Mossworth could feel his forehead tightening. "Thank you, Annalisa. Yes, as always, yes."

"But Dr. Mossworth," started a young man's voice, "What about why the work is thought good now but wasn't then?"

At that moment, Mossworth could hear the door at the back of the room opening and someone entering. Peering into the darkness, eyes dazzled by the projector, he could not make out who it was. "I'm sorry," grunted Mossworth with a louder tone, "we're not quite finished with the room."

Mossworth thought he heard a voice say, "Just observing," and assumed it was a student.

"Ah, ah...well...very good. Welcome. Right, " and here Mossworth clicked to bring up his presentations next slide: one of Monet's water lilies paintings, "here we see where Monet has taken that talent for incorporating his optical sensations..."

"But Dr. Mossworth, what about the critics?" asked a student.

Another: "And why we should care about someone's optical sensations?"

"Yes, yes," started Mossworth, again, glancing about, trying not to blind himself from the projected light, "the critics, particularly those of the 1880s, or some of them anyway, sought to liberate the staid work of the Academy in France from its, ah, staid, formulaic...traditions. So, they decided that those traditions no longer fit and art needed to go in a new direction, one of their own choosing, of anyone's choosing. They were given some shows, after rejection by the art establishment, and they went on to, er, establish shows of their own and a new style which was soon...uh, growing in, ah, popularity."

Mossworth had never actually spoken aloud that particular short version of the Impressionist movement. There flickered across his mind an unentertained thought that the story of Impressionism sounded fairly-to-completely idiotic: did they not just substitute their own preferred styles for ones they rejected? However Mossworth had no time to indulge his mind in original thinking as questions began anew.

"Are optical sensations better to paint than actual objects, or historic events?"

"Did Manet really think it was all just paint on a canvas?"

"Who says this art is better than the Realists? Or the Academic painters?"

"If it is about their optical sensations, why can't I like whatever sensations I find pleasurable?"

"Okay, okay, very well, very good, good questions, good questions," Mossworth squeezed out through firmly clenched teeth. A large vein that apparently carried not quite enough blood into Mossworth's brainpan began to throb prominently upon his forehead. "I am getting to your questions. One at a time, please, children! I mean students."

A mumble resonated from the darkness.

"Very well," started Mossworth, "optical sensation was thought by the Impressionists to be a better way, to, ah, to make art and to grasp, um, at the, that is to say, the more authentic optical experiences of, the, uh, individual." Flickering on the edge of his vision raised an arm. Mossworth sighed. "Yes?"

"But Dr. Mossworth, why did the critics not approve of Impressionism and why does our book assume it is great? What makes it good? Do you think they are good? What if we think...?"

Mossworth paused and took a deep breath. His head vein throbbed more and his face flushed. "It is art. Art is paint, and marble, and architecture. It's about what moves you emotionally, about what artists, great men and sometimes women have thought is great. What they understand is not what we understand. Critics also have some of that genius, if they are great critics and understand the aesthetics of greatness, or, that is, great, uh, aesthetics. They work with the artists and if the artist is a great one, and produces great work, then the critic, if he has been properly trained, or, at least, has an insight, will see that greatness and it will be, that is, commented upon and find its way into prominence and galleries and museums. It's just not that complicated."

The mumble from the darkness droned, filling the room with a kind of painful sound. Mossworth squeeged his forehead with his hand and squinted into the crowd. "And so, the next generation of artists, conveniently enough, has been termed the post-impressionists. It was..."

"Excuse me, Dr. Mossworth."

"Can this wait?"

"Well, I mean," said the student, "not really."

"Very well."

"What do you mean by great?"

Mossworth lifted his hand in despair and dropped his precious green laser pointer onto the floor. Bending quickly over he felt more than heard the fabric on the back of natural white linen trousers give way from stem to stern. He straightened, whistled through clenched teeth, made fists, started to open his mouth... and flung his green laser pointer over the heads of the students. They heard it smashing against the back wall, bits tinkling on the floor. "Great?! Great? Are you kidding? You understand nothing! Really? I've been explaining it over and over again and you aren't getting it, none of you are getting it. Are you really that stupid? Is that it? Are you unable to comprehend even the simplest art concepts? Why are you even at Hardley?

What did you think it was going to be like? It's about hard work and dedication and seeking, yes, seeking what is great! Just go, just get out. Get out! Think hard about what you hope to accomplish in this class and in your pathetic lives!" With that, Mossworth grabbed his aged file of notes and stormed out of the silent room down to his office, slamming his door.

In his office, Mossworth tossed his file onto his desk where it slid knocking a variety of fountain pens and accessories onto the floor, threw himself into his chair, and reached jerkily for his pipe.

"Damn them! Damn the students!"

He lit a match. One drag and the leaves warmed.

"Damn them! Who do they think...?"

Two drags and they began to glow.

"I am their teacher!"

Three drags and there was a knock at the door and Dean Marlboro entered.

"Heya Champ, I..." and then Marlboro noticed that Mossworth had a lit pipe in his office. "Well...uh...Sport. Hm. I guess now I'm even less sure of where to begin."

Mossworth jerked to attention, scattering matches across his desk. He quickly extinguished his pipe by covering the bowl with his thumb, profoundly burning the appendage. "Dean, Dean, how are you? What brings you to my, ah, humble abode? I, ah, um, sorry, sorry, here, please sit."

The Dean sat and looked at Brian. "Brian, you do know that smoking is not permitted in any campus building?"

Mossworth licked his lips, and then briefly sucked his burnt thumb. "Well, uh, of course, of course, and I, would not want to think that you thought, ah, this was a sort of regular occurrence. I have just come, you know, from an, um, not very good class experience. So, when I hastened back here..."

"I know, Brian, I was there. I came in to observe you after the complaints from students. Did you not know I was in the room? Did you not see me enter? I told you I was there to observe." Dean Marlboro threw up his hands. "I'm flummoxed, plain flummoxed. What am I supposed to think, Sport?"

Mossworth swallowed several times and shifted his feet about. "Ah, well, yes, you see..."

"What the hell, Champ, what the hell?" Marlboro paced back and forth. "This is hard for me, dammed hard. I mean, you've been a part of us for, what, seventeen years? That's a long time, a long time for a man to apparently utterly misunderstand his employer's mission. A long time." Marlboro took a deep breath and reached for the door. "You'll be hearing from me. Soon."

Mossworth fumbled about with his pipe and licked his wounded thumb. "Stupid...stupid..." he quietly muttered. He stood up and moved over to his window. Outside students shuffled by, trees went about their business growing green leaves. "Seventeen years! I know! Why can't they just accept that I know what I'm doing? I didn't just fall off the turnip truck! Bloody hell, blu-uh-uh-dee-hell!" Crossing his office he stepped towards his file cabinet. "I'll show them." He opened up the lowest drawer as far as it would and reaching into the very back recesses, fetched out a tiny bottle of whiskey. "I'll show them!" Mossworth slouched into his chair, directed his browser to place him on Ebay, and began to drink and shop.

Just before he awoke the following morning, Mossworth's subconscious busied itself with a dream. He dreamed that on a bright morning he had awoken, shaved, washed, breakfasted, and dressed all the while accompanied by a strange man standing behind him. He could not see the man's face and the man did not seem to inspire fear, at least not a childish fear. When the dream brought him to the end of his morning routine he discovered that he was still not awake. His dream continued with him again awakening, going through his morning ritual, the quiet man standing behind him. Then he arrived at school, stood in front of students only, again, to find that he was not yet awake. Finally, he dreamed that again he had awoken, prepared for the day, made his way to work, stood in front of his students, and opened his mouth only to find he was unable to speak. The last thing he could recall before he actually woke up was a voice, perhaps that of his father, maybe even that of the strange man, saying clearly, "wake up!" At that he lurched out of bed and onto the floor shouting, "I'm up, I'm up, okay, okay!"

Standing produced a most unpleasant throbbing in Mossworth's head. He glanced about the bedroom at the several empty bottles. He slowly noticed that his plaid pajamas were still neatly folded on the chair and he had slept in his underwear, both legs in one leg hole, a tee shirt, and one black dress sock and that it was a quarter to nine. The good thing about it being that late was that it provided Mossworth little time to contemplate. His exceedingly hot shower revived him a bit. After dressing he rapidly checked his marinating lamb. His mind filled itself with only thoughts of the impending evening and of Charolais.

"Yes, yes, all coming together."

Backing the Morris out into the warm morning, one suggesting anticipation of summer, only confirmed to Mossworth that this would be his day, a day to remember.

All thoughts of difficult-to-answer questions, Marlboro, the obnoxious class, and his own culpability dissolved, like wisps of mid-morning clouds under a relentlessly burning sun. He even managed a bit of a smile. And then he went for his second colonoscopy.

Mostly, Mossworth remembered little, other than the humiliation of wearing a wretchedly thin gown and the slowly, painfully awkward awakening. As his eyes focused he noticed his doctor standing in front of him. "Well, well, how are you? No, no, don't try and answer just yet. I'm sure you are groggy. Okay, well, first of all, these procedures go much better for all concerned if you do not drink a lot the night before. Having said that, the good news is that we did not sedate you fully so your recovery will be faster and we should actually have you back at work in a couple of hours. The bad news..."

Mossworth's heart skipped a beat.

"Well, Dr. Mossworth, the truth is, and I've got to tell you... I've never had quite this sort of a situation before, but the truth is, we could not get the camera properly inserted and we'll have to give it another try. I've got one of my secretaries on it; she's calling the manufacturer to see if they make a smaller diameter camera. Not quite sure what happened...it just, well, you know, it just...we just couldn't get it through your sphincter."

Driving directly from his appointment, Mossworth rendezvoued with Couch in front of the Coffee Cup.

"So, when will you have to go back?" asked Couch.

"I daren't even think about it," said Mossworth.

"But you've got to get it done"

"Yes, I've got to get it done."

They entered the shop and stepped up to the counter.

"I'm buying today," said Couch, "after what you've been through."

"There's a good man," said Mossworth, "I'll have a double-cappu-latte-mach-i-total with a shot of orange, no whipped cream, and 1/2 ice." Mossworth looked up to see if the tattooed lad behind the counter was familiar. He was not. "And extra chocolate sprinkles, please."

"Anything for you, Doc Mossworth," replied the young man. Mossworth could not place the face.

"Sorry, have you been in my classes?"

"No sir, no, I just know about you from the posters...and the rally." Couch looked up from the cookie display.

"What rally?"

The young man looked a bit confused, then embarrassed. "Oh, uh...the one for today, in front of the art building." Then he mumbled something about chocolate syrup and disappeared into the back. Mossworth picked up his coffee and glanced at Couch.

"You know anything about this, Old Boy?"

"No, didn't hear anything this morning," replied Couch, "but I drove here, too. Haven't been near campus."

"Hm," said Mossworth.

In a few moments the two professors were carefully toting their drinks up the sidewalk, past the empty lot with the huge live oak, and towards the art complex.

"I say, Couch, you don't suppose this is about that competition to which I submitted my book?"

From ahead they noticed a droning noise. As they continued up the walk, the art building came into view along with several dozen chanting students. A few had cheap printed signs that read, "Why pay for incompetence?" and more cleverly, "Mossy doesn't grow on rolling minds." Presently Mossworth and Couch were able to make out the chant.

"Hey, hey, ho, ho, we ought not pay for what he don't know!"

"Brian, this is terrible. Maybe we should, I don't know, avoid it?" asked Couch.

Mossworth took in the situation. Straightening his tie, and buttoning the first button on his summer weight, pale brown Harris tweed sport coat, encouraged him. He recalled that this very morning he had shaved extra well and used his most expensive after shave. Mossworth stood tall. He took a manly slurp of his tolerably good iced coffee and with chin jutting out said: "Nonsense, they are students. What do they know?" And he quickened his pace towards the art building.

The first person to notice Drs. Couch and Mossworth sported a series of silvery studs along his left ear, a noble effort at a soul patch, and a tightly fitted black tee shirt that clearly displayed his efforts at the Health and Wellness Center. "You, you professor you!" he shouted at Mossworth, and then Couch. Mossworth paused and looked at him.

"Yes?"

"Yeah, right, yeah," the studded fit man growled, "Yeah, you professors, you and your, you know, bad... yeah!" And he shook his fist in rage.

"C'mon, Brian," said Couch, leading through the gathering crowd.

But Mossworth didn't budge. Instead, looking again at Stud Head, he asked, "Do you have any idea why you are here?"

"Shut up, man!" began Stud Head. Several other students, now in a crowd, assented their agreement. "We're here, because we care! That's why!"

"Really," said Mossworth, "what is it you care about?"

Stud Head looked around at the others students gathering. "We care about what you have done! How you, you know... We care!"

Mossworth gathered his upper lip. "I think you haven't the slightest idea as to why you are here, why you are here protesting, nor even who I am. Are you even a student?"

Stud Head looked around. "No. But I stand up for what is right!"

The crowd grew quiet at this exchange. Stud Head moved back into the mass of students. Mossworth took this as his opportunity. "Indeed, I, ah, suspect not a one of you really knows what is going on. I do not. You see," and here Mossworth turned fatherly: "You don't wish to be just a gaggle of pathetic, spoiled brats who come to school to play, not to get serious about life. No, uh, no. If for only just, just a second, really, just one second, you could see a much larger world, one resplendent…"

But a quick interruption to the pervasive eloquence was delivered to Mossworth's head in the resplendent shape and manner of a brick tossed. Grazing his brow it gashed well enough to cause a prodigious flow of blood and knock Mossworth to the ground. The crowd of students vanished in moments leaving Couch shouting.

"A brick, a brick! Could have killed you!" Couch offered Mossworth his hanky for the bleeding.

Mossworth mumbled quietly, "I'm fine…I'm okay…"

Couch helped Mossworth to his feet and into the building. "I'm stunned, when admin gets wind of this, well, there will be hell to pay. Students throwing bricks! Here, Brian, keep pressing the wound. I'm going to call campus security."

Mossworth stumbled into the men's room, dampened a paper towel, and tried to clean himself up a bit. Starring into the mirror he noticed that one drop of blood had trickled down past his eye, appearing as a long, red, teardrop. Mossworth dabbed at the drop and smeared it away. Then, suddenly, he threw his soiled paper towel into the waste can. Then he kicked the waste can (with his good foot) sending it flying across the room. Then he repeatedly kicked the door of the stall. An echoing crack bounced in the room at every kick.

In short order, Mossworth was in his office, seated, Dean Marlboro on one side and Chuck Ricks, the head of campus security on the other. Mossworth's head was wrapped with gauze.

"So, Dr. Mossworth, did you recognize anyone else in the group?" queried Ricks.

"No," said Mossworth, "and neither did Couch. I'm sure he would have mentioned it."

"Thanks, Chuck," said Marlboro, "I'm sure Brian will let you know if he thinks of anything else." Ricks nodded and left the room. "Now look, Sport, I know you've been through a lot, a hellofalot, but I had some business with you and seeing as you are doing okay, I just want to get it over with."

Mossworth nodded. "Gravely."

"Yep," grunted Marlboro, "the very one. Her claims are serious and documented and there will be a hearing. I'm letting you know that when the board meets next week the incidents with her, as well as what happened in class yesterday, oh, and the smoking thing, will be addressed. The letter ought to have gotten to your campus mailbox today. I'm also letting you know that you are to have no contact with Gravely."

"I should hardly worry about that," mumbled Mossworth.

"Right. The Trustees also know of this situation. I'm not sure where this will end for you, Kiddo. It's time for you to sort out what you are doing here and how Hardley can help you in fulfilling your whole person. We've a mission, we're to educate, this is a demanding and supporting environment and we want to make fully functioning, whole persons who grasp the social, environmental, spiritual, and psychosexual needs of today's world. Know what I'm saying?"

Mossworth shook his head. "No, not really. Well, that is to say, yes, yes, I know exactly what you mean and I'm there with you. I just...I'm not expected to teach today, am I?" he asked.

Just then a frantic Charolais burst into the room. She took one look at Mossworth's bandaged head, ran to him, and cradled his head to her bosom. "Dean Marlboro, is this how low Hardley has fallen? Is this what students do here now? What are you going to do about this? What happened to the Hardley I knew from years ago?!"

Marlboro raised an eyebrow. "Mm. I guess I didn't know about you two." With a nod to Charolais, he left Mossworth's office.

A constant flow of soothing words from Charolais, complimented by the proximity of her prodigious bosom, began to calm Mossworth. "Oh. Oh, my Charolais. You are such a dear, such a dear."

"How could they do this, Brian, how? Little brats. Like we work for a lot of money, like we do not have enough other things to worry about, department responsibilities, publishing...sometimes...and parking permits... it never ends! And now this?" Charolais continued in this manner for some time until eventually Mossworth found himself offering calming words. Then it grew silent. Charolais still cradled Mossworth's head closely. Mossworth noticed that Charolais' heaving bosom heaved a bit differently. He realized that his own breathing pumped a bit quicker. The room spun about Mossworth. Looking up he noticed her cheeks were flushed. Suddenly he sat back and then stood, unsteadily.

"The lamb, the rack of lamb! I've got to go!" He grabbed his briefcase in one hand and his umbrella in the other, even though it was sunny. "Darling, tonight. Tonight I shall make for you the most elegant and perfect dinner of your life. My heart races with anticipation at the perfection that shall await you, and me."

"Brian, sweetheart, are you in a condition to drive?" Charolais' dark brown eyes starred into his own, appealingly.

"Yes, yes, thank you, quite alright. Small nick. Flesh wound, merely. I've got to get home. The lamb must needs go into the oven to have enough time for the juices to fully saturate." Mossworth moved towards the door. "Thank you, thank you, precious lady. Your gentle ministrations will aid in my preparations for an even more perfected evening together. Until this evening. Oh, and get the door, please." And Mossworth left the office.

Charolais sat for a moment, her eyes lingering upon the doorway. Then she stood up, smoothed her dress and pushed back her hair.

"This had better be some damn good lamb."

Rushing down the hall towards the front of the building Mossworth at the last minute remembered his mail. He turned to enter the main office and was confronted with Professor Van Engelen-Van der Bauwede retrieving her own letters.

"Hello. Brian."

Mossworth froze in place, palms up.

She took him in with one glance and raised an eyebrow at the gash and bloodstains.

"I guess some professors struggle more than others with their teaching."

"Look Evangeline…" and yet she was already down the hall.

Mossworth hissed out a breath, shook his head, adjusted the bloody towel on his face, and turned towards the mailboxes. Several letters as well as book catalogs were stuffed in. He grabbed the lot, stuffed it into his coat pocket, and exited towards his car. One of the letters fell out and Mossworth noticed it was typed on official Hardley College President's office letterhead: his annual review letter. He tore into it to learn that due to 1) Student complaints, 2) No notable professional achievement and 3) A bad attitude, he would not receive any additional compensation for the coming year yet he ought to remember that compared to peer institutions Hardley offered a benefits package that reached to nearly the twenty-third percentile of some of those peer schools. Behind this was another letter, one with an impressive signature:

Dear Dr. Mossworth,

It is our understanding from the ongoing investigation and complaint filed by Cynthia Gravely that no position of satisfaction has been reached. Ms. Gravely's complaint is of such a substantial nature that it behooves this body to convene a disciplinary tribunal. It is the aim of this tribunal to seek the accuracy of the allegations of a hostile classroom environment as well as those of professional incompetence. During this tribunal you are strongly urged to have legal council. The first meeting of the tribunal is set for June 7 at nine a.m. The tribunal hopes to quickly resolve this matter to the satisfaction of both the complainant and the defendant.

Sincerely,

The Rev. Dr. A. W. N. Boodlemeyer III
Hardley Board of Trustees
Disciplinary Tribunal Chair

Mossworth raised the letters above his head, shaking them at the sky, his lips clenched, venting, hissing, only to look down at his car and notice that most of the windows had been graffitied with the word, "LOSER" excepting the driver's side window, which had been smashed completely onto the driver's seat. "Buuwaa...mmm...fff," buzzed from Mossworth's mouth as he brushed broken glass off the seat and sat. "Mmuh, muha!" he exposited, and then started the Morris. Driving with much fury as possible in a Morris, Mossworth made it home with plenty of verbalizing but not a single word and only a slight abrasion to his left buttock.

All of his agitation instantly evaporated upon entering his house and stepping into the aroma of roasting lamb. Mossworth transported himself on the fumes of greasy mutton. "Ah, ah, jolly...wonderful...mmm..." With a grand, sweeping gesture his whipped open the door to his spare room, threw his coat, papers and briefcase inside, kicked off his shoes, closed the door, twirled himself to the kitchen, opened a top drawer, flipping out a red and white striped apron, and attempted to slip the ties over his head. But the ties were just a bit too narrow and knocked his glasses to the floor.

"No matter, no matter," he grunted as his bent to fetch them.

"It's fine, it's all fine."

Straightening himself he completed tying the back tie to the apron and then surveyed his realm. "Yes, yes, but first..." and he moved towards the wine rack, pulled off a particularly terrible Chateau de Marmot Merlot, and proceeded to work the cork with a puller. "Ah, yes, and..." reaching into another drawer he found a remote. Soon the clipped tones of a recorded 1953 BBC newscast filled the room. Then, a glass of red in his hand, a final adjustment of his glasses, and several deep breaths (followed by several deep draughts) found him ready to work.

At precisely seven-thirty the door bell rang just as Mossworth's grandmother clock on the mantel chimed the half-hour. "Oh, my Charolais is nothing if not punctual," chirped Mossworth, speeding towards the door. Mossworth had brilliantly prepared everything, except himself, for what awaited him at the door: there stood a gleaming Charolais, resplendent in a black gown accented by white, her flipped hair glistened, red, succulent lips beckoned and the deeply plunging neckline revealed more of her feminine character than Mossworth had imagined. Deeply, longingly, slowly Mossworth drank in the vision before him; Charolais paused to permit him such a glimpse, yet after such a long gaze she began to smile. Mossworth saw the glow of her perfectly white large teeth and smiled back.

"Wooo, I wasn't expecting quite such a reception," she said.

"Oh..." moaned Mossworth, "oh, my..."

"A girl might catch coooold out here, Doctor."

Without another word Mossworth pushed open the door and swept his arm, inviting her in. Charolais stepped up smiling, pinched Mossworth's cheek, and then walked across the threshold. The smile grew larger as she took in the dining room. "Oh...Brian..." In a glimpse she saw the pristine Doulton china, the Waterford crystal goblets and glasses, the wine, the rustic basket of fresh buttery rolls; all of it illuminated only by the flickering golden light of countless candles burning.

"For me?"

"For none other."

With a deft flick of his wrist Mossworth activated the hidden sound system. The eerily haunting tones of *Für Elise* fell slowly to the floor. He drew Charolais' shawl off, draped it across the nearby sofa, and pulled out her chair. Silently, she smiled again, and sat. Moving across to the other side of the table, Mossworth first picked up a Waterford crystal-handled carving knife and fork ready to attack the huge lamb rack dominating the center of the table. Then, his smile flickering somewhat, he hastily placed them down again. "Forgive me, but the sight of you..." Then he whisked himself into the kitchen to return immediately hoisting a very carefully arranged green salad cradled in a sparkling glass bowl. "Would, Madame...?"

"Please," replied Charolais.

Mossworth served. Then he reached for a rustic oil and vinegar set; with the utmost care he dripped the balsamic and then drizzled the oil. Shortly, the salad remains were removed and Mossworth was back, with another set of tongs, serving a buttery roll to Charolais. Again, he made to reach for the serving knife and fork but remembered something else in the kitchen and rushed off. This time he returned with a carefully wrapped (in an Italian linen tea towel from Florence) bottle of *Chateaux du Boeuf 1997 Beaujolais Villages*, perfectly room temperature. After delicate pouring, Charolais picked up her glass. "To us!" said she...to Mossworth's back as he exited the room.

"Brian, come and sit. Here, have a drink," she called after him.

Quickly he returned, and sat. "My apologies, dear lady. I had hoped to make this a night to remember," he said, looking over his wine glass.

"Oh, Brian," said Charolais, raising her glass higher, "it is. Already it is. This is just lovely. I can't believe...sooo much trouble."

Mossworth lifted his own glass. "To us, indeed," and just as the glass made contact with his lips a mechanical beeping started in the kitchen. "Ah, ah, yes. Goodness, me, I nearly forgot!" and Mossworth leapt up and ran to the kitchen. This time it was a few minutes before he returned. Before he sat, the tiny plastic remote was subtly aimed at the sound system; *Für Elise* started over. "No worries, none at all." A lavish bean casserole, dripping with delicate cheeses, was served. Now, where were we?"

"We were drinking," said Charolais with a grin.

"Yes, of course," said Mossworth, and lifted his glass again.

"Brian, this, this... I am astonished. And is that the lamb that smells divine? Did you make the entire...?"

"Oh, good heavens," blurted Mossworth, "the lamb!" With that, Mossworth stood again and took up the crystal carving set. Delicately he placed the fork just so between the ribs, sliced straight downward, and produced a perfectly proportioned serving. Flipping the knife to the side he gripped the meat to set it right at three o'clock on Charolais' plate. Then, setting down the implements, he reached for a tiny silver ladle and scooped into the drippings, below the grease, and then poured it carefully over the lamb he had just served. Charolais stared.

"May I?"

"But of course."

Mossworth shivered with pleasure to note that Charolais reached for the outermost set of her dining silver. Cutting in, Charolais watched Mossworth's face as she did not switch hands but used her fork flipped over to lift the bite to her lips. "Mm," they both intoned together.

"Now, Brian, please, eat something."

"Yes, dear lady, terribly sorry. I just want it all to be..."

"...perfect?" she asked, eyebrows raised.

"Mm, indeed. In fact, I very nearly forgot..." and he stood and moved towards the light switch near the door. Without a word he flipped it and a small gas fire popped to life in his fireplace.

"Well, that is impressive, but so is this lamb." Charolais brought another bite up and savored. "Brian, it is stunning. You must have spent hours." Mossworth lifted his knife and fork, cutting a wedge of dripping lamb. The succulent bite made it halfway to his lips before being placed down onto the plate.

"It wasn't that hard, really. Once the lamb is suitably prepped, tied, one merely administers the sauces over a several hour period. Mostly," he continued, "it's just a matter of time." Then he lifted that bite again only to replace it again. "But you...you make me...forget time." Mossworth's eyes rested on Charolais'.

Charolais reddened slightly. "Brian...you...your... you are too kind. And I've been selfish. Besides the cooking, how has your day been? That business at school. I almost forgot all about it."

Mossworth sat back in his chair. The glow in his eyes flickered and he reached delicately towards the bandage on his scalp from the persuasive brick. Then, with a practiced, motion he had *Für Elise* begin again. Delicate tones moved through the candlelight. He attacked his bite of lamb. "Yes, well, yes...what can one say? The day is done, the week is done, and now I'm here with you and it is all perfect."

"Well, I'm confident that the student who assaulted you will be caught. Marlboro won't stand for that sort of behavior," encouraged Charolais.

Mossworth helped himself to an extended session at his wine glass. "Marlboro...that git has helped little."

"But he hasn't had time, just give him time. I have every confidence in him."

Mossworth took another leisurely tip from his glass. "Hm, confidence in him. Yes, of course, of course. We all have confidence in Marlboro."

"Oh, tsk-tsk," scolded Charolais, "now you are growing testy. That was bad form on my part to bring up work. I shan't do it again."

Lifting the bottle, Mossworth refilled his own glass and topped up Charolais'. A single drop of the red fell upon the white tablecloth. Mossworth promptly stood. "Dammit!" He moved to leave the table. Charolais reached for his hand.

"Brian. Brian. Just leave it. I'll get it out later. A bit of soda water..." Mossworth looked straight, or mostly straight, at Charolais. He wobbled just a bit.

"Yes, yes...whew...that wine...whew..." Still holding her hand he walked, slowly, around the table behind her. "Yes, it can wait. We can...eat...yes," he mumbled off. Then, standing behind her, his right hand holding hers, he reached in his pocket for the remote and began *Für Elise*, anew.

"Again?" asked Charolais? "Wow, you really like Beethoven, don't you?" Mossworth moves his hands to the sides of Charolais' head, gently stroking her hair.

"I believe what I...really like...is you." His hands moved to her shoulders. Deeply he leaned down, moving his quivering lips towards her bare neck. With the gentlest of brushes his lips met the tingling flesh of her neck. Again, he kissed her but slightly lower towards her shoulders. An intense, deep, quiet moan escaped from Charolais' mouth. The third time as he kissed her even further down, his lips touched something. Before he moved to kiss her neck a fourth time, Mossworth casually glanced downwards. He spied, settled there on her neck, right where he had kissed, a mole. Starring, now, intently at the mole, Mossworth furtively wondered, "why has she a mole on her neck?"

Mossworth stood and moved, not too quickly, back to his chair, smiling at Charolais. "Well, goodness, how are you finding the lamb?" He stabbed his fork into the lamb and attempted a cut but pushed to hard and managed to slop sauce off his plate. "Well, well...how about that? First some wine and then the sauce..." Mossworth dabbed his napkin on the stain. Then he finished the cut and shoved a huge dripping bite into his gob.

Charolais sat, quietly looking at him. She reached for a roll, buttered it, purposefully and methodically, taking her time. After taking a leisurely bite she wiped her mouth with her napkin and, again, look at him. Mossworth had his head down and chased the lamb sauce about his plate with a roll. "Brian."

"Well, yes, yes, I must say," started Mossworth, "I think the stress of the day...I'm feeling a bit...you know, it's been something of a week..."

"Sure, Brian, sure," said Charolais standing.

"I certainly hope..."

"Oh, no, no, not at all," said Charolais, reaching for her shawl. "Don't think about it. Just take care of yourself. I'm sure you'll be fine. No, please, don't get up. Thanks for an almost lovely evening."

"Uh, I, uh, well, uh...shall I...?"

But she was gone.

Mossworth sat heavily back in his chair. He lifted his wine glass. Empty. Fill it. Smiling, Mossworth downed it in one go. Then he threw the glass across the room into the wall. Mechanically, Mossworth stood and moved his shaky legs to the kitchen, opened the pantry door, removed the broom and dustpan, returned the dining room, turned on the lights, and started to sweep up. *Für Elise* played quietly. When all the pieces were swept up, Mossworth returned to the kitchen, dumped the broken glass into the bin, carefully wiped out the dustpan with a damped paper towel, put that in the trash, then replaced the broom and pan back in the closet. Next he moved down the hall and removed from the closet a small vacuum. He carried that back to the dining room and began a methodical and loud sucking. When he finished, and made sure the nap of the carpeted portions of the room all faced north, he noticed that *Für Elise* was no longer playing. He replaced the vacuum and returned to the table.

"Damn mole." He mumbled. Then he picked up a meaty lamb rib with his fingers and took a huge bite. While he chewed, he wiped his left hand upon his napkin, picked up the wine bottle, and drank from it. "Mole." Then he reached for the asparagus almandine, now cold, clotted; he pinched a spear in his fingers and then shoved the whole thing into his only half empty mouth.

Later, when the second bottle was empty and food remains long dried stuck around his mouth, Mossworth lay quietly on his sofa. Both the volume of wine and the size of the brick from earlier in the day made his head ache. He stood, crumbs falling off his shirt. Slowly, greasy hands reaching for the walls to steady himself, he walked down his hall towards the spare room. "Brideshead...Fawlty Towers...yes, something funny...Are You Being...or maybe good old double-u, double-u two..." But when he opened the door his eyes fell upon his jacket, umbrella, briefcase, and items piled on the floor. "Oh...," he said and moved to pick up. As he bent, he fell, and landed with a thud. "Charolais. Dear lady... Mole." Mossworth's eyes blinked rapidly. "Uhaaaaahhhhhhhuuuu, Gravely... stupid...students and their...what the...art...mole..." And then after a low guttural howl Mossworth's eyes filled and he pulled his knees to his chest and began to shake until a kind of sleep overtook him.

Mossworth felt himself underwater. He looked up and could see the surface, his eyes caught the dancing sunlight, but he felt nothing and did not move towards it. From far away he heard what sounded like bells.

"No, not bells," he thought, "more like music, like the music from the smash eighties UK television show, Top of the Pops."

Then he awoke, recognized the song as his very own ring tone, and rummaged about the floor for the device. As his hands searched his mind realized something was quite wrong for, one thing, he had awoken from the floor and he was still dressed, but for another, night had not yet ended. He found the phone. "Hello?"

There was a long pause. "Uh, yeah, Johnny."

"What?" asked Mossworth.

"Who?" came the voice. And then: "I need Johnny. Johnny! Johnny? That you? Johnny, we've got to talk."

Mossworth took a deep breath. His body shuddered and his head throbbed. The phone read 2:34. "Johnny...?"

"Johnny, this is Nick. I'm not...okay, I mean, I'm probably not..."

"No Johnny. Here. You've...wrong number."

"Oh, man, right. Go to hell, Johnny." Then the voice hung up. Mossworth made an attempt off the floor, but could not manage it. He reached for his overcoat, still lying in a crumpled heap, and managed to pull it across his bottom half. After a few sniffles he slept once again.

Later, the quiet chiming of his mantle clock awoke him. Mossworth, sniffed, and rolled over to his other side and discovered, half-way under his head and somewhat covered in tears, other letters. The allure of the post gave him energy to drag over and flip on a desk lamp. The first letter, from the BBC, informed him that while his correspondence was very much appreciated the BBC still had no plans to produce a documentary upon the making of Kenneth Clarke's, Civilisation. The second letter cleared Mossworth's head instantly; it was from Bleary.

Dear Mr. Mosswroth,

Bleary College thanks you for your resent application to its opened position in economics. We appreiciate the efforts you put into writing your application. When professional professors as you make the effor tto apply, it means alot to us. Thanks for your time and consideration and we all wish you the best of luck in your future endeavors.

Sincerely,
Dean Ahrupthaboopia

Below that was hand written:

PS: You did not get the job. But the attached interview evaluations may help you in your blossoming hopes for future employment.

Mossworth crumpled the letter. Much against what little of his judgment remained, he turned to the first page of the interview evaluation. A piece of black construction paper held a drawing, in grey pencil, of a sad, bearded face with one tear. At the bottom, written in letters cut from magazines, it read: "Expressing Feelings After Mossworth Interview: He won't ever be a part of the Bleary Family." The evaluation pages that followed were written with a purple crayon. With a shuddering sob, Mossworth shoved the letters away, knocked the lamp, breaking the bulb, and waited not long for sleep to drown him.

Neither the ringing of a phone nor chimes of a clock woke Mossworth the next. Rather, a still, small, unyielding light of dawn prodded at his eyes. Determinedly, it found its way to him on the floor via a low horizon, through scanty tall trees in front of the east-facing window, and reflecting from an antique mirror on the west wall of his spare room. Painfully he glimpsed the intense refulgence before jerking his head out of its reach. His first conscious thoughts were not pleasant. Then his eyes followed a tiny sliver of the light to where it fell directly upon one of the unopened letters, upon its blue and gold seal. He could just barely make out the words, *Dominus Illuminatio Mea.* Something deep in his memory lurched. He tore into the letter.

Dear Mr. Mossworth,

We would like to thank you for your recent application to Oxford University. It is with great privilege that we offer you a place in the entering class this autumn. Shortly you will be receiving more information appropriate for international students. Furthermore, you have been provisionally accepted, pending your high school grade transcriptions, to Fochashite College, one of Oxford's youngest and fastest growing. Fochashite has authorized us to inform you of your status there as a College Fellow with all the rights and benefits that designates.

On behalf of the University, please let me wish you a hearty welcome.

Very Sincerely Yours,

Owen H. W. W. Henderson, O. B. E.
Oxford University Matriculation Chief

Mossworth stared, confused and amazed. He read the letter again, and again. With thumping head and pounding heart he stood and twirled and danced and roared and wept tears of recrimination, satisfaction, and utterly childish joy.

PART TWO

COURSES OF EMPIRE

I was entirely happy in a subdued fashion during these first two terms, doing all that freshmen traditionally did, purchasing a cigarette box carved with the college arms and the popular printed panorama of the Towers and Spires of Oxford; learning to smoke a pipe; getting drunk for the first time; walking and bicycling about the surrounding villages; making an unremarkable maiden speech at the Union; doing enough work to satisfy the examiners in History Previous. But all the time it seemed to me that there was a quintessential Oxford which I knew and loved from afar and intended to find.

Evelyn Waugh, *A Little Learning*

A sudden high pressure in his ears sent Mossworth's head to aching and he awoke. With effort he rubbed, and then opened his eyes, and then yawned. His train had just entered a tunnel. Disorientation gripped him. The windows were dark. Was he on the plane? But the next moment his eyes reeled from a burst of sunlight as the train shot out of the tunnel.

"Ah, oh, yes, United Kingdom, England, Gatwick, Victoria,...Oxford... ," Mossworth muttered, and then blinked rapidly hoping to keep himself awake. His head lolled about as his jet-lagged mind struggled for consciousness. "Ugh," burst from his dry lips and then he sat upright and shook himself. Warming him nicely, Mossworth's matching grey Harris Tweed suit struck a note of daring on the train: it was August. Next to him, on the seat, was his repaired Swiss Army suitcase and a new rolling duffle. Under his knees, on the floor, carefully positioned for security, lay his black nylon, rubberized suspension, ergonomically designed laptop carry-case. On his lap sat his briefcase glowing with fresh wax.

Mossworth kept his arm across the stacked representatives of the Swiss Army on his left and another arm wrapped around the briefcase on his right. With a quick look around, Mossworth noticed only three other people in the compartment. A young man and a young woman were carefully engaged, near the back of the car, in intimate examination of each other's oral areas. Near the center of the car, just a few rows behind, a middle-aged man with a pierced lip wearing dirty blue coveralls and a ratty denim jacket, sat starring directly at Mossworth.

Starring back, Mossworth gave the gent a curt nod. The gent gave Mossworth his middle finger. With a reassuring grip, Mossworth cuddled his bags even tighter. Then he fell soundly asleep.

Appearing before Mossworth's jetlagged mind grew an image of him, taller than in life, certainly younger and thinner, and seated nearby a humbled and much less attractive Dean Marlboro. Behind him stood Professor Van Engelen-Van der Bauwede, dressed as a waitress. "So you see, Dean...or should I just call you Marlboro...man?" Mossworth let the jibe hang in the air. Dean Marlboro kept his eyes lowered. "Well, Three-Pack-a-Day-Pack-Man, I know that my destiny is elsewhere. Furthermore, this little school that you are so fond of is nothing, it's too small, it is nowhere. Just look at those buildings. They are so, so, so not-Oxford. They are pathetic. And as for you, Professor Van Engelen-Van, Van...Van-Van Man, you can just stuff this job up your theoretical gendered space. This is what you get for trying to scuttle my career! So, because I know my talents, while they are of course needed here most, they are welcomed elsewhere. Thus my resignation. Yes, yes, that is it, right here. Take it and be glad I don't sue Hardly."

With this Marlboro, tears in his eyes, fell to his knees. "Please, please, Brian...

Behind him, Professor Van Engelen-Van der Bauwede wept quietly, hand reaching out, "Brian, please, listen."

"Call me Dr. Mossworth, dammit."

"Please, Dr. Mossworth, we need you! You can't see it! We are so desperate for your gifts and abilities..."

"I know, I know."

"...and we can't run the college without you. Please, please reconsider."

Mossworth tapped his fingertips together and starred out the window.

"Believe me, Marlboro Man, I do understand," started Mossworth, "but no longer may my gifts be used only to the service of Hardley College. It is time for me to move on. My future lies elsewhere. Ours is a high and lonely destiny." With that a shooting pain ran up Mossworth's leg.

"Ow!"

"Watch your feet there, love."

These words came from the obese and slightly greasy attendant attempting to push the tea trolley through the kneecap of the now mostly awake Dr. Mossworth. He yanked his leg out of the way.

"Sorry, love, sorry. What about something from the trolley then, pet?" said the tea lady, just as she wiped her damp upper lip with her sleeve.

"Hm," grunted Mossworth, suddenly appeased by the attention and the accent. "Very well. I should like a cup of tea and a digestive biscuit, please."

"Hob Nob?"

"Even better."

With a quick flip the hot water streamed into a single metal teapot, a bag was dumped in, a mug was produced. Mossworth flipped down his small tray and reached for the mug and pot.

"And your hob nob," said the tea lady.

"Thank you, indeed."

"That's three pound forty, please love."

"Of course." Leaning up, Mossworth reached for his wallet in his back pocket. After a brief frantic searching he remember that he had put it in his jacket pocket. He reached in the left pocket, then the right one, then his other back pocket. A gnawing panic began to grip him. "I...uh...I..."

"What's wrong, love? Got no Pounds yet?"

"No," said Mossworth breathlessly, "I just exchanged five hundred this morning." His hands moved more quickly in all of his pockets, again.

"Five hundred?" asked the tea lady, "Bloody..."

"It's gone, stolen," said Mossworth, "my wallet has been stolen."

"Oh, love, that's rotten luck."

"Wait a minute, wait a minute," Mossworth exclaimed, "there was someone else here! He must have seen." Looking over his shoulder, Mossworth saw the pierced-lip man still starring straight at him. "You, sir, you there. Did you see someone steal my wallet?" The tea lady looked back at the pierced man.

The man raised his eyebrows and shrugged, "Didn't see nuffin, mate. Rough blow." He continued to stare ahead.

"Sorry love, sorry," said the tea lady, "the trains can be a bit rough at times." With that, the tea lady reached across Mossworth and removed the teapot and mug from his tray and set them down in an interior drawer on her trolley.

Mossworth looked up, pleadingly. "Oh, my tea. I thought..."

The tea lady then reached across for the Hob Nob, still in Mossworth's hand. For a brief moment it appeared Mossworth would not relinquish the plastic enshrouded crunchy biscuit. "But..."

"Thank you, love," said the tea lady, as she put the Hob Nob back on the rack. "Enjoy your visit in England." Mossworth watched as she pushed the cart back to the next passenger, the pierced man. "What about you love? Anything from the trolley?

The pierced man stopped starring at Mossworth and sat up.

"Yeah, a hot cuppa and bickie," said the pierced man.

"Three-Pound forty, love."

Pierced man reached into his jacket and removed a very crisp twenty-Pound note. "And a pack of Wrigley's."

As Mossworth deliberated what his next move would not be, a voice sounded over the speaker. Mostly the voice sounded like someone trying his hardest not to speak the word, "Oxford." The train began to slow.

With appealing eyes, Mossworth looked around the train. Neither the tea lady nor the pierced man looked back. "But I...the...my..." Then the train stopped. Pushing and shoving managed to get the Swiss Army into the aisle. Leg over, other leg out of the seat, and then the duffle. Handles up, computer case and briefcase on top, another muffled announcement, growing tension, uprights flipping sideways in the aisle, duffle slipping, huge step and then a graceless flop onto the platform as the doors closed. With a grunt, the train began to move away and Mossworth got a quick view into his compartment in time to see the tea lady and the pierced man roaring with laughter.

Down the gentle ramp away from the station, through a mostly empty puddle, Mossworth attempted to pull his suitcases; a handle in each hand, computer atop, briefcase on the strap across his shoulder. He had a vague notion as to his direction from looking at maps in his nineteenth-century architectural histories of Oxford. So, from the train station he turned and headed exactly west on the Botley Road towards Botley. With little but perceived goodness ahead of him, and no wish to dwell on the loss of his wallet, he indulged a few thoughts in his already manipulated perception of events that brought him up to Oxford.

Early the morning after receiving the admissions letter, Mossworth marched into Marlboro's office, very hung over, and tendered his resignation, or would do as soon as he had one written. As it was, he merely stood there empty-handed and told Marlboro he was leaving. He could not quite recall if Marlboro came across as furious and resigned or sad. The rest of Mossworth's life wrapped up surprisingly quickly after that. Term ended without incident. He no longer faced the Council nor Cynthia Gravely. Only once in the final months of the semester did he see Charolais from afar. Her deep brown eyes looked at him and then promptly turned away. Mossworth's house sold quickly in June; he moved out in July. What he didn't put into storage, he sold or simply threw out. Six boxes of his most precious books were delivered to the post office to be shipped surface to Oxford. Four boxes of clothes were also shipped. Quivering with anticipation, Mossworth had strolled into Couch's office the day before he left town. After a short chat, some kind words, a manly handshake and half-hug, Mossworth's goodbye's were done and elation over his seeming freedom lifted him upwards. He drove the Morris, slowly, from Arkansas to an elderly aunt's home in eastern Pennsylvania. He was in no hurry. The aunt had offered to keep the Morris, along with a few other boxes of clothes and books, in a dusty barn. By the start of August his bags were packed and he was ready to go.

And here he was, in Oxford, clad in a variety of Hebridian tweeds, including his calf-length grey great coat. In spite of the heavy clouds, the warming August day began to take its toll as he attempted to find his way. The two cases rolling and bumping along behind him lent a sort of rhythm to his journey, neatly matching the ups and downs of his little beating heart. "Where," he pondered to himself, "are the gleaming spires and towers, the dreaming city of stone?" The only large visible buildings were an office supply shop, a Toys-R-Us, and a concrete and green glass Volvo dealership. He kept walking.

Soon the heat grew unbearable and Mossworth had to stop. While catching his breath he mused, "Oh, for a hot cup," but then remembered the unpleasant incident on the train, that he didn't have any money, and quickly put any thoughts of beverages out of his mind. Carefully Mossworth removed his great coat, folded it neatly, and placed it in an exactly-enough-sized spot within his Swiss Army suitcase. He took a deep breath and resumed his walk. The houses grew larger, with larger gardens. Cars on the street began to move faster. Still, not a single dreamy spire in view.

Clouds scudded across the sky quickly, opening silvery glimmers. Seriously warmed up again after three more blocks, however, Mossworth stopped. He removed his sport coat, folded it neatly, and placed it in another exactly sized spot in his other Swiss Army suitcase. He stood up from his labors, placed his hand to shade his eyes and gazed west. "Bloody...where is the place? I know exactly..." Just then a large white bird flew past. It was just unusual enough to catch his eye and he followed it moving east. Gasping, Mossworth discovered his path had been in exactly the wrong direction; to the east, framed by dark clouds, leapt the stunning, shinning, and indeed dreamy golden towers and steeples of the University.

A gentleman walking the opposite direction slowed and then stopped. The man wore a linen sport coat, was of medium height with a high and intelligent forehead and peered at Mossworth with penetrating, yet kind, eyes. With a friendly tone he inquired, "Just arrived in Oxford?"

"No, not really," said Mossworth, "I, ah, that is, I rather..."

"If you don't mind my asking," asked the gentleman, "what is your ultimate destination?"

Mossworth considered for a moment. Could he tell this man he was an undergraduate at the university? "Oh. Well, Oxford."

The man laughed a warm chuckle and then put out his hand. "Sorry for the laugh. It was not your answer. It was my question. I am at St. George's, the vicar, Theodore

Dunlop. Pleasure." He shook Mossworth's hand. "I realized that my question could have been taken in a metaphysical sense." He laughed again. "Hopefully Oxford is not your ultimate destination."

Mossworth strained a smile.

"Perhaps," said Theo, "perhaps I could call you a cab? Would that help?"

"Ah, well, yes. Very kind, very kind, Reverend Dunlop." Mossworth nodded.

Theo popped out a cell phone and dialed. "Not at all. And please, call me Theo." After a short conversation the taxi was ordered. "Well, I do hope that helps and, please, if you ever find yourself in need of a Sunday service, or a friendly chin wag, I trust you will find your way to St. George's." Then with a friendly wave, Theo continued his way down the street.

A few minutes later a taxi screeched to a halt just next to Mossworth. "Want a ride, mate?" asked the driver.

"What? Oh, no, but thanks."

"Right," shouted the driver, "then who called the bloody cab?"

Mossworth looked around, "not me."

The driver shouted something incomprehensible and the taxi sped away. Mossworth started his rhythmic plod, east this time. "I don't need a taxi, thank you very much," he grunted.

Soon, even warmer than before, he passed the station from whence his adventures had started and began up Hythe Bridge St. Just before the bridge proper he stumbled across a quiet street, Upper Fisher Row, and then he began to wrestle his luggage over the lumps and bumps of the bridge itself.

He carried on across Worcester onto St. George, growing more confident of his direction. "Right, and then upwards, past the Odeon and, there, St. Giles at last." But his eyes also espied Waterstone's in all its glorious three stories of stories. Mossworth stood for a moment staring up at the great curved facade of the bookstore. "Surely," he reasoned, " a short break from a long day would not hurt..." But then he remembered his suitcases, his briefcase, and the fact that he no longer had a wallet. "Plus," he considered, "I ought to be getting to college. No doubt it will take me some time to get settled in." He set off again.

He moved along St. Giles properly: approaching the stately Randolph hotel he spied the pastiche of classical grandeur that composes the Ashmolean. His appreciation of the Ashmolean's denticulation prevented him from quite paying attention when crossing busy Beaumont Street; stopping for safety on the traffic island he neglected his right Swiss Army suitcase, leaving it about eight inches in the roadway. A speedy BMW neatly clipped the edge of it and, his hand still firmly gripping, the bag spun about in a wide arc, narrowly missing an old age pensioner, and catching the metal safety rail full on.

After a two or three second pause, while Mossworth's confused mind tried to put what had happened together, the pedestrian traffic started to move again accompanied by a few clicks and clucks, a "hard luck mate," and an encouraging, "BMW git." Fortunately, the Swiss did their work well; the bag only suffered from some scuffs and a bent wheel. A bit more aware, Mossworth started again, less smoothly.

But a mere hundred steps more and he was brought up short. Above his head hung the sign for the Eagle & Child. Welling up in his narrow chest, fueled by a lack of sleep, a long walk wearing woolen attire in August, and a near brush with death, was his proximity with greatness. He entered, one smooth rolling suitcase and one wobbly, into the dark and woody pub. Immediately his senses were assailed. The assailant in this case was a smoky haze from some misbehaving chip fryer back in the kitchen. His luggage could not quite make the narrow hall so he ran one back to a recently emptied table in the Inklings room, then went to fetch the other. As best he could, both bags were managed into a corner with him in front. Finally, he sat, weary, thirsty, hungry, and waited for a waitress. His eyes grew heavy.

"Hello, may I help you," said the cheery voice. Mossworth snapped awake.

"Oh, yes, please, yes. Fish-n-chips, please, and a pint of cider."

"Right, my love, anything else?"

"No," said Mossworth dreamily, "I have all I want." The waitress departed. Mossworth gazed upon the grainy photos of Lewis, Tolkien, and the other Inklings. Was he not now a part of this group? He was here, in this pub, wasn't he? And then he fell asleep again.

"Excuse me, love, here's your food," chirped the waitress.

"Oh, my, sorry, I'm, uh, jetlagged," explained Mossworth, snapping awake.

"Don't mention it. Happens all the time here. Six-Pound-thirty, love."

"Oh. Oh...I just remembered: I don't have any money."

"Sorry, love," replied the waitress, "I can't give you the food for free."

"My wallet was stolen!"

"I'm sorry, love. If you were a student, that would be different. We could open an account for you."

"Splendid," said Mossworth, excitedly, "I am a student!"

"You?"

"Yes."

"A student?"

"Yes."

"A University student?"

"Yes, yes."

"Which college?"

"Fochashite," replied Mossworth. The waitress roared with a burst of laughter, spilling a few chips from

Mossworth's plate. "Really, truly," said Mossworth, "it is Fochashite College, that is the one, Fochashite." Still the waitress laughed, even harder. Mossworth tried again: "Fochashite. Foch-a-shite." With that, the waitress screamed with laughter and dumped the entire contents of her tray not quite neatly, but completely onto, Mossworth's table.

Mossworth looked up at the waitress with softened eyes and while maintaining the forlorn gaze slowly lifted a single fat, greasy chip from the table to his lips. The waitress raised her eyebrows. "Alright, love, alright. Student, eh? Well then I'll just start you an account." She reached behind the counter for a thick notebook. "Name?"

"Brian."

"Figures," she mumbled, "but I mean your surname."

"Mossworth," he said. "And thank you, thanks very much indeed."

"Righto, love," the waitress chirped as she stepped towards the bar. With a glimpse over her shoulder she added: "for future reference, it's pronounced 'foo-Ka-shee.'" But Mossworth's jetlagged brain didn't hear as the chips and fish that had not landed on his lap began a quick trip to his gullet.

Thirty minutes later, satisfied with the allotment of grease rolling about in his innards, Mossworth slowly slogged his belongings down St. Giles. By this time the temperature outside had further warmed. Mossworth found his tweed trousers growing itchy and his head aching from the second pint of cider. Hardly a hundred paces later a blaring voice split into his head. "Hallo, hallo, and how are you today, sir? Lovely day, certainly, and nothing better to do on a lovely day than rummage through the mysteries and histories of yesteryear. Why don't you rest your weary feet, take a break from the heat? Step inside, it is neat! You are in, for a treat!"

Mossworth looked up to see an elderly, semi-toothed, chipper man in a bright red waistcoat standing in the doorway of a shop. "What do you say, sir? Nice break from the day's struggle? Why not let me give you a hand with those bags?"

The word, "no" began to form on Mossworth's lips when he looked up at the shop facade and read: "MacInney's Antique Books & Oxford Oddities." A huge cloud that had been drifting across the sky moved aside to allow a beam of sunlight to fall upon the subtitle: "Specialists in unusual Historic Hand-Fashioned Harris Tweeds." Mossworth could only stare.

"I, I...I didn't know shops like this...," he mumbled.

"Yes, sir, yes, sir. Many folks do not. Please, here, let me take those bags. And might I add, sir, that that is spectacularly delightful tweed you yourself are sporting today. Birdseye 147 or 148. That is a 1994 or 1995 weave, I believe. Right this way, right this way." And Mossworth permitted himself to be led right that way.

Mossworth spent several brain-addled hours in the shop, stumbling about with jet lag. Mr. MacInney proved to be an absolute delight and a most understanding person. Mossworth explained that he'd been pick-pocketed but also that he was now a student at Fochashite; Immediately MacInney had started an account for him and immediately Mossworth had charged two new pre-owned Harris Tweed "vintage" sport coats, a rare Harris waist coat, two fountain pens from the fifties, (MacInney assured Mossworth that every incoming student back then used them), and a set of prints, reproduced from original nineteenth-century plates, but somehow still rare and costly. (Mossworth's brain didn't follow that too closely.)

In the end his new MacInney's account showed a debit of seven hundred and forty-eight Pounds.

In a rarely seen state of bliss, Mr. MacInney showed Mossworth the door, assisted him with his neat paper-wrapped packages. "Please do come back, Mr. Mossworth, sir. We need people like you to keep Oxford alive," MacInney stated cheerily as Mossworth headed up the sidewalk. By this time the sun cast long shadows and Mossworth's mind, the part that wasn't mostly asleep, directed him to step it up and get to college.

Stepping it up, Mossworth crossed St. Giles to situate himself on the Banbury Road. His knowledge of Oxford directed him out the Banbury but the details on the exact distance remained vague. As he passed the Pitt Rivers ("ah, yes, the Pitt Rivers...museum...") and then Wycliffe Hall, he realized that his last few dozen steps remained a blank in his mind as he had fallen into a sort of walking sleep. Recognizing the danger of this, he looked about for a pedestrian with a friendly face to ask for directions. An elderly woman carefully balancing plastic grocery bags caught his eye.

"Pardon me, might you be able to tell me how far it is to...Fochashite College?"

The woman stopped and looked up at him with large, reddened eyes. Slowly she shifted her bags. After a long intake of breath she said, "No, English," and set off again down the street. Mossworth gripped his bags, took a few short and intense breaths of his own to clear his head, and continued out Banbury. Towing his various bags, his leather briefcase, and now two large bags from MacInney's, Mossworth found the going increasingly intolerable. His head spinning he used the last of his wit to hail a cab. A speeding yellow Passat screeched to a halt. Mossworth didn't even try to put his bags into the boot. He opened the door and fell into the rear seat mumbling, "Fochashite College, my good man."

What finally woke Mossworth were the incoherent shouts of the taxi driver, a man of secondary English acquisition. Mossworth sat up in the rear of the Passat, noticing it was now night. "Okay, okay, we here, now you awake, sir, now you must pay!" Looking at the meter, Mossworth saw it totaled fifty-eight Pounds.

"Fifty-eight Pounds?" he asked the driver, sleepily.

"I ask you want the tour, you say yes," replied the driver, "so you get it. Good tour, good tour. Two hours! Now I go. Fifty-eight Pound, please."

Mossworth stood up, his body swaying, his head spinning. "Yes, well, yes, I..." He looked over his shoulder towards the college, or what he thought might be the college. "You see, I was robbed this morning, pick pocketed, and I have no money right now and..."

"No money? No money? What is this no money? I have give you the ride. I give you tour. You ask for tour! Now no money?" shouted the irate driver.

"But this is my college," said Mossworth, "I'm sure I can get you money here." He looked behind him but saw nothing in the now darkness but a shadowed mass of glass and metal. "Fochashite, that's my college, is this it, is it here?"

"Yes, yes, Fochashite, yes this your college. Go, ask for the money. Go!"

As Mossworth stepped from the cab, his feet did not feel quite right. Head awhirl he moved, slowly, towards an aluminum framed glass door. No lights were on. Another step revealed to his blurry vision a bit of light behind the glass and some figures. Next, he could make out above the door, cut freehand into a piece of raw steel, the words "Fochashite College." He turned back to the driver. "Are you sure...?"

"Yes, yes, Fochashite, Fochashite, everyone knows it is it. Now knock, get my money."

Mossworth knocked. In a few moments a white-haired gentleman appeared at the door but did not open it.

"Yes?" he asked through the glass. Mossworth tried to focus his eyes on the man.

"Are you the porter?" he asked.

"Yes, yes sir. We're closed now, however, visiting hours don't begin until ten tomorrow morning," said the Porter.

Mossworth tried to speak, words were slurring a bit as the Porter faded in and out of focus. "I'm...I'm...I am Brian...Mosswroth...I'm a fellow."

The Porter looked at him knowingly. "I see, sir, I see. But Old Fellows aren't permitted in college except during commencement or during normal opening hours."

Mossworth shuffled his feet to steady himself. A sudden sharp pain in his abdomen brought back the greasy fish and chip and pints he'd enjoyed earlier. He grabbed his stomach. "I am a Fellow, now, I'm Mossworth, I'm a Fellow, a Fellow. I'm a student." While the Porter looked at him in wonder, Mossworth suddenly heaved, emptied the contents of his stomach mostly onto the glass and aluminum door, partly on his own tweedy self, and then collapsed in a nasty woolen heap onto the concrete.

The Porter stared and shook his head. "Only a student..." He began unlocking the door. The taxi driver walked over with Mossworth's bags. Stepping out of the open door, the Porter looked at Mossworth and then up at the driver, "whatcha, Ali?"

"Hi, Jimmy," replied Ali, with less of an accent, "did he say he was a student?"

"He did, indeed," said Jimmy, "And, I must say, bit of a stunner."

"Here are his bags," said Ali, flopping the various bags and his recent purchases onto the sidewalk. "He can pay me later. I know where he is."

"And drunk already," said Jimmy, shaking his head and bending down to assist Mossworth. "It's not even September."

"Damn the student!" said Ali.

"Damn him indeed! He wasn't sick in your cab!" replied Jimmy with a chuckle. With that, Ali gave a friendly wave and hopped back into his cab. With practiced hands, Jimmy got under Mossworth's arms, careful of the mess, and dragged him in through the aluminum and glass door, down the hall, and out into the small tool shed in the garden quad. He gently placed his head on a dirty floor mat. After moving his bags inside and relocking the door to the college, Jimmy walked to the Porter's Lodge tearoom and put the kettle on. As the comforting noise of heating water began, he walked back to the front desk to consult a large registry. After a moment, Jimmy gave a mild shake of his grey head and looked out towards the tool shed. "Welcome to your first year, Mr. Mossworth."

Slowly, slowly, awareness came upon Mossworth. With a wave of pleasure he remembered that he was in Oxford. Quickly the pleasure wave receded as Mossworth caught the scents of motor oil, mildew, and dried stomach contents. Next he noticed a severe pain radiating from his neck down. Then he opened his eyes. All his bags, and his self, were nicely arranged on the dirt floor of a small shed. Grunting with effort, Mossworth sat up. Dust fell from his shoulders and hair. His Harris Tweed trousers streaked with vomit were also now caked with dirt. Mossworth stood carefully.

A tepid light filtered through the shed's one window, a window framed by an elaborately carved stone quatrefoil. Around Mossworth stood implements of yard maintenance and their smelly accoutrements. Moving closer to the window, Mossworth peeked out. It was raining. He ran a dusty hand through his hair, straightened his tie, and opened the shed door.

Across a short swath of deeply green grass lay an open door to a large, dull grey brick building. Mossworth stepped across and entered into a small office suite. He vaguely remembered it from the previous evening. "Ah, there you are, sir." came the voice of Jimmy, emerging from another of the small offices. "Sorry about the accommodation. Best we could manage on short notice."

Mossworth looked at the approaching Porter. "Yes, well, thank you. And I do apologize for my condition last evening. Very sorry, very sorry."

"Don't mention it, sir. Happens all the time around here. We are prepared for any contingency. I believe that is our school motto," said Jimmy with a wink. "Now that, Mr. Mossworth, how may I help you today?"

Mossworth blinked a few times. "Oh, yes, well, I should very much like to simply move into my, er, digs today. I am ready!" Mossworth smiled for good measure.

"I see, I see," said Jimmy, "and I'm sorry to say, but there is a problem: Term does not start for another three weeks. The college is, besides the grounds crew, and myself, closed. Not to mention that the rooms are being painted, asbestos is being abated, and there is some serious plumbing repair. All that is to say, with apologies, we do not have a room for you just yet."

Mossworth's head spun about. "Is this not mid-August? Do I have the dates wrong?"

"Oh, no sir, this is indeed August the fourteenth. A grand day, to be sure. The problem is, we do not begin term until September. The prospectus has the dates..." Mossworth waved his hand.

"Well, I am here. Can I not just, you know, have my room, any room?

Jimmy shook his head sadly. "No, sir. Besides the work there are liability issues."

"But, but...what do I do between now and the start of term? Where do I live?" pleaded Mossworth.

Jimmy pondered for just a moment. "Well, sir, there are many fine hotels in Oxford, perhaps you saw the Randolph just across from the Ashmolean? Lovely place. Very comfortable."

"What does that cost?" blurted Mossworth.

"Oh, I should not think more than a hundred and fifty. It includes breakfast!" said Jimmy.

Mossworth hung his head, still awhirl from jetlag, slowly. "I, uh, well, right...right." He turned to the door. "I'll just get my things."

"Here, sir, I'll lend you a hand." Jimmy the Porter led Mossworth out the door and towards the shed. It was then that Mossworth received his first full glimpse of the splendor that is Fochashite.

Rising eight stories behind the shed, a bold, humanist statement to the 1960s assaulted the sky. Its utterly unembellished concrete facade declared the glories of Modern architecture in a way only British architecture from the mid-sixties can. Democratic in conception, each window of the building, starting exactly at ground level, was exactly door sized. The effect dazzled the mind and made the actual entrance door difficult to find. While any normal person would have assumed that the pedestrian middle aperture hosted the entrance, that person would be sadly mistaken. As it turned out, however, the actual entrance easily stood out. A thoughtful Fochashite student had some years before spray-painted the words, "bloody door" on the wall above the veritable doorway. Mossworth gasped in a way that caused Jimmy to stand back. "Coming up again, sir?" Jimmy asked.

"Where...where is the rest of the campus?"

Jimmy looked up at the monolith. "Yes, well, sir, that is all of the college in one building. Inspired by Corbu, the lot that built this was. Thought folks just wanted to be closer and that pure geometry and egalitarian concrete would make them happier."

Mossworth rubbed his temples. Then he looked up again at the eight stories of tribute to concrete and the Swiss. "I was under the impression that Fochashite was founded in the eighteenth century. Where are those buildings?"

"Right you are, sir, right you are," said Jimmy, stopping on the concrete path. "See, just there sir, the wee shed in which you spent last evening. You may have noticed the traceried window. Well, that is all that is left from the original campus. Of course, we've the Blitz to thank for some of that. Was the Germans that hit the original library. The remaining nineteenth-century buildings were torn down in nineteen fifty-nine. Some thought as how "cut stone celebrated a bourgeois aesthetic ill-fitted to a post-war democracy.'" For just a moment Jimmy appeared wistful. "I guess I ought also to mention that in nineteen seventy-three another building stood, right over there, by that ginkgo tree."

"What happened to it?" queried Mossworth.

"Well, that one...part of the movement, you know, conceptual. It was built entirely out of compressed paper."

By this time they had proceeded into and through the doorway and found themselves at the front gate, the one through which Mossworth had entered last evening. "Well, sir, very nice to meet you. I look forward to seeing you during Start, that's the name for Fochashite's first day, in three weeks."

His mind slightly more clear now, Mossworth gathered his things from Jimmy and asked, "Jimmy, might you know of a hotel, or perhaps a B&B, that might be more suitable for a, ah, student?"

"Right you are, sir. I'm forgetting that a man your age is, well, your age, and a student. Sir, may I recommend the Nanford house? It's a wee B&B right out the Iffley. Straight on into town, out the High, and then across the Magdalen bridge. When you come to the roundabout you take the second shank to your right, due south. Bit of a pace down to Nanford but very affordable rates, indeed. Cheapest bed in Oxford, I believe."

Jimmy held the door opened for him. Mossworth looked to say something, shrugged, and arranged his bags, briefcase, and two bags from McInney's into order. As Mossworth started down the street he could hear Jimmy chirp, "Goodbye."

Forty minutes later, standing in front of a typical terraced house in a typical English neighborhood, an even further disheveled Mossworth arrived at the door of Nanford House. There had been some issues crossing the street, he inevitably looked the wrong direction, but a ring of the bell a very dark and short man with a non-English accent opened the door.

"Eh?"

"I wonder if I may inquire..." started Mossworth.

The man gave Mossworth a quick up and down. "Thirty quid, no sick."

"What?"

"Thirty. Thirty quid a night and you get breakfast, hot. Egg, sausage, toast. Hot." The man looked Mossworth up and down. "But no sickness. You sick in Nanford, you clean it up!"

"Oh, yes, certainly. No, uh, sickness," said Mossworth.

"Right, come in you, come in." Waving his hand, the man led Mossworth back, through a long hall, across what was at one time red carpet, to the rear of the house. They entered a larger room filled to the ceiling with older computers, hulking, bone and beige, all humming and buzzing. Wires draped across the ceiling. In seconds a receipt was printed up. "Here, mate. Thirty Pounds."

Mossworth took the receipt. "Yes, um, I was actually wondering about a longer stay..."

"How long?" inquired the man.

"Ah, well, yes...three weeks..." mumbled Mossworth.

"Right, ten percent for weekly stays. You pay first week now. Second week halfway through first. Third, quarter through second."

Mossworth shifted from foot to foot. "Yes, yes, very good, very good. Um, I was, ah, wondering..."

"What? What you wonder? Money?"

"Yes, money, right. See, I was pick pocketed and..."

"It's not worry, mate, not worry. When you get money?"

Mossworth shuffled his feet. "I'm not sure. I've got to contact my bank in America."

The proprietor pursed his lips for a moment. "How long you stay? Three week?"

"Oh, well, yes, it's three weeks until term starts..." began Mossworth.

"Term start? You, you old man, you student?"

"Uh, yes."

"Oh, student, yes, student. I see. Okay. Student good, really good, yes?"

Mossworth nodded, "yes, yes, of course. I mean..."

"What college?"

"Oh, er...Fochashite."

The proprietor nodded, paused, and then briefly looked away, gazing out the window. "You got computer?"

"Yes," replied Mossworth.

"Here's we do: you give me computer to hold until you get money. You give me money, I give you computer."

Seeing as he had little choice Mossworth agreed. The proprietor, who went by the name of Ricardo, had Mossworth fill out several forms and ended up taking not only his laptop but also his passport. It seemed ages but really only a few minutes had passed and, at long last, the vomit encrusted Dr. Brian Mossworth was led to his room.

Ricardo led him not upstairs in the house but out the front door from which he came, down the steps, and along the sidewalk and then up into the front door of the adjoining house. Down a short, dark passage he fumbled with a key ("you don't lose key!") opened the door ("always lock!") and then with a flourish of his hand gestured for Mossworth to enter.

The room was about nine by nine feet with one large window opening onto the back garden, an area strewn with bits of disassembled washing machines. On the walls of the room was vertically striped wallpaper dating from the early twentieth century. A bent iron queen bed took up most of the floor space; delightfully festive in a variety of bedclothes it sagged in the middle only mostly. On the side of the room opposite the door was fabricated a chamber with an ill-hung sliding door leading to what could only very poetically be termed a bathroom. Proper use of the facilities would require one to step over the commode to enter the shower stall. Mossworth, however, noticed none of this immediately as at this point his olfactory sense took primacy and carefully discerned the odors of insecticide and cat urine both competing quite competently with his own stench.

Holding his head high, Mossworth tried not to inhale. He glanced about the room, shook his head and said, "I'll take it."

Mossworth slept for a day and a half. His third day in Oxford was spent briefly at the bank sorting his financial matters followed by eating to make up for the previous sleeping. As his eating consisted mostly of the greasy fried breakfast his proprietor set out and several packets of cheese & onion crisps from the corner shop, he spent the fourth day also in his room, mostly in the bathroom part. During those two days he became acquainted with English morning television and by day six he was hooked wondering what British celebrities (of whom he had never heard) would be commenting about political issues (of which they had never heard) or which American celebrities would be cracking the same old jokes about the meteorological conditions in London. Shortly after yet another greasy breakfast on day seven the post arrived with his replacement credit cards. He looked about his room, counted twenty-seven empty packets of cheese & onion crisps, and recognized it was time to sally forth. Besides, he had yet to get his suit cleaned.

Thus it was on a bright and cheery August morn, more than two weeks before the start of term, Dr. Brian

Mossworth set out in earnest, washing in hand, on his first exploration of Oxford. He made a brisk pace towards town. Less than a block later, however, he narrowly missed tripping over a man kneeling in a peculiar way on the sidewalk. "Oh, sorry," said Mossworth, "I didn't see you there."

The gentleman, a tall middle-aged chap with a dark tan, thick black eyeglasses and obviously dyed hair, stopped his prostrations and stood up, wiping his dusty hands on his ill-fitting, silver spandex pants. "No trouble at all, sir. I'm sorry I was in your way. Probably seems odd my kneeling here but it is part of a research project I'm working upon: history of kneeling. I'm sure you are aware…" But Mossworth didn't stop and walked a bit more quickly down the Iffley Road.

The sun broke through the clouds illuminating even the dullest of the terraced houses. Mossworth stepped a bit lighter. Birds chirped. The automobiles sped by in a more orderly and melodious fashion. Even more lightly did Mossworth step. Upon reaching the roundabout at the Magdalen Bridge, Mossworth took a right to locate the cleaners as suggested by Ricardo. After dropping off his fetid garments, Mossworth made his way over the bridge and glanced longingly at the slow drifting Cherwell, vowing in a quiet voice to return soon. Up the High Street he marched, even faster: there, the small entrance to the Oxford Market. Once, on a high school trip, Mossworth had actually stumbled into the Oxford Market. Three things he could remember from that trip: a never ending stomach flu that kept him in a variety of English toilets, his striking out with the perky Missy Loveblood, and the instant of the very first bite he ever had of a pork pie. Following his nose, Mossworth moved quickly through the dark and dank passages arriving soon at one of the Market's butchers. Spread out before him in rows: the mother lode of meat pies.

"Yes, sir?" the man in the white apron inquired.

"Ooo," said Mossworth, "I, uh, ooo."

"Yes, rather, sir. I take it you are desiring a meat pie?"

"Oh, uh, uuuuggghhhh," slobbered Mossworth.

The man in the apron nodded. "Yes, sir. I quite understand. The meat pie has that affect upon most men."

"Aghuh," nodded Mossworth.

"Might the good sir know what sort of pie he would like?" The man in the apron made a sweeping gesture taking in what appeared to be hundreds and hundreds of golden, flakey crusts. His eyes flickering about, Mossworth pointed at a nice medium-sized pie.

"Mrrguh."

With a deft flick, the man slid open the back of the glass case, reached inside with a pair of shinning tongs and gently extracted the pie. "Yes, the Lancashire hot-pot. Inspired by the original. A splendid choice, one of our best sellers. Sure to satisfy."

"Brrawah?"

"Yes, sir, beef."

"Hmm, greeugh?"

"Well, in that case, perhaps I ought to suggest a pie? Let me see…yes, what about one of our specialties? Here, see this one? See the T on the top? That stands for "Tikka" as in Chicken Tikka Masala. Our version of an Indian classic."

Mossworth just stared. A small line of dribble moved down his chin.

The man in the apron deftly flicked open a brown paper bag and accepted three Pound coins from Mossworth. Before he handed over the bag, however, he caught Mossworth's eye. "Sir, if you don't mind my saying, I have made and sold pies in Oxford for nearly twenty years. Remember that while they look delicious on the outside that is merely flour and water; it's what on the inside that counts."

Mossworth nodded as the man handed over the bag with a wink. Before he had even turned fully about, one of

Mossworth's hands was fumbling to open the package. Three steps later, just as he emerged into a flash of Oxford sunshine, the Tikka pie hit its mark and Mossworth found himself transported to a new realm of culinary nirvana. Flavors exploded, crust crisped, juices dripped. It was all nearly too much for mortal man. Mossworth did not slow down until there were but crumbs about his mouth and jacket. He now greatly desired to slack his thirst.

The most important job of the day accomplished, Mossworth realized he was very close to Waterstone's and thus a few blocks from that utterly convenient source of liquid refreshment, The Eagle & Child. Having been there once, Mossworth already considered it something of a second home in Oxford. Within a minute he found himself pushing open the door, entering the dark passage, shouldering past the other patrons, and ordering a pint at the bar. With his cooling jar firmly in hand, Mossworth maneuvered back towards the Inklings room. He was pulled up short by meeting a roomful of Japanese tourists, all chittering excitedly about, presumably, the Inklings. Standing dully for a moment, Mossworth was rescued by the sound of English, real English English, from down towards the back end of the pub. He moved that direction and found an empty table. Settling himself down into a decidedly not 1930s chair, Mossworth performed the perfunctory solo pub ritual: pint set down, condensation from glass on hands is wiped discretely on pant leg, quick glimpse up and around the room, face back down, right hand around the jar, jar lifted gingerly to appear as if one is sniffing the aroma of the cider, approving smile as if one is sensitive and discerning enough to know if a cider is good by the mere scent, a slow, slow, sweet and satisfying sip, and finally the ever so subtle nod that lets those around you know, if they have been watching carefully, that your tasteful evaluation of the drink was correct.

Having establishing his territory in the pub, Mossworth could relax slightly and take in the other patrons. The

English he had heard in the Inklings room came from a table in the corner at which sat two grey-haired gentlemen. Both had grey flannel trousers, well worn. One had a thick, wooly cardigan, in spite of the summer warmth. The other wore a tweed jacket, shades of brown, with the left side pocket bulging with pipe and tobacco pouch and the other pocket mostly torn off. Pint jars of pale ale shimmered in the grip of each. The first was tall, but would have been slightly stooped standing. His thinning hair stood back neatly combed on his head. He leaned into the table towards his friend with a focused intensity. The other gentleman, Mossworth thought, gave an impression of frailty. Wispy bits of white hair drifted about his mostly baldhead, his skin was pail, translucent even, and his eyes watery. But behind those eyes, however, Mossworth dimly perceived a ferocious kindness, gentility, and intellect. Mossworth caught a few words: "But John, there was no sense in Geneva without a proper grounding. It's all very well to speak of 'human rights' but from whence?"

The other man, still leaning in, spoke. "That is the point, exactly, of course, and we made it as best we could. It was not the fault of our group if the committee could not grasp where international human rights originated, Tom." Both nodded their heads, one sighed, and the other had a long draft of his beer. They were probably retired academics, Mossworth surmised, but more than that they carried themselves as men of substance, gentlemen of conviction and character. Mossworth hated them.

At the other table, Mossworth observed, sat an older couple, much better dressed. The man wore a rich blue doubled-breasted jacket with white, sharply pressed trousers. Mossworth could see that if the man stood he would be tall and trim. He could also make out that the stripes on the man's necktie must mean some school affiliation but it was one he could not place. The man's hair was white, thick, and waved over his forehead and handsome face. His neck muscles were pulled tight, constantly, perhaps a sign of fitness but it lent him the appearance that he had spent his life constantly trying to reach something with his head and yet never quite attained it. The woman wore a matching blue blazer, adorned with sparkling brass buttons, a smartly pleated white skirt, and was notably handsome and well preserved. Several large bracelets of varying metals clinked and clanked as she gestured. "No, no Richard. You want the sports, remember?" She flipped through a large edition of the Times and pulled a section. Folding it in half she held it out towards the man. At the moment the man seemed to be preoccupied with something on the wall, although Mossworth was unable to discern just what that might have been. "Richard. Richard!" the woman shouted, unusually loudly for an Englishwoman. Richard snapped to and looked at her.

"I say. I say. Rain again." The woman handed him the sports section. Immediately the man nodded and then placed the pages under his bottom. Before Mossworth could make much of the situation, a waitress appeared at their table.

"Whaddya have, love?" she asked.

"Of course, I shall have the onion soup and the crepes. Richard would like the lamb chop."

"Sorry, ma'am," said the waitress, "Truck never made it in this morning. We do a nice fish and chip."

Richard fiddled with the salt and pepper shakers on the table. "Richard, darling, they are out of the lamb."

Looking again at the wall, Richard sighed, "well, whatever the solicitor thinks is most efficacious."

The woman, never turning to the waitress, said, "and the fish and chips," and dismissed her with a wave of her hand. The waitress moved in the direction of Mossworth's table.

"And what about you, Fochashite, what you having?" Mossworth then realized the young woman was the same who had waited on him during his first day in Oxford.

With a broad smile, Mossworth nodded, "yes, yes, quite well. Oh. The, well, fish and chips."

"Oh, ready for another go, eh?" she asked.

"It was very good the first time, so, uh, you know…"

"Right-o, love." And she was off.

Smiling after her, Mossworth glanced about just in time to catch Richard starring intently at him. Mossworth nodded slightly and averted his eyes. "What you need, sir, is a Bodleian!" said Richard in what toddlers understand to be an outdoor voice. Mossworth looked up to see if the comment were directed towards him. It was. Before he could acknowledge the remark, Richard's wife spoke.

"Richard, leave the young professor alone, will you? He is trying to have lunch." Richard lowered his eyes. The wife turned to Mossworth. "Very sorry, sir, for interrupting your luncheon. Please don't let this ruin the afternoon for you."

"No, no, not at all, not at all," replied Mossworth. "Please enjoy your lunch…on."

"And," said the wife, apparently not hearing Mossworth, "it is the Bodleian, not 'a' Bodleian. You know that, Richard."

Mossworth glanced about the room but no one else seemed to notice the couple or Mossworth. He returned to his drink.

When his fish and chips arrived, the waitress neatly set down the plate and then a bottle of ketchup. "Anything else, love?" she asked, her eyes lingering upon Mossworth's for just a moment. Mossworth starred.

"Uh, yes, yes. No, no, I'm fine, thank you."

"Paula."

"Um. Sorry, what?"

"Paula. My-name-is-Paula."

"Oh. Pleasure. Brian Mossworth." Mossworth smiled again. "And malt vinegar, please." Paula reached around to the back of her apron and instantly a bottle of Heinz' best appeared. She leaned in low, providing Mossworth with a glimpse of her feminine charms, and placed the vinegar on the table. With her mouth closer to Mossworth she spoke.

"Eight."

"Eight what?"

"Eight o'clock."

"Yes, eight o'clock. What?"

"Eight o'clock is when I get off work." Paula looked at Mossworth with a smile. "Love, for an Oxford student you don't seem to be all that bright."

"Oh, no," said Mossworth, "no, I mean, yes. That is, you know…"

"Yeah, yeah, I know love. No pressure. Just thought you may like to know." With that, Paula turned and left the room. A bit of wheezing brought Mossworth's attention to the English couple at the next table. Mossworth, fork halfway to his mouth, looked up in time to see the wife standing just as she glanced his way. He offered a smile and a nod. She ignored him. Her hand went out to Richard who latched on, then grabbed his cane. Just as Richard managed to stand entirely upright his left hand slid up between his wife's legs. Without slowing down her movement, Richard's wife lashed out with her right knee and shoved it neatly between his legs, then left him there, bent over, moaning, gasping for breath. He began slowly shuffling towards the door after her. Before he exited the room he twisted his neck about to see Mossworth, still holding his fork.

"A Bodleian," came his strained whisper.

After lunch, such as it was, Mossworth strolled around the town, attempting to get lost among the aged walls. With Richard's admonition still in his head, it did not surprise him to find, about an hour later, himself standing outside the entrance to said Library. A young woman looked up at him as he approached.

"Yes?" Then she looked back down at the magazine on her desk.

"Oh, uh, I would like to…" said Mossworth.

"Next tour is in four hours Five Pounds," she said without looking up.

"Well, yes, but I would prefer not to…" started Mossworth when he was interrupted.

"If you do not have a membership card you are not permitted into the library nor to use any of the library's facilities," the young woman stated blandly.

Mossworth looked behind the girl towards the massive doors. "This is a library, right? I mean, aren't libraries…"

"No. Sir. These are private collections of the University of Oxford and they are not general libraries do you want a ticket for the four tour five Pounds."

Mossworth shuffled his feet a bit. "So, the library is for, ahem, you know, students?"

The young woman looked up at him. "Yes, students of Oxford university do you have a card if not you are not permitted would you like a tour five Pounds."

A five-Pound note appeared and the young woman initialed something on a list. "Please be here seven minutes before the tour starts or you may miss your spot thank you for supporting the Bodleian library and the Oxford Libraries system it is a costly endeavor to operate so ancient buildings and we are grateful for your contribution good bye."

By four forty-five Mossworth was back out on the streets, his head reeling from delicate traceried stone, aged painted beams, and the musty reek of old leather volumes. Slowly, dazed, Mossworth made his way back down the High Street, across the bridge, out towards Iffley and Nanford House. Ideas for grand research projects danced in front of his eyes but he could not quite focus on any one in particular. Greatness whirled about him. He knew it to be his destiny. But at that moment all he cared about was a Chinese take out and some quality television viewing.

THE SAVAGE STATE

The clever men at Oxford
Know all that there is to be knowed.
But they none of them know one half as much
As intelligent Mr. Toad!

Kenneth Graham

Sunday morning dawned, and Mossworth awoke with a mild spiritual conviction that he felt best fulfilled by church attendance in historically significant architecture. He decked himself out in one of his new historic tweed jackets, a pair of crisp black wool trousers, and his brown bucks. He hesitated when it came to his Bible. Did one carry such to church here? For the life of him, he could not remember what he had learned from BBC films. He decided upon a nice pocket version, a 19th century New Testament. For good measure, in his other coat pocket he loaded up with Foxes mints.

He recalled the vicar's invitation, reminded himself as to the location of St. George's, and set off. As he walked, the sunlight flicked between the clouds. "Hm, yes, what is with the cobbles?" Mossworth then mused about the ages of the cobbles and the comfort of his shoes upon them. "Mm," he grunted as he moved past St. Giles and down around Christ Church College, "ought they to have coffee shops on the High? A disgrace!" A few more blocks and Mossworth found himself facing the modest arched doorway of St. George's. He checked his watch, popped in a Foxes mint, and tried to quietly open the door. A pretty young woman stood in the narthex, smiling, and held out her hand. "Good morning and welcome to St. George's." Mossworth nodded, shook hands, and accepted the proffered order of service. Then he quickly, and quietly, moved through the doors and took a seat in one of the rear pews.

Safely ensconced, Mossworth looked up and around and then sighed audibly. Beams of dusty light flickered down the nave, across the heads of the congregants, illuminating silver heads, smiling faces, and warm handshakes. Mossworth noted that the anticipated Gothic arches and vaults were not a part of St. George's brick, paint, and wallpaper. Sneering, he turned his attention to the order of service. "Humph," he wondered, "why are they not following the autumnal schedules? And what is with the Bernardo's appeals? Money, money, money." Interrupting, a hand dropped down in front of his face.

"Good morning. Mossworth, was it? Remember me, taxi caller?" Reverend Dunlop smiled warmly.

"Oh, yes, Mossworth, correct." Mossworth shook Theo's hand.

"Well it is very fine to see you here, Mr. Mossworth. I do hope you find our worship service useful. Please, let's chat during tea in the hall afterwards." Then Theo moved off to greet others in his fold.

"Mr. Mossworth, indeed," thought Mossworth. Then, catching himself, he realized the precariousness regarding his situation. Of the consequences for revealing himself as a doctor of letters, a professor, he had no clue. "I could lose my place at college!" He resolved then to mention his past to no one.

With a great squeaking noise a wheezy organ started up soon to be followed by even more squeaky voices in song. It appeared that nearly all joined in the singing. It was loud. "Does not a single person grasp even the most rudimentary concepts of tone, pitch, or key?" When the singing ended and they sat, Mossworth realized that someone had joined him on the pew. Out of the corner of his eye he took in the over-dyed hair, polyester dress with much-too-large flowers, a jangling bracelet with obvious glass instead of jewels, the well-worn overcoat, and the most extraordinary knee-height boots with elastic side bands.

"Good lord," thought Mossworth.

The service ended. With a friendly smile the flowered woman bade him farewell. Before he could fully escape, Theo appeared with a wife and two small girls and introduced them. Everyone shook hands and Mossworth forgot their names. He could not quite get why the young girls were so ill-behaved, climbing on their father, clinging to their mother. As he left the building he considered the event. "Yes, no doubt they try hard. What they need is some real leadership. Well, perhaps this is why Providence saw fit to place me here. I'll do what I can." Mossworth strolled up towards the High Street in anticipation of a palatable lunch.

Later that afternoon, Theo and his wife, Amanda, sat in their kitchen, lunch finished, washing up done, fresh mugs of tea in hand, and the two girls playing quietly in the next room.

"What did you make of the American, Mr. Mossworth?" asked Theo.

Mrs. Dunlop paused for a moment. "An unconscionable bastard," she replied. Theo looked sternly at his wife and then smiled.

By the end of his second week in Oxford, with yet a week until Term began, Mossworth had settled into a daily routine. He would rise at seven, sharp, stumble next door to where the Nanford served exactly two eggs, two sausages, and two slices of mostly burnt wheat toast. Satiated, he would return to bed and arise again no earlier than ten, wash and be ready for the day, promptly, by eleven, at which time he would stroll down the High Street and arrive at the Bodleian. Typically, it was half-eleven when he made his entrance, past the snippy counter girl, into the lobby, past security, through card-check, and then up, up and into the reading room. His research there consisted of his finding a quiet corner, sitting thoughtfully for a moment breathing in the dusty scents, and then reaching randomly up behind him for a book. Reading usually lasted fifteen to twenty minutes, less if it was in any language other than English. After this exhausting regime he was ready for the afternoon programme: lunch with Paula, strolling through the Ashmolean, tea with Paula, dinner somewhere with Paula, then a walk, arm-in-arm with Paula to her apartment. A quiet and meditative walk, whilst smoking his pipe, through nighttime streets and alleys of Oxford brought him back to the Nanford to catch the ten o'clock news and the rebroadcast episodes of, Are you Being Served?

On this particular day, the Saturday a week before he would be permitted entrance to his Fochashite rooms, Mossworth found himself slightly behind schedule, on his way to the Eagle and Child. It was 12:35. As he entered he was surprised to find that he did not have to elbow his way through a crowd to get to the bar. He stepped up.

"Hello, love," said Paula with a smile. "What you at today?"

Mossworth sat himself down at the end of the bar. His seat, he liked to think of it. "Oh, real breakthrough today, Paula. Some good work done, to be sure," said Mossworth. "Mm, and I think that deserves…"

"A pint of bitter?" asked Paula, reaching for a glass.

"Indeed," said Mossworth, with a wink. He monitored Paula as she pulled his pint. Carefully he considered her buttocks, particularly as they were prodigious and jammed into black trousers at least two sizes too small. A blurry thought sparked across his mind that, perhaps, Paula existed as a real person in a real city with a real life and, in fact, real emotions. "But of course," he mused, "of course this is a real city and she is real. I do not wish to hurt her, nor for anything but her friendship, her company, her companionship. She is a grown woman and must know that." Then his thoughts were redirected as a patron entered the front door. "Good heavens," thought Mossworth, "that man could be the son of Tolkien!"

Mossworth hung about a bit until Paula's shift ended. Together they walked hand-in-hand down St. Giles towards the High. They walked this route often during their evenings. Mossworth, after a bit of hunting, had found an Indian restaurant down near Christ Church; tonight they would dine amid the exotic smells and sounds of the subcontinent. Their evenings together consisted entirely of lovely walks then even lovelier dinners. While the former were rather of a bargain, the latter cost Mossworth a hefty sum. To date, while at Oxford Mossworth had thought about his money situation exactly once, eight days earlier during the purchase of an antique saddle. For a moment his mind danced across lots of numbers but when it came, quite quickly, to three thousand Pounds, he immediately reflected that compared to the eighty-two thousand Dollars he had gained from the sale of his house it was but a small percentage. "And really," he muttered aloud in his room, "it is only money. Oxford is a once-in-a-lifetime experience!"

Over a ridiculously spiceless vindaloo, during a quiet moment, Paula smiled brightly and toyed with her fork. "You're a piece of work, you are, Mossy," she said.

Mossworth chomped at his onion bhaji, grease smearing along his beard. "Me?" he said with a grin, "no, not I. I am but a poor undergraduate, a student."

Paula grunted a laugh, "I hope not, love, or we'll be doing a runner." Mossworth smiled back, dully, and continued eating, dipping yet another piece of toasty naan into the remnants of his vindaloo. "You know, Brian, you've never explained to me what you are doing here at Oxford."

Mossworth paused, briefly. "I'm just a student."

Paula looked down, then smiled and looked up. "Yes, yes, just a student. But what did you do before? I mean, obviously, you are more...mature...than your classmates." Here she paused for a moment and her eyes flickered about before resting upon Mossworth's own. "I want to know what you been doing for the past twenty years."

Clattering just a bit loudly, Mossworth set down his fork. He picked up his napkin and, carefully, delicately, cleaned the corners of his lips. "Yes, yes, well...it is a bit complicated, you know."

Paula kept looking at his face, unmoving.

"Right, well, you see...sometimes in life. That is to say...there are moments when one finds that, you know, life, life can take...directions..."

"Look you," said Paula, "I like this. I like being here, being with you. You are kind and gentle and, and...but you are a bit of alright. Two weeks nearly now we've been eating out, walking, talking. Nice and like...but I don't know you." Paula's eyes attempted to look deeply into Mossworth's.

With something like the cross between a lemur and a kitten, Mossworth tilted his head just so, gazed at Paula, and smiled ever so gently. "Yes, these weeks have been...a sheer delight. It feels like..." and his voice trailed off. He reached for the naan.

Paula grabbed the naan basket and held it close. "Sometimes, love... Are you interested in me at all? Are you hiding something? Are you gay? Why are you in Oxford, at your age, at our age? Is this a kind of game, just for fun, for amusement, the Oxford experience, reliving youth?" At this her eyes dropped. After a pause, she continued, "Brian, I've been hurt before, dove. I'm just trying...not to be stupid."

Mossworth cleared his throat. He looked past Paula and noticed an antique print of Bombay on the wall. He looked at Paula's hair. "Was she graying?" he wondered.

Then he removed his glasses and took a hanky from his back pocket and began to clean them. He cleared his throat again. Just then a shuffling noise, followed by the sound of someone standing up, putting on a sweater, sniffling, and then walking away, came to Mossworth's ears. He slowly put on his glasses.

"Ah," he breathed upon noticing that he now sat alone, "yes, well...perhaps it is for the best. There is work, important work, to be done." Mossworth picked up another piece of naan, sloshed it in the cold vindaloo juice, and shoved it in his gob. "Mm, my first Oxford romance," he mused. "Tragic, dramatic, happiness cut short." Mossworth raised his hand for the waiter and ordered another beer. And another basket of naan.

After the curry, Mossworth, feeling that a bit of moodiness would be appropriate, did not immediately head back to Nanford House. Instead, he worked his way up to St. Giles, crossed over by St. Johns so as not to walk past the Eagle & Child, and strolled. Carefully, and due to the appropriate level of post-romantic moodiness, he packed a new bulldog pipe with a blend he had yet to try: Evening Stroll. A match sparked to ignite the tobacco and he puffed contentedly. With a flash of insight he realized he had not enjoyed his afters. He looked about while thinking. "No doubt, smoking is more appropriate to the moment," he considered, "but there is equally no doubt it was a romance not to be. Tragic, indeed, deeply moving. A sweet would make the moment...more deeply bittersweet...like bittersweet chocolate. I wonder, was it Wordsworth who said...that poem about love...?" He then looked up in time to see the Chateau Rouge, a confectioners, still open. "Yes, my instincts have again served to guide my path."

Crossing the street, Mossworth neatly snuffed his pipe and entered to find a small shop, much too warm, with nearly every surface covered in red or black Formica. For a moment he stood, wistfully, by the display case and took in the magical colors of the tarts, cakes, cremes, cookies, pies, and meringues. A small, dark-haired woman behind the counter looked over at him with something like disgust, then smiled, put down her newspaper, and asked, "You like something?"

Just as she spoke, however, Mossworth heard, shouted, from the other side of the shop, "Bodleian!" Mossworth, ignoring the voice, turned to the woman to order.

"You, sir!"

Mossworth peered his head around as minimally as possible. Frantically waving, in the corner, sat the elderly gentleman he had seen at the Eagle and Child.

"Yes, yes, you. Bodleian man. Come here."

Mossworth looked to the woman behind the counter. Then he looked down at the edibles. The woman raised her eyebrows.

"Here, I say, come here," the man shouted.

Mossworth obeyed.

As he approached the table, Mossworth noticed first that the man's wife was not about. Second, he noticed that the man was wearing a most extraordinary tweed jacket. Getting closer, the man grew increasingly animated. "Yes, yes, yes, my boy, that's it, come here, come here," the man intoned. Mossworth came by and the man motioned to a chair. "Yes, here, sit. The Bodleian, did you get one?" he asked conspiratorially, leaning in much too close, as Mossworth sat. The man's breath reeked of onions, liquor, and cigarettes.

"Well," began Mossworth, "I did go there as you recommended..."

"Oh, hurrah! You got one! I knew you would!" exclaimed the man. Then, suddenly, he turned back towards his newspaper and half-eaten meringue. With his right hand he grabbed the meringue and shoved most of it into his mouth. Crumbs spilled about his person.

Mossworth looked up quickly to see what the other patrons were doing. The dark-haired woman had disappeared and the only other patrons were a young couple starring intently into each other's eyes. Shuffling in his chair, Mossworth made to stand, but then sat. Then he put out his hand. "Good evening, I am Mossworth."

The man turned quickly, his face lighting up. "Mossworth, eh? Pleasure old boy, pleasure." Then the man stuck out his right hand and grasped Mossworth's firmly, shaking up and down. "Delighted, delighted, I say. And what crew are you again?"

Mossworth blinked a few times. "Ah...crew..." But just then was interrupted by a snapping voice.

"Richard! Richard, damn you, what have I told you... Oh, good lord you are a stupid git." Pulling back her chair at the table, Richard's wife, the woman Mossworth had seen before, sat down. "I do apologize Dr...?"

"Mossworth."

"Mossworth. Yes, I do apologize. My husband thinks he knows people when he really does not. It was different before, I assure you. When Richard was Master of Magdalen, well, then his wits were earned and he had a name and really did know everyone and everyone knew him." She paused a moment, watching Mossworth. "And you are of course a lecturer here? Which college?"

Eyes darting about, Mossworth used his precious conversational seconds to make a quick decision. "Please, may I order us some tea?" he asked. The woman nodded. Mossworth stood and extended his hand. "I'm terribly sorry, but I have not introduced myself properly, Brian Mossworth."

Hand extended, wrist bending just so, the woman nodded her head as Mossworth took her hand. "Cordelia Tolkein. The pleasure is all mine." Mossworth blinked rapidly a few times before releasing her hand. Cordelia merely smiled pleasantly.

Mossworth backed slowly away and moved to the counter. After taking a second look into the counter he ordered from the dark haired woman a pot of tea and, in a moment of haste, a kilo of assorted cookies. He then returned to the table and attempted to start the conversation over.

"So...am I to understand...?"

Cordelia nodded. "Yes, Tolkein. A name with substance, if I may say."

"Well, I must say... and, um...Dr. Tolkien served as Master of Magdalen...?" asked Mossworth.

"Yes," said Cordelia, throwing a sideways glance at Richard, "for more than fifteen years he ruled the unruly. Richard ran the ship well. In spite of his being an unadulterated ass."

At the sound of his name, or perhaps the insult, Richard looked fully upon Mossworth. "Tell her, tell her you got the Bodleian."

"What?" exclaimed Cordelia. "Richard, you idiot, the young man is a lecturer here. Of course he has access to the libraries." With a sweet smile Cordelia addressed Mossworth, "and which college are you presently at, Dr. Mossworth?" But just then the dark haired woman arrived with a steaming kettle and a very large box full of assorted cookies.

"Biscuits!" exclaimed Richard, "goodness, look at them. How did you know, lad?" Without hesitation, Richard tore into the box and grabbed a handful. More carefully, he then began to examine them one by one, carefully nibbling the ends and the placing the remaining portions into his jacket pockets.

Cordelia reached across and slapped his hands. Richard went spilling onto the floor. "Good god, Richard, you know better! How many times... I do apologize, Dr. Mossworth." Quietly, with two hands, Richard lifted one of the cookies he had managed to keep a hold of to his lips. For a moment he appeared contrite, Mossworth noticed, until Cordelia returned her attention to Mossworth. At that point, Richard winked at Mossworth and stuffed three cookies into his gob, and then quite audibly ventilated his trousers.

Cordelia sat quietly looking at Mossworth and ignoring Richard. He, smiled, somewhat, and then reached for the teapot. "May I?" Cordelia nodded. Mossworth poured cups for the three of them. He shook a bit while doing so.

"And your college, Dr. Mossworth?" again asked Cordelia.

"Oh, ah, well, that is an interesting question..." said Mossworth.

"Oh, my good doctor," began Cordelia, "they are all part of the University system. We are all family here. Each has their history to..."

Richard cut her off. "No, they are not all family. Particularly not that Fochashite rubbish. No one with an ounce of respect would work for them. Ah, but that beautiful concrete masterpiece... How they got funding for that baffles me. Cookie, anyone? American?" Cordelia took one from the offered box. Mossworth held his teacup with two hands and kept his face in it. Richard set the box down and took two more cookies.

Before anyone could ask any further questions, the door to the Chateau Rouge opened and in walked a well-dressed, middle-aged couple. The man was lean and fit, dashing in a formal suit with tails. A pair of thin wire glasses lent him a perceptive, furtive appearance. Next to him, however, was a vision in shimmering purple and gold silk, presumably his wife. Tall and exceptionally thin, the dress clung to her form, accentuating her womanly charms but with propriety and decorum. Her pronounced cheekbones lifted even higher as she smiled at a quip from the man. The smile threatened to outshine the artificial illumination in the cafe. Both of them were black.

Attempting to take his eyes from the couple, Mossworth heard Cordelia mutter, "When did they allow in the darkies?"

Richard grunted. And then with a mouth full of cookies he said, sotto voce, "Isn't this the Chateau *Rouge*?" He snorted with laughter and Cordelia joined him. Mossworth kept his teacup to his lips.

"Well, Dr. Mossworth, I must say it has been a pleasure," said Cordelia as she stood up. "I'm afraid we must be going now." At that, Cordelia stepped firmly upon Richard's left foot. A gasp of Richard's breath brought a slight flush of color to her cheeks. Richard slowly raised himself to standing. He then put out his hand to Mossworth.

"Thank you for the bikkies. They were splendid." He shook Mossworth's hand several times. "Your contribution to the college is much appreciated. I do hope we may luncheon together sometime."

Mossworth just smiled but, at the mention of lunch, Cordelia paused in gathering her things. "My dear Dr. Mossworth. I do believe Richard has made sense at last. Indeed, what about luncheon at Willington Hall, our estate just outside the city?"

Rubbing his hands, Mossworth twitched his lips and imagined the delights of Willington Hall. "Oh, oh, well, lovely, yes, thank you. Thanks you, alot." He inwardly shuddered at the malapropism.

Cordelia snapped her fingers under Richard's nose. "Toad. Card." Richard reached into his jacket pocket and produced a thick-papered, elaborately imprinted business card only partially crumpled and tea-stained. "Let us say, luncheon on Friday. And, Richard, what do you say to the Doctor?" But not waiting for a reply, Cordelia flatly stated. "And please do bring the wine. Richard prefers French." Without another word, but with a vague wave, she moved to the door, opened it and exited, letting the door slam back into Richard. When the door was fully closed Richard turned to look at Mossworth. He gestured with his hand, encouraging Mossworth closer.

"Lad," he said quietly, "no doubt you have discerned that she is a total bitch but, let me assure you, she gives a very satisfactory rogering. Oh, most satisfactory." Richard then tipped a non-existent hat and exited.

Mossworth merely stood at the door, swallowing several times and licking his lips. He slowly removed a striped hanky from his back pocket and rubbed it across his forehead as he walked back to the table.

The black couple was deep in intimate conversation.

The dark haired woman raised her eyebrows at him.

A delicate patina of cookie crumbs covered Mossworth's table; all the cookies were gone, and the tea was cold. Mossworth paid the bill and discovered it included sandwiches and drinks the Tolkein's had earlier enjoyed. Quickly he exited onto the streets of Oxford, dark with the mystery of a late summer evening and a measure of personal angst.

Strolling towards darkened Cornmarket Street, the wind tugged at his hair for a moment, attempting to pull his thoughts elsewhere. Flashing through his mind, but on the edge of his perception, he felt something like desire, something needing response, a feeling that he ought to remember something significant. With a sudden shift, the wind whipped about in another direction and carried with it the sound of a church bell. He lifted his eyes and noticed that Cornmarket stood in shadows, void of persons. A few pieces of tossed paper spun about nearby. Raucous laughter came from down an alleyway. Mossworth stopped walking and pulled his jacket up. The wind had cooled. Glancing into one of the shop windows he noticed an illuminated display of watches and clocks. A glowing sign read, "Got Time?" Mossworth leaned in to have a closer look but just then another tower bell, much closer, started ringing the hour. Startled, he jumped just a bit and made a minor screeching noise. He continued on his way, nagged by that feeling, that need that he could not quite grasp, which followed him all the way down the High, out the Iffley and into his smelly Nanford room.

Late Saturday morning a week later, Mossworth dreamt he floated in golden light high up among the tremendous stone vaults of a hall. Somehow the architecture reminded him of Oxford but stronger, deeper, more solid, more alive. Illumination poured in from windows; he could not look directly out the windows to see the source of the light. Music seemed to linger in the very air but it could not be heard. Clouds drifted about, brightly colored birds flittered. His eye, or his floating body, began to gently move down from these heights. Flickering rainbows danced around him, through him, beneath and above him. As he moved down the light began to dim and he could see, now, the walls covered with what appeared to be artworks. Sliding along the wall with a shock he realized the art works were windows, visions onto moving, living scenes. Further down the light lessened and the movement stopped yet the images continued to astonish with their sheer verisimilitude. Assorted other images, flat in their perspective, but recognizable, somehow connected with life, mixed in. He kept descending, the light from above dimmed further, the images changed again to optically recognizable yet unintelligible forms; even further down, the images flattened out entirely. As he approached the bottom, in the dimmest light, he could barely make out sheer fields of color, pale, washed-out.

Grimacing, Mossworth braced himself to hit bottom. Instead, his non-corporeal self landed upon a tepid gelatinous mass, absorbing his fall, cushioning him, and then rolling him about. He came to rest on his back and noticed that the substance cooled him just enough to insure he would always be cold, never warm, should he remain. Far above he was able to glimpse in the dizzying heights, flashes of, he perceived, an intelligible light.

Mossworth awoke with a start, gleams of morning sun invading his face, the dream still fresh. Shielding his eyes, he ignored the light and sat up, trying to orient himself. Sitting on the edge of his bed, he caught sight of a small black wooden box atop the tiny Nanford table. Smiling, then frowning, then smiling again, he reflected over the previous afternoon and evening.

Yesterday Mossworth had taken advantage of the Tolkein's invitation. He had stood, awaiting the number twelve bus, in one of those miserable misty Oxford drizzles, warm, but wet. His Swayne-Adney-Briggs umbrella had been left behind, lost in the increasing pile of things at Nanford; a three-Pound flimsy crimson one, purchased in a rush from a newsagents, kept a portion of the moisture from his head. In his left hand he grasped a brown paper bag.

Forty minutes later, and with a kindly grunt from the driver, Mossworth exited the number twelve at the end of a leafy, green, overgrown lane, nary a house, or any other structure, in sight. He strolled up the lane as it appeared to be the only direction in which one might travel. "Where," he wondered, "might the impressive edifice of Willington Hall be?" Avoiding the largest of the puddles, he kept on the lane as it slowly began to curve about and descend. As he came about he caught, through the damp leaves, the glare of artificial illumination and he pressed on. Soon he discovered a smaller path leading off, back into the overgrown trees; at the start of the path was a rotting wooden postbox with the letters, "Tol" on its side and the letters "k, e, i, n" scattered about on the ground underneath. Four minutes trudging up an ill-kept path brought him to the front of a modest brick house. Mossworth soaked up the ivy covering most of the facade and the half-hung shutters. He noticed that among the ivy grew some sort of flowering weed, one that reeked, and that behind the half-hung shutters were windows so opaque he had at first assumed they were blinded instead of merely filthy. Several cats milled about under the porch and approached Mossworth eagerly as he stepped up to the door. He reached for the knocker, a long, thick, bronze device, and rapped.

"Hello, Bodleian," said Richard as he opened the door. "Welcome to Willington. Please do come in." Richard shook his hand and took the wine in one gesture then sweepingly invited Mossworth to enter. Inside were books. Covering every wall, top to bottom, bookshelves of every type were jammed, crammed full of leather bound matching sets, yellowed, crumbling paperbacks, massive antique folios, ribbon-tied boxes of prints, and decades-long collections of journals. Mossworth drank up the musty odors and reveled in the patina of richness the chaotic collection suggested to him. He sneezed a few times.

"Oh," said a plumy new voice, rich with that accent peculiar to the English clergy, "are you also a reader?"

Mossworth turned to find that a small, squishy man had invaded his personal space. The man was about five-foot-five, late fifties, had a thick head of golden curls, a pugnacious nose, and perfect, and perfectly white, teeth; his pants were an absolutely black, thick sort of woolen fabric, and the purple intensity of his silk shirt made Mossworth's head ache. Before Mossworth could answer the man's question, the man took a long drag on his gold-foiled Gitane, and blew the smoke straight up, like a factory furnace venting. Then he lifted an unusually large wine glass up and tipped a good half of the glass into himself. Mossworth shuffled as the man's eyes took him all in, inspecting, it seemed, every inch of Mossworth.

Breaking his own tension, Mossworth quickly replied, "Yes, yes, reader. Who isn't a reader? Just look at...this place... I love reading. You?" He put out his hand.

The man took another long drag, very cleverly slipped his cigarette under one of the fingers holding his wine glass, and took Mossworth's extended hand into his own. As he spoke his inhaled smoke exhaled through his nose and mouth. "Pleasure, I'm sure. Leslie Smith-Davies, Reverend Doctor."

Smith-Davies' hand felt like a stale piece of bread. Mossworth pulled back slightly but Smith-Davies hung on. "But you haven't told me your name, darling," said Smith-Davies.

"Oh, yes, well, Mossworth, Reverend. Brian Mossworth."

"Well my dear Mossworth," began Smith-Davies, taking Mossworth by the arm, "you must tell me all about what you read and how you know Tolkein." For the first time, Mossworth noticed something odd about how Richard and Cordelia's name was pronounced. Before he could ponder it much, Smith-Davies led him into another even larger, book-strewn room, one hung with a myriad of modern colorfield prints, faded now, and mostly colorless, and began speaking, lovingly, about the history of publishing in Oxford, as well as his own glorious time behind the pulpit at St. Gertrude-on-the-Middens, a small country church on the edge of Oxford. Then Richard entered, chittering away, slightly drunk, and was followed by a tipsy Cordelia. A large glass found its way into Mossworth's hand, and then to his lips, and soon he, too, was a buzz with the excitement of whatever it was that they were talking about.

After this point, Mossworth's memory of the evening grew less clear. He did recall Cordelia's friendly comment about the bottle of Saint-Estèphe, Petit Verdot. Mossworth could remember that he had paid thirty-three Pounds for the bottle but not if he had been served any. There were flashes of a luncheon indoors but Mossworth distinctly remembered occasional sunlight at the windows, then a long, very sleepy period, a more awake moment after some coffee, then a dinner, something vegetarianish, a sort of nut roll with boiled cabbage. The pudding (as Smith-Davies called it, to Mossworth's pleasure) featured two small scoops of ice cream and a banana. Smith-Davies roared with laughter and said in Turkey it was called "young girls delight." Mossworth remembered laughing although he didn't quite get the joke. There was also that bit of unpleasantness during which Richard brought out some of his Victorian "ladies" as he called them, Mossworth recollected with a smug frown. Richard had demanded that they all go to his study to see more of his collection; Cordelia slapped him and then kissed him quite violently.

Frowning a bit more, Mossworth recalled the way in which Smith-Davies constantly invaded his space, taking his arm, putting his arm about him. There had been much laughter about other topics Mossworth didn't quite remember, or get. And Cordelia had once, after dinner, when Smith-Davies and Richard were in the study, moved very close and wanted to "read his eyes." But that memory lost accuracy to the effects of the wine.

Late into the evening, the four of them moved outside into the chilly back garden. The sky had cleared and a pale moon shown limply down through the branches of the trees, lending the small group a unique and mystical privacy. Smith-Davies had sucked on his cigarettes furtively, outlining the decline in church membership, cultural shifts, oppression and intolerance, and movements in the arts. Mossworth did not recall any specific statements that Smith-Davies had made but he was certain they were of an important nature. Of course, at the mention of art, Mossworth waded into the conversation. Citing both Renaissance examples as well as a few from the nineteenth-century, he provided illustrative weight to Smith-Davies comments. Or, at least, he thought he had. No doubt, his contributions lent a more engaging air to the deliberation, pulling the group even closer together. After that, perhaps it was Richard, who said, "but don't you see, this is exactly what is being missed in the schools. No longer are their minds being opened." And then Smith-Davies suggested, "it is only through open minds that open-mindedness can evolve." Mossworth proffered: "When the axis of the regnant paradigms shifts towards authority, then is when engagement towards wholeness must seek to renege upon any basis for meta-narrative." (Mossworth remembered that line perfectly, as it so impressed him, then and now, that he was able to use so many big words even when mostly drunk.)

Approbation followed Mossworth's comments, as did more wine. Only flashes of memories followed: Some more eating of cheeses from Shropshire, wild dancing in front of a roaring fire, readings from Whitman, and then the end of the evening. Someone had called a cab for Mossworth. (Fitfully, Smith-Davies lay passed out, mostly nude, upon a Persian rug.) Then a particular moment that Mossworth did well remember. In the quiet expectation of the ending intimacy of a group, Cordelia stood and moved, almost ceremonially, to one of the shelves, pushed aside some dusty books, and removed a small and narrow black wooden box. She came over and stood in front of Mossworth. "Brian, darling, we want you to have this."

He took the box carefully. Atop the box, in carefully inlaid letters, spelled the name, Tolkein. Mossworth rubbed a tiny bit of dust from the letters. "That box," said Cordelia, "was given us by our uncle. He was a great writer." Mossworth looked up at Cordelia, eyes deep with emotion.

"Yes," he whispered. Mossworth stared at the box.

"Darling, please, open it. I know that uncle would have wanted you to have it. You are like family now. Richard, is Brian not like family now?" asked Cordelia.

Without hesitation, Richard piped up, "Family, indeed. What a night. Is there more wine?"

Mossworth, fingers atremble, turned the box around in his hands, finding the lid that slid back. He pushed it with his thumb. The box began to open. "I don't know what to say," he said.

Cordelia looked at him with large, glassy eyes. "Treasures are not treasures lest they be passed on. That is what uncle said."

Shaking his head with this sage wisdom, Mossworth moved the panel partway down to reveal a small, carved head. The face was long, stylized, clearly not a portrait. It had a vague African technique about it. As the lid continued to open, Mossworth realized that the head of the figure was attached to a body that ran the length of the box. Now the chest area revealed a bit of detail in the musculature, as much as could be contained in such a narrow design. Mossworth found the technique enchanting, at least in its relationship to Tolkien. Finally, as Mossworth moved the lid down past the figure's mid section, a powerful spring flipped up a gigantic phallus. Mossworth screamed and dropped the box.

"Ha!" shouted Richard, "what are you doing?" He leapt to pick up the box from the floor. Mossworth composed himself and bent down to aid Richard, but Richard had gathered up the box and was reloading it. "Here," he said, holding up the box, "it works better like this." Richard pulled the lid down more quickly. Wooden private bits sprung.

Mossworth moved his lips about but could not quite find the words.

"Oh, bollocks," shouted Richard, "don't you see, it is a pen, a writing instrument!" Now he removed the lid completely to reveal both the figure and the phallus as well as the fact it was all a wooden pen. "Uncle used to write with this pen every day! He loved it. Now it is yours."

A horn honked outside.

"Ah, that is your cab." Cordelia had Mossworth's coat at the ready. She kissed him on the cheek. Richard slapped his back.

"We must do this again."

"Soon, my dear Brian, soon."

"Safe home."

And so, Mossworth sat on the edge of his bed the next morning, gazing upon the black box, a box with a pen used to write every day by Tolkien! Who would have thought that he, Brian Mossworth, Ph.D., would have connected to Oxford insiders with such speed. Warmness filled his being even as his head continued to pound from the red wine. He stood and attempted to move to his micro bath and then, even with feelings of emotion from the previous night, his eyes espied his calendar. Mind spinning even faster he realized he had forgotten what he now remembered: today was moving-in day.

Mossworth started to pack. This afternoon he would enter Fochashite, his college, his new home. Mossworth put the tiny two-cup kettle on to boil for his morning tea. Reaching in to the room's built-in wardrobe, Mossworth began to extract his nicer clothes; these now seemed to be more in number than he had remembered purchasing. Yes, the first day's purchase at MacInney's, the two suits and waistcoat, then there was at least one more trip back. Those shirtings...bought from the gentleman's shop just off the High Street? Several other pairs of tailored flannels as well as at least six pairs of various dress shoes he could not quite account for. Carefully the shirtings were packed, then some of the suits, but in short order his two Swiss Army suitcases were full. Quite a large pile of shoes, socks, and Marks & Spencer's underpants remained. Mossworth removed one of the full bags from the bed and set it near the door. When he reached for the second one he managed, quite accurately, to catch his elbow on the just whistling kettle, knocking it cleanly into the wall where upon the impact caused the lid to pop off and steaming hot water to spray about the room and partly onto Mossworth's surprised, annoyed and then extraordinarily pained face. "Ow, dammit!" he exclaimed as he leapt to the miniscule sink, flipped the tap, and splashed his cheeks and nose with cold water. "Oh, oh, aw, oh...bloody..." Reaching blindly he felt about for the face flannel, soaked it, and gingerly laid it upon his face. Slowly the cooling of the water spread across his cheek; quickly the tightening of his post-burn skin spread across his cheek.

When he felt brave enough, he risked a looked in the mirror. Through squinted eyes he noticed an increasingly red splotch across his cheek and forehead. He also noticed that the flesh was still in place and not blistered and thus he would survive. Packing recommenced with the assistance of several Sainsbury's plastic bags.

Then, a few minutes later, just before ten, Mossworth heard the honk of a horn. His taxi was here. For a moment his heart skipped a beat. He imagined his reflection upon this moment years from now, grandchildren on his knee, mountains of books, of his own writing, upon his shelves, young students needing impressing, diploma upon the wall, and then the horn blew again. Hurrying, Mossworth grabbed the two official Swiss Army suitcases, his laptop bag, his WWI reproduction Army Air Corp briefcase, another canvas satchel he'd picked up somewhere, the antique saddle, and his great coat, and carefully maneuvered to the door. The taxi driver had his boot opened and helped Mossworth load everything. "Ah, yes, one moment more," said Mossworth as he ducked back inside. This time he came burdened with six large orange plastic bags of mostly his new clothes, his six pairs of shoes, another new overcoat, a dramatic (and presumably) historic academic regalia cap, two nineteenth-century prints of now extinct Oxford buildings (framed), and a small collection of antique books.

The driver looked at the load and then at his rear seat. He muttered something and went around to again assist.

Mossworth just dumped it all upon the sidewalk and headed back to his room. "Oi, mate. The boot is full..." cried the driver.

"Just the key," shouted Mossworth over his shoulder. Leaping gaily over the threshold Mossworth took a last peek into his first Oxford home. He decided it no longer smelled of insecticide but did of feline urine and that he would miss it just not that much. Upon locking the door he turned quickly towards the front of the building, mis-stepped just in time to trip face forward into another room's just-then-opening door, neatly preventing the door opening with his left eye. The startling falling sensation and more startling pain jerked Mossworth about, whereupon something confusing happened with his legs, and he twisted valiantly, bashing his nose right square onto the finial on the neighboring stair railing. Someone screamed. The taxi honked. Stars flickered about Mossworth's eyes and he made a quick decent towards the floor.

"Sir! Sir!" came the distant voice. Both the taxi driver and the occupant of the other room, a young Asian woman, stood over him.

"Right smart fall there, mate," said the driver, "if I hadn'a seen it I'd not have believed it possible."

"Uggnna," groaned Mossworth.

The young woman stared at his with astonishment. "I am very sorry, sir, I just had no idea you were there. I didn't mean..."

Mossworth focused a bit and raised his right hand. With his left he began to hoist himself up. "Oh, just a minute, " said the young woman as she ducked back into her room. Three seconds later she returned with a handful of tissues. "Here."

Starring uncomprehendingly at the tissues, Mossworth reached out and then noticed his hand was covered in blood. Looking down he noticed so, too, was his front. He looked up at the cabbie.

"Bloody, bloody nose, mate."

Mossworth dabbed at his jacket and shirt first. He tried his nose once but decided that was not a good idea. Groaning, he forced himself to his feet. "Got to, got to...get a cab."

"Right. That's the spirit, mate. Here we go." The cabby lent Mossworth a hand down the hall and outside.

"Sorry, sir, really," came the quiet voice of the young woman as she closed her door.

"Okay, mate, now in you go," said the cabbie as he gingerly assisted the dazed Mossworth into the vehicle, and then not so gingerly attempted to close the door pinching Mossworth between it and the pile of plastic bags filling the rear seat. Hopping around the front of the car the cabbie took his place, twisted the key, and they were off.

Mossworth rolled down the window and let the chilly breeze clear his aching head. Gingerly he gave his nose another try, dabbing carefully. He managed to remove most of the blood off his front. Or, at least, to smear it in well until it nearly disappeared. Then he sat back, breathed deeply, and attempted to enjoy the moment.

Pulling up to the front of Fochashite, resplendent in its concreteness, the first thing Mossworth noticed was a procession of students, clad in the dark and contrasting light-greys of Fochashite College, marching back through a rough-hewn gateway, into the college grounds. They were followed by what appeared to be the Fochashite faculty. As the cabbie began dumping Mossworth's items onto the sidewalk, Mossworth looked up at the face of the last faculty member in line.

"Pardon me."

"Yes," said the Professor. Then seeing Mossworth: "What in God's name..."

"Ah, yes, sorry. If I may ask, what, er...is..." queried Mossworth.

"The procession? Start. First day welcoming and orientation ceremony for Fochashite students, freshmen.

Now if you will excuse me." And quickly the man moved to rejoin the group.

Quickly paying the cabbie, Mossworth grabbed as much as his trembling hands would permit, shouldered his way into the receiving room, dumped everything, gave a quick nod (and received one) from Jimmy, and returned to fetch the rest of his things. Upon reentry, and redumping, he shouted to Jimmy, "I need a gown!" Jimmy, with a smile, lifted his arm to reveal a gown he'd been holding.

"I knew we'd see you, sir. Here, let's get this on you." Whereupon Jimmy helped Mossworth off with his bloodied jacket, into the grey gown, and managed to produce a damp cloth which he dabbed, with small effect, at Mossworth's face.

Mossworth's mind was awhirl with questions. Why had he not been informed of the assembly? When did it start? When did it end? Would he be able to hold his bladder long enough? As he managed the long zip up the front of the gown he asked: "What is this made of?"

Jimmy gave a quick eye over the way the gown fit on Mossworth, put a firm hand behind his back, opened the rear door, and began guiding him out. "Down to the south end, sixth door on the right, past the Moore sculpture." As Mossworth stumbled away Jimmy added, "recycled paper."

"Sixth door, sixth door. Why the sixth?" Mossworth mumbled as he bumbled. As he neared the end of the first building he espied a much larger central yard, one surrounded by what appeared to be a hundred portals. Looking intently he found the Henry Moore, one that looked much like all of Moore's other pieces, and started counting. Veering quickly, with a bit of a slip on some wet grass, he crashed into the door, gown flying. The door, a mostly aluminum affair, banged loudly as it whipped open down near the front of a rather large lecture hall, one filled with the Fochashite faculty, upperclassmen, and the new freshmen class. Four-hundred and seventeen heads turned to look in his direction. Spinning about, Mossworth took in the scene, stood tall, adjusted his gown, and moved not too slowly down the side aisle towards the empty seats in the back, every eye upon him. So it was that Brian Mossworth made his grand entrance in a culminating moment in his life, nose bloodied, black-eyed, cheek burned scarlet and late for his first ever Oxford collegiate event.

That evening, long after the welcome ceremony and a wretched affair called "dinner", Mossworth took a breather from moving into his room. He leaned back into his desk chair in time to notice, standing in the open door, a young man, medium height, dark hair, handsome face and mesmerizing thick and angular eyebrows that danced as he smiled. He held out his hand. "Charles Reed. How do you do?" Extending his own hand took Mossworth a few seconds more than would normally be considered polite. "I believe," Reed continued, "that we are sharing these rooms." During the course of lugging his myriad of personal affects up six flights of stairs, making an attempt at cleaning the blood off his face, and starting the substantial unpacking process, he had utterly forgotten that his stark room, their stark room, must be shared.

"Sorry, sorry. Brian Mossworth." Mossworth pumped his hand several times, reflecting over how exceptionally young Reed looked. "I, ah, had something of a hiccup this morning...with a door...you know...some...blood."

With an indifference that was neither practiced nor rude, Reed nodded and then moved to the hall to gather his things. His things consisted of a light blue Adidas tote bag that cinched at the top with a dirty thick cord and a creased black leather jacket. Mossworth had already mostly filled the room by spreading out his own things. Quickly he moved to pull his suitcases out from under Reed's bed. "That's no bother," said Reed, kicking off his shoes and then neatly easing into his bed, "I travel light. Hope you don't mind. I'm only just back from Nepal and totally shattered." With that, Reed fluffed his pillow and went promptly to sleep.

Mossworth, not knowing quite where to look, tiptoed quietly over to the polished flat of stainless steel set into the wall of their room and inspected his face. His eye now glistened dark blue, his cheek bright red. At least, he thought, most of the blood had been cleaned off. Studying his face, for a moment he took in his eyes, mostly the one that was not blackened. He squinted and made the crows feet appear and then disappear. Was he old now? Glancing over his shoulder he observed Reed's relaxed face. He looked back to the mirror and noticed that his own skin seemed thinner, less hearty, more disassembled. It looked old. With a monumental yawn, a great weariness crashed upon him, one fueled by three weeks of dining on fish and chips, too much cider and beer, overspending, keeping up with the Tolkeins, sleeping in an unfamiliar bed, a soured relationship, public humiliation, and several grievous bodily wounds. He moved to his own bed, threw himself upon it and managed to remove but one shoe before falling deeply into his own sleep.

THE ARCADIAN STATE

[Oxford] whispering from her towers the last enchantments of the Middle Age . . . Home of lost causes, and forsaken beliefs, and unpopular names, and impossible loyalties!

Matthew Arnold

Mossworth woke to a completely naked Reed toweling himself off. Mossworth rolled to face the wall and pulled his pillow over his head.

"Morning, matey," said Reed. "Ready for your breaky?"

Mossworth took the pillow off of his head. "Morning," was all he could mutter.

After a moment Mossworth heard Reed shout, "Decent now" and then the door creak open. "The dining hall is legendary for its wonderfully fried breakfasts," began another voice, a female voice, with an accent of breeding, money, and tradition. "Bacon, eggs, ham, real sausages, even fresh scones. Oh, and the fruit table is astounding." Mossworth, still facing the wall, licked his lips while he mind attempted to sort out who this source of vocal enchantment was and why she found herself presently in his room.

"Really?" said Reed.

"Really?" said Mossworth from the pillow.

"No," said the melodious female voice, "not really. But let's go anyway." Then door opened and closed and Mossworth relaxed into the quiet. Only he now noticed that quietness did not quite exist. From the hall came a quiet rumble of conversation and steps, between the walls roared water pipes, and from the lawn outside buzzed mowers.

Mossworth sat up and then realized that his back was a bit stiff mostly due to the particular vintage of the mattress. He stood. Some sort of crumbly material fell off of his bloodied clothes from yesterday. A closer examination showed the crumbs to be yellowed matter squeezed out of the mattress. It smelled like fetid socks.

Standing there, Mossworth briefly mused over a matter of grammar. He was certain that his invitation letter had said he would be given rooms at college. Mossworth had taken that to mean, rooms plural, not room. He sat up and looked towards the window for the first time. Outside a grey sky lumbered. Noticing that the window seemed an odd construction, Mossworth moved towards it. His hand went up to the wall, which protruded just slightly. He tugged and, presto, that part of the wall swung back to reveal a tiny space beyond measuring about three by two feet. Kindly, someone had thought to provide it with a sitting bench. The bench was made of machined aluminum.

"Rooms."

Mossworth closed the panel and prepared for the day. He rummaged in his wardrobe for his clothing and washing kit. At that moment it dawned upon him that the washroom and toilet were not in his room. "Ah. Ah, yes. Down the hall."

Later, attired in grey flannel woolen trousers, a crisp white oxford shirt with Fochashite necktie (colors taupe and yellow), and his very best deep navy blue jacket Mossworth entered the dining hall. Unlike the other rooms Mossworth encountered at Fochashite thus far, this one clearly learned from very recent ideas in architecture. The east wall stood about three stories, resplendent in grey concrete punctuated every few inches by a variety of colored glass bottle bottoms. Above, the ceiling descended from east to west, from three stories to one, and was carried by, Mossworth later learned, recycled iron trusses from early twentieth-century London tube stations. The layers of rust had been maintained in order to, "preserve an iconic layer of prescient history." Food trays,

Mossworth saw, emerged from a narrow slot in a wall constructed out of recycled automotive tires.

Mossworth headed towards the slot. He watched the other students take their trays and then go and sit. His turn came. "Ah, yes, I wonder…" and a tray popped out leaving Mossworth a second to grab it. "Oh, ah, thank, thank you." After a quick glimpse about the room he carefully moved away towards a table. Sitting, Mossworth examined his tray to find a stainless steel tea pot steaming nicely, a stainless steel drinking mug with an unidentifiable juice, a stainless steel plate piled high with a substance Mossworth identified as either oats, grits, or chili, two slices of toasted bread, and a plastic fork and spoon. He bit the toast; Mossworth looked up, then, to see what others were doing and eating. It appeared that none of the dozen or so students nearby touched their gruel. Mossworth took a spoonful and lifted it to his nostrils: salty, woody, and stainless steel. He moved the spoon towards his mouth.

"Hold on there, mate," came Reed's desperate voice from behind him. "Let's not do anything foolish." With a sneaky grab Reed ripped the spoon from Mossworth's hand, dipped it back into the oats/grits/chili, slopped a heaping load onto it, gave a furtive scan of the hall, and flicked the whole lot onto the southern wall, where it neatly stuck fast next to hundreds of other similarly stuck spoons. "Now, why don't you come and join me?" Reed pointed, and then began to move, to a table at the far end of the hall, near the wall, brilliantly illuminated by the multi-colored bits of glass.

"Oh, oh, well, thanks very much. Indeed," said Mossworth. Then looking at the collection of stuck spoons he asked, "doesn't anyone like the…er…breakfast?"

Reed didn't look back. "No." At the table Reed settled in next to a yellow-haired young woman, with glowing fair skin, an inviting smile, and far-away grey blue eyes. "Brian, Susan. Susan, Brian." Then Reed picked up the football scores of the morning paper in one hand, his cup of tea in the other, and had a long drink.

Mossworth hesitated, then put down his tray, then sat, then stood, then straightened his tie, then put out his hand. "Oh, uh, nice to meet, you, pleasure, pleasure." Susan placed her perfectly smooth and warmly delicate hand into his.

"Charmed, Brian, I am sure." intoned Susan in the most delicious English accent. At the sound of her voice, Mossworth forgot to breath. Mossworth sat. He put his hand on his chin and then his elbow on his toast as he very poorly tried not to stare.

"So, Brian, Charlie tells me you are also in our esteemed college. What are you reading?"

"Oh, yes. Yes. I do love a good read," replied Mossworth, smiling, squishing his elbow even further into his toast.

Susan looked at him and his elbow. "Well, perhaps this is a subtle difference in American and British English but what I mean to ask is: what subject will you be studying at university?"

Mossworth blinked a few times. Then he coughed gently. "Studying is good at university, to be sure." At this point Reed looked up from his newspaper.

"Mossy, mate. Pass the…anything." Mossworth looked lazily at Reed as he reached for his fork. As he attempted to hand it over, he lifted his elbow off his toast, to which it attached itself; halfway through the maneuver the toast fell off his elbow and onto the floor.

"Sorry, sorry," began Mossworth, "I… I didn't…" And then Mossworth picked up the toast and handed it to Reed. Reed flicked the toast over his shoulder.

"Mossy. Do you have any classes today? Tutorials?" asked Reed.

Mossworth blinked a few more times, then swallowed, then looked away, then picked up his tea and had a long drink. "Yes. Yes I do. I…no, no wait, I don't know. I've not signed up for any classes. I only just arrived." Looking at Susan he added: "Well, I mean, I've been here for a while but, that is to say, I have been in Oxford, but I only just came to Fochashite today. Er, yesterday…"

Susan stood up. "While this has been lovely, thank you Charles, I do have a tutorial. Medieval lit with Dr. Pewtardsky-Bowles. It starts in ten minutes and I only have the vaguest notion as to where her office is located. Brian, brilliant meeting you. Hope you sort out how to eat breakfast. Charles, as always, ta." With that Susan left the table and then the hall. Mossworth rubbed his eyes.

"I need to get classes, ah, Charles."

"Charlie."

"Right, Charlie. Thanks."

"Indeed."

"From where do you know Ms… Susan?" asked Mossworth.

"My younger sister did dressage for a few summers and Susan and she shared barns or something," explained Reed. "She came up to the room this morning while you were still asleep because…hm, well I'm not sure why. Anyway, hope that wasn't a bother. She doesn't know anyone else at Foosh."

"Oh, well," said Mossworth, "that was kind of you."

"Mm," said Reed.

"Might I ask," started Mossworth, "where I go to register for classes?"

Reed looked at Mossworth, started to speak, thought the better of it, drained his tea, and stood. "Better if I show you."

An hour later Mossworth understood, at least on a rudimentary level, the asymmetrical interior arrangement of the Fochashite college buildings, how his first term schedule would be filled, and that he was, now, ten minutes late for his first tutorial. Reed had tried to explain the various levels of the educational buildings and their recurring number patterns. "They are a base six instead of ten so as not to privilege any traditionally western number systems," but gave up after seeing Mossworth's expression when confronted with a third door numbered A247b^2. Reed just led the way. Shortly, Mossworth found himself outside of B1138x. "Good luck," said Reed and turned away down the hall.

Without much time to consider his other course choices, Mossworth, slightly out of breath, knocked on the door. "Come in," rang out a man's voice that rather rattled Mossworth's head. He turned the unfinished aluminum handled and opened the door. Directly across from him, behind a modest but solid oak desk, starring intently, sat Dr. Arthur Postlewait. Mossworth had but a moment to take in the dark desk, the shelves filled with hundreds of volumes, and the Turkish carpets.

"Mossworth, is it?" asked Postlewait.

Standing, still holding the doorknob, Mossworth nodded.

"Right," said Postlewait, "first let me say, please come in and sit. Second, welcome to Fochashite. Third, you are ten minutes late for my tutorial and you have come with neither pen nor paper. That will not happen again." With that he paused. Postlewait had not moved his eyes from Mossworth. Looking up, and then around, Mossworth licked his lips and sat, saying nothing.

Postlewait stood and came around his desk. Of medium build he was dark haired, of indeterminate age, trim and fit, lightly bearded, with an intelligent forehead, and eyes that focused intensely. He stood in front of Mossworth and extended his hand. "Arthur Postlewait. Please, call me Art. You are Mossworth?"

"Ah, yes, Brian. Brian Mossworth. D... Brian Mossworth," muttered Mossworth. For good measure he added, "I'm new here."

"Indeed," said Art. "Tea?" Without awaiting a reply, Postlewait reached around to a small side table next to his desk, produced an electric kettle that had recently boiled, and started preparing tea. "So, Mossworth. Non-traditional?"

Mossworth shifted in his seat and adjusted his glasses. "Well, ah, that is, no, I think that tradition has an important role to play."

"Sorry. My apologies," said Postlewait, "perhaps an American and British English issue. Non-traditional means that you are not of a traditional age for a university student."

Mossworth relaxed in his chair a bit. "I see, I see, yes, once at my college...er...my high school, there was a man...he, uh. He...you know, he returned..."

Postlewait reached for two tea mugs. "Milk?"

"Yes, please. And sugar."

"Very good." Postlewait pulled another smaller side table out so it was positioned in between them. He placed the mugs upon it. "So, Mossworth, why do you wish to learn about the history of art?"

With his mug halfway up, Mossworth paused. "Well, you see, art to me is revelatory of the greatest emotional insights of the human race."

Postlewait took a sip of his tea and gave no indication of what he thought.

"Didn't Picasso say," started Mossworth, "that art is a lie that makes us realize the truth? So, art is a means by which we seek our truth, our emotional truth, it takes, that is to say, it expresses our own authentic reactions to the world around us, good, bad, ugly. It captures those splendid, awful, terrible experiences, placing them in paint and canvas, brick and mortar, marble, or even dance and music. Many suggest that art is hard to define; I believe that art is emotional expression made willfully visible." Mossworth sat back, cleared his throat, and took a sip of tea, and permitted himself a tiny bit of a smile.

Nodding his head, Postlewait pursed his lips, then stroked his beard. "Pyramids." He took another sip of tea.

Mossworth nodded. He crossed and then uncrossed his legs. "Well, yes…pyramids…splendid things…"

Settling back into his chair, Postlewait rubbed down his moustache. "Why did the Egyptians build the pyramids? To express their emotions?"

"Oh, ah, well, you see, yes…"

"To suggest that they built the pyramids for emotional ventilation not only crosses the boarder between farce and stupidity, and by the latter I mean to say, a lack of what the historical record suggests, but it also manages to utterly denigrate and deny, indeed visits violence upon, the Egyptian's own motives for considering and making the pyramids."

Mossworth blinked a few times. "Dr. Postlewait, I…I…the pyramids stimulate in the viewer a sort of…"

"Which viewer? A contemporary tourist? You? Or the ancient Egyptian? What they made him consider was the value of life, how the eternal order was kept in such state by the benevolent moderation and control of the Pharaoh, how to seek that eternal was every man's duty and purpose. To deny otherwise is to not only impose some other value upon them, but one that denies duty and purpose, that denigrates the pyramid, indeed all work, to the merely aesthetic." Postlewait looked Mossworth in the eye. "Are we getting this, Mossworth?" Without waiting for an answer, Postlewait continued. "Week one: Plato." I should like you to read everything you can find this week on what Plato thought about art and beauty. Five pages for next week." Then Postlewait stood and opened the door. "Goodbye. And again, welcome to Fochashite. I wish you every success."

A kind of whirring echoed about Moss's head; he stood shakily. He mumbled "thanks" and left the room. Previously, when faced with substantial challenging, Mossworth had taken solace within the confines of his own ego and aided by liberal spending habits. Down the hall a bit, father from Postlewait's office, he brushed his sleeves down, ran his hand through his hair, adjusted his tie. "Fine. Pyramids…" he grunted. "He was a…a…real…" Just then a pair of professors approached up an awkwardly placed staircase Mossworth had not noticed he was standing next to.

"Ah, good morning," one chirped to Mossworth. "Perhaps you might direct us to Professor Dr. Shekeshvaherfar's office?"

Looking askew, Mossworth tugged his jacked down snappily and then brushed his hands across his lapels. "No, I'm afraid I cannot. I'm on my way out." He turned his back on them and strolled down the hallway.

In fact, it took Mossworth more than an hour to find his way out of the building and then another twenty minutes or so to find the entrance to his own room. He arrived to find five large boxes in the hall next to his door. They were his books just arrived from America. Vigorously, uninterrupted by any other tutorial, Mossworth spent the rest of the day unpacking and arranging.

Just before teatime, Reed returned to find every inch of shelving filled with volume upon volume of both art historical texts and first editions from a myriad of English authors. Mossworth had also managed to hang several of his prints. In the corner sat the saddle. The laminated wardrobe leaned precariously due to the weight of Mossworth's collection of tweed. Mossworth appeared to be nearly asleep.

Reed looked about the room and then flopped onto his bed. For a few moments nothing was said. "Mossworth…" began Reed.

"Susan!" shouted Mossworth, leaping awake.

"Hm," said Reed. A few more moments of silence passed as Mossworth rubbed his eyes.

"Oh, um, Charles," said Mossworth, "hope you don't mind about my things, old boy."

Reed looked over at Mossworth. "No, not at all. Makes the place look...Olde World-e."

"Right," said Mossworth.

"You like Oxford, don't you?" asked Reed.

"Well, of course. I mean...it is rather a dream for me. Back when I was an und... under, under a...very bad...captain...in the army, I knew that I, you know, hoped, to get away to somewhere as lovely as Oxford. Dreaming spires."

"Dreaming spires."

"Yes. Indeed." Mossworth laid back on his bed and put his arms behind his head. "Yes...dreaming S... spires.

"Mossworth?"

"Yes?"

"I need a pint and you need one worse. Let's go. The Raven's Head."

Reed, who Mossworth would later learn possessed an innate sense of direction towards any pubs, led them both back towards the downtown, past the Eagle & Child, around the Martyrs Memorial, and down one of the even more narrow alleyways. Mossworth found himself utterly turned around but before he could voice any concern Reed ducked into a low doorway. Mossworth entered to find himself in what he later considered to be "the womb of England." Low beamed ceilings threatened, in a charming and rustic sort of way, to bash one's head. A dark, very dark bar at one end of the room glimmered with brass, polished wood, and a myriad of pulls. Windows, with blurry, diamond-shaped leaded panes, looked out onto some body of water drifting by; a real fire crackled in a rusticated stone fireplace. In front of the hearth, curled on a large pillow, lay a smelly, yellow retriever. Mossworth stood for just a moment and inhaled deeply.

"Mossy, whudda having, mate?" asked Reed. Mossworth looked across the room to Reed.

"Cider, dry."

Reed procured the liquid refreshment and chose a table near one of the windows. Without awaiting Mossworth, he tucked his upper lip into his pint. Eventually, Mossworth joined him.

Reed looked over. "How was the tutorial?"

After a few good droughts of his pint, Mossworth put his glass down. "Great, fine, I, uh, you know, thought he was…nice."

"Postlewait?"

"Yes, the very man."

"I heard he is a pretentious git."

"Ah," mused Mossworth approvingly, "that mightn't be amiss. Seemed to think he knew more than…uh…then…you know, then I would have thought, er…"

Reed looked up. "What?"

"Oh, you know, nothing. I just…yes, pretentious git. That is just right." And with that Mossworth buried his nose in his jar.

"Hm," grunted Reed. "will you read art history?"

"Oh, yes, assuredly," replied Mossworth, "it is what I came here to do."

"And what will you do with a B.A. in art history?"

Mossworth stopped drinking and, for a moment, looked thoughtful. "Well, you know, something in art. Graduate school, I suppose." Across Mossworth's mind darted long term planning and the lack thereof.

Reed's eyes were following something behind Mossworth. Reed sighed. "Oh, lovely."

Mossworth looked up, "What?" Then he turned to look around. Just entering the pub, taking off her wet Burberry waxed cotton hunting jacket, blond, slightly dampened locks hanging just so about her cheeks, which were ruddy and fresh, stood Susan.

"Uhhh," said Mossworth.

"Hm," grunted Reed. "Listen, Mossy…," started Reed, but Mossworth had already stood and begun waving his arms.

"Susan, Susan, over here!" he shouted. Susan looked up and smiled and the room, from where Mossworth was standing, grew brighter.

"Oh, hello Brian. Charles. Mind if I join you both?" Susan's eyes twinkled, or at least the light in the pub made it seem so. Mossworth pulled a chair out for her.

"Please, ah, here, Susan. And what may I get you to drink?" Mossworth reached for her dripping jacket, took it, and placed it across the back of another chair. Susan looked at the jacket and then up at Mossworth.

"Thank you… Brian. Gin and tonic, please."

"Yes, oh, yes, of course," answered Mossworth and moved to the bar to order.

"So," began Reed, "Susan…"

"Yes, Charles?" replied she, with an innocuous tone.

Reed glanced over to the bar and then waved his hand in that direction with a casual gesture. "Nothing at all, nothing at all."

Susan reached into her purse and removed from it a packet of fruity chewing gum. With a practiced move she unwrapped and then inserted the florid pink matter.

Charles looked at her over the edge of his glass. "I don't know how you can chew that rubbish. It smells like…child."

Susan smiled in time for Mossworth's return. "Here you are, Susan. I also picked up a few packets of, chips, crisps. Steak and onion flavor." Reaching across, Reed snatched a packet.

"Thanks, Mossy."

Mossworth's eyes briefly flicked to Reed before returning to Susan who at that moment was shooting her gin and tonic. Once it was dry, she reached for a packet of crisps. "Brian, you are too kind. And steakers, my favorite." She smiled at Mossworth. Then she chewed her gum some more. Then she shoved a great mass of crisps into her mouth. Quite before Mossworth could consider this event Susan stood, waving to someone across the room.

"Mm, sorry, sorry," she mumbled as the crisps broke in, around, and down from her mouth. Susan grabbed her Burberry, smiled at Reed, and then patted Mossworth on the cheek. "Ta, Brian."

When she was gone Reed stood. "I need another pint. You?" Mossworth, touching his cheek, slowly looked over at Reed. "Yes." Moments later he returned. Mossworth still was touching his cheek.

"I need this pint, Mossy, to get that awful childish smell of her away."

"Mm, quite, yes…"

Reed quaffed a few droughts and then wiped his mouth. "Yeah, ah, you know, Mossworth, you think this is how first term will go?"

"Mm, quite."

But the start of this term, this first day, was far from complete. Arriving back at their rooms later that evening they found a party in the Common Room (which at Focashite was referred to as the Uncommon Room). Not only did Mossworth discover the compelling mysteries of binge drinking with those just past adolescence but so too did he learn of Clubs. Only slightly mostly inebriated he signed up for football, tennis, orchestra, numismatics, debate, the gay mens choir, and rowing. Fortunately Reed, who found himself less drunk, managed to remove Mossworth's name from all but the very last.

"Ladies and gentlemen, I present to you, Dr. Brian Mossworth, Ph.D., as of late a distinguished student at…one of the distinguished colleges of Oxford. Now Dr. Mossworth of course is well known in academic circles, but what is less known about him personally, even unknown as of yet to the good doctor himself, is that we have just received word he is to receive his O.B.E. from the Queen upon the morrow. Please join me in congratulating Dr. Brian Mossworth!" The crowds neatly arranged in the Sheldonian rained down applause upon Mossworth. He sat down at the front, in the high-backed gilded chair, gently nodding and waving one handed. Soon roses began to tumult towards him. The applause thundered and Mossworth began to find it increasingly painful to his hearing, then his head, then his brain, and then he awoke. "What? What!" His buzzing alarm read 5:00. "Five?" It was still dark. Reaching awkwardly, he turned off the alarm and noticed as he did so, a piece of notepaper stuck in the top of his clock. Mossworth rubbed his nose bridge and then turned on his reading light. The note read:

Although I am ever certain you will retain no knowledge of the event, last evening you enrolled in the rowing club. Your (new) teammates made it eminently clear that failure to show up at today's practice would result in both ejection from the team and a myriad of accusations to the effect of your being a sodomite. Cheers, Reed

The note had a small drawing with directions to the launching area. Mossworth leapt out of bed, then grabbed his head to steady himself. A glimpse over at Reed showed him laying on his back, mouth closed, not a note of worry on his face. He appeared, in this state, as a terribly young man, Mossworth mused. Some sort of vague warning welled up in his breast as he gazed on so vulnerable a person. Then he espied his wardrobe and rummaged for appropriate attire.

In a deliriously overheated and overhung condition, Mossworth arrived near the appropriate point on the Cherwell just before dawn. A light mist hung about the river. From it Mossworth could make out the shouts of the others. He approached as the sun peaked over the horizon to reveal his white trousers, blue wool sweater with large "O," and yellow and blue beanie. A sudden hush from the team fell as they espied Mossworth, glowing. Then a voice shouted, "Oi, coach, give us a hand," which was followed by a roar of laughter.

Mossworth, mostly thinking about his splitting head, called back, "I'm on the team!" For his comment he was grabbed by the rough hands of his teammates and quickly dispatched into the chilly river.

"Alright, alright," came a gruff voice, "get the sir out of the drink." Mossworth, with hardly a moment to think, found himself grabbed again, dragged to his feet, dripping, and facing a shortish man with very close-cropped grey hair. "My apologies, sir, for the lads' abuse. They take their sport with to'al respect. To'al Respect."

"I, I...isn't this...the rowing..." asked Mossworth, teeth chattering.

"Wait a minute coach," shouted one lad, "I recognize that man. He was at our party last evening. I mean, our study session." Several others then grunted assertions.

"Right," said the coach, "he was at your part-e. And...?"

"I..." shivered Mossworth, "am on the team." The coach raised an eyebrow.

"Is that so? I'm afraid the team ain't open but to students, sir."

"But I am, I am a student, a Fochashite student," said Mossworth.

"A Fochashite Man!" shouted one of the lads.

Another raised his fist and then flipped it down onto his own head in a sort of salute. "Huzzah for the Focashite Man!" The coach lowered his head and mumbled something. Then all the lads on the team organized themselves around Mossworth, one hummed a C, and the song began, in rap style:

What does it take to be a Foch-a-shite?
A man bigger than the other man, man?
Sure ain't money, sure ain't class
Ain't 'bout who can bust a cap in yo' ass.
Foch-a-shite 'bout bringin' it down.
Down, down, down...

And at this point the song went into an early twentieth-century collegiate acappella form.

Fochashite, Focashite, to you we will be true.
No one else loves Foch-a-shite
And that's because you suck.

At the end of this verse the team's long, crooning faces suddenly changed and they reached for Mossworth, lifted him high above their heads while chanting, "Fochashite Man, Fochashite Man!" Then they threw him in the river.

Later that evening after a tedious lecture on bioeconomics and an even more tedious speech in the Sheldonian regarding ethnic cleansing in northern Sweden, Mossworth settled in at the Raven's Head with a pint of bitter at his left elbow and Reed at his right. Next to Reed, cup of coffee in front of him, sat another student from their floor, John Marshall.

"Three times into the river?" asked Reed, between draughts.

Smiling just a bit, Mossworth wiped his upper lip with the back of his hand. "Four, actually. You see, I did such an awful job rowing, and even managed to break one of the locks, that they decided to throw me in once again for doing poorly and then a last time since it was my first time to row." He took another drink. "But, all in all, a good day."

"Here, here," said Reed.

"Sounds awful," said Marshall.

"However," started Mossworth, with an elderly tone, "so as not to have another painfully sore head as this morning, I'm going to have a short night tonight." One more quaff and Mossworth's jar emptied. He stood. "Good night, Reed."

"Good night, Mossy. Oh, and I hope you don't mind: Marshall wanted to know what you made of Postlewait's tutorial."

A grimace passed over Mossworth's face. "Not much looking forward to it, Old Boy."

Marshall perked up. "Postlewait? I've heard him lecture before. Fantastic. No doubt, provocative."

"No," said Mossworth, "in fact I find him to be a pretentious git."

"Ah, well, I'm sure you'll do swimmingly," replied Reed.

Mossworth grunted, waved and exited the pub. Walking back towards St. Giles he found himself on an unexpectedly empty street. A light breeze blew a cold wind against his cheeks, attempting to stir him. Reaching into a jacket pocket, he removed a newly purchased pipe, a handmade Blakemar apple, and began to pack it with Three Nuns, a blend the High Street tobacconist said C.S. Lewis smoked. Once lit, Mossworth gripped the pipe tightly in his teeth, put his hands in his pockets, and inhaled the intellectualism. He strolled down towards the Martyrs Memorial wondering how it was Lewis tolerated such awful tobacco when he heard his name shouted. It was Smith-Davies and Richard.

"Mossworth old man, how are you?" beamed Smith-Davies, "what about joining us for a drink? Richard rather stared off into space.

"Oh, well, I..." began Mossworth.

"Nonsense," said Smith-Davies, we are here at the Bird and Baby and so we must stop in. Here, Richard, get the door for Mossworth."

Richard looked up directly into Mossworth's face. Then he stepped closer invading personal space. "I am Richard Tolkein, T-O-L-K-E-I-N. And you are?"

Mossworth smiled, then frowned, then smiled again, then looked at Smith-Davies.

Smith-Davies, without missing a beat, grabbed both Tolkein by the arm and Mossworth by the hand and dragged them into the pub. A burst of heat, pub stench, and cheering greeted them when Smith-Davies pushed his way inside and instantly Mossworth imagined himself part of a group of significant persons.

Soon Mossworth established his post-Nanford routine. Rowing practice at dawn, tutorials in the mornings, lectures on the occasional afternoon, reading, or writing, alternate afternoons, and most other times drinking in the Raven with Reed, the Bird & Baby with Richard and Smith-Davies, or seeking out Susan. Most Sundays he attended services at St. George's. When he discovered, much to his annoyance, that they met in the youngest church building in all of Oxfordshire, he realized he would ultimately have to find a real church to nourish his profound spiritual needs. "All things taken as one," Mossworth mused one particularly damp evening, "this is a rather nice life." However, a single exception to this blissful undergraduate life remained: Postlewait. While Mossworth found his other courses much as what he expected undergraduate education to be, the memorization and regurgitation of factual data, he was surprised, and then annoyed, to discover that he could not succeed in Postlewait's course this way. When once Postlewait asked him about the shift from Romanesque to the Gothic,

Mossworth instantly recited the technical aspects of rib vaulting, flying buttress and stained glass from Saint Denis; Postlewait listened patiently and then asked, "So what?"

Mossworth groused over this exchange far into the evening so much so that whilst attempting study he burst out with, "So what!" and pounded the table with his fist. At the moment this was not a wise thing to do as this particular rainy evening found him reading, or supposedly reading, in the great hall of the Bodleian library. Several patrons heads popped up to glare. Being sensitive to peer pressure, Mossworth packed up his books, into his leather briefcase, and headed back further into the stacks. The previous week Mossworth discovered an odd corner of the library, one where he could sit between stacks and behind an ancient desk and not be seen. Flopping down his briefcase, Mossworth pulled out his books, glanced around, and then installed himself at the desk. After a long inhale of the dusty leather scent, Mossworth got to work sitting back in his chair and doing nothing. Soon his chair tipped back and his feet went up and he slipped into a dreamy sleep involving Susan, running in slow motion, through sunny fields of lush red flowers.

With a start, Mossworth's mind told him to stop running in the flowers and get himself balanced, but it was too late. In a more alert frame of mind, Mossworth found himself on his back, now interestingly sore, on the floor of the library. While recovering his breath and weighing his next move, he glanced up. His eye caught sight of something odd underneath the elaborate oaken moulding on the wall: a scrawled arrow. Following the arrow, his hand traced a line towards the corner of the wainscoting. He reached up towards the corner, fumbling about, and soon discovered a recessed button. "My, my," he mumbled, pushing the button. With a soft "thwang" a panel, previously hidden by the contours of the moulding, sprung open. Hardly breathing, fingers trembling, he reached into the narrow dark compartment and grasped a small, tatty book. He held it up to the light, this way and that, then brushed the dust from the front and read aloud in a hushed voice: "Keble Building Notes." Mossworth got himself up off the floor and furtively looked about. Trembling, he sat down at his desk to think, and to read. Carefully turning the pages it grew clear to Mossworth that this small book held new information concerning the history and design of Keble College. He even recognized a few of the names mentioned. Slowly, a plan formed in his mind: he would keep the book hidden, study its contents, write a publishable essay, and then before submitting it he would reveal the book to the Bodleian authorities. He would confirm himself as first out of the gate in regards to what the journal contained, get all the credit for the research and also for finding the book.

Looking about again, still trembling, Mossworth carefully replaced the book. Once the hidden door was latched, he drew a deep breath, and then coughed repeatedly from the dust. Gathering his things and replacing them into his briefcase, Mossworth grimaced just a bit and quietly spoke, with a particularly venomous tone, one name upon which he would have the sweetest academic revenge: "Postlewait."

Next morning, at dawn, as Mossworth arose for rowing he realized revenge would have to await publication of his essay. "Damn it," he grunted, quietly so as not to awaken Reed. Then he tied his shoes with a particularly tight set of knots and set off to row, or run, or, more likely, repair and wax the skulls. Mossworth opened the door to the hall and discovered a disheveled Susan.

"Hello!" said Mossworth. His heart skipped. Her hair was mussed.

Susan leapt back, gasping, "bloody…!"

"Sorry, sorry."

"Oh, Brian, good Lord, you frightened me!" Susan pushed her hair back. "Chas up just yet?"

"No, sorry, afraid not."

Something flickered across Susan's eyes. "Well, damn." Looking up at Mossworth she moved closer and patted the giant O on his chest. "Off to rowing?"

Mossworth inhaled as her proximity increased. Intoxicating effusions of stale liquor, sweat, cigarettes and some lurking musky odor teased his nose. "Oh…"

"Brian, really, we must stop meeting like this."

"Har. Har, har, yes. Oh, yes, rowing."

"Father rowed, you know, for St. Johns."

She called her father, "Father," considered Mossworth. "Yes, St. Johns…"

"Right. Well, I'll check in on Chas later, Brian. Ta, ta."

"Bye. Susan. Susan." And he headed down towards the river, a variety of mostly lusty thoughts dancing about in his head.

As Thanksgiving approached, except not, Mossworth's plan was nearly complete. His research had revealed an elaborate story to the construction of Keble, one that involved some graft, a torrid love affair, a complicated attempt to cheat building codes, and the real reason architect William Butterfield chose the amazingly unique "streaky-bacon" style of masonry: He liked streaky bacon. At the end of October he had a draft of his essay submitted to half a dozen journals of moderate reputation and abstracts to several conferences. True, he'd not managed to make any intellectual impression with Postlewait, but on the other hand, he was quite popular with most of the students, including Susan. Many was the evening, Mossworth reflected, during which he purchased rounds for the really terrific lads down at The Raven's Head. Those were some great times. He smiled.

At the moment, Mossworth's reminiscing and smiling took place in the 1st class carriage of the Eurostar about to emerge from the Chunnel. He sped along on his way to Paris, to an international conference at which he would present his research for the first time. The only way he could get invited to read at the conference was by using his credentials; this was a risk but he doubted Postlewait, or any of the profs he was currently studying under, would be attending. Still, he applied as: B. J. Mossworth so as to make his name less known. As the train suddenly shot into the moderately dazzling sunlight of the French coast, Mossworth looked again at the program: "The Third Annual Symposium of Erotic Structure and Aesthetic Desire." Mossworth snorted just a bit before mumbling, "Erotic structure…" Then he flipped again through the list of sessions and papers to read his own session and then the title of his own paper: "Keble in a New Light: Elongated Meaning through Variegated Patternage of Neo-(Homo) Vaginal Ensconced Brickwork." Tuesday at ten. Mossworth leaned more deeply into his leather seat. He'd splurged a bit, given the magnitude of what was to be accomplished in Paris. First class carriage to Paris, a room at the Hotel D'Aubusson, and he knew of several historic restaurants near the conference center in need of a discerning palette.

Briefly Mossworth reflected over his own undergraduate education and the fact that his student penury then did not reach the level of funding he now enjoyed. He did not consider that selling his house provided the means to such funding.

Eventually the train pulled into Gare du Nord. Mossworth traveled light on this trip: two new hard-shell Swiss Army suitcases and his trusty briefcase. The chilly autumn weather demanded, Mossworth thought, that he buy a new tweed overcoat and he had done so three weeks earlier, in London. During the same trip, his purchases included the coat, a morning getting trimmed at Geo. Trumper, a pair of custom leather gloves, and some spectacular handmade bluchers. Mossworth exited the train station, into blinding sunlight, and realized, with a start, he had no idea where he was going. Never had he been in Paris and his French mostly did not exist.

"Ah, uh, pardon monsieur, possible…" started Mossworth to a man outside the station selling sunglasses. The man looked at him and mumbled something Mossworth did not catch and gestured towards the street: Taxis. Wheeling both suitcases, Mossworth called out for a taxi and a grizzled, middle-aged man doffed his cap and came to get his bags. Mossworth climbed into the back seat. The driver carelessly threw the two suitcases into the trunk, came around and entered the cab, started the engine, and began driving down the boulevard. Smiling as the slums near the station rolled past his window, it was some minutes before he attempted to ask the driver where he was going.

"Uh, monsieur. Dove…?"

"Dove? Really? I'm not Italian. But would you sir like to see the city before I take you to your hotel?"

"Oui," said Mossworth, "moi hotel."

"Oui," said the driver.

Two hours later, a very red faced Mossworth stood outside the Hotel D'Aubusson, shouting at the driver. Upon inspection at the hotel, Mossworth discovered two scratches in the painted finish of one of his new suitcases. Mossworth became so animated that eventually the liveried doorman came over.

"Sir, may I be of some assistance?" the doorman queried.

Mossworth looked up. "Yes, please. This man carelessly tossed my brand new luggage into the trunk, the filthy trunk, of his taxi. Now he has scratched the finish on them!" Then turning again to the driver, Mossworth shouted, "Do you have any idea how much these bags cost?"

The driver said something to the doorman in French. The doorman nodded and turned to Mossworth.

"Sir, he is very sorry for the damage. The taxi belongs to his son who normally drives it but is today at the hospital for testing."

Mossworth suddenly was still. He pushed his hair back and cleared his throat. "I see."

The driver spoke again to the doorman.

"Sir," began the doorman, "the driver again apologizes, he begs your pardon, but he must get back to work. If you would be so kind as to pay your fare…"

"Yes, our, yes," said Mossworth. "How much?"

The doorman asked and then reported, "Two hundred and twenty-three Euros."

Mossworth shook his head in disbelief. "Two hundred and… that is crazy. This city is bigger than I thought." He removed his wallet from his breast pocket and counted out two hundred and thirty Euros. "Here, here. Keep the change. And I do hope your son will soon be well again."

The driver bowed, then he brushed off Mossworth's jacket and bowed again. Mossworth caught many "mercis" as the driver hopped into his cab and took off.

"May I, sir," as the doorman, gesturing to Mossworth's bags.

"Yes, please."

As they walked up to the rotating front door, Mossworth asked the doorman, "is there a quicker way to get to the train station?"

The doorman studied Mossworth for just a moment. "I am sorry sir: quicker than what?"

"Oh, well, a taxi."

"Oui, Monsieur. Walking. Do you see, there? That is Gare du Nord. The train station is across the street from the hotel."

Mossworth opened and closed his mouth, sighed, and entered the hotel slightly bent. When he arrived at his room, took in the expansive size, lush bedclothes, spotlessly clean bath, and view of Paris, things looked up.

Later in the day, he visited the Louvre with noisy school children, enjoyed a spectacular dinner at the Maison d'Larche where he dinned on unidentified fish parts, and realized, after his second bottle of wine was opened, that he would most likely make a huge splash with his research and paper.

The three-day conference only took two days due to low numbers. Mossworth's reading came along late on the second afternoon: of the six members in his audience, two left before the Q & A, an elderly and extremely large woman in a red hat, who arrived late, slept through most of the session's papers, snoring loudly. The remaining three in his session nodded frequently but did not speak English. He received no questions. For his part, Mossworth attended two sessions, one on images of the phallus in ancient pre-Columbian rock art and another concerning something about women's sexuality, the ontological movement of ovum, and warfare as menses in the male. The latter session featured one reader who didn't show, another who read in French, and the last whom Mossworth could not follow due to an impressively never ending stream of poststructuralist euphemisms (mostly death related), the lack of an understanding of English grammar, and the speaker's several narcoleptic fits. His weekend ended poorly when, after a particularly rich meal of buttered sausage crepe, he found his way to the hotel blocked by two transvestite street mimes who sexually assaulted him.

"So, Mossworth, are you certain that you grasp the issue?

Mossworth sat, again, in Postlewait's office. Postlewait sat in a chair directly opposite Mossworth, their knees almost touching.

"Ah, yes," came Mossworth's reply. He licked his lips.

"Good. Let's have it back then in next week's paper. Have you a topic in mind?"

"Sure, yes."

"And, may I ask what that topic is?"

"Oh. The architecture of Keble college."

Postlewait paused.

"Probably Van Gogh's boots. Or…Picasso."

Postlewait sat back in his chair and reached for his tea. "I see."

Mossworth shuffled about slightly, not meeting Postlewait's gaze. After a moment, Postlewait stood and walked to his window. He cracked it and allowed the frigid December air to float in. Soon the room chilled enough for Mossworth to see his breath. He looked up to find Postlewait starring directly at him. Mossworth pulled his jacket closer.

"Mossworth," said Postlewait in a quiet voice, "are you cold?"

Mossworth looked up again. "Yes. Yes, of course."

Postlewait nodded and then grunted, "uh, um." Mossworth shivered a bit. There was a bit of a crackle as Postlewait struck a match to light his pipe.

Mossworth did not move but kept glancing about.

"And," started Postlewait, after blowing a huge cloud of smoke, "what does one do when one is cold?"

Mossworth stood up suddenly and reached for his overcoat. "I guess one bloody well puts on a jacket!"

Postlewait nodded again and reached for the window. "Or, one may merely close the window." And he did so.

Putting on his coat, Mossworth muttered, "is that all for this week, sir?"

"Oh, yes," said Postlewait moving to open the office door. He paused before Mossworth left. "Mossworth, do you understand my point?"

Adjusting his scarf Mossworth looked over and shook his head.

"Well, my point is that I see my career much less as pointing out the design and form of the window and much more about hoping students will learn to keep warm."

Mossworth nodded and left the office, closing the door with a bit more verve than usual, and after it was closed, rushing down the hall eventually making it to the second level, third access stairs whereupon he kicked into the wall with his not previously broken foot, seriously bruising three toes, as he had forgotten in his rage that walls in England are made of plaster and not drywall. He then limped down the three other staircases and across the landing, through the hall (short) and then the access tunnels (A7 and D2) to end up near the mid-level baths. He looked up the hall. Nothing. He looked down the hall.

"Well, goodness, if it isn't Brian. Hello darling."

Susan.

Mossworth's face contorted up, then down, smiling, and then frowning. He took a step towards Susan, forgetting his injured toes, and grimaced in pain. "Ow!"

Susan immediately reached for him, locking her arm in his, helping to support him. "Brian, you seem to have injured your foot."

"Yes, I…that damn…sorry."

"Can I lend you a hand? Heading to your rooms?" Mossworth had not been heading to his rooms but, for some reason, this seemed an ideal time for him to go to his rooms.

Susan turned out to be eager to chat about this and that, relaxed, funny, and of course, very helpful to a man requiring care to his sore toes. She helped him to his bed and off with his shoes, brought him some ice, and spent several hours talking him through the pain. Then, when lunchtime arrived, she managed to fetch a curry and a bottle of Pimm's.

"And what did he mean, 'you close the window?'" asked Susan, laughingly.

"No bloody idea," replied Mossworth, but I can tell you that at my school…uh, you know, public school, they would not have tolerated that kind of rubbish."

"I should hope not," said Susan. "You know, sometimes it rather surprises me as to how some folks can finish graduate school, much less get jobs at university."

"Oh. Oh, yes, yes, you have got it…"

A moment of silence passed between them, but Mossworth found it surprisingly unawkward.

Susan stood and started putting on her jacket. "How are the toes?"

"Very well. Thank you, Susan. Thank you for your kindness, your very kind, kindly…"

"Brian, stop it. You might embarrass me." She zipped up her jacket, something Mossworth noticed, particularly as when her chest rather pushed itself one direction and her bottom another. Susan moved right next to Mossworth. "Thank you Brian. Lovely afternoon." Then she leaned in and kissed him on the cheek.

Watching her go, Mossworth leaned back more fully into his pillow and sighed. "Oh," he whispered, "A damn fine girl. A damn fine girl. Oh." He drifted, but not off to sleep.

The next morning Mossworth woke to a steady rain and a chill in the room. He moved to sit up and felt sudden pains in his back and more yellowed mattress crumbs on his pajamas. He got to his feet and stumbled to his bulging wardrobe. In trying to remove a pair of trousers, Mossworth managed to dislodge a pile of undershorts, which cascaded onto the floor. He swore quietly and threw them all back into the wardrobe. Gathering his toiletries and clothes for the day, he set off down the hall to the showers. The only shower open had been used heavily that morning; Mossworth could not find a dry surface upon which to place his things and the chamber smelled even more damp than usual.

Later, breakfast went down miserably, but that was only to be expected. The lack of company made it worse. No one seemed to be about. Mossworth's English History tutorial went badly; he'd mistakenly written on the wrong topic and then managed to gripe about his own error aloud in an accusatory manner. His two tutorial mates were shocked into silence. Professor MacBarren glared at him, demanded an apology, and then piled on two topics for the following week. As the tutorial mates were included in increased workload, they made it clear that Mossworth ought not join them at The Raven's Head. With heavy heart and hurting back, Mossworth lugged his carcass to his rooms. Along the way he happened into Jimmy who, smiling, handed over a personal letter. "From America, that is," he said, "and personal." It was on Hardley stationary and from Couch via Mossworth's aunt in Pennsylvania. On the way back to his rooms, or the way Mossworth assumed to be in the general direction of his rooms, he read:

Dear Brian,

I do trust things are going well for you at Oxford. Sorry for not writing sooner. Our system has been down due to a profound water leak in my building. (Remember how terribly the drains worked. It's been pouring rain.) Westley in biology is leaving at the end of the year. He got his dream gig at the NSF. Did you hear about the football team? Big press to change the name. Apparently Cowboys isn't inclusive enough. I don't get that as women aren't permitted to play anyway. Well, a host of names were suggested. First, Marlboro did some digging and learned that at one time our team was once called the Red Savages. Obviously not acceptable. Suggested were the obvious Cowgirls, the, Cowpersons, followed by the Bovine Boys, then the Beefy boys, even less polite, the Beefy Girls. Went downhill from there: Vegetarian Hominids and, in a nod to UCSC, the Worms. In the end the name was chosen not by the faculty, of course, but from an anonymous committee. Are you ready? Winners. Because, "everyone is a winner!" Hardley Winners, get it?

We'd love to hear from you and learn how things are going. Must be exciting to be living the dream. Been to all the Harry Potter film locations yet? Sure hope the experience is all you hoped for. Lots of folks missing you. Coffee better there?

Best regards, John

In his room, Mossworth quietly folded up the letter and set it on his desk. Then he opened up his hinged wall to his other "room" and went and sat on the bench. The rain dribbled down the windows. He sat there for nearly an hour before he packed off to the Raven's Head.

After several rounds, on the opposite side of the room from his tutorial mates, Mossworth found himself at the center of a group of unfamiliar Fochashite students and at the center of a disagreement. The issue under discussion concerned the history of the colleges and their original buildings. Mossworth had immediately waded into the chatter, throwing out a few dates. More beers were ordered so as to better judge the accuracy of Mossworth's claims. Well into rounds seven or eight, the group of Fochashite men realized that the only way to settle a critical matter of history was to head directly to Brasenose College and see for themselves. When they arrived at the gate, and had to show their student cards to gain entrance, a brief exchange ensued between two students, Zandi and Conner, as to why they had chosen Brasenose and what it was that they were to see. Their attempt at logic was promptly shouted down and the group moved into Brasenose chapel.

Suddenly, a hushed tension descended upon the eager young men as the history and beauty of the chapel closed in upon them. Several sat in the rear benches. A few put their drunken heads down to sleep on the benches. Mossworth, standing tall, grasped his chin thoughtfully, and stared intently at the aged portraits hung above the entrance. He then followed something, perhaps it was the huge painted pointing white hand, across the room. Then he looked back. His hand went up to trace an invisible line from that wall to the other. He also held up his two hands in a kind of frame and gazed intently through it. While gazing he swayed and had to step to catch himself from falling.

"Yes!" Mossworth's voice echoed across the ashlar walls. The others stood and gathered around him. "Don't you see, don't you see? The hand! Main! Hand in French!"

A few of the lads murmured in stunned amazement. A few others were slapping each other. One remained sleeping peacefully on the benches.

"But what to do? What should we do?" asked Mossworth.

Tension built. Glances were exchanged. Something was about to happen and they were all going to be there to see it.

"Okay, look...uh...the Brasenose architects were unknown members of the Knights Hospitaliers, a Captain and a lieutenant, both from Paris, they were priests... I think. Well, they traveled to Rome to see if they could learn more about what Luther was, uh, you know, teaching. There they learned about the new style of architecture from Bernini, or about Bernini, at San Carlo alle Quattro Fontane: Charles of the Four Fountains!" Mossworth took a breath and waited for gasps of astonishment from the group. One gasped while another was sick in a corner, gasping.

"So...yes! The hand, the hand, in French...and it is pointing to..." and here Mossworth's unsteady hand traced the line again across the room to the wooden benches. "There!" Triumphantly he stood back, shaking his head.

One of the lads, Duncan, Mossworth thought, kept rocking back and forth and burst out, "but what? What do we do? What do we do?!"

Mossworth blinked after having fallen asleep for a few seconds. "Wha...? Oh, yes, we get it! The hidden... Secret! We get the treasure!" With that he ran over to the corner of the room and pulled off one of the benches. Seconds passed and the rest of the lads, excepting the sleeping one and the one still being sick, ran to Mossworth and began pulling out the benches, then stomping on the wooden platform under them. "Here, look, see. Hollow!" No one could lift the platform and no one seemed quite to know what to do until one of the lads picked up a nearby iron candlestand and started to thrash it. Another candle stand was quickly had and the work accelerated. Splinters flew, larger bits fell, and the noise echoed loudly enough that no one noticed the wide-eyed Brasenose porter.

"Oi!" he shouted. "Oi! What in the name of..."

Silence fell and Mossworth immediately stepped up.

"Sir, I do apologize for how this must appear. Please allow me, allow me, to introduce myself. I am Dr. Brian Mossworth, professor of art history. My colleagues and I," and here he waved to the nearby drunken lads, "we, we...we are conducting a research project. You see, that, that white hand, or in French, Blanc Main, directs us to the, the...well, you see, it gets complicated very quickly what with the Hospitaliers and Rome, you know. Right, so, what is buried here, I, you know, the hidden, that is, treasure. See?" Here Mossworth gestured again to the gaping hole opened in the splintered bench platform. "See?"

The porter looked at Mossworth and then at the hole. Then he took off his cap and scratched his head. "Sir," he started slowly, "you believe there to be treasure under this platform?"

Mossworth, wobbling just a bit, nodded. "Indeed!"

Putting his cap back on, the porter rubbed his chin. "Sir, you are not on my register for work. Have you any papers?"

At this a few of the lads began slowly to back away from Mossworth. Looking over his shoulder, and at his Fochashite brothers, Mossworth faced the porter. "No, I'm afraid I do not. Great, great historical, uh, research, does not, um, papers..."

"Very, well, sir. If you would not mind giving me just a minute." With this the porter pulled out his radio.

A scuffle occurred near the door caused by all of the great men of Fochashite attempting to get out as quickly as possible. Mossworth blinked a few times, watched the porter glance towards the doorway, and then something deep within stirred his aged legs to move, move, move. Out the doorway and towards the gate, Mossworth scampered, now suddenly desperate to catch up with his classmates. Legs pumping like they had not in years, he would have made it had it not been for a simple change in the level between the sidewalk and the street: a misstep, a moment's weightlessness, and then blackness.

Hours later, Mossworth awoke, slowly, on the floor of the holding tank in the Oxford city jail. As his mind cleared, and his consciousness returned, Mossworth tried to remember what had happened. Rolling off his belly, he gingerly moved to his knees and then sat up. "Ahhugh," escaped his clenched teeth as the world began to revolve around him. His blurry eyes noticed McGill, Bruce, and some other chap, heads down, among other less savory gentlemen, in the holding cell. VanWinkle and Lovick sat starring blankly at each other. Smith still snored and was resplendent in what Mossworth hoped were the contents of Smith's own stomach. Duncan just sat rocking back and forth.

"Morning me' lovers," boomed the voice of a huge and sweaty uniformed man pushing a cart. "Time for tea."

Mossworth reached for a bar and leaned towards it. His trembling hand reached out towards a steaming plastic cup. Even the burning sensations in his fingers could not dissuade Mossworth's joy at the approaching hot cup. From his own side of the bars, a much larger hand reached out towards Mossworth's cup and a much boomier, and scarier, voice said: "fanks, mate," as another, very large and very smelly man took Mossworth's cup.

"My pleasure…sir," said Mossworth.

Reaching for the second cup, interruption came by way of a different, professional voice. "Mossworth. Let's go, mate." A dark suited gentleman stood impatiently by the cell door as the uniformed man fumbled his keys.

Mossworth straightened his rumpled clothing as he left the cell, tucking in his shirt and running his hand through his hair. Before he could speak he found himself in a small office, received a quick lecture from a sergeant with raised eyebrows about public intoxication, signed a few forms, and was shoved into a waiting area where, waiting, stood Susan and Reed. Susan took his arm and Reed handed him a steaming plastic cup of tea. Mossworth smiled a grim smile.

"I...I am grateful." Susan and Reed nodded and waved it off. They walked for a few minutes in the morning sunshine, quietly, with Reed breaking the silence.

"What was with the white hand?"

Mossworth sat, fidgeting, in Postlewait's plaid side chair. He was much relieved that Postlewait had mentioned nothing of the incident at Brasenose, an event Mossworth thought certain to be widely discussed among faculty. Finishing with his latest paper, Postlewait looked up.

"Well, not quite what I expected."

Mossworth brightened.

"In fact," Postlewait continued, "It is exactly what I expected. You have again brought up your discovery at the Bodleian, more on Keble, more on the affair of Butterfield's assistant and the Bursar." Postlewait stood and walked to his window.

Mossworth stared at the floor. His right hand quivered slightly and his left eye twitched. "But, sir, that is, that is original research. No one knew that before me. No one. That is the best work I've done in years." Mossworth coughed and amended, "the best thing I've done, since, since, my old life, you know."

Postlewait gazed at Mossworth a long time saying nothing. He packed his pipe. "I wonder," he began, "if you could explain to me what you mean by 'best'?"

"Certainly," said Mossworth, sitting up straighter. "Best refers to the best that has been done, the best thought and done by men. Arnold, you know."

"Yes, I know. But you have not explained anything. You have provided a nothing argument, a tautology, circular. Can you do better?"

Mossworth shuffled in his seat. "Of course. Best is that which is most well done, most original, that which most clearly expresses those innermost desires and passions of the human condition."

"Ah," said Postlewait, " you mean, like pornography?"

"I, uh, no."

"Does it not express innermost desires and passions? And is it not of a technical level of photographic quality? Some of it, surely, is highly original?"

Mossworth sat for a moment with an open mouth. "But…yes, technical, but…it objectifies women!"

Postlewait sat down across from Mossworth and took a long drag on his pipe. He blew to smoke slowly. "Mossworth, is it wrong to objectify women?"

"Yes."

"Prove it."

Mossworth shook his head. "This is all very, very interesting, but it has nothing to do with art! What are we doing here? Are you not supposed to be teaching me art history? A subject that I know very well?"

"You know it well? No, Mossworth, you know a bunch of meaningless facts and trivial postmodern clichés. That is not art history." Postlewait scratched his chin and stared out the window. "Hm, well, I suppose, tragically, that is art history. Just not the art history that I do or that is worth doing."

Mossworth opened his mouth, then closed it. After a moment's awkward silence he blurted out: "But all that philosophy and religion we've been discussing, all term, all of that has nothing to do with that art? Art is about, aesthetics! We're talking aesthetics!"

Postlewait quickly crossed the room, dragging a chair right up next to Mossworth. He sat and leaned in closely, almost conspiratorially. "Exactly, and that's the problem. Don't you see? Turn it around: all that art has nothing to do with philosophy and religion? See? See?"

Mossworth gaped and shook his head. "This is, this is… astonishing! Art history, and art, is what it is. Who do you think, I mean, who are you to change art history?"

Postlewait stood, checked his watched, and moved to open the door for Mossworth. He shrugged his shoulders. "Mossworth, I am no one. I'm just a teacher trying not to waste my own nor anyone else's time. I believe that, today, we made some great progress."

Mossworth left, quickly, without any goodbyes, shuffling down the hallway, mumbling all the while about "progress."

DESTRUCTION OF EMPIRE

"Well, he has just come from Oxford, you know," said Mr.
Townsend: "and at the present moment Oxford is the most dangerous
place to which a young man can be sent."

Anthony Trollope, *Castle Richmond*

By the end of term Mossworth faced only two final
papers, one in English poetry and the other in Postlewait's
art history. For the poetry course the professor had
permitted the students an option: a written exam for two
hours or an interpretive dance based upon one of the
poems studied during term. Only Margaret, a young
woman in a wheelchair, had opted for the written exam
(and that was against the advisement of Professor LeBouf
who insisted Margaret "expand her boundaries").

Mossworth reclined on his bed, pondering his fate in
both English Poetry and art history, attempting to think
about the paper for the latter. Reed suddenly opened the
door, fresh from the bath. "Morning, Mossy."

"Hello, Reed. Sleep well?" Reed grunted and started
dressing. "Reed, have you any projects due next week?"

"No. Finished for maths and that sociology course.
You?"

"Quite. Poetry. And art history."

"Postlewait?"

"Yes, afraid so."

"Hm, Jolly bad luck that."

"Yes. That, that…"

"Snarky weasel?"

"Right."

"Mossy, I've been meaning to ask: what are you doing
for Christmas?"

Mossworth sat up in his bed and rubbed his neck. "Christmas, yes…That is coming up, isn't it?"

"Yes it is. Same time every year."

"Christmas…"

"I'm heading home."

Mossworth gave Reed his full attention. "Well, Reed…that's good. I hope your holidays are very nice."

"Right, okay. Mossy…," started Reed, "did you need somewhere to go for the hols?"

Smiling, Mossworth removed his glasses and cleaned them with his tee shirt. "Reed, you are kind, and your family, but I've work that needs doing and I've got to get to it. Plus, I'm sure to find some Christmas cheer here. Maybe even at church."

Reed shook his head. "Right, well, I'm off. Cheers, Mossy." Reed put on his jacket and hoisted his grip. Mossworth waved his hand. Reed nodded and quietly closed the door as he left.

An hour or so later Mossworth wandered down to the washroom. Only a few of the lads were about, none of who Mossworth knew well. Walking back to his rooms he noticed the quiet that had already descended upon the hall. Mossworth entered his room and looked about: the shelves sagging, the wardrobe bursting, the floor strewn with his shoes. He sniffed a few times and then reached for the door to his other micro room. Several books and some papers fell to the floor as the tiny space was revealed. Mossworth started to reach for them but decided to kick them out of the way instead. Then he sat, gazing out across the grey and severe buildings of Fochashite. He flipped open his laptop and put on some music. British Big Band tunes from The War. "There'll be blue birds over the white cliffs of Dover..." Then he turned the music off. "Damn quiet," he murmured, "who can stand it?"

He stared out the window at the flagging daylight, noticing no one on the tiny green space between the halls, then stood and reached for his cell and telephoned Richard Tolkein.

"Hello?"

"Richard, hello. This is Brian Mossworth, how are you?"

"Who?"

"Brian, Richard. Brian Mossworth. Mossy."

"Brian Richard Brian, eh? Well I can assure you, sir, I know no one by that name. And if you think I owe you money, I do not."

"Richard, please remember: Mossy. We meet at the Bird & Baby on Thursdays for drinks with Smith-Davies."

"Ah, yes, Smith-Davies." A long pause ensued.

"Yes," started Mossworth, "Smith-Davies…"

"Smith-Davies isn't here. Goodbye."

Mossworth briefly looked at his phone and then threw it across the room. He got dressed without shaving and went out.

His first destination was down St. Giles and towards the Oxford Market where he walked right up to the butcher.

"Morning Mr. Mossworth, sir," said Tom, the proprietor.

"Morning, Tom."

"Usual, sir?"

"The usual, please."

Mossworth took his treasured Tikka pie and turned up towards Cornmarket and strolled. A burst of greasy and spicy delight steamed up from the bag as he lifted the pie out and to his mouth. Mossworth dove in with a huge bite, crust crumbs scattering about his chin, his tweed long coat, and the sidewalk. But with this first bite did not come any ecstasy rather a queasy, fatty, unhealthy nausea. He threw the whole package into the nearest rubbish bin. As he was wiping of his chin and coat, a familiar voice spoke.

"Mossworth, how delightful." Theo stood near, hand extended, smiling.

"Oh, hello. How are you?" asked Mossworth.

"Fine, fine. I was rather hoping to run into you. I do not have your phone number, I'm afraid, so I could not contact you. One of my dear friends teaches at Fochashite but I've not see him and neglected, I am sorry to say, to call."

"Oh, well, that's fine…"

"If you do not have plans for Christmas, what about spending it with Amanda and I?"

"Yes, well, uh, that is…"

"Amanda is making a lovely goose. She's rather a whiz in the kitchen. Said that if I invited enough she would even put her hand to mincemeat tarts and a Yorkshire pudding." Theo laughed, "She assured me it would not break any laws to have a Yorkshire pudding with goose!"

Mossworth found himself smiling. "Well, I don't know what to say. This is very kind."

"A real traditional English Christmas! We'll have crackers and the girls will do a bit of a panto. Say yes!" said Theo.

Mossworth smiled more and shook his head.

"Great," cheered Theo, reaching and then shaking Mossworth's hand again. "Amanda will be so pleased. This means a full house, a full table, and we like to do that for the 'orphans' we come across. You know where we live so we'll see you elevenish on Christmas. Drinks will start then. Now, sorry to say, I've got to run. An elderly parishioner is having some difficulties in relating to her cat, apparently. Cheers Mossworth." And Theo was gone.

Standing for a few moments, grinding his shoe in the trash near the bin, Mossworth grunted and huffed, muttering "orphan" and "so glad I could round out your table." He hacked and then spit on the ground and then headed for the quiet halls of the Ashmolean.

Mossworth was relieved to find the museum nearly empty. Everyone here also seemed to be already departed for the holiday. Past the entrance stairway, Mossworth worked his way up, up, to the top floor, where he liked to start, and prepared himself for some serious contemplation of aesthetic splendor. As he came around to the first hall featuring Elizabethan ceramics and painting, he noticed a man sitting quietly. It was Postlewait. Instantly Mossworth changed direction but even as he did so he heard the voice of a small child say, much too loudly, "Daddy, who was that sad man?"

Mossworth ducked into an adjoining hall and put several suits of armor between he and Postlewait and the child. He managed to, very clearly, hear Postlewait's voice: "Darling, there is no one else here." And thus Mossworth realized the inevitability of his situation. Soon the pitter-patter of sneakered feet coming around the corner were followed by a freckled face of a five-year old girl with penetrating blue-grey eyes. She gestured, but did not point, at Mossworth.

"Here he is right here, Daddy."

Postlewait came round the corner and spotted Mossworth. "Indeed, pet, you have found a gentleman. This is Mr. Mossworth. Mr. Mossworth, please allow me to introduce my daughter, Verity." The young girl stepped up and offered her hand to Mossworth.

"It is a pleasure to meet you, Mr. Mossworth," said Verity.

Mossworth shook hands. "Oh, I, yes, charmed."

Verity turned to look at her father who gave her a meaningful nod. "Mr. Mossworth, I apologize for saying that you were sad. I...I ought not have said that...out loud."

"Oh, well, quite alright," said Mossworth. "In fact, I, you know, was a bit sad but came into the museum to get happy."

Verity looked at Mossworth, then her father, then back to Mossworth. "Daddy says that one ought not go to art for happiness but for wisdom." With that, Postlewait stepped closer and whisked Verity up in his arms.

"Thank you, Verity, but that will be quite enough."

"But Daddy, that is what you say," she huffed.

Postlewait put out his hand to Mossworth. "She is…interested. And interesting. We must be off now, Mossworth. I have promised her luncheon. A curry. She likes chapattis. Looking forward to your paper. Good luck." Mossworth stared and Verity stared back, looking over her father's shoulder. She blew him a kiss.

He turned back to the art, walking quickly in this gallery and then moving immediately on to the first room. But there he found little to interest him, stopping for a moment at an Elizabethan console, glancing at a few tapestries, lingering for a second in front of a sculpted stag. Mossworth then stepped quickly to the other side of the museum, looking for something. "Now, let's see, where was it? West wing?" he mumbled. "Ah, yes. No, wait, what was it?" Stepping in front of a window he happened to look down and catch Postlewait and his daughter exiting the museum. Postlewait, he noticed reached into a jacket pocket, pulled out a pipe, and without lighting it put it into his mouth and began to smoke. Mossworth heaved with fury: he kept his pipe lit just sitting in his pocket! He left the window and stomped off down one wing feeling Edwardian faces staring. He remembered he always wanted to actually just have time to take in the building itself so he sat, at last, in the entrance lobby, and looked up, however, he could not recall why he'd been interested in the architecture. Other avenues exhausted, he found his way down to the basement café, thinking about a hot bowl of tomato soup. But when he arrived he found the menu made no mention of soup and the café was yet to open for lunch.

Mossworth checked his watch, even though he'd just checked it a minute before. Back up the stairs, through the lobby, and then onto the streets of Oxford. Without much thought, he wandered down West from the Ashmolean, past the theatre, then back through the bus station and onto George Street. A chilly wind blew down the sidewalks so he headed into a coffee shop and ordered a latte he didn't want and a peach danish he didn't need. A sip told him the coffee was tepid and poorly made. He didn't even bite the danish. Back on the streets he wandered through the long alley behind St. Peter's, then out by New Road. A few tourists milled about, pointing and chittering excitedly, but the chill wind did not invite anything but moving quickly. Back up the High Street, Mossworth turned left onto Cornmarket and walked back down towards St. Giles. This time, however, he headed straight for the Bird & Baby.

No one was working whom he recognized, nor who recognized him; he had learned long ago to avoid the hours Paula worked. Inside was warm and the bitter was cool. In moments he had a pint and seated himself in the prime corner seat of the Inklings room. He reveled for a moment but then noticed the pub sat mostly empty and very quiet. Other than two workingmen having lunch and a youngish couple speaking intimately, no other customers could be seen. Before he could quite finish his pint or work up a really profound bad attitude, the door burst open and in walked Smith-Davies.

"Smith-Davies!" Mossworth shouted across the room.

Smith-Davies looked up and waved. After ordering his jar he came and sat with Mossworth.

"I say, Old Man, you are looking a bit grim. What's the word?"

Mossworth sighed. "Thanks, you are the second person today who has told me that."

"Who was the first?

"A five-year old girl."

"Ha," burst out Smith-Davies, "a child with insight!"

"Postlewait's daughter."

"Postlewait? Postlewait. Art history?" Smith-Davies looked askance. "I hate that arsehole."

Mossworth raised his glass. "Here, here." He drained half of it. "And I've a final tutorial with him Thursday. My last one. Well, until next term. Can't wait."

"And, Mossy, what about the Yuletide? Plans? Richard and Cordi were talking about renting a cottage for the holiday." Smith-Davies finished of his first pint and moved to the bar. He returned with two more pints. "A cottage by the water, rich friendship, lots of drink..."

Mossworth nursed his pint. "I, well, I tried calling Richard today and was quite shut out. Plus, do you not have some church responsibilities for Christmas?"

"Christmas? Good heavens, no. My parish, thanks to me, does not go in for that nonsense at all. And Richard, don't let him throw you. His is such a finely attuned mind that he often seems to us, mere mortals, as distracted. But, believe me, he means well. I'm sure he'd love you to be there. Cordelia just said the other day how much you mean to them." Smith-Davies reached over and patted Mossworth, high up on his leg, in a genial manner.

Mossworth considered the kindness of Richard and Cordelia, and the fact that they were related to Tolkien. He mused briefly over Smith-Davies "proclivities," as he thought of them, but so far it had not been an issue. Mostly running through his mind was getting away from the pressure of Theo's version of spirituality "and just being another number" for their Christmas table. Mossworth nodded, "It sounds lovely. Shall I call Richard?"

Smith-Davies shook his head. "Not at all. I'll let them know. I believe they are leaving early Christmas morning. They were to pick me up at my house. Why don't you just meet me there at eight?"

"Great plan. And thanks for the pint but now I'm off. Studying to do." Out on the streets, Mossworth noticed a severe drop in the temperature. He turned up his collar and shoved his hands in his pockets and, for a moment, found himself troubled by his decision to not attend

Theo's Christmas. But his mind leapt ahead, telling him he didn't know Theo that well, that Theo's spiritual ideas were inaccurate, that he pressured him too much, that he really didn't like Theo's wife, whom he'd only met in passing at services, and that the notion of spending the Christmas holidays with a bunch of religious people seemed to miss the point. Besides all of this, he knew his faith journey was progressing because, his mind informed him, here he was, living in Oxford and being a much nicer fellow than he had been. Walking more quickly against the cold, his step lightened as his subconscious painted even more alternative worlds. "Yes, yes," he spoke aloud, "this would be a meaningful Christmas, a truly meaningful holiday."

And thus Mossworth's first term at Fochashite and Oxford came to a close. He submitted his final papers for Poetry and Art History by the end of the week before Christmas and since marks were not out until the New Year he could safely put it all out of mind. That weekend before the holiday he found out about an opening in London, an artist he actually met once, a deeply moderate Christian man. Held in a long-closed but preserved Victorian underground gentlemen's toilet, the art installation featured various groups of carefully made ceramic cylinders about three inches tall. The artist briefly spoke about his faith, which meant he suggested that being raised in a minister's home had profoundly denigrated his ability to believe in God. When Mossworth tried to speak with the artist, the man could not remember ever having met neither Mossworth nor ever having been to Arkansas. Mossworth left the opening early and took the last train back to Oxford, disappointed in knowing that he could not get his £45 shave and skin treatment at Trumper's in Mayfair as the next day was Sunday.

He forgot about the opening soon enough, then forgot about London, bloody Geo Trumper, his ridiculous art history course, his pathetically overstuffed dorm room, the idiotic layout of Fochashite, his overspending, indulgent, directionless life, and his lust for Susan, and focused on Christmas. Unlike every other Christmas in his life, as an adult, Mossworth mused, this one would be different, better, more wonderful, emotional, exciting, and get in touch with that really, real Christmas realness. Thoughts of a wonderfully cozy Christmas cottage began to expand and got Mossworth through the missed Sunday service at St. George's, the lack of any other company in the dorm, and a rift in the time-space continuum that made Monday, Christmas Eve, at least twice as long as it ought to have been. Sugar plum visions actually danced around Mossworth's head as he went to sleep, with help from half a bottle of scotch.

Christmas morning Mossworth arose like a child, a child with a pounding hangover, to glimpse out the window. There had fallen a light dusting of snow and in the distance church bells pealed. No need to pack as packing was completed two days ago. One of his Swiss Army bags stood at the ready. No matter what Smith-Davies said, Mossworth knew to bring something. For Smith-Davies he'd found a lovely antique tie with the crest of a now defunct Cambridge historical society. Cordelia's gift, a delicate necklace of silver from one of the vendors in the weekly Saturday market, made in Turkey he'd been told. Selecting the right gift for Richard took some time but in the end Mossworth discovered an historical engraving technique practiced by some long suffering Pakistani immigrant and purchased from him a set of handsome personalized note cards. Finally, in addition to all of these Mossworth filled up with some chocolates, a few tins of caviar, coffee, scotch, and several bottles.

Attired in his bright red woolen waistcoat under his contrasting grey Harris Tweed sport coat, topped with the Fochashite school scarf, Mossworth exited the college, and soon rolled smoothly along down towards St. Giles. The sun popped up casting long shadows from the towers and deliriously cheerful oranges beams along eastern facades. Bells began to ring again from every direction. A few happy faces greeted Mossworth with cheery greetings of, "Merry Christmas!" Carefully avoiding St. George's by several blocks, Mossworth felt his anticipation growing with each step, particularly those steps away from St. George's. Even the frigid breeze did not chill Mossworth's thrill and within another ten minutes he stood outside of Smith-Davies' house ringing a much smaller bell.

But no one answered. Mossworth rang a second time, and a third, and then began knocking. A moment's panic quickly died as a window from the upstairs room opened and a disheveled Smith-Davies peeped out. "I say, what is the bloody racket? First the bells and then...oh, Mossworth? Is that you, old bean?"

"Merry Christmas, Smith-Davies!"

Smith-Davies waved his hand and nodded, "yes, yes, Merry whatever. And, ah, Mossworth, did you come all this way to merely wish me greetings?"

Mossworth smiled and laughed. "Naughty Nellie! Richard! Cordelia! Cottage! Let's go! And let me in the bloody house. I am freezing!"

Smith-Davies' head disappeared and the window closed and momentarily he appeared at the door, in his much-too-short mauve housecoat. He waved Mossworth in and then headed back to the kitchen. "My dear fellow," started Smith-Davies as he put on the kettle, "I had utterly forgotten about the plans. My deepest apologies. Here, let me get the tea going and I shall call Richard to confirm. I'm sure it's no trouble."

Mossworth blinked a bit and then sat at the kitchen table, a rickety affair loaded with books, magazine, clipped articles, several overflowing ashtrays and empty wine bottles. As Smith-Davies escaped to call, Mossworth busied himself looking for two clean tea mugs. He found none. From the other room Mossworth could hear Smith-Davies on the phone. Lots of mumbling and then the occasional shouting suddenly ended. Smith-Davies called in, "I'm just upstairs to the bath. Mind putting my cuppa outside the door?"

With a twinge of anxiety, Mossworth steeped the tea, washed out two mugs, and marched a hot cup upstairs. He discreetly passed the mug to Smith-Davies who was inside the bath, splashing about.

"So," said Mossworth, sitting in the hall outside the bath, "are the Tolkiens picking us up…er…soon?"

"Ah, yes, well that is some matter of delicate planning," came Smith-Davies' echoing voice. "I'm afraid Richard is having another episode and Cordelia is working him through it. It may take a few hours but I'm certain they will here before luncheon." After a long pause from the bath Smith-Davies added, "please, help yourself from the larder."

Just past two, Cordelia pulled up in their creaky Austin Princess and honked. Smith-Davies, who had been watching tele, leapt up and practically ran out to greet her. Mossworth wheeled his suitcase out to the sidewalk just in time to see Smith-Davies speaking to Cordelia through her window and to see Cordelia's face turn from scowling at Smith-Davies to smiling at Mossworth. Richard was in the front seat; one side of the rear seat was piled high with what appeared to be dirty laundry. Smith-Davies ran around to Mossworth, then noticed his suitcase. "Ah, yes, the luggage." He shouted to Cordelia, "Darling, the boot please." Cordelia shouted something back and Smith-Davies nodded. "Look, old bean, what about we just take what you'll need and leave the rest here?"

"But, ah, I thought, that is, aren't we to stay the night?"

"Yes, well, that is…"

"I'll just sit it on my lap."

Smith-Davies opened the passenger door and revealed Richard, enraged, and with no pants. "Who the hell are you?"

So it was Mossworth found himself crammed into the back of the Austin, crushed by his suitcase, which also soiled his trousers, and surrounded by a pile of musky laundry. For the next forty minutes Mossworth and Smith-Davies sat in silence as Richard talked.

"Damn those Labour MPs. Why ought we pay for all those Paki brats?"

"Damn the Yanks. Who are they, anyway?"

"Damn Thatcher and her privatization! What will the miners do?"

"Damn the university administration!"

"Damn!"

But soon relief showed itself via a dirt road leading into a very dark wood. Even Richard sat silent as massive oaks and elms went past. The road grew bumpy, and muddy, and then, just as Cordelia sucked in a huge breath, the trees thinned and a cottage came into view. It sat, a bit crookedly, next to a small, muddy pond. "Well," said Smith-Davies, "about time." After a few minutes persuading Richard to remove himself from the car, Smith-Davies and Mossworth extricated themselves from the back seat. Richard stood starring at the cottage.

"Cordi, darling," he shouted, "will we be having sex here?"

Cordelia ignored Richard and went right to the front door. Mossworth, dragging his suitcase across the soft turf, looked around as Smith-Davies followed Cordelia.

"Ah," said Mossworth, "Shall I get the luggage?"

Cordelia held up a plastic, clanking bag, opened the cottage door, and entered. Richard followed. Smith-Davies looked around and pointing to his head replied, "The only baggage I have is up here."

Mossworth entered last and came upon Cordelia and Smith-Davies speaking in hushed tones. They stopped as Mossworth approached. Cordelia stepped towards him. "Brian, love, I'm afraid the arrangements aren't quite what we were led to believe." She gestured towards a doorway, "here is where Richard and I will stay." Waving towards a door directly opposite she said, "and here is the room for you and Leslie." The room contained a single queen bed. Mossworth looked at Smith-Davies. Smith-Davies shrugged.

Settling in took only a few moments and then the foursome gathered in the tiny front room, a dull green affair decorated in the latest trends from the seventies. There was one puce armchair, two dark wood table chairs, and a small, short stool. Richard immediately took the armchair and went right to sleep, Cordelia and Smith-Davies sat in the table chairs, and Mossworth perched himself on the short stool. The silence rather hung about until Mossworth lurched himself to his feet. "Well, right, the day is nearly done but we can at least enjoy a bit of Christmas cheer." He scampered off to his room, gathered his things, and returned. "Here you are Cordelia, and one for you, Smith-Davies, and... Richard." For the last he merely placed the gift on Richard's lap. "Merry Christmas and God bless us one and all."

Smith-Davies tore into his immediately. "Thank you, Brian. It's just what I wanted." Then he set the tie on the floor next to his chair. Cordelia gave a rather thin smile and cooed slightly, holding up the necklace. "Thank you, thoughtful boy." She then wrapped it up again, neatly, and set it on the floor, too.

Mossworth looked about eagerly. Suddenly he stood again. "Well, what about some food. I'm famished."

Cordelia looked at Smith-Davies and then at Mossworth. "Oh, Brian dear, well, we typically don't prepare much for this day. I mean to say, darling, there is so much work involved and we do make an effort to avoid the sentimentality and consumerism."

Mossworth blinked a few times.

"However," continued Smith-Davies, "we do bring drink."

"Well, wait a minute," said Mossworth, "I brought a few things, a few food things, and we can eat those. Right?"

"Oh," started Cordelia, "yes, fine, lovely."

Mossworth fetched his things and returned with an armload of cheeses and crackers, the caviar, and wine. Smith-Davies produced a bottle of vodka. Cordelia returned from her room with a bottle of vodka. She looked up at Mossworth. "Brian, darling, you didn't happen to bring glasses, did you?"

That night, after they'd all retired to their beds, mostly to keep warm as the cottage had no source of heat, Mossworth began to reflect on the day. As the events went over in his mind he had a sudden flash of the dining room at Theo's house, spread out with a feast of riches: roast goose, Yorkshire pudding, mince pies, happy laughter and the squeals of children. The rumblings of Smith-Davies' stomach, and the particularly pungent vodka odor from his body, right next to his under the thin blanket, reminded Mossworth of his present condition. Conspiratorially, Mossworth whispered, "But SD, why don't they have food? I just don't get it."

"Because it isn't that sort of a party," hissed Smith-Davies, angrily.

"But this isn't a party," whispered Mossworth, "it is Christmas."

Before Smith-Davies could reply, a long, low moan came through the wall from the other room, then a thumping noise that repeated with great regularity. Various other shouts and cries, grunts and bumps followed. Mossworth pulled his knees up to assume the fetal position and moved his pillow to put it atop his shaking head. Before he could cover his ears, Smith-Davies patted him gently. "Look, Brian, so there's no hard feelings, so to speak. I know those desires are natural, normal. But my dear fellow, I just do not have them. I'm just not attracted to you."

Mossworth clenched his fists, then relaxed, curled himself even more tightly and fell into a deep and utterly silent fury.

The next morning, Mossworth did not stir as Smith-Davies got out of the bed and got dressed. He did not leave the bedroom when he heard the others in the main room not eating breakfast. He planned his trip to the bathroom when he heard the others go outside. He did not speak as they all climbed into the car. He said not a word during the trip back to Oxford. At Smith-Davies' house, he removed himself silently from the car but stood for a moment looking at Cordelia and Richard. Cordelia waved a hand and said, "I'm sure you boys had a wonderful time." Then the car pulled away.

Smith-Davies fumbled with his door keys. "Well, Mossy, another awful Christmas behind us. Wretched holiday. I hate Christmas." But when Smith-Davies turned, Mossworth was gone.

With a last gasp of effort, Mossworth got his suitcase up the third stairs in his rooms. He then dragged it, banging it frequently and purposefully into the wall. Opening the door, Mossworth took in the crowded sloppiness and then picked up the suitcase and hurled it at the desk. Books and papers, pencils, and pipes went scattering in every direction. Mossworth kicked at the things. Taking a deep breath, he prepared himself to let loose a profoundly lengthy series of curses, however, his lungs just emptied with a wheeze. He fell into his bed and began to shake, then quiver, and then cry, big fat tears.

The luxury of self-indulgent sorrow ended abruptly with the slamming of a door down the hall. As Mossworth had seen few students over the past week, his curiosity beat out his anger and frustration; he cracked open the room door just in time to be seen by the student, a student with a face swollen and even more red with crying. It was Susan and she noticed him and she stopped. A mild aroma of fruity chewing gum clung to her. She wiped a hand neatly across her cheeks and smiled. She kept smiling. Mossworth rubbed a hand across his eyes and smiled back.

Prior to this moment, as Mossworth's hair danced in the frigid blast of air coming over the windscreen of Susan's Aston Martin Vantage cabriolet (with buffalo hide seats), he never knew that his depths of despair could change so quickly, instantly, to ecstasy, to impulsive freedom. Susan's now-gone tears had been related to the ending of a failed relationship. Mossworth, being in the state he had been, commiserated easily and soon Susan confided much. Very quickly a friendly and exciting intimacy was achieved, one Mossworth found much desired and, apparently, so did Susan. Mossworth bemoaned the events of Christmas with the Tolkiens which, via Susan's golden laughter, transformed the tragedy to a shared amusement. Shortly after that Mossworth opened a bottle. Forthwith they both felt a bit better and then, blissfully, Susan suggested a drive, then a trip. She had Mossworth quickly pack a small bag and then they ran, holding hands, roaring with laughter, out of the dorm and down, around to the back of Fochashite. Still laughing, Susan lowered the roof, turned up the heat and gunned the Aston Martin for all it was worth.

They stopped for dinner at a converted eighteenth-century tollhouse, the sun casting its last rays right in front of them. When the proprietors lit the candles, and dancing light tickled their eyes, Mossworth assumed things could not be better.

"So, Brian, you've not asked me what I plan to do with you."

"Alas," he replied, "I do not care as long as you have rescued me from Oxford."

"I thought you loved Oxford."

"I do, but, ah, that is, some things about it."

"Well, anyhow, you know what today is?"

"The day after hell?"

After a bit of laughter, and more drinking, Susan continued. "Today is Boxing Day, of course, the day the servants open their prezzies."

"Yes, yes, I knew that!" giggled Mossworth.

"Well, I don't have a box for you, and you are certainly not my servant, but there is something I can offer you."

"You have my attention."

"I'm taking you home."

Mossworth swallowed hard and took another sip. Susan's glorious eyes teased at him.

"Ha, naughty boy! I mean to say, darling, I'm taking you to my home, my family's home, Watlington Hall, the estate."

Mossworth opened his mouth, then closed it, then smiled. He smiled all the way.

Watlington Hall turned out to be, of course, all that Mossworth had dreamed. A pair of monumental gates rose up to meet the Aston Martin. Waving to the empty gatehouse, Susan ran the car quickly across the grounds. Down past what Mossworth was certain had been a landscaped pond, alongside horse pens, over a Roman bridge, came the vista. Sitting on a hillside, three windows aglow, stood the house. Although difficult to take it all in at night, Mosswoth caught glimpses of a stately ashlar pile, classical symmetry, extended wings, and a curving white-stone drive in front. Susan drove up the drive but then continued around the side towards the back of the house, under a more recent porte-cochere, and parked.

"Brian, let me show you to the guest house. It's late now but I promise to take you round the entire house in the morning." Susan led Mossworth towards an arched doorway at the other end of the porte cochere. She opened the door and turned on the lights to reveal a cozy, beamed, low-ceilinged sitting room with a very large stone fireplace. Mossworth gasped at the medieval double-post chairs, a lavish Flemish tapestry of St. George, and a small portrait certainly by Reynolds. Flanking the dark-green marble fireplace stood two oaken bookcases, floor to ceiling, filled with leather folios and bound volumes of prints. Across the flagstones lay a thick Turkish carpet with deep reds and heady blues.

Before Mossworth could take in more, Susan cleared her throat. "I'm sorry, Brian, it's not much." She moved to the prepared fireplace and, striking a handy match, lit the already prepared kindling. "I'd rather you were in the main house but many of the rooms are closed up and the heat is not on. And mother and father are not here." For a moment Susan paused. "They prefer to holiday in Nice."

"Oh, Susan, this is just fine, just fine."

Susan smiled. "Here," she said, moving towards the inner door, "In here is the bedroom and the bath beyond that." Susan looked at Mossworth. "I hope it suits." Mossworth merely smiled.

Susan stepped on her tiptoes and kissed him on the cheek. "Goodnight, Mossy, and thanks for being a friend." She left Mossworth and, after a deep breath, he ran into the bedroom and threw himself upon the bed. The oval baroque ceiling above him filled his eyes with an illusory fresco that Mossworth assumed to be an allegory of an ancient ancestor. A minute later he was in the bathroom, eyes even wider at the fully sunken tiled tub, which sat in front of yet another marble fireplace.

Wisely, given his sleep-deprivation and slight drunkenness, he forwent drawing a bath and opted for his pjs and reveling in the luxury of the spacious, queen-sized, elaborately carved, wooden bed.

"A bed, a real bed."

For a moment, after he turned off the lights to find silvery moonlight spilling into the room through leaded window glass, he feared his excitement would prevent him from falling asleep. And then, just as his conscious self dissolved into blissful respite, he recalled the last time he had enjoyed a comfortable sleep was in his Arkansas bed.

Mossworth, dreaming, walked quickly through an endless hallway, some goal driving his mind ahead. Regularly spaced windows, so tall he could not see the tops, allowed brilliant sunlight to spill onto the floor. These bright-lighted beams, shimmering orange, contrasted with the very dark shadows in between. Each of Mossworth's steps brought him either into illumination, brilliance and warmth or darkness and cold. Voices, Susan's, Postlewait's, Theo's, all spoke, words of direction and attraction. Mossworth could not tell from which direction they came but all urged him towards some end. As he walked past one window he noticed a painted landscape by Poussin. The next looked Raphaelesque. But the light from the next window tickled his eyes and he awoke to a sunny day.

"Oh," he stretched and twisted across the entire bed, "oh, that was good, a good sleep. I've not slept that well since…" He sat up in bed and glanced out the window to see a massive lawn shimmering under a bright sun. He looked at his watch and gasped to find it was half past one. He washed and dressed quickly and then opened the door. Sitting neatly in a chez lounge, bundled up with a thick pink duvet, sat Susan reading a magazine.

"My, my, aren't we the lazy one?"

"Sorry, sorry," he replied, "I had no idea of the time."

"Of course you did not. You were asleep." Susan smiled. Mossworth shrugged. "No worries. Come along you Oxford student and let's get you some breakfast." She stood and looked over her shoulder at Mossworth. "Or lunch."

Susan led Mossworth through a series of room, some small, most empty, windows covered up, the few furnishings draped with sheets. At one point she turned and winked at him, throwing up a pair of massive moulded doors to reveal a pristine example of an eighteenth-century great hall replete with arched windows, a central fireplace, French wallpapers, gilding, and that sort of quiet stillness that comes with good masonry, age, and square feet. Very slowly Susan walked, leading Mossworth, then suddenly she started to run down the hall. Mossworth laughed.

"I did that all the time when I was young. Or, at least, I did when mother and father were not around, which was often."

A few more rooms and they entered a large dining area and then the kitchens. "There is no milk but I found some juice and tea and some not-too-stale Hobnobs. Will that do?"

"Wonderfully, especially the tea," said Mossworth.

The kettle boiled, the tea steeped, stale Hobnobs disappeared. Neither said much. Susan smiled. Mossworth smiled.

"Brian, thanks for coming."

"Thank you. I've not slept that well since, since…for a long time."

"Good."

"And I'm very pleased to have seen the house. Amazing." He looked over at her. "Oh, and of course, it has been lovely getting to know you better."

Susan looked away for a moment. "Thanks, Brian. I, you know, just hate…staying in this house alone."

"Of course, of course." More silence. "Susan, is there no, ah, staff?"

"No, not during the holidays. We used to give the servants Boxing Day. Now we are the ones to have the day off. From food. And the next day."

Mossworth stuffed another Hobnob into his gob. "It is a nice day, isn't it?"

Susan nodded and looked out the window. "A lovely day."

"Did you ever see that episode of Faulty Towers where Basil had the work done to his house, but tried to do it on the cheap?"

"Faulty Towers? Ha! No. I wasn't born! But was that a good one?"

"It was brilliant. You see, Basil never wanted to spend money on anything..." and Mossworth continued, for several hours, to revel Susan with retold, and sometimes reenacted, episodes of the Beeb's greatest sitcoms of the seventies and eighties.

Susan stood and stretched. "Brian, you are funny. I wish we had more time."

"Must we go somewhere?"

"I've got to get back to campus. I'm working on a project for Dr. Swindon. Did I not tell you?"

"No."

"It has to do with indigenous groups in West Africa during the early Victorian era. There are documents in both the Bodleian and..."

"Yes?"

"I'm boring you, aren't I?"

"Not at all."

"Well, anyway, I've got loads to get done and I need to do so before term starts."

"Of course, of course," said Mossworth, standing. "Do we need to leave just now?"

Susan stood and started to lead Mossworth back the way they'd come. When they reached the great hall she stopped and took his hand. "Brian, I am very grateful to you, I hope you know that."

Mossworth felt a tremble go through him but wasn't sure if it were from her or him. "It has been, beyond doubt, my pleasure."

"After Christmas..."

"I know. I know."

"Having you here, listening to your stories, well, it has meant the world to me."

Mossworth smiled.

"I could talk to you about anything."

Mossworth started to lift her hand up, just slightly, perhaps, maybe, possibly thinking something that could not remotely…

"May I…may I ask you something?"

The hand lifting stopped. "Yes."

Susan hesitated for just a moment. "What did you do before coming to Oxford?"

The smile melted from Mossworth's face. He turned to look for a moment out one of the windows and in so doing released Susan's hand.

"I'm so sorry, Brian. I ought not to have asked."

He turned back with a smile. "No, not at all. But, I, well, I think, you know, that I am not ready to talk about it yet. It was…a lifetime ago."

Susan nodded. "I understand." She started to walk again leading Mossworth down the hallway. "I must say, however, that it only shrouds you further in mystery."

"Mystery about what?"

"Mystery about what sort of jobs you've done."

"Do you have any guesses?"

Susan smiled, brightly, glowingly. "Pirate."

They laughed all the way back to Oxford.

The glow for Mossworth lasted exactly until he opened his dorm room.

Strewn about sat the results of his last emotional outburst from the previous day. He spent three hours sweeping, picking up and putting away and returning it to its normal overstuffed and crowded state. "Great, lovely, wonderful. Lovely room." Moving to the panel he slid it open and took a look out the window in his other mircro-room. "Splendid." He closed the panel and carefully selected a book from his shelf: *Meditations* by Marcus Aurelius. In less than a minute he had his shoes on and headed down the stairs for The Raven's Head.

A growing restlessness followed Mossworth for the next few days. He put it down to his "relationship with Susan" at first, and the fact he had not see her since the trip to Watlington. Later he assumed the problem to be stress related, having to do with his extraordinary exertion in his classes the previous term. He finally settled on Postlewait as the source of his stress. This directed his passions and fueled his anger, for a while.

In an effort to distract, he decided he ought to go to return church. Just after he had dressed for vespers he remembered how he skipped out on Theo and his family at Christmas. Mossworth sighed and slumped back into his room. "Right," he grunted to the room, "I'll just, that is...hm." He sat on his bed. With a sudden movement, Mossworth went to his knees next to his bed. He cleared his throat and folded his hands. "Lord, Our Most Heavenly Father of Glorious Realms...We beseech thee for thine most beneficent attentions and wonderous blessings." Mossworth shuffled a bit. "Lord, I am in need of help. You are a good and great God and I am an unworthy supplicant...and I...You can guide me in, in how to, that is, in how to deal with such unfair people. Give me wisdom to understand why other people are so selfish and self-absorbed. It seems, to my pale, human mind, that I am to be punished. So, teach me to be patient. I want to be better, to be good. I promise to follow your teachings, to be a better person, to try to be more sincere... and I hope that..." But at this point the door burst open and Reed walked in.

Quick as a wink Mossworth was off his knees and rummaging under the bed. "Oh, hello Reed. You've not seen my, er, brown bluchers, have you?"

"Hi, Mossy. No. And I'm not sure what a blucher is. Nice hols?"

Mossworth paused for a moment. "I... Hm, good question. Why don't you tell me about yours first? Then I'll tell you mine over a pint."

"Why don't I tell you mine over a pint?" asked Reed with a wink.

Reed, to Mossworth's mind, opened up a bit and shared some details of his family and their warm and festive Christmas experience. For his own part, Mossworth told Reed of the miserable Christmas experience but said not a word about Susan. Reed drained his jar. "Nothing but booze? Sure it sounds good, but I mean, really."

"Nothing," said Mossworth, "and no gifts. What is Christmas without gifts?"

"Sound like some real types, bloody bastards."

Mossworth paused at that comment and pursed his lips. "Another pint? I'm buying."

Reed nodded. "Mossworth, sorry that you didn't come to my Christmas. Well, there's always next year."

Mossworth smiled and went up to the bar to order another round. "Next year..." he thought. He stood at the bar for a moment, a pint glass in each hand. Reflecting back at him, in the mirror behind the barman, shimmered his own face. "Next year," he mumbled and welling up before his mind grew the thought of another year on the wretched dorm bed, another year of cramped quarters, another year of horrible dining hall food, shared bathrooms, and another year of...

"Mossy, where's the pint, mate?" shouted Reed.

Slurping and slopping his own glass, Mossworth worked his way back to Reed.

"Cheers, mate."

"Cheers."

And Mossworth started warming again to Oxford. He warmed more as this, his second pint, neared the bottom. By his third life looked up; by the fourth he and Reed decided it would be possible to head on the midnight train to London, than catch a cab, and still get served dinner at Green's. For good measure both slammed down their fifth jars and headed to the train station. The evening went well, the train riding part, but that was due mostly to Mossworth's falling asleep. They arrived into Paddington just past one, stumbled to a kiosk that seemed to offer taxi services but in fact only sold umbrellas and pashminas. Reed said he learned from a janitor that a taxi stand operated just outside the station. Fearlessly, the two of them found the stand and, boldly, asked for a taxi. A few minutes later their taxi pulled up in front of Green's. Mossworth's head no longer spun about so Reed suggested before going to order steaks they needed another pint and pointed to the nearby, King's Groin. Mossworth agreed and suggested whiskies instead of beer. Each tried three different blends, commenting intelligently after each shot. Around two o'clock Reed led Mossworth to Green's and found it soundly closed. In a fit of desperation and being attracted to bright lights, soon they found themselves entering the gleaming Kaghan Valley. A smiling Pakistani man led them to a quiet table and suggested items they might like. Feeling a bit of an evening chill coming on, Mossworth asked, "do you have anything hot?" The proprietor assured him they did offer substantially hot food so Mossworth ordered all that the man had suggested and said, "I want it hot." Then he fell promptly asleep.

A prodding from Reed re-animated Mossworth and his eyes opened to a table filled with colorful dishes. Steaming, exotic aromas crept into Mossworth's sinus, lingered, and rather singed. Mossworth looked blearily at Reed who was smiling and holding a huge portion of naan bread. "The ragan josh is bloody fantastic. I love Pakistan, Mossy."

And the eating then began in earnest. Mossworth tried dish after dish, each seemingly richer, more satisfying, and spicier, than the last. Mossworth held strips of bread in each hand; lines of orange, red, and yellow sauces dribbled down his chin and across his shirt. Vaguely he grew aware of a stinging sensation in his esophagus and its environs but found if he continued eating the burning grew less. Some sort of sweet drink also found its way down Reed and Mossworth's gullets; it kept the burning at bay.

Reed looked over at Mossworth, a long brown smear of curried sauce across his cheek and naan in each hand. "Oh, Mossy. I'm…this…curry…"

Mossworth nodded, then fell asleep with an onion bhaji halfway to his mouth. When his head started to flop over he awoke suddenly. "Yeah, curry." Down his shirt dripped fresh stains. Briefly, and sloppily, he attempted to rub them off with the back of his shaking hand but only managed to drip more from the end of his bhaji onto his profusely stained trousers. "Heh, you, you know, uh…Reed…"

"Ah, yeah…what? What? Mmm, that is good. What?"

Mossworth's red eyes looked at Reed. "What?"

"No, you. You what?"

"Me? Me what?

"You. More vindaloo? Loo, loo, loo."

"Reed, you are great, really great."

"Loo."

"Really great."

"Loo. Lulu."

"You know…I'm in love with Susan."

"Loo…loonie." Reed stuffed another curry soaked naan into his mouth.

Mossworth sniffed and drank some more water, or that sweet liquor. "Whew, hot. Susan. Am I bad?"

Reed shook his head. "You're great, lad, great lad. Susan..."

"Susan."

"She's…she's a whore."

"Yes. What?"

"Whore. Susan. That girl you love. Whore."

"No. No." Mossworth lifted a piece of beef to his mouth with his fingers. "You don't say that. She's an angel."

"Mm, what? Angel what?"

"Angel?"

"No."

There was a long pause as Mossworth rubbed his chest, burped a bit, wiped his mouth and looked around. He tried to focus on Reed. "Stop jumping."

"Not."

"I'm…I'm done. Are you done?"

"Uh…bloody hell, yes."

There then developed nary an issue with their bill nor the paying of it. Mossworth handed over his credit card and told the proprietor, a lovely chap named Mr. Singh, to just add his own tip. Mr. Singh was happy, Mossworth was happy, Reed was happy, everyone happy. Lots of smiles. Then Reed and Mossworth entered onto the street and Mr. Singh and his cohorts immediately closed the restaurant and turned off the lights.

Mossworth stood, shakily, looking at a bright street light on the next block. Reed scratched himself.

"Mossy?"

"Yeah?"

"Mossy?"

"Hm?"

"What. Uh, what do we do?"

"Taxi? Taxi!" But instead Mossworth walked towards the light. Reed followed. The light emanated from an all night disco. They kept walking. Neither reflected upon direction nor method. Avoiding the darker streets, following the lights, they wandered, their heads clearing a bit, towards shadows they took to be something other than they were. Exhaustion overtook them as they neared a set of large steps.

"Stop!" shouted Mossworth. "I just…fell asleep. Stop."

Reed just sat on the second set of steps and then lay down. Mossworth lay on the step just below and fell into blissful repose.

Bliss was short-lived as a constable discovered them, on the steps of St. Paul's Cathedral, around dawn. Some prodding awoke Mossworth to the rising of the sun on a clear morning over London, over St. Paul's. Then he experienced a unique sensation in his stomach. Reed sat up as the constable poked at him with his nightstick. Mossworth, feeling worse by the second, looked at the cop, then around. "Sir, a toilet? I think…" and then it didn't matter.

A few minutes later the cop called a cab and they were on their way to Victoria utterly forgetting that trains to Oxford did not leave from there. A hot cup of tea was all either could manage as they awaited a train. Neither spoke. Soon their train departed and immediately the two fell asleep. An hour later Mossworth awoke and ran towards the loo only to find it in horrible condition and, then, to find himself in worse condition with fascinating and deeply troubling burning sensations. When he could, he stumbled back to his seat next to the sleeping Reed. They missed their transfer stop, had to buy a ticket from the conductor, at higher prices, and then fell asleep again and awoke in Manchester. There a kindly, but firm, conductor shook them awake and promptly showed them the exit.

Head spinning, Mossworth stumbled out of the station followed by a glassy-eyed Reed. "Mossy, Mossy, wait lad, wait. We need to get return tickets."

In spite of the tremendous effort it took, Mossworth stopped walking and turned to look at Reed. "No," he gasped, "hotel." Within view stood the stately, Manchester Arms, a solid, Victorian pile. Mossworth raised a tremulous arm and pointed. Together they crossed the street and entered the lobby, or tried to. A huge fellow in a long coat immediately stopped them.

"Sirs, may I enquire as to your business at the Manchester Arms?"

Mossworth blinked several times, then stood up a bit straighter, pushed his matted and dirty hair back with a curry-stained hand. "We are seeking…we are…we are seeking accommodation."

The large man looked at Mossworth and then at Reed, then shook his head. He leaned in a bit closer. "Sir, what you do is your own business but, ahem, we are not that kind of a hotel." The man nodded towards Reed.

Mossworth raised his hand and sucked in breath preparing to speak.

"And, sir, not meaning to be rude, but, you stink."

Mossworth's mouth moved around, soundlessly. Reed stood by shakily. "C'mon Mossy...ruddy hotel. Bastards... I don't have any money."

Mossworth wiped his lips smearing aged stains of brown and red onto his sleeve. The, slowly, he turned about away from the hotel and fell to his knees, heaving into the gutter. Reed helped him up and back to the train station.

The ticket agent looked at them both. "No, I'm not selling you a damn thing until you clean up. Toilets are down the way. On your bike." He waved them off.

An hour later, head slightly cleared, face slightly washed, sitting on a dank, moldy train station toilet, feeling his innards burning as they rushed out of him, Mossworth first began to consider his situation. His mind wandered over several possibilities as to who might be to blame for his present condition. The name that popped up first sounded like "Postlewait" and yet almost immediately the thought occurred that, right at that moment, he was having a genuinely authentic experience. As vague as the workings of his mind were at the moment, it did occur to him that no matter how authentic this experience had become it still was qualitatively hell. Grimly he smiled as he realized he'd connected hell and authenticity, something he assumed Postlewait would consider an accomplishment.

From the neighboring toilet came varieties of unpleasantness. "Oh...oh god...oh my god..."

"Reed, are you, are you going to be okay?"

"Uhhhhh. I hate Indian. Never, never again."

"Never again, Reed, never again."

After stopping at the newsagent for antacid tablets they shuffled quickly to get the next train, gave the new conductor ten Pounds to awaken them at Oxford, ate six antacid tabs each, and then slept, arriving into Oxford at ten and Fochashite at ten-twenty.

The next morning Mossworth awoke to a tremendous stench in the room and realized with a start that it came from him. Reed slept like the dead. Mossworth caught sight of himself, still in his clothing from two nights earlier, and silently whistled. Quietly, he gathered clean clothes and toiletries and opened the door right into Susan.

She looked him up and down gasping between gum chewing. "What the hell happened to you?"

Mossworth looked this way and that. His cheeks flushed. "Oh, oh, this was, you know. Reed and I…there was this train… it was London."

"Brian, you look a mess, a really awful mess. Whew, and you smell a mess."

"Sorry, sorry…Manchester train…"

"Right," said Susan, nodding her head, "right." Susan looked away, eyes reddening.

"Susan, what's wrong, what's the, ah, matter?"

Shuffling her feet, Susan looked down the hallway. Then she looked up at Mossworth. "Brian," she said quietly, "I saw Michael today in the Raven. I…he…" she sniffed. "Brian," this time whispering, "I'm just feeling…a bit lonely, you know."

Mossworth nodded, then he stumbled just a bit.

"Brian, I'm sorry, go get cleaned up. We can talk later." She gave him a wee pat and moved on past him down the hall.

Thinking over this encounter, Mossworth decided it could only be a good sign. He heaved himself down the hall towards the baths and got to work. Returning to his rooms an hour later he found Reed sitting up in bed, bleary eyed, shaking, smelly. Reed looked up. "What are you so happy about?

"Nothing like a freshly brushed mouth and clean knickers after a shower to make one feel all is right with the world," said Mossworth brightly.

"Hey, ah, what day is it?" asked Reed.

"Oh," said Mossworth, "it is…um…Tuesday…?"

Reed turned on his laptop. While he was waiting for it to warm up he reached around and flipped open the tiny vent window.

"Thanks," said Mossworth.

"Don't mention it," said Reed. "Okay, Wednesday. Tuesday must have been Manchester day." Reed looked up at Mossworth.

"Manchester?"

"Yep. Manchester Arms."

"Manchester Arms. Wait a minute, Wednesday?"

"Yes."

"I have tutorials starting tomorrow. Don't you?"

Mossworth scrambled for a paper schedule under a pile of files and neckties. "Here, yes, yes. Oh.

"Tomorrow?"

"Yes."

"Postlewait?"

"Of course."

Reed gingerly got out of bed, looked in the mirror and shook his head.

"I'll wait for you in the dining hall."

Over tea and buns little was said. Reed stared off towards the windows. A light, grey, chilly rain fell. Mossworth chewed slowly.

"Ever been drunk like that before?"

"No. Never."

"Why did we do that?"

Mossworth sipped his tea. "Maybe, maybe thought it would make me feel younger."

"Hm. Made me feel older…but not smarter."

"It was fun, wasn't it?"

"No."

"Yes, no."

Reed was quiet for several minutes as he gnawed on his bun. "I think what we sought, and found, was an aesthetic experience divorced from an ontological aim."

Mossworth nodded slightly and then frowned.

"What?"

"Sounds like something Postlewait would say."

"Really? It's from my philosophy course. My tutor's take on Plato. I don't think I understood it until last night."

"Monday night."

"Yeah, Monday night."

"But," pondered Mossworth, "ought an aesthetic experience have an ontology?"

Reed nodded, "no, it doesn't have to, but then how do you know the good from the bad?"

Mossworth considered for a moment. "I guess the experience would have to be authentic…oh."

"Authentic? To what?"

"Yeah, never mind. Tutorials tomorrow? I'm going shopping." Mossworth stood, waved to Reed, and left.

Reed stared after him. "Authentic what?"

Mossworth set a brisk pace down towards Cornmarket Street. He told himself he had much to accomplish today. It began with a stop in the Next store to see what was on sale. He found an entire wool suit for under a hundred pounds and some socks and underwear that were colorful. Afterwards he practically leapt just up the block to Marks & Spencer's. By then had tuckered himself out and needed to stop in for a pastry and coffee at Nu Coffee. He found the coffee weak and unstimulating. Mildly satiated he moved quickly down to the High Street and in rapid succession bought two new sweaters, various attractive pens and pencils, a special red Moleskine calendar, a delightful etching of Oxford dated 1845 and guaranteed to be authentic, and a brand new pipe, an extraordinary Blakemar with near perfect grain, from Trantor's on the High. The pipe cost more than Mossworth liked to spend on pipes but the proprietor, who called him, "Mr. Mossworth sir," effused so kindly and threw in a tobacco pouch, and several tins of tobacco, that he could hardly refuse.

Heavy laden, Mossworth trudged back up George Street to Street Giles. Store fronts that normally beckoned he ignored. His feet ached, his back hurt, and his arms were beginning to weary from the weight of his bags. "Hm," thought Mossworth with each step, "serious shopping, yes, Oxford...good...Oxford...whew, tired. Susan...what...what does she want? Oxford. Good..." And these profound thoughts kept with him all the way back to Fochashite and his rooms. A bit of evening sunshine managed, somehow, to greet Mossworth as he opened the door to his rooms, splaying out across the desk, his bed, and the wardrobe. "Nice," he said aloud, "Oxford." He sat on his bed and lingered in the rays of light for the few minutes they lasted. "Right," he grunted, as he stood, and then got to work putting away all his new things. Only there did not exist space in the wardrobe, or under the bed, or in his second room, or on the floor to fit any additional required items. With tremendous aplomb, Mossworth balanced several pairs of woolen trousers on top of his suitcases, which were in turn sitting atop the sagging wardrobe. Low creaks emanated from the finely wrought compressed wood furnishing. He placed two of his plastic shopping bags from today on the foot of his bed. When all settled he realized there ought to be two more elements: "Tea and music," he said aloud as he carefully worked his way across the packed room to his desk and started the water boiling. Instead of music, however, he soon was shuffling through his DVD collection and settled upon one of his favorite BBC series:

The Souls of All Souls, a period drama from the post-war years set in Oxford concerning the lives and loves of ambitious young Oxonians. Soon his massive Oxford University mug steamed with really hot tea. He wormed his way to his bed, grabbed a handful of biscuits enroute, pulled up a thick duvet, and cozied himself in front of his laptop.

Hours later, utterly snug, Mossworth drifted into a fitful sleep where he perceived himself dressed entirely in tweed, including oddly comfortable tweed shoes, walked slowly upon a tweed sidewalk in a tweed version Oxford. A tweedy sort of sun shined rays of light upon the city. Mossworth smiled and yet a great unhappiness settled upon him. His tweed felt heavy, weighing him down. Looking up towards the tweedy top of the tweedy High Street he noticed a person, dressed entirely in tweed: Susan. Her blond hair waved about her head in slow motion, her sparkling teeth glistened in the tweedy light. She held out her arms towards the direction in which Mossworth stood but her eyes did not alight upon him. He started to move towards her but between he and she stood his teachers, all his teachers he had ever sat under. He recognized a few, Mrs. Ferguson, his first grade teacher, another middle school English teacher, Mr. Harvey, and two of his first year college teachers. But in front, and closest to him, stood Art Postlewait and Theo. With a strange foreboding and wonder he looked at the two. Besides their clear identity he noticed their tweed was different, somehow an older weave, an ancient pattern. Mossworth grew desirous of that weave. As he watched it grew in his mind that Postlewait and Theo were waving at him, calling, or was it singing? Before his mind could sort this out the quiet entrance of Reed into the room gently awakened him.

Feeling self-conscious about his purchases, and persnickety about the way he had laid out all of his things, he feigned sleep. Gnawing away at the back of his mind, quite from nowhere, were doubts about Reed's friendship. "He never really liked me," drifted up and started to foment. Mossworth listened but only heard Reed undressing. Then he felt Reed very gingerly lift his laptop off of Mossworth's lap and pull the blanket up under his chin. As Mossworth was processing this event he heard Reed take a step, about all one could manage in the now full room, and knock over several of his books and DVDs.

"Bloody hell," he hissed.

"I knew it," thought Mossworth, and lumped himself into sleep.

CONSUMMATION OF EMPIRE

I wonder anybody does anything at Oxford but dream and remember, the place is so beautiful. One almost expects the people to sing instead of speaking. It is all…like an opera.

W. B. Yeats

Mossworth awoke, stretched, knocked a few pairs of shoes off of his bed onto other shoes on the floor, and breathed deeply. First day of term. He was ready. Gathering up his toiletries, the ones he really needed, took a few minutes of rummaging through various boxes. Down the hall in the bathroom he shaved, scrubbed, brushed, combed, buttoned, buckled, tied and straightened to good effect. If one thing were going to happen today it would be his making a good impression upon Postlewait. This term, well, this one began better and would not be like last. He found himself, in the shower room, moderately happy.

He returned to his room to see Reed sitting at the desk holding his phallic Tolkein pen.

"Hello, Mossy."

The smile slid off Mossworth's face. "Ah," he said, "my Tolkien pen."

"What is a Tolkien pen?" asked Reed. "It looks more like a penis pen."

Mossworth stepped towards Reed, knocked over a pile of trousers and books, and put his hand out impatiently. "It is a pen that once belonged to Tolkien." He took the pen and gently placed it back in its wooden box.

"Tolkien? J.R.R. Tolkien? The author?"

"Yes, of course, why else would it matter?"

"That's amazing," said Reed, "how did you come by it?"

"It was given to me as a gift by his niece, or niece-in-law, Cordelia," replied Mossworth. "I, ah, am personal friends with them."

"Them? The Tolkiens?"

"Yes, that is, friends, yes. I have spent some time at their house. I spent Christmas with them... at a country cottage."

Reed shook his head. "Those were the Tolkiens? Well, you never fail to impress."

Mossworth sat on the edge of his bed, looking at shoes, deciding which pair to wear. He nodded, "Tolkien was Master of Magdalen, you know, thirty years."

"The author?"

"No, no, his...uh...nephew. Yes, his nephew."

"For thirty years? Would that not make him quite elderly?

"Yes, Richard is, ah, perhaps seventy-five years old."

Reed dressed and remained silent for a few minutes. "Mossy," he began, "I...that is..." He looked at Mossworth. "Never mind, it's not important."

"Please, Reed. What is it?"

"I'm sure you know more about this than I but, well, Tolkien's siblings have children, of that age?"

"Yes?"

"Really, or would they not be a bit older than that?"

"Yes, yes...maybe, I'm not sure, actually."

"And would he, a devout Catholic, have a pen like that?"

"Well... that is... but then, who did I have dinner with, Christmas?"

Reed shrugged.

Mossworth scrambled to the desk and started rummaging about. "Wait, I've a card, his business card. Here...here!" He lifted the card up triumphantly. "Here, see, right here. 'Richard Tolkein, Ret.' See?" The card was passed.

Reed looked at it. His eyes lifted to Mossworth's slowly.

"What?" Mossworth demanded.

"That's not how Tolkien spells his name. His is T-O-L-K-I-E-N."

Mossworth just starred.

"Sorry, Mossy, sorry. I think maybe it would have been better if I'd said nothing."

Mossworth sat on the bed with a frown. Then he looked up at Reed, smiling. "No, no, not at all. I was, ah, fairly sure, you know, that they were not, that is, you know…"

"Sure, mate, sure. Listen, I've got to run. My nine o'clock with Stuart."

Reed left.

Mossworth snapped the pen in half, threw it on the floor and stomped on it several times. Then he stomped on it again. "Stupid Reed."

On his way out of the building, Mossworth found himself face-to-face with the porter, Jimmy. "Hello, Mr. Mossworth. Hope your new term is off to a good start."

"No."

"Yessir, splendid. Well, I just was coming up to find you and ask you to sort out your post"

"Post?"

"Yessir, your post has not been picked up, ah, well that is, ever."

"Well, er…where…?"

"Right this way, Mr. Mossworth." Jimmy led him back to the office area, down another hall, out through a tiny outdoor courtyard filled with dead plants, and then to a larger room with rows of tiny aluminum postboxes. Mossworth gazed in wonder. Jimmy went past them and back to a door with a window. He knocked and a spectacled head popped up.

"Peter."

"Jimmy."

"This is Mr. Mossworth."

"Ah, Mossworth." Peter notably frowned and then disappeared. Half a minute later he popped up again with a big box, one that covered all but the top of his head. "Here. Remember to check your box."

"Thank you," said Mossworth, gasping with the weight.

Jimmy led him back to the front entrance. "Goodbye, Mr. Mossworth."

"Mm, thanks Jimmy, thanks," said Mossworth over his shoulder.

Up in his room, Mossworth dumped the box out onto his bed. Inside he found catalogs, most for pet clothing and toys and women's undergarments, innumerable credit card offers, several bills, and some very important notices from banks and other financial institutions. After opening the first one, Mossworth moved quickly to the desk, knocking books and papers about, looking. "C'mon, c'mon. Ah!" He grabbed the laptop, got it warmed up, and logged into his Oxford email. Messages, past, present, and future loaded up. "What, what? Nothing!" Mossworth looked at the first bank letter again. He opened another. More bad news. Tearing into several other notices Mossworth's befuddled face turned to understanding, and then fear. He had neglected to change his email address for his bank and credit cards; they had been sending emails to his Hardly address. The long and short unfolded in a second: his money was gone. Well, not all of it, but enough of it to make Mossworth grasp that his high living must now end.

After throwing most of his belongings around his room in the vain hope of some sort of positive emotional release, Mossworth took himself down the stairs, and the other stairs, and walked purposefully directly towards the Bird & Baby aspiring for a different sort of release. As soon as he walked inside, the warmth of the wood and rooms cheered him up. "Sure," he thought, "money is tight but, well, I'm fine. I'm but a poor student in Oxford!" He ordered a pint of Blackthorn and moved back to the Inklings room. For half a pint Mossworth duped himself into the illusion that he wasn't bankrupt, that he belonged in Oxford, and that he had a purpose. Shaking him from this reverie were the contents of a large tray that formerly supported two burgers, a fish and chip, two glasses of water, a pint of lager, and a bag of crisps; without warning those items fell, totally and completely, onto Mossworth's front and lap. Looking up, he focused on the feigned surprise of Paula.

"Oh, my. Sorry, sir. Here, let me bring you a towel. I'll be back." After she had taken a few steps she turned and looked at Mossworth. "In just a minute."

Mossworth stood, looking at his soiled front, slack jawed. Slowly he walked, bits of food falling from him, towards the back of the pub to the toilets. No paper towels. Mossworth resolved to dab at his tweeds with wads of toilet paper. Less soiled, he moved, slightly glazed, out into the pub away from Paula's section and towards the rear of the building. Still holding, and nursing his pint, he came round the corner expecting to sit in the very far corner, alone and safe from angry barmaids. Instead, he turned into the back room and found himself in front of a table at which sat a young woman with her back to Mossworth. At the same table, across from and facing Mossworth, sat Postlewait. Hesitating just a moment caught Postlewait's attention. He looked up with a smile.

"Ah, Mossworth. How are you? Am I not seeing you later this afternoon?"

Opening his mouth to say, something, anything, Mossworth was cut off as the young woman turned abruptly about to face him.

"Mossworth? I don't believe it! Hi!"

It was Cynthia Gravely.

Mossworth's eyes focused in and out. He mumbled some excuse, stumbled towards the door, and then he ran.

He ran and he ran. Down Cornmarket. Near the High Street his age caught up and he winded himself. Then he turned down the High, up several alleys, and found himself outside of St. George's. Utterly out of breath, he sat on the steps, head spinning, lungs aching, heaving. "Cynthia…" he muttered.

"Mossworth?" With a half-bitten jam sandwich in one hand, a very concerned Theo looked down at Mossworth. "What brings you to St. G's?"

Blinking, rapidly, Mossworth looked at Theo's necktie. He held up his hand, still panting.

"Everything…okay?"

Mossworth nodded. Then shook his head. Then nodded.

"Oh. Well…"

Mossworth rubbed his cheeks. "I'm…I'm just… waiting."

Theo nodded and took another bite. "I see."

Thanks, thanks," Mossworth panted, "waiting…"

Theo sat down. He stuffed the rest of his sandwich in his mouth and chewed it up slowly. He pursed his lips. "My dear fellow, for what are you waiting?"

"Ah," said Mossworth, standing, "just catching my breath, thanks."

Theo stood and looked directly at Mossworth. He extended his hand and reflexively, Mossworth took it and immediately attempted to disengage. Theo held his hand firmly until Mossworth, who had yet to look in his face, raised his eyes to Theo's.

"Mossworth," he said very quietly, "you aren't really waiting, you know. Perhaps you have never learned waiting. You are running."

Nodding, Mossworth pulled his hand quickly, grunted some words, and then slid away. Down by the High he turned out towards Magdalen and walked more quickly. Over the bridge he took the only route he knew, down the Iffley Road, and soon found himself approaching the

Nanford House. Suddenly he crossed over to the Nanford and entered and found Ricardo and with few words paid up to get his old room. Ricardo, shook his head, grunted, and took Mossworth's credit card numbers quickly.

Mossworth moved quickly down the hall and remembered the awkward movement of the key. He entered the room to find, to his moderate relief, that the same overpowering stench of cat urine and insecticide remained. He inhaled deeply and smiled and threw himself on the bed. Tears leaked out of his eyes as he rolled himself in the same bedspread, presumably still unwashed. "Home," he whispered. He closed his eyes, shaking slightly, seeking sleep. It did not come. He tossed. He turned. He crawled out of bed, too hot from being dressed, and stripped. With one step he moved to the shower, turned the spray on, and then got into the hot, hot water. But five minutes in the warming heat and he turned the water off. He dressed and turned on the tele. He flipped the channels and then flipped it off. Mossworth started pacing the room. This meant he took two steps between the wardrobe and bed towards the window and then turned around and took two steps back towards the opposite wall.

After kicking the bed a few times and knocking the television off the table, he left and started walking, this time with a very specific goal in mind. A few blocks back towards town Mossworth made his first stop: the Oxford Blue. "Two whiskies, please." Feeling not particularly at home, Mossworth moved down Iffley to the next pub and then decided, after another two whiskeys there, upon a plan involving every pub within sight and lots of grain-based liquids. Gradually, Mossworth's sadness grew less and his numbed mind began to enjoy the perception of popularity he thought he enjoyed.

Hazy thoughts drifted in and out of his mind, faces laughed and, Mossworth perceived, enjoyed themselves. The evening came on, the light dimmed, and eventually, stumbling, Mossworth entered The Raven's Head. "Hey!" he shouted to the crowd he did not yet recognize, "how is everybody?" A few lads shouted back, recognizing him. He bought them all, everyone, a round, and ordered a whiskey for himself. More cheers went up. "Heh, heh," said Mossworth, "I am great, I am great." Some of the patrons right next to him snorted. He looked at them, unfocused, "I am, I know it. Dr. Mossworth, at your service." He raised his glass.

"Brian?"

Mossworth flicked his eyes towards every direction looking for the voice. It was not until a pair of very smooth hands grabbed his chin and directed his gaze to her that he recognized Susan. "Hello, lady," he said.

"Brian, where have you been?"

"Uh...Oxford. Oxford is good."

"Yes, darling, but where have you been in Oxford. Charles called. He was a bit worried about you. I needed to talk…"

"Talking is grand…talking."

"Brian, everything okay?"

"Peachy. Peachy keen. Drinky keen…drink?"

Susan stood close and looked intently into his face. "That bad?"

Mossworth glanced at his drink. "Scotch is…better…"

"Postlewait?"

Dropping his face, Mossworth, shuffled his feet a bit. Then he slammed down his drink and smiled, grimly. "Everything. Everything is…everything's great! Barman, another whiskey! And one form the lovely girl…woman…Susan!" Drinks instantly popped up and Mossworth handed one to Susan. "Cheers!"

Susan sniffed and smiled and lifted her glass, "cheers!"

And the drinking began for Susan and continued for Mossworth and very shortly they were in the street singing, arm-in-arm. Mossworth enjoyed her proximity as much as he thought he would, the fragrance drifting off her hair roaring through his alcohol-fueled senses.

Susan led the way to the next pub, a rough affair, rather more working class. Mossworth, unsteadily stepped right in, pushed past several patrons, and at the bar, in a very loud American voice, said, "Bartender, we, we...Susan...the lady and I...we want, two, whiskeys. Bourbons whiskeys. From Bourbon...Kentucky." He looked, unfocused, at Susan, "right?"

Susan, wavering slightly, nodded, then leaned heavily into Mossworth, pushing her head up against his shoulder. The golden glasses arrived and they went down quickly. Susan laughed loudly, then stumbled a bit knocking into a few patrons. Mossworth noticed, vaguely, that some faces gave off unwelcoming expressions. He led Susan out, carrying her a bit.

"What, what Mossy, what?"

"Not a good place, Susan...they're...they're...not happy."

"Oh, Mossy. You're a good listener..."

They wobbled down the street, wandering without direction, Susan hanging onto Mossworth. After a few blocks, Mossworth stopped, stood shakily, looking up the street and down the street. Susan looked at him.

"Why did we leave, Mossy?"

They weren't nice...not nice..." and then he snorted with laughter, "... and we're drunk"

"Oh...you saved me from them!"

"What?"

"Rescued me!" She threw her arms around his neck. "My hero!" It took Mossworth's foggy mind a moment to realize her lips were firmly planted upon his own. He found this not disagreeable; when her tongue worked its way through his lips Mossworth felt his knees go weak and he had to lean on Susan not to fall down. Susan then leaned very hard into him and moaned slightly.

A tiny conscious, minority of his mind sent out warnings to the majority drunken mush between his ears. "She's not old enough." "You cannot have sex with her." "Would she want to have sex with me?" "Man, am I drunk." "You can't have sex with a drunk girl." "You can't have sex with anyone." "Why can't I have sex with anyone?" "But I don't want to have sex with anyone, just Susan." "How does she do that with her tongue?" "She is so drunk!" "Hell, I'm forty-eight and this totally hot college girl is into me." "I am so amazing." "I wonder what her breasts are like?"

With his last gasp of self-restraint Mossworth developed a plan that, at the time, seemed utterly perfect. He led Susan to a nearby bus stop where they hopped on the next bus to Headington and to The Kilns, the former home of C. S. Lewis. Susan leaned close to him on the bus. "Where we going, Mossy? A hotel?"

"Oh, a great place. A place where people don't have…"

"Ha! What? Kiss me!" Susan snuggled very close to Mossworth and put her tongue in his ear. At that very moment Mossworth realized he stood on the edge of an ethical abyss and that he no longer cared. With wild abandon he reached over and slid his hand up Susan's shirt. She giggled. He giggled. They giggled.

A sense of consciousness dribbled down into Mossworth's pounding head. His face pressed against something very hard and very cold that felt much like a stone gutter; his eyes stuttered in their opening, encrusted with, he perceived, blood. For a moment, Mossworth thought he was blind. As his eyes adjusted he could see, just not clearly. The area was artificially illuminated; dawn had yet to arrive.

Rolling over, then sitting up in the street, Mossworth discovered new sensations comprised of a profound hangover on the inside mixed with mild head trauma on the outside. Besides the blood, the front of his jacket and shirt stiffened from dried vomit. He did not grasp where he currently sat. Rising, carefully, Mossworth could tell by the strange shadows nearby stood one of the colleges, perhaps Merton. There appeared in the dim streetlight a sort of alley between the buildings; it seemed the way to go. He carefully stepped, holding his wounded and aching head. With each step more of the previous evening, fragmented, chaotic flashes, fell into disorderly place. A heaviness descended as events reconstructed in his mind. His cheeks flushed.

He and Susan had ended up at The Kilns well past midnight. The neighborhood stood quiet and dark. He remembered being consumed with desire, wild with reckless passion. Susan panted, breathing hotly on Mossworth's neck, urging him on. They fell to the neatly cropped lawn at the front of the Kilns and rolled on top of each other. Mossworth had a memory of Susan wrestling her pants off, then rolling on top of her, and then the attempt at consummation. All he had desired and dreamed about, everything he wanted, the perfection he so longed for, lay beneath him. The simple rhythmic movements began and, uncontrollably, Mossworth began to shout, "Exeter! Hertford! All Souls! Merton! Keble! Magdalen!" But consummation did not bring fruition as, Mossworth vaguely recalled, interruption came in the form of a dazzling light blasted into his face. Headlight? Policeman's flashlight? All he could remember after that was fleeing blindly away from Lewis' house and the light. How did he avoid capture?

Now he plodded along an alley that presently turned into a sort of path. Mossworth hung his head and continued slowly, step-by-step. Other thoughts and plans and failures drifted past and around him but he could not put them in place. Gradually he noticed a lightening, graying of the sky and sorted out that he was winding his way along Dead Man's Walk, feet crunching on the rough gravel path. His shoulders hung heavy.

At Rose Lane he turned towards the north and the High Street. On the High he could make out Magdalen tower as a looming presence, a great solid. He made towards it, as if drawn. Clearly grasped now, he had possessed no real destination.

The night porter looked up as Mossworth entered the lodge. "Sorry, sir, but we are closed to visitors." Mossworth held up his student badge. The porter took the badge and looked intently at it, then at Mossworth, then at Mossworth's stained appearance. Mossworth twitched and kept his eyes down. "Sir," said the Porter hesitantly, "are you sure this is the best thing right now?"

"Yes," Mossworth replied, quietly. "I just need to get on the walk, the way."

The porter drew a deep breath.

"Please. I need this."

Shaking his head, the porter handed back the badge and waved Mossworth in. "Remember, sir, this is quiet hours."

Mossworth entered the college. He weaved around the chapel and under the quad vaults, steps echoing lightly. New Buildings loomed in the pre-dawn; the sturdy gate to Addison's Walk lay just to the right. Mossworth turned, passed through the gate, and started the path. The silence grew moody. Thoughts assailed Mossworth. Doubts, fears, hopes, and dreams, all danced around his head, none landing, none grounded. Each step he took down the path slowed, his feet moving heavily. Presently Mossworth stopped. The path lay in the dark. Above him, breezes tickled the uppermost branches of the aged trees. He looked up but could not discern what lay in the heights. Then, quietly, almost gently, he passed out.

A dream descended upon Mossworth. People played a game. A man asked Mossworth why he was unhappy. His reply made no sense. The man smiled and told Mossworth to get dressed. Frantic, for some reason, Mossworth searched but found nothing. A whistle blew. In a classroom Mossworth sat in a very uncomfortable desk. The same man, now dressed in tweed, asked Mossworth if he were in the right class. Mossworth did not know. This time the man looked down and touched Mossworth's shoulder in a kindly way and said he needed to be in the right class to do well. Then a light breeze accompanied him out of the dream and gently moved the branches above, making them creak an aged tune.

Shaking with the pre-morning chill, head still pounding, Mosswoth rolled to his back and looked up. A lightening sky announced dawn. The oaks and elms on the sides of the path appeared dull and colorless. He glanced to the side, past the trees, into the fields of the inner park, the grasses, the silhouettes of shrubs. He saw no tone in that predawn moment, no depth, just shadow. For a moment he listened and he found that he had grown sad at the quiet. He waited for something. A hush, pronounced, descended upon where he lay. He dared not move. Without warning, a rushing wind bent the branches above him, creaking and snapping. The sky lightened perceptibly and in the distance a bell rang out. Mossworth witnessed. The outlines of the trees nearest him darkened, the shadows firmed, and shrank. Rays of golden illumination fell across the glistening field, then upon the aged tree trunks and the path, and then onto Mossworth himself. He rolled over and pushed himself to his knees, looked out across the fields and realized he could see color and shape, he could see forms. Finally, an authentic experience, not of his own invention, descended upon Mossworth and with a moment of inspiration gentle as a whisper, he perceived that he could see all because of the sun. Plato, Christ, Miss Wendy's ginger scones, and something in the beauty of

Oxford grew a tiny bit intelligible to him and that small bit of Grace comforted. He fell on his face and wept.

A moment later he lifted his head at the sound of voices. Perhaps he would not have noticed them; what gave them away was their large and generous laughter. He made out two men headed up the path towards him. Illuminated by the sun, Mossworth for the first time clearly recognized the two: Art and Theo. Before he could sort out what to do, the men found him. Kind and gentle hands reached out to him. With many a, "my dear fellow," and, "not at all," the two got him to his feet, one on either side, and began assisting him back on the Walk, along the way, back to College.

They settled Mossworth on the first bench available. Theo dashed off to fetch a hot reviving beverage; Postlewait sat quietly beside Mossworth. A few silent minutes passed.

"I didn't know you two knew each other, Dr. Postlewait."

"Please do call me Art. Yes, Theo and I have known each other for years. We are very old friends."

Mossworth rubbed his chin, "I guess I never saw the connection."

Art nodded, "No, many do not. I'm glad you have."

Theo returned with tea. Mossworth sipped and found it greatly encouraging. He turned to Postlewait. "Dr… Art, I mean, I wonder, that is, I think that perhaps I ought to explain…"

Art held up a hand. "No, this is not the time. We'll have time for business later."

"Indeed," said Theo, "We shall help you home."

Mossworth looked at both their concerned faces. A wave of envy passed over him when he thought of the open and easy friendship between them. With warmth previously unknown, he relaxed, and the envy passed as he realized that what they had was shared with him, freely.

"Home," said Mossworth, "yes, please.

DESOLATION

By religious experience we ought to mean an experience which is religious through and through – an experiencing of all things in the light of the knowledge of God. It is this, and not any moment of illumination, of which we say that it is self-authenticating; for in such an experience all things increasingly fit together in a single intelligible whole.

William Temple

Two days later Mossworth received a written summons, delivered by Jimmy, to meet with the Chancellor of the University. Mossworth asked, and Jimmy, with the utmost propriety, laid out the directions. The summons required Mossworth to be at the office promptly at one, suitably attired. Jimmy left just as Reed returned from the bath. The two had not spoken since their last encounter.

"Morning," said Mossworth. "Have you a minute?"

"Sure, of course."

Mossworth sat and directed Reed to sit opposite him. "Well, first, I am very grateful for how you cleaned up my mess. That means a great deal to me."

"Not at all, Mossy."

"Second, I want you to know, well, I am, grateful for your friendship, your kindness."

Reed smiled and waved his hand.

"There are also, ah, probably things I should say about how I ought not to have taken you on a dangerous drinking binge in London, about how I should have listened to you about Susan, about how I should never have filled up the room with my shoes and books…"

"…and tweeds…"

"Indeed, and tweeds!" Mossworth laughed at himself.

"Yes, tweeds. Oh, Reed, I am sorry for being such a… git."

Reed laughed easily, too.

Mossworth paused for a moment and the smile changed. "And…me. I'm fairly confident that I shall be leaving Oxford."

Reed, serious, asked, "Sent down? I didn't know you'd done anything that serious."

"Ah, yes, well, it's not actually about what I did. It is more about, well, who I am." Mossworth shrugged. "You see, I'm afraid that I ought never have been permitted into Oxford in the first place. The plain fact is I am, ah, was, a college professor."

Reed looked at him, "but how…?"

"Good question. I have no bloody idea. But here I am. And here I go." Mossworth stood and put out his hand. Reed stood and they shook.

"Thanks, Reed."

"Best of luck, Mossy."

Promptly at one Mossworth received a nod from a chipper, middle-aged secretary and entered through a doorway into a darkly paneled lobby. Illustrative trefoil windows in this space led him through an elegant door into a Georgian foyer with no windows but very large white columns. From there a white door opened into a vestibule covered in pale yellow chintz, with pale yellow carpet. On a plinth, in a glass cabinet, sat the University's mace; on a door at the end of this room hung the University's crest. Mossworth walked up to the door but before he could knock, a voice called out, "is that Mossworth?"

"Yes, sir."

"Enter."

The office delighted Mossworth more than perhaps all the other rooms he had seen in Oxford. Scarcely did he drink in the Jacobean ceiling beams, the display niches in the heavily enriched walls, the slightly-ajar-but-otherwise-hidden closet in the paneling revealing a glimpse of lush gowns, and the desk…

"You, Mossworth. Sit there." A small, fit, and very intense man directed Mossworth to the only chair in the room not behind the desk. Mossworth sat. The man looked at papers for a moment and then looked at Mossworth.

"You are old."

Mossworth nodded.

The man then stood. He pursed his lips. "Oxford…" Then the man held up a finger and moved to the other side of the room and opened a window. "Sorry, but I've got to have a smoke." He pressed a part of the paneling under the window and it opened up to reveal a hidden rack of elegant pipes. Mossworth leaned a bit to see inside more. The chancellor heard him shift in his seat and looked over. "You…you aren't a pipe man, are you?"

Mossworth smiled, "yes, indeed I am, sir."

Soon the Chancellor had a cloud of smoke about him, sitting back in his chair, chewing on the stem of his massive Turkish meerschaum sultan's head; Mossworth held a loaned briar, a delightful poker, plain in design yet he found it smoked evenly. After a few moments of mutual reverie the Chancellor cleared his throat.

Mossworth spoke first. "Sir, if I may. I am very sorry about how things have gone. I never meant to embarrass the university.

"Embarrass? I've no idea. The thing is… who the hell is Marlboro?"

"Marlboro?"

"He has been ringing and ringing. My secretary is rather annoyed."

"Marlboro? You mean Postlewait."

"And we've received faxes and letters…"

"Marlboro?"

"… and even several packages filled with, what do you call it? Caramel corn?"

Mossworth blinked. "Caramel corn? Marlboro? Dean Marlboro? From Hardley?"

"Um, yes. Hardley, that's the one."

"Hardley? Marlboro?"

"And caramel corn."

"Well, uh, what…?"

"Yes, what," said the Chancellor, "well the what has to do with, as nearly as I can tell from Marlboro's endless ravings, is that he wants you back, back at Hardley."

"But…that is, what?"

"Yes, so, of course we looked into you, your record here at Fochashite, and found that you are a freshman, a first year, yes?"

"Yes, sir."

"And not a particularly good freshman."

"Ah, no, sir."

"And you are also a professor?"

"Yes, sir."

The Chancellor creaked back in his chair, thoughtfully. "Well, we made a bloody pig's breakfast out of that, I suppose."

Mossworth considered the past nine months and remained silent.

"Any idea how?" inquired the Chancellor.

"I applied to a summer program."

"And we let you in as a first year?"

"Yes."

"Hm, well, sorry about that. I suppose you know that you really can't stay."

"Yes, sir, I know that."

The Chancellor chewed on his pipe silently and for such a time that Mossworth grew uncertain if the meeting were over. Without warning the Chancellor stood and moved around the desk to Mossworth, offering his hand. As they shook he looked at Mossworth squarely. "I was rather wondering what would bring a middle-aged and experienced professor to throw off his life, quit his job, to start at Oxford as an undergraduate."

Mossworth looked at his feet. "I guess, sir, that at first I came because I loved Oxford but, that is, it wasn't Oxford I loved, it was a shadow of Oxford."

Still shaking his hand, the Chancellor pulled Mossworth conspiratorially closer, "And now?"

Mossworth looked up and smiled. "Now... Now I am beginning to know what it means to love Oxford...properly."

The Chancellor released Mossworth's hand and then patted him warmly on the back. "Well, you were only here for a year but it appears we have given you an education after all."

Mossworth returned the way he had come, back through the antechambers, and it was not until arriving at the reception area where the secretary sat that he realized the Chancellor's pipe remained in his hands. Before he quite sorted what to do, the secretary announced, "The Chancellor said you may keep the pipe."

Later that evening, Mossworth called Arkansas and got through to a very excited Marlboro who cut right to the chase and informed Mossworth that the brick that struck his head on that dreadful day came from the hand of a delinquent trustee's son, one who had been directed in the assault by none other than Professor Van Engelen-Van der Bauwede, with whom he had been carrying on an oddly asexual affair. Marlboro assured Mossworth that he no longer had any worries about Professor Van Engelen-Van der Bauwede as, because of her unprofessional and criminal activities, the college had decided to offer her an administrative position. By way of settlement, the college desperately wished to offer Mossworth his old job as well as his salary for his time absent (which they would term "recovery period/sabbatical"). Marlboro capped the deal by informing Mossworth that the college so very much desired his return, to see him teaching, and to have him not sue, they had purchased his old house.

He never even thought about refusing.

A few mornings later, Mossworth went down to Postlewait's office during what would have been his normal tutorial hour. The door was open and a smiling Postlewait greeted him.

"Ah, Mossworth, I'd hoped to see you." They shook hands. "Feeling better, I trust?"

"Thanks, yes."

"Jolly bad luck what with your being sent down."

Mossworth nodded. "Yes, ah, Art, but it was also luck that brought me here."

Postlewait smiled again. "I don't believe in luck." There was a bit of silence as Postlewait fussed with a kettle and tea accoutrements. "Mossworth, what will you do now?"

"Oh," started Mossworth, "I, ah, thought you knew…"

"Knew? No, all admin said was you needed to withdraw from the University. Sorry, I don't mean to pry."

Mossworth sat with a confused look. "But, I thought, Cynthia, you know, when she saw me."

"Cynthia? The young American student? You know her?"

Mossworth shook his head, "yes, I know her. She was, well, one of my students."

With that Postlewait smiled, then laughed. Mossworth joined him.

"My dear fellow, you are a teacher!"

"Dr. Mossworth, at your service."

"A fellow professor, I see, I see. But, hm, why…?"

"Why? This is Oxford. This is spires and aged stone, quiet alleyways, strange people, the golden sunsets, Headington park, intimate woody pubs…meat pies…"

"Yes," said Postlewait, "Oxford is those things, but those are the surface, the visual, the aesthetic, the shadows."

"But the aesthetic is good" said Mossworth. "I love the aesthetic."

The kettle boiled and Postlewait stood to prepare the tea. He stepped back with the steeping pot and two mugs.

"Isn't the aesthetic good?" asked Mossworth.

Postlewait poured the tea and handed Mossworth the steaming vessel. "Mossworth, when your tea is finished, where will the aesthetic be?"

"In…in my belly?"

"No doubt you like the aesthetic. But you love something else. Let me put this another way: when the tea has been drunk, what use is the aesthetic afterwards?"

Shrugging, Mossworth enjoyed another sip and then smiled.

Postlewait remained serious. "Tea is good. This, you and me here, aspiring to catch a glimmer of wisdom, to "chase the fox truth," this is better. Hm, or put it this way: what is it about the aesthetic that pleases you?

Mossworth thought for a moment. "Those things, those aesthetic things, they are…better."

"Better than what?"

"Better than, ah, normal."

"If there is a better, might we assume there is a perfect?"

"I guess… I never quite…"

"We all desire perfection."

"Ah, well…"

"But perfection, in a manner of speaking, has a source. Perfection can only be so if it is timeless, eternal, whole, complete…"

A silence gently fell. Mossworth grew aware of some long dormant mechanism deep in his mind lumbering towards movement.

"God?"

"Right. But if it is about God then our desire has an object and thus a goal."

"Oh, then our desire for perfection is really one for God!"

"And is God aesthetically pleasing? Or is God beautiful?"

Mossworth had no reply.

Slowly a smile spread across Postlewait's face and he then burst into laughter.

Mossworth frowned slightly. "I thought I was on to it."

"My dear chap," said Postlewait, still chuckling, "you have it. I laughed as we have, at last, become teacher and student."

The following Thursday Mossworth's packing concluded. Marlboro emailed travel arrangements: first class from Heathrow. Reed gave his farewell as easily as his introduction: a handshake, a smile, and a "cheers, mate." Two taxis arrived to load Mossworth's luggage. Jimmy lent a hand and then gave Mossworth a friendly wave. At the bus station, after an argument with the driver about the number of bags and boxes, Mossworth looked around, took a deep breath of the polluted Oxford bus station air, then climbed up and took his seat. Heavy grey clouds weighed down the air. A wave of conflicted thoughts washed over him and he lost himself to melancholy. Then the door closed and Mossworth slouched down in his seat. With a lurch the coach started to pull out of the station just as a cloud slid aside and permitted the silvery atmospheric glow of sun and rain, cheer and gloom that only England can produce. Mossworth looked out the window in time to find Theo and Art, splendid in dark tweeds, Art with wisps of pipe smoke about his head,

Theo with a long green scarf flipping in the breeze, and both smiling and waving. He raised his hand, waved, and sighed. "Beautiful Oxford," he mumbled.

Twenty-three hours and three bad meals later a sleepy and moderately grumpy Mossworth made his landing at Bill and Hillary Clinton National. Wondering whom Marlboro sent as a driver, and if their vehicle could manage with his four Swiss Army suitcases, two luggage trunks, five nylon duffels, historic leather riding saddle, and a wooden crate, Mossworth rode the escalator looking for someone holding a sign. What he found, resplendent in a shimmering brown and tan suit, was Charolais, smiling, and holding a very hot cup of coffee.

"Helloooo, Brian," she intoned kindly.

"Hello."

"Welcome home."

"Thank you. Thank you, indeed."

"Before you ask," said Charolais, "I brought the pick up."

Mossworth laughed. Charolais extended the cup. "Coffee?"

He took the cup, held it up, inhaled the steaming fragrance, and drank deeply.

"That," said Mossworth looking Charolais in the eyes, "is a beautiful cup of coffee."

EPILOGUE

Education consists mainly of what we have unlearned.

Mark Twain

Midway through Autumn, Mossworth typed furiously in his office, a bright Arkansas sun shining through his window. Only the previous week had his old house been organized to his comfort. His furnishings from storage were shipped back, the walls received some fresh paint, several hundred new, old, and dusty books found shelving, and even the battered Morris received a thorough service. That part of his life settled nicely into place; what drove him at the moment were the words of an essay. The last part of the summer Mossworth delved into several tomes recommended by Postlewait. With a sudden, and splendidly productive burst, Mossworth's thoughts came to life and sought paper and ink. The current work explored connections between Classical philosophy and how the understanding of art, beauty, and pleasure led to advance or decline in western art.

"No doubt, it is wildly broad," thought Mossworth, "but I'll pin it all down as I go." And he typed until eleven-thirty. Then he paused, carefully selected his Oxford pipe, filled it with the last of his Kingsbridge tobacco and headed outside. As the bowl warmed nicely, Mossworth walked his new daily route across the campus. It included a pass by Charolais' building where, more often than not, he could catch a glimpse of her smiling face, offer her a wave, and receive a blown kiss in return. Indeed, today, she smiled brighter and waved more lovely. As Mossworth continued down towards the forested part of the campus, a voice called out to him.

"Dr. Mossworth, Dr. Mossworth." A winded Gina, the department secretary, ran up to him. "Sorry, I just tried your office: you have a small package."

"Well, thank you, but you needn't have troubled yourself," said Mossworth.

"No trouble. I thought you'd want it immediately," she said breathlessly. "It's from Oxford!" Gina handed Mossworth a mailing tube, one labeled "Royal Mail," posted with stamps of the queen, and covered with a variety of other labels that made it clear the tube had done some traveling.

"All those notices…" said Gina.

"Ah, yes," said Mossworth with a smile, "they assumed the AR stood for Arizona. Ah, look here. It was posted more than six weeks ago!"

"But what is it?" asked Gina.

Mossworth fiddled with the tube ends finally prying one out with his tiny pocket knife. He then shook the tube and a rolled up parchment slipped out. Gina held the tube while he carefully unrolled the document and found, written in an elaborate script:

"To whom it may concern: May all hereby and forthwith recognize that Brian Mossworth is graduated from the College of Fochashite, Oxford University, with the degree of Diploma in Collegiate Studies and is guaranteed all the rights and privileges thereto. Signed this day of our Lord…" And after the date came the signature: Arthur Postlewait, D. Litt, M. Phil, D. Phil.

"What does it mean?" asked Gina.

Mossworth rolled it back up and gently placed it back in the tube. "I suppose it means I am a graduate of Oxford." And then he laughed long and loud and, though she didn't quite get the joke, Gina did get that Mossworth was laughing and seemed not to be the cranky bastard she remembered from previous years so she joined in.

By the next afternoon the diploma sat in his special glassed-in shelf, itself framed and matted, next to some of his other Oxford treasures. Mossworth gathered his notes and his second-best laser pointer, gave a chuckle as he looked again at the diploma, shut his office door, headed down the hall to his classroom, took a deep breath, and began.

ABOUT THE AUTHOR

R. A. Miller is Professor of Art History at Hendrix College. He is married to a supremely lovely and patient woman and together they attempt to raise their three clever and beautiful daughters.